IN HER SHADOW

www.**transworldbooks**.co.uk

Also by Louise Douglas

The Love of My Life
Missing You
The Secrets Between Us

For more information on Louise Douglas and her books,
see her website at www.louisedouglas.co.uk

In Her Shadow

Louise Douglas

BANTAM PRESS

LONDON • TORONTO • SYDNEY • AUCKLAND • JOHANNESBURG

TRANSWORLD PUBLISHERS
61–63 Uxbridge Road, London W5 5SA
A Random House Group Company
www.transworldbooks.co.uk

First published in Great Britain
in 2012 by Bantam Press
an imprint of Transworld Publishers

A CIP catalogue record for this book
is available from the British Library.

ISBN 9780593070215 (cased)
9780593067093 (tpb)

Addresses for Random House Group Ltd companies outside the UK
can be found at: www.randomhouse.co.uk
The Random House Group Ltd Reg. No. 954009

The Random House Group Limited supports the Forest Stewardship Council (FSC®),
the leading international forest-certification organization. Our books carrying
the FSC label are printed on FSC®-certified paper. FSC is the only forest-certification
scheme endorsed by the leading environmental organizations, including Greenpeace.
Our paper procurement policy can be found at
www.randomhouse.co.uk/environment.

Typeset in 11.5/15pt Sabon by
Falcon Oast Graphic Art Ltd.
Printed and bound in Great Britain by
CPI Group (UK) Ltd, Croydon, CR0 4YY

2 4 6 8 10 9 7 5 3 1

For Kevin, with love

CHAPTER ONE

I looked up and she was there. Ellen Brecht was standing just a few feet away from me, so close that if we had both reached out our arms, our fingertips would have touched.

'Ellen?' I whispered, and it was as if the past twenty years had never happened. For a moment, life became dazzling and exciting again, and I remembered how it felt to be young and strong and healthy, and without loneliness or regret. My desiccated, useless heart came back to life, pumping relief through me like some sublime narcotic. For the first time in two decades, I felt truly alive.

'Ellen!'

I wanted to touch her, I wanted to reach out and take hold of her hand and never let it go. I wanted to ask her why she had gone away like that, why she had left me alone for so long, why she had let me believe she was lost – but before I could move, the lights began to fade and she had melted away into the darkness. Then I knew it was too late. I had lost her again. She was gone.

The day I saw Ellen had begun much like any other. I had woken at the usual time and gone to work in the Brunel Memorial Museum in Bristol. The morning had passed quickly and without drama. I'd eaten a tomato and mozzarella panini for lunch and then John Lansdown, the Curator of Antiquities, had asked me to assemble some materials for an illustrated lecture. One of the objects he needed was a jade amulet that was kept in the Egyptian Gallery on the mezzanine floor. Normally I would have asked our intern, Misty, to fetch it, but she was off that day and in any case I felt like stretching my legs. I picked up my keys and left the cramped backstage rooms where the academic staff worked, crossed the museum's cathedral-like main hall and trotted up the sweeping marble staircase, its wide steps patterned with lozenges of coloured light reflected beneath the grand glass dome.

On the mezzanine, I wove through the tourists and visitors crowded around a visceral display on the science of embalming, and stooped to go through the low doorway designed to resemble a pyramid entrance. A narrow tunnel led into the gallery, which was a recreation of the interior of a tomb. It was dark inside, a deep and heavy darkness, black as pitch. This was broken by muted spotlights which were on timers; so as one faded, another would come in, and the jackal face of an eight-foot-high statue of Anubis would disappear as a rag-skinned mummy emerged grinning from the gloom. A soundtrack of a mournful wind played low in the background. The visitors spoke in hushed voices, and although I was used to the gallery, its claustrophobic atmosphere never failed to unnerve me.

I moved slowly amongst the displays while my eyes adjusted to the gloom, and when I found the relevant cabinet, I crouched to unlock it and disable the alarm. The glass door swung open, I reached inside to pick up the ancient amulet, closed my fingers around it and cupped it carefully in my palm. I shut the door and relocked it, stood up and straightened my back, squinting as the spotlights grew brighter – and that was when I saw her.

Ellen Brecht was there, in the chamber.

Ellen Brecht. My best friend. My nemesis.

She was wearing a green raincoat with the collar turned up, the red lipstick she had favoured when she was trying to look sophisticated, and her eyes were dark in her pale face. Her hair was damp. She was wearing her mother's necklace, the treble clef charm lying in the hollow beneath her throat.

'Ellen,' I whispered, but before I could say anything more, the lights faded again. As the artificial darkness fell, I remembered what had happened to Ellen and me all those years ago, and my joy was replaced by fear. Panic crept up behind me and grabbed me by the shoulders. It shocked me back to my senses.

I took a few steps away, and then the lights came up again and I cried out in alarm because she was closer to me now, standing beside a display of canopic jars. Now I could see what I had missed before: Ellen's gaze was fierce – her eyes bored into me and I was afraid of her, and of what she wanted from me. She hadn't come to forgive me, she had come to punish me. She wanted to hurt me as I had hurt her. She had been waiting, all these years, to claim her revenge – and now the moment had arrived, it was almost as if I had been expecting it. I had known it was not over between us.

Cold fingers of dread tightened around my throat.

'*Go away!*' I pleaded. '*Go away! Leave me alone!*' But she didn't move; she stood and stared, and her eyes burned into mine, as if they could see into my soul and read its awful secrets.

I tried to back away but my legs were useless, like newborn legs. I tripped, bumping into a sarcophagus in the dark, and it seemed to me that the body inside in its ancient brown bandages was looming towards me. The floor was tilting, the chamber spinning. The lights faded again and I didn't know where Ellen was. I turned and pushed into the tunnel entrance, scrambling and blinking back into the light. I ran along the edge of the mezzanine, holding onto the balcony rail, then I clattered down the sweeping staircase and into the main hall. A crowd was gathered in the shadows beneath the suspended Tyrannosaurus skeleton. My elbows knocked against adults with toddlers on their hips pointing up at the remains of the huge creature and I tripped over children flapping their educational quiz-sheets.

'Excuse me!' I cried. 'Please, *please* let me through!'

At the far side of the hall, I stumbled into a dimly lit corridor leading out of the atrium. The passageway was low-ceilinged, and narrowed by lines of Victorian glass display cabinets containing threadbare stuffed animals. At the far end was a door labelled: *Staff Only*.

I looked again, over my shoulder, and made out a figure at the entrance to the passageway moving slowly towards me. The light was bright behind, turning it into a faceless silhouette. With a sob, I fell against the locked door and fumbled over the security code. After three attempts, drunk with panic and weak with fear, I felt a hand on my shoulder. I cried out, my heart pounding, and slid to my knees, covering my face with my hands, and then a kindly voice said, 'Hannah, dear, what on earth is the matter?' And I looked through the cage made by my fingers and saw the concerned face of my colleague and friend Rina Mirza.

Rina helped me to my feet and took me through the door and into her office. It was tiny and overcrowded, a professorial burrow. I sat on a rickety chair squeezed in between filing cabinets piled high with bundles of paper and shivered while Rina made tea in the staff kitchenette. She returned and passed a mug to me. It was only half-full, even so my hands were trembling so badly that the liquid slopped around. I tried to contain it, holding the mug cupped tight in the palms of both my hands, steam curling from its surface. I felt icy cold inside.

Rina rubbed my back.

'What happened?' she asked, peering at me over her half-moon glasses. 'Has somebody hurt you? Were you assaulted?'

'No,' I said so quietly that Rina had to lean forward.

'What was it then? Something's given you a shock.'

I looked up at the older woman, her kind face, her anxious eyes, black hair wisping out of its bun.

'I saw somebody who used to be my friend,' I said.

'And that's a bad thing?' Rina asked.

I dropped my head forward, so that my hair fell over my face. The years since I had recovered from my breakdown, years that had formed a protective carapace of new memories and experiences around me, were crumbling to dust. I felt vulnerable as a newborn mouse, blind and squirmy and naked.

'Hannah?' Rina asked again. 'Why did it upset you so much to see your friend?'

'Because Ellen Brecht is dead,' I said. 'She died almost twenty years ago.'

CHAPTER TWO

The story of Ellen and me began in the 1980s in the Lizard Peninsula, a wind-blown, storm-tossed, rocky Cornish outcrop. That was where I was born and where I grew up and where I knew Ellen. As far as I am concerned, she was only ever there. It has always been difficult for me to imagine her anywhere else, out of that context.

There was a time before Ellen, when it was just me, of course. That time is further away and harder to conceive, but it's possible; I can still go back, in my mind, to my early childhood in all its Hipstamatic brightness. Most of my memories pre-Ellen are a muddle, like snapshots jumbled in a drawer, but there's one September afternoon when I was eight years old that I recall with perfect clarity. It was the only time I ever spoke to Ellen's grandmother, and if I hadn't, there would have been nothing to connect Ellen and me later. Perhaps, if that afternoon had played out another way, we would never have become friends and, that being so, I would have had a different and, most likely, a happier life. Before Ellen, things were easier and less complicated. They were either good or bad, right or wrong, black or white, and I understood the difference. Since Ellen, everything has been coloured in shades of grey.

This is how it was that afternoon. The school bus had dropped off its last passengers – the Williams twins, Jago Cardell who lived in the cottage next door to mine, and me – at the stop in the lay-by on the Goonhilly Road. It was cold; the shadows were lengthening. A promise of fireworks and frost and spiderwebs hung in the air, and swallows sat like small dark sentinels on the telephone wires waiting to go somewhere warmer. The Williams boys ran off down the lane that led to their farm, and Jago and I went across to the stately horse-chestnut tree that overhung the boundary wall of Thornfield House. There were hundreds of conkers up amongst the big papery leaves just out of our reach. Jago dropped his rucksack on the grass, found a stick and jumped up and down, hitting the branches. I watched for a moment, then I had an idea. I picked up the rucksack, swung it by its straps and threw it into the air. It hit a branch and several prickly green cases fell, splitting as they bounced on the lane and releasing their glossy brown nuts. Jago whooped with delight and pounced on them. Made confident, I threw the rucksack again, but this time it fell the wrong way, over the wall and into the garden of Thornfield House, which we had always called 'Haunted House'.

Jago turned to look at me. 'Fuckin' hell, Spanner,' he said. 'You've been and gone and done it now!'

I remember the feeling of dread in my stomach. It was more than a quarter of a century ago, but I feel it now so clearly. I feel it in my bones. At the time, I was afraid of the old lady, Mrs Withiel, who lived alone in the house. We half-believed she was a witch, and we were scared of getting into trouble, but with hindsight it seems obvious that this premonition was of something far worse than a childhood scolding. I knew something terrible was going to happen inside that house. I knew it even then.

Thornfield House was like no other house in our part of

the world. It sat square at the top of the hill, surrounded by a wall, its upper windows overlooking the fields that led to the coast on one side, and the flat, marshy lands spreading out towards the satellite station at Goonhilly Down on the other. It was not the sort of place where normal people would want to live. It was too big, too severe, not hunkered down, white and wind-worn like most Cornish houses, but standing tall with its big proud windows and grand door, its steeply sloping roof topped by a weathervane shaped like a schooner riding a billowing wave.

That afternoon, I crept along by the wall to the gap where the huge, wrought-iron gates stood ajar, rusting on their hinges. I looked around the edge of the wall and I saw the old lady standing at the door looking out. I was the one who had thrown the rucksack, so it was up to me to go and ask for it back, but I didn't move. I looked across to Jago. I knew he would help me because he always did. He didn't hesitate. He stepped forward into the garden, he went right up to the witch, and he talked to her.

Jago was two years older than me, a scruffy, skinny boy. From behind, his ears stuck out and so did the dark flame-coloured hair his aunt hacked with her kitchen scissors. His neck was long and thin with the hair tapering down on one side, his shirt was too small and his trousers were worn and scuffed at the hems. His hands, which seemed too big for his arms, hung at his sides.

I crept forward and stopped a few paces behind him.

The witch, Mrs Withiel, was stooped and trembly. She wore a long grey cardigan over a powder-blue dress with the buttons at the front done up all wrong, and grubby old tennis shoes. Her hair was thin and white.

'Why do you children always run away from me?' she asked. 'Whenever I try to talk to you, you run away.'

Jago looked at his feet. He couldn't tell the old lady we ran away because we thought she might put the evil eye on us.

'I like children. I have a daughter, and a granddaughter,' said Mrs Withiel. She looked at me. 'She'd be about the same age as you, dear.'

'That's nice,' said Jago politely. 'Do they live in Trethene?'

'Oh no. No, no, no.' She wrung her hands. 'They're long gone. The devil came and took my daughter away. He stole her away from me, her and the child. I don't know where they are. I don't get a card at Christmas. Nothing. He's evil, you know, evil through and through.'

The old lady's voice rose as she spoke until it was so high and reedy it almost faded away. I felt sick. I thought perhaps Mrs Withiel was soft in the head with her talk of the devil and evil. Or maybe she really was a witch.

Jago glanced at me. I tried to convey, with my eyes, that we needed to get away.

'That's a shame you don't see your family,' said Jago. He toed the weeds that were growing through the gravel on the drive. Then he asked: 'Is it OK if I get my rucksack now?'

'Yes, yes,' said the old lady. She waved him towards the bag with the back of her hand, then she looked at me. 'You'll come back and see me, won't you?' she asked me. 'Come back and talk to me. I'm so fond of children, especially little girls. Next time I'll have some biscuits ready for you, dear.'

I tried to smile but my face didn't feel like smiling.

'Chocolate Bourbon biscuits,' she said. 'Those were my daughter's favourites. Do you like Bourbons, dear?'

I nodded.

'Don't forget then. Come back to see me. You will, won't you? Promise me?'

'Yes,' I said in a very quiet voice. Jago was dragging the rucksack through a large patch of dying nettles by one of its straps. When he reached me, we turned together and walked slowly back to the gates. We waved goodbye to the old lady, and as soon as we were hidden by the wall, we began to run as if our lives depended on it, to the crossroads and then down the hill that led to Cross Hands Lane, where we lived.

Jago and I amused ourselves for some time afterwards, pretending to be the witch.

'I'm so fond of children,' Jago used to say in a crackly, creepy voice. 'Especially . . . *for breakfast*!' And he'd reach out his hands which he'd made into claws and pounce on me. He used to make me cry with laughter and fear.

I never did go back to see Mrs Withiel, although I passed Thornfield House almost every day. I was too ashamed to look up to the window to see if she was watching, waiting for me, hoping I would go in and talk to her, and I tried not to think of the biscuits she would have bought specially going stale and soft in their packet.

CHAPTER THREE

I couldn't recover from what I had seen at the museum that afternoon, couldn't pull myself together, so Rina took me home. Her small car laboured through the city and into Montpelier, pulling up outside the building where I lived. My flat was on the first floor of a house that had been converted for multiple occupancy, squeezed between a trendy flower shop and one that sold second-hand clothes. The pavement to one side was cluttered with clothes-rails hung with brightly coloured dresses and shirts, and on the other with dark green plastic buckets filled with lilies, daffodils and tulips.

Rina helped me out of the car, put her arm around me and bustled me up the steps to the front door of my house, into the untidy communal hallway and up the narrow, carpeted staircase that led to the first-floor flat.

I felt better there. Everything was pale, muted, neutral. It was calming. My little grey cat, Lily, wound herself around my ankles and I picked her up and pressed my face into her soft fur.

'Go and lie down while I make you a drink,' Rina said.

'I'll be fine now.'

'Do as I say. Let me look after you for a little while.'

Rina gave me a gentle push towards the bedroom. I drew the curtains, lay on the bed and was immediately overwhelmed with a fatigue so intense it seemed as if a great weight had been placed on my chest. I pulled the duvet over my body, let my heavy head sink into the pillows, felt the mattress absorb my angles. The cat pawed at the duvet, her little feet patting, tugging. I tried to relax but my mind would not stop spinning. When Rina came into the room some minutes later with a glass of camomile tea, my eyes were still wide open.

'Were you very close to this friend of yours?' Rina asked, leaning over me, stroking my forehead as if she were soothing a child with a temperature. I could taste the mintiness of her exhaled breath.

'We were like sisters. Closer than sisters.'

'It must have been hard when you lost her.'

'Yes, it was.'

I turned my head to look towards the window. The top sash was open a foot or so and the cream-coloured curtains lifted softly in the air and then collapsed again, as if they were breathing. Outside were the familiar noises of traffic, children, music, dogs and the clatter of the kitchen being prepared for service in the restaurant down the road.

'What did you say her name was?'

'Ellen Brecht.'

'What happened to her, Hannah?'

'It was an accident. She drowned.'

'Oh, how dreadful. Were you with her?'

'No. I was in Chile. I only found out a long time after.'

Rina smoothed the bedlinen. 'So you never had a chance to say goodbye?'

'No.'

Rina gave a sad sigh. I looked up at her. I wanted her to understand.

'We didn't part on good terms, Ellen and I,' I said. 'The last time I saw her . . . The last time we spoke . . .'

'Yes?'

The memory was like a pain inside me, like a fist clenched around my heart, bleak and cold as winter. I couldn't put it into words. I couldn't describe what had happened.

'It was a misunderstanding,' I said, although that statement was nowhere near significant enough to describe what had happened between Ellen and me. 'I thought we'd be able to put things right, I thought there'd be plenty of time – but there wasn't.'

Rina sighed. 'These things happen. Young girls can be very passionate.'

The palm of her hand was flat on the bed.

'Did something happen today to remind you of Ellen?' she asked.

'I dreamed of her last night.'

'There you are then.'

It wasn't unusual for me to dream of Ellen, though. I dreamed of her, and Thornfield House, most nights. The previous night I'd dreamed the big old house was derelict, burned-out, the roof caved in, the window-glass broken, the curtains grey and torn blowing through the shards, the trees and plants in the garden black and skeletal, cobwebbed, covered in ash. I was inside, searching the empty rooms, withered flowers scattered on bloodstained floorboards, looking for Ellen. I knew she was there somewhere – I could hear her crying in the distance – but in my dream, I couldn't remember where I was supposed to look. I was walking blood through the house; it was wet on the soles of my bare feet; my hands were covered with it – each time I touched a wall I left behind a red smear. All the time the piano music was playing, winding round me like a mist; it was a requiem. And then the music faded and all that remained was the sound of Ellen crying as if her heart was breaking. '*Ellen!*' I called. '*Where are you? Ellen?*'

She did not answer.

*

Rina said: 'Hannah, shhh, it's all right now,' and I realized I must have cried out.

'Sorry,' I mumbled.

Rina looked concerned.

'Perhaps you should have a break,' she said. 'You work so hard, dear, and I don't remember the last time you had a holiday. Why don't you take a few days off?'

'Yes,' I said. 'You're right. Maybe I will.'

'That's good,' Rina said. 'Think of somewhere nice you can go. The countryside maybe? The coast?'

I lay warm and comfortable in the bed and allowed myself to be calmed by Rina's presence. I knew I would eventually sleep. Lily crept up onto the pillow beside me, turned several circles and tucked herself up. I watched the gentle billow and lift of the curtain at the window and remembered the first time I saw Ellen, how it had been a bright, sunny day, how it was the day when everything began, and began to end, for both of us.

CHAPTER FOUR

It was a long time ago, but not so far back as before; nearly two years after Jago and I spoke to Mrs Withiel. The memories are clearer now, sharp in my mind, the snapshots organized, if a little faded around the edges. It was the school summer holidays. I was ten and Jago was twelve. Jago still lived next door to me with his uncle and aunt, Caleb and Manda Cardell, and we were still the only children in Trethene village. Mrs Withiel had been dead for some time and Thornfield House had been boarded up and abandoned – left to go to pot, my father said. It had been sliding towards dereliction.

There had been a fight at the Cardells' the night before. Dad had been out, working a late shift at RNAS Culdrose. Mum and I were at home, stoically trying not to listen to what was going on next door. Perhaps if we had had a phone Mum would have called for help, but none of the local authority-owned cottages in Cross Hands Lane had telephones in those days. It probably wouldn't have made a difference anyway. People in Trethene didn't interfere in other people's business.

When something, or someone, crashed into the wall that divided the Cardells' cottage from ours with such force that the pictures on our side had jumped on their hooks and fallen crooked, Mum said, 'I can't listen to this any longer,' and put on her coat with some unspecified plan in mind – but then the shouting had stopped. Mum and I had gone upstairs to look out of my bedroom window and we saw Mrs Cardell in the back yard, all blue and silver in the moonlight, shivering in a thin cardigan and slippers and smoking a cigarette. Mr Cardell had come out and the dog had hidden under the rabbit hutch. Mr Cardell had put both his arms round his skinny wife and held her tight and kissed her frizzy yellow hair. The two of them stood together, rocking. I could see the red light at the end of the cigarette that Mrs Cardell had dropped, winking up at her through the night.

After fights like this, Mrs Cardell wouldn't come out of the house for a few days. She'd send Jago to fetch her packets of Embassy from the village stores.

But this was the next day, the morning after. I was pushing my bike up the lane when Jago fell into step beside me. He started to act out the plot of a film he'd seen on television. He shot at imaginary adversaries concealed in the rambling rhododendron bushes that lined the lane, swaggered and blew the smoke from the barrels of his finger-guns. I held onto the handlebars of my bike and watched.

'You're a nutter,' I said.

He laughed. He was happy because after a big fight, things were often better at the Cardells' – for a while.

At the top of the hill, we turned left and I leaned, panting, over the handlebars. I was proud of my bike. It was a BMX my father had bought from a man in the Royal Naval Air Station. I rang the bell a couple of times with my thumb but Jago didn't take any notice.

'Have you got any money?' he asked.

'Nope.'

'You should have. We could have got an ice cream.'

I pulled a face at him and then we stopped together. We'd reached the entrance to Thornfield House and for the first time in months it looked different.

After Mrs Withiel's death, planks had been nailed over the windows, and the gates had been propped up and padlocked. Wisteria grew rampantly over the walls and the garden became so overgrown that it was impossible to make out the features that had once been there, the lawn, the path, the drive.

But that day, the gates had been removed and the shutters taken away from the windows; some of them were open. Nettles, brambles and saplings had been cut down and piled high in one corner of the garden, and the flagstone path that led to the front door had been cleared.

Jago and I exchanged glances. He scratched behind his ear.

'We ought to go and have a look,' he said. 'To make sure nobody's inside, thieving.'

His face was serious, one eyebrow slightly raised, and his thumbs were tucked into the sides of his jeans. He was pretending to be somebody from a film. Jago was always pretending to be somebody he wasn't.

'What if there *is* someone inside?'

'Then we'll tie them up and get a reward.'

I propped my bike against the wall.

'I don't think we should go in,' I said. 'We'll be trespassing.'

'It's OK,' Jago said. 'I'll go first.'

He crept forward, light as a cat in his tatty old trainers. I followed at a distance. The garden around the drive was so green and dense with overhanging branches and plant-life that I had the impression of falling into water. Bees buzzed in the heat and the air was heavy with the scents of flowers.

Jago pushed at the front door. It creaked beneath the palm of his hand and when he pulled it away, flakes of old green paint were stuck to his skin. He wiped his hand on the side of his jeans.

'Hello?' he called softly, then more confidently: '*Hello-o!*' but there was no answer. He looked at me over his shoulder, beckoning with his eyes. He went into the house and I followed.

It took me a few moments to accustom myself to the gloom of the interior. The hall floor was tiled, the walls were tall and elegant with ceiling roses and fancy cornices. The air that had been trapped inside for so long smelled stale but a faint, summery draught was breezing through, chasing away the mustiness. A fly corkscrewed through the hall, and Jago and I stepped carefully forward, looking into each of the abandoned rooms. The odd piece of furniture remained shrouded in dust-sheets, casting shadows in the huge oblong shafts of mote-filled sunlight that fell through the windows. An enormous grand piano had been uncovered and stood proud in the centre of the front room.

I knew Mrs Withiel had lain dead in the house for three weeks before her body was discovered, and wondered where exactly she had been and if I would recognize the spot when I saw it by the aura of unquiet that must hover over it. The thought of the old woman lying there, alone in the dark, sent a chill of horror through me. I knew I'd walked past Thornfield House many times when she had been inside, dead, and the knowledge frightened me. What if I'd looked up and seen her ghost watching through the upstairs window? I wrapped my arms around myself and shivered.

'Come on!' Jago called under his breath. He ran upstairs and I followed him into one of the large front rooms. The walls were covered with floral pink-and-green paper, the pattern mostly faded but still strong in the places where the furniture had protected it from the sun. Jago dropped to his hands and knees and peered into a mouse-hole in the skirting board. I went to the window. Wisteria blooms hung like paper garlands, framing the view. A lorry slowly passed by on the lane beyond, and stopped. I could see the top third of it over the wall. And then I sensed, rather than heard, somebody come into the room, and I turned and there was a girl: Ellen.

She was close to me in age and about the same height, but that was where the similarities ended. She had dark hair, a fringe, dark eyes. She was slightly built, long-legged, wearing denim shorts and a sleeveless green T-shirt and although her feet were bare, her toenails had been painted bright green. I was pink and fair, big-boned, round with puppy fat, sticky with sweat and dressed in a pastel-striped T-shirt and towelling shorts.

I had never seen anyone my age as self-composed as this girl and felt childlike in comparison. I tugged at the legs of my stupid, babyish shorts. The elastic was tight around my tummy. I wished I hadn't put my blonde hair into pink bobbles that morning. I wished I wasn't so hot.

Jago scuttled to his feet, brushed himself down and cleared his throat. He licked his lips, anticipating trouble. Adult voices rose up from outside and the rumble of a heavy-duty engine. '*Left hand down!*' someone called. '*Mind the wall!*'

'Who are you?' the girl asked. 'What are you doing here?' Her accent was strange and attractive, her words more precisely enunciated than ours.

'We're just checking everything's OK,' Jago said in a formal voice. He was pretending to be older than he was. He was trying to impress the girl. I frowned at him. 'What about you?' he asked casually. 'Why are *you* here?'

The girl laughed a little artificially and pushed her hair back over her shoulders. She was showing off too. 'I'm Ellen Brecht. This was my grandmother's house but now we're going to live here.'

'The old lady was your grandma?'

'Yes.'

'She told us about you.'

Ellen's eyes widened. 'Did she?'

'She said you never visited.'

'I couldn't.' Ellen wandered over to the window. She held back the net, accidentally replicating the exact pose her grandmother used when she looked out. 'My mama worried about Grandma all the time. I told her she would be all right. She was, wasn't she? She wasn't lonely?'

Jago and I exchanged glances. Jago scratched the eczema on the inside of his elbow. Was it possible Ellen did not know the circumstances of her grandmother's death?

'She looked fine last time we saw her,' Jago said. 'Only . . . she said some weird things.'

Ellen dropped the net. 'What things?'

Jago gazed round the room. 'I dunno. About the devil keeping you away from her . . . and stuff.'

'That's silly! We couldn't come and see her because we were living in Germany, that's all.'

I felt embarrassed. I frowned at Jago. He pulled a face back.

'What are your names?' Ellen asked.

'I'm Jago and she's Spanner.'

'Hannah,' I said, and I pushed his arm.

'Are you her brother?'

'No. We live next door.'

Ellen examined us for a while, as if to get the measure of us. Then she said: 'Come and meet Mama.' She looked at Jago. 'Only don't tell her about the devil stuff.'

We followed Ellen downstairs, where her mother, slight and glamorous, was leaning on a stick, and her father, who looked to me like a film star in skinny black jeans and a black shirt, was waving a cigarette around and directing the removal men as to where to place the chaise longue with which they were struggling.

Ellen's mama was about as different from my mother as it was possible for another woman to be. She was young, slight and beautiful. Shiny hair slip-slid down her back, falling in lovely brown curls over a dress the colour of terracotta. She wore cherry-coloured lipstick and her teeth were small and straight and white.

'Hello,' she said. 'Who have we here?'

'This is Jago and Hannah,' Ellen said. 'They were friends with Grandma.'

'You knew my mother?' Ellen's mama asked, and without waiting for a reply she stepped forward and embraced me, and then Jago, sweetly and tenderly. She smelled exotic and her skin was soft as silk against my cheek. She stepped back and looked at us with her head slightly to one side. Her sunglasses were pushed up onto her forehead, holding back her hair. She wore gold hoops in her ears and a chain with a treble clef charm around her slender neck, and she would have been perfect if it hadn't been for the joints of her fingers and wrists, which were badly misshapen.

'I hated the thought of my mother being in this monstrous house on her own,' she said, straightening her back with difficulty and making the bangles on her arm chink. 'I didn't know she had young friends. And you,' she looked at me and smiled a smile that warmed me inside, 'you must have reminded her of Ellen, mustn't she, Pieter! How perfect that you were there to look after her!'

Ellen's father gave a little mock bow and graced me with a smile so devastating that my stomach flipped and my cheeks burned. I had never met anyone like him in my whole life. Never.

'We didn't exactly look after her,' I said.

'Of course you did!' said Ellen's father.

Just then, a shorter, stocky, older woman, dressed in dark clothes, came through from the back of the house. She was carrying a box of ornaments, wrapped in newspaper, which she placed on the small table beside the telephone. Ellen's father backed away from the woman, like a snail retracting from salt. He moved into the shadows and watched from under his hair, rubbing his chin.

'Are these children bothering you, Anne?' the woman asked Ellen's mama.

'Not at all.'

'You should sit down. You're overdoing it – you need to rest.'

'I'm fine, thank you, Mrs Todd,' said Ellen's mother.

'Your mother needs some peace and quiet,' Mrs Todd said to Ellen. 'Go and play somewhere else.'

From behind Mrs Todd, Ellen's father rolled his eyes. I put my hand over my mouth to contain a giggle. Then he beckoned me over to him. He took a wallet out of his pocket and removed a five-pound note, which he gave to me. He closed my fingers around the money. 'It's for sharing,' he said, enclosing my hand in his fist and giving it a squeeze, and then he leaned down and whispered, 'But you, adorable Miss Hannah, must be responsible for it.'

'Thank you,' I whispered. He winked at me. I held the note very tight in my hand. Nobody had ever called me 'adorable' before.

Outside, Jago, Ellen and I were tongue-tied. We walked along the lane in silence for a while. I kept looking at the money to make sure I hadn't lost it.

'Your parents are very nice,' I said eventually.

'Mmm.'

'Who's the other lady?'

'Mrs Todd? Oh, she's our housekeeper.'

'Is she a servant?' Jago asked.

'Kind of. She does the cleaning and cooking and looks after Mama.'

'Hannah's mum's a cleaner too,' Jago said.

It was true but I wished Jago hadn't said anything. It took all the shine away from the morning. I didn't want Ellen knowing that my mum wore a housecoat and spent her days scrubbing floors and toilets and that her fingers were rough and her arms meaty and that she smelled of bleach. I wanted her to think we were the same.

Ellen looked at me in a curious way but I turned my head and didn't elaborate.

We bought iced lollies at the garage and then walked to the church and sat on the wall looking out over the sparkling sea beyond the fields. Ellen peeled the paper from her Fab fastidiously, and dropped it behind her, into the graveyard.

'Where do you two live?' she asked.

'Down there.' Jago pointed. You couldn't see Cross Hands Lane from where we were, or the pebble-dashed cottages, only the slate-grey colour of the roof-tiles way below in between the leaves of the trees.

'Our houses are semi-detached,' Jago said.

'Joined together,' I explained.

Ellen was impressed by this. I licked the bottom of my lolly, which was melting down my hand, and smiled at Jago. He smiled back. Ellen was watching. I moved my leg a little closer to his, scraping my thighs on the wall.

'Tell me about your families,' Ellen said.

'My mum is dead of cancer and my dad is gone away,' Jago said without looking up. 'I live with my uncle and aunt. He's a bastard and she's a bitch.'

'Oh,' said Ellen, her eyes widening. 'That's so sad!'

Jago shrugged.

Ellen sat for a moment, swinging her legs and processing this information. 'I never met anyone whose mother was dead before.' She turned to me. 'What about you?'

'Nothing really. Boring. One mum, one dad, that's all.'

'Same as me,' said Ellen. She smiled at me then and it was a friendly smile. This was something we had in common. It wasn't much, but it was a start. It was enough.

CHAPTER FIVE

Darkness was swirling around my legs like fog and my bare feet were cold. I was hiding in the back garden at Thornfield House. It was dusk, or dawn perhaps, and the sky was bruise-coloured. Trees and bushes were illuminated by the shadowy light of candles flickering in jars made of barbed wire hanging from the branches. We were playing Murder in the Dark and Ellen was the killer. She'd already found Jago and her father and Mrs Brecht. Only I was left, pressed against the trunk of an old willow tree hidden in the swaying umbrella of its long fronds. '*I'm coming, Hannah!*' Ellen called softly. '*I'm coming to get you!*'

I peeped through the willow leaves and saw her approaching through the twilight. She was smiling a charming, chilling smile and her hands were behind her back. I crept backwards as she came forwards, holding my breath, feeling the ground beneath my feet: toes, sole, heel, treading as carefully as if I were walking on glass. '*I know where you are, Hannah!*' Ellen called. '*I can see you!*'

I was careless – my foot slipped and I fell backwards, tumbled down and I was suddenly falling through water and Ellen's cold little hands were holding onto my ankles, her fingernails digging into my bones, pulling me down away from the daylight, down, down, down. Too late, I realized she had tricked me, and as the light faded in my head I could hear Ellen's voice whispering: '*You can't get away, Hannah. You know you can't. Not now! Not ever!*'

I opened my eyes wide and thanked God I was in my bedroom in my flat in Montpelier, and there was the antique vanity mirror over the chest of drawers with the shell necklace Jago had given me hooked over the stand; there were my Klimt prints on the wall, the picture of my parents – and the beams of light sent by passing cars outside were sliding over the corner of the ceiling as they always did. Everything was in order, everything was normal. Everything except me.

I pressed the heels of my hands into my eye-sockets.

I wished I could get Ellen Brecht out of my head.

I had to stop her tormenting me in this way. I couldn't go on like this.

The room was almost dark. Dusk had fallen while I slept. Lily was still beside me, but Rina had gone. The day had died and the ghosts of my past had come creeping in through the open window.

The telephone was ringing. Had that been what woke me? I counted seven rings, then it fell silent. I turned onto my side, pulled the duvet over me and tucked myself into a foetal position. Sleep had not refreshed me; rather I felt exhausted, emotionally battered. The telephone rang again. I didn't want to move, I felt safe in the cocoon of the bed, but I craved company; even a voice at the end of the line would be better than nothing. I slipped out of bed, turned on the lights, went into the kitchen and picked up the phone. I could see from the caller display that it was John Lansdown, my colleague from the museum.

I answered, tucked the phone between my ear and shoulder, filled the kettle and plugged it in while John apologized for disturbing me. 'Rina said you'd had a bit of a turn,' he said. 'I wanted to make sure you were all right.'

'What did she tell you, John?'

He hesitated a moment. Then he said: 'She told me you thought you'd seen a ghost.'

'It was a migraine,' I lied. 'They affect my eyes.'

'I thought it must have been something like that. How are you now?'

'I'm absolutely fine, John. It's kind of you to ring but you don't have to worry about me. I'll be back at work as normal in the morning.'

'I know you will, Hannah, that's not why I called. Actually I wanted to ask you a favour.'

'Oh yes?'

'Charlotte's out, the girls are at a sleepover and there's no food in the house. I was going to go out for supper and I wondered if you'd like to join me.'

I hesitated.

'It would be a good opportunity to talk about the plans for the new museum annexe,' John continued. 'And I thought after the day you've had, you probably wouldn't be in the mood for cooking either.'

Still I hesitated. I had little doubt Rina had somehow engineered this invitation to make sure I was not left on my own that evening.

'Low blood sugar is very bad for migraines, you know,' John said. 'Although if you have other plans . . .'

'No,' I said. 'No, I'd love to come.'

'Great,' said John. 'That's great. I'll pick you up in an hour.'

I tried to pull myself together before John arrived. I showered, dried my hair and dressed, then listened to a recording of Beethoven's *Prelude for Piano* as I wandered about the flat barefoot, with the cat winding around my ankles. The gentle music soothed me. The Brechts had taught me the alchemy of music. They were experts in the subject. They knew precisely which music would comfort and which would cause pain, and how music's echo lives on in the mind long after the record has finished.

I didn't want to think about the Brechts. The curtains were drawn, all the lamps were lit. I was in my home. I could choose to listen to whatever I wanted, or I could choose silence. I felt safe. When the buzzer rang, I slipped on my shoes and picked up a jacket. John was waiting for me on the pavement outside the front door.

I'd known John for eight years, since I'd taken up my position at the museum. Rina had told me he came from a wealthy background, and he'd obviously had a good education, but he was so down-to-earth that it was easy to forget his privileges. It didn't matter that our upbringings could hardly have been more different; they never interfered with our friendship. I enjoyed his company and respected his methodical approach to work. We shared an interest in ancient history and often John lent me books, or forwarded links to articles or discussions he thought would interest me. He also enjoyed circulating quirky or funny cuttings and pictures – he found humour in many things and it was largely due to his buoyancy that the museum was such a happy place to work in. The whole team liked John, but I believed I was closest to him. He teased me, gently, if ever I became too immersed in a project or took something too seriously. He told me off if I worked too late. I always felt as if he were looking out for me, and I reciprocated.

John was one of the most highly regarded academics in his field but it was not unusual to find him standing in the museum involved in an earnest discussion about the comparative ferocity of different dinosaurs with a group of small children. He wasn't being patronizing, he was genuinely interested in their opinions and ideas.

John was wonderful.

I didn't feel the same about his wife. Charlotte worked in the Admissions Department at the University. I'd met her on many occasions at functions and events, and she was the kind of woman who made me feel uncomfortable – all cleavage and innuendo. She was a keen and apparently competent showjumper and, as far as I could tell, she only had two topics of conversation: horses and sex. Everything about her was loud and colourful, she was a peacock of a woman, and she was happiest when she was surrounded by admirers.

I'd heard her talking about John at the launch of the museum's summer exhibition. 'He's so obsessed with his job that I honestly think he'd pay more attention to me if I was a fossil!' she had said, with wide eyes and a melodramatic shudder. 'I bought some new lingerie for his birthday and was draped in the doorway like so . . .' she adopted a provocative pose, 'and when I asked him if there was anything he fancied, he said: "Yes, the *Panorama* special"!'

Everyone had laughed; everyone except me.

Worse still, it was impossible to be part of a team that worked so closely with the University staff and not hear the rumours about Charlotte. I didn't know what was true and what was not, and a person who flirted as obviously and as much as Charlotte did was bound to be the subject of gossip, but I believed there must be some substance in the speculation that she had had, and was still having, a series of affairs. John was one of the most honest and honourable people I'd ever known. I could not bear to think of him being hurt and humiliated. That was why I avoided Charlotte where possible. That was why I could not stand her.

That evening, he had taken the roof off his little sports car and I felt more like myself as he drove me through the quietening streets of St Paul's and into the centre of Bristol.

The city wind was warm in my hair. I closed my eyes and felt it on my face and I smelled the smells of the city and was grateful to be out with John and not in the flat, on my own.

When we stopped at the traffic-lights, I looked at him. He turned to smile at me and I smiled back. His gentleness was balm to me. That evening, and not for the first time, I wished he and I were together, a couple, so that I could reach my hand out and take hold of his. If he was mine, he would tether me. He wouldn't let me go. In a world of in-consistencies, John was a constant, somebody who could be relied upon. For the thousandth time I wished he and Charlotte had never met, never married, never had children. If things had been different, if it had been me instead of her, then perhaps . . .

'*Don't even think about it, Hannah!*' Ellen's voice whispered in my ear. '*He wouldn't look at you twice.*'

I turned away from John and intertwined my fingers, and as he pulled away from the lights, I concentrated on watching the city go by. I did my best to ignore Ellen, but she was there; all the time she was there, with me like a persistent ache. I sensed her presence in the golden stains seeping across the twilight sky; I glimpsed her reflected in the glass panes of shop windows; I heard her voice in the breeze.

'*I won't go away, Hannah,*' the voice whispered. '*You know I won't. Not now. Not ever.*'

CHAPTER SIX

That first summer, the summer the Brechts moved into Thornfield House, I went there almost every day during the school holidays. My parents were both out at work, Jago was helping at the farm and I was bored at home. There was nothing for a young girl to do in Trethene, and anyway I loved going up to the house to call on Ellen and her parents. I liked seeing how they were settling in, how the rooms were being redecorated and the garden cleared, and how traces of Mrs Withiel were being painted over and scrubbed away. Mr and Mrs Brecht were different from other adults. They made me feel welcome in their home, as if I were special. They were more sophisticated than the Trethene people I'd known all my life. They didn't have mud on their boots, their skin wasn't red-raw from being outdoors too much and they were interested in other things besides the weather, the tourists and the tides. They were glamorous, attractive and exotic, and they made me feel like I was one of them – almost. I wanted to spend every moment I could with them, hoping some of the gold dust of their perfect lives would rub off on me.

Ellen's father was German but had gone to university in America on a music scholarship, and he spoke with a sophisticated accent, like a film star. Whenever I went to Thornfield House, butterflies of anticipation would flutter in my stomach at the thought of being close to Mr Brecht with his long legs, his teasing, his cigarettes and his pointy-toed boots.

'Our little English rose is back!' he would exclaim when he saw me, pulling me in, captivating me with his smile, the twinkling, easy warmth of his manner. And, God, he was handsome. He had good, straight white teeth and dark, soft hair that fell over his almond-shaped brown eyes. He rolled up his shirt-sleeves and the hairs on his arms were dark and his wrists were bony, his fingers long and square. He teased me all the time, played little jokes on me, pretended there was a spider on my back, tickled me, serenaded me, made me jump, made me giggle, made me almost faint with happiness.

'Come on, come on,' he would say, clapping his hands and squinting one eye to protect it from the smoke of the cigarette burning between his lips. 'I've got fifty pence here for the person who does the best handstand!'

I wasn't very good at handstands. Ellen could stay up for ages, she could even walk on her hands, or flip her legs right over to make a crab; I normally collapsed after a few seconds, but I did my best to please Mr Brecht. He always declared the outcome of such competitions a draw, except for the times when Ellen had played up, shown off or otherwise misbehaved, and then I would win. Fortunately for me, she did this regularly.

Ellen was nine months younger than me, but sometimes she acted like a baby. She also told terrible lies – she was always making up stories, sometimes when there was no need for them. She couldn't seem to help it.

'What sort of place did you live in when you were in Germany?' I asked her once, and she said, 'It was a castle.'

I pulled a face.

'It was,' she said. 'It was a proper castle with a moat and a drawbridge. My father's family is related to royalty. So you'd better be nice to me, Hannah Brown, or I'll have you put in a dungeon and chained up with the rats until you die!'

I went home and told my mum, who warned me not to be so gullible.

Another time, we found a dead dove in the pond at the back of Thornfield House. Ellen fished the bird out and held it dripping between her hands, its head hanging lifeless between her fingers. Mrs Todd came out and asked what had happened.

'I drowned it,' Ellen said. She held the bird up to her face, and kissed its beak.

Mrs Todd grabbed Ellen by the arm, said she was a wicked girl, and took her indoors. The bird fell back into the pond and I went home.

Later, Ellen told me that her father had beaten her with his belt for killing the bird. I was so upset by the thought of Ellen being beaten that I burst into tears and Mrs Todd, hurrying to console me, assured me that Mr Brecht hadn't laid a finger on her. She said it was just another one of Ellen's stories and not to take any notice.

'She didn't even kill the bird,' I wept. 'It was already dead when we found it,' and Mrs Todd shook her head and said, 'Those lies are going to get that girl into real trouble, one of these days.'

When Ellen was in disgrace, Mr Brecht paid special attention to me. I basked in the glory of being with him, and not having to share him with her. I alone would perform a dance routine I'd spent hours practising, or pretend to be amazed by his magic tricks, or listen to him singing silly, and sometimes rude, lyrics to popular songs and clap my hands with genuine delight. His irreverence excited, seduced and appalled me; and being appalled by Mr Brecht was a thrill in itself.

At those times, Ellen would hide away somewhere for as long as she could bear to be alone, but eventually she always turned up, sucking a strand of hair, scowling. Mr Brecht would pretend he hadn't noticed her for a while then suddenly he'd leap over to where she was standing, pick her up and swing her round; he danced outrageously with her, she holding on for dear life as he galloped around the garden. *My girl!* Mr Brecht would sing, leaning forward so Ellen had to arch her back, and usually by this time she would be laughing, no matter how hard she tried not to: it was impossible to sulk when Mr Brecht was trying to make you happy. '*Dancing round with my girl!*' he sang, waltzing around the pond swinging Ellen until she was flushed with dizziness and joy.

Mr Brecht had employed a local man, Adam Tremlett, to work on the garden, and he and Mrs Brecht would laugh as they watched.

'It's so good to be back,' Mrs Brecht would say, and she and Adam would exchange smiles.

I used to spend hours wondering what I could do to make Mr Brecht so pleased with me that he'd dance with me like he did with Ellen. There had to be something that would make him look at me the way he looked at her, with such love, with such complete adoration.

'I am the luckiest man in the world,' he used to say. 'I have the most beautiful wife and the loveliest daughter, and I will never, ever let anyone hurt them or take them away from me!'

A few weeks after we first met, Ellen and I were playing upstairs, when she sent me to fetch some juice. In the passageway outside the kitchen, I overheard Mrs Brecht and Mrs Todd talking in suspiciously quiet voices. I crept to the door, put my ear to the crack and listened.

'Hannah's such a nice, uncomplicated child,' Mrs Brecht

said. 'She's a good influence.' I felt a clutch of pleasure in my stomach. 'Don't you think Ellen seems calmer now, Mrs Todd?'

'She has settled down,' the other woman agreed. 'But it's not Ellen's fault she's precocious.'

Mrs Brecht laughed. 'You always defend her, but there's a fine line, Mrs Todd, between being precocious and being an over-indulged little monster!'

I went back upstairs without the juice, but I did not forget what Mrs Brecht had said about Ellen. I kept her words in my mind and turned them over and looked at them from different angles, and each time I came to the same conclusion. Ellen must have a great capacity for being bad, for her own, gentle mother to speak of her like that.

CHAPTER SEVEN

John took me to a small Turkish restaurant tucked away in the back streets of Easton. It was packed with people, its cave-like interior twinkling with red and gold fairy-lights that matched the decor. We were shown to a small table, beside the wall. A candle flickered inside a glass jar the colour of blood. The tablecloth was decorated with spangles that reminded me of a shawl Ellen had given me for my fourteenth birthday. I used to wear it wrapped around my waist when I went to the beach. I remembered the dazzle of sunlight on the glass diamonds sewn around the hem, and a picture came into my mind of Ellen tanned, lying on the sand, shading her eyes from the glare with one hand, leaning on her elbow, smiling at me, and the teenage Jago standing behind her, wet from the sea, watching, dripping, with a towel around his bony shoulders dotted with acne.

I blinked the image away, slid into the seat, unfolded the paper napkin on my lap. John ordered wine. The waiter brought a bottle, opened it and filled our glasses then fetched a large plate of meze. I broke off a piece of warm pitta bread and dipped it in the hummus.

'So how are you feeling now?' John asked.

'I'm OK. Just a bit tired.'

John looked at me, but did not push it. I knew I could trust him, but I could not tell the truth about what had happened in the Egyptian Gallery without explaining my past. I didn't want him to know how, after I returned home from Chile, twelve months of suffering from increasingly acute anxiety had culminated in what used to be called a nervous breakdown but would now be termed a psychotic episode. Along with the psychosis there had been delusional paranoia – voices in my head and hallucinations. I had, at the time, been so convinced that Ellen had come back from the dead to haunt me, that I admitted myself to a psychiatric hospital, pleading with the staff to make her go away. I stayed for several months until a combination of drugs and counselling had restored me somewhat, before being handed over into the care of my long-suffering parents. It was not a picture of myself I wanted to paint for John.

'Really, I'm fine,' I said.

John nodded. 'I'm lucky. I've never had a migraine in my life,' he said. 'Charlotte's mother is a martyr to them.'

I smiled politely. 'How awful for her.'

The waiter returned and put a hot tray on the table between us. He laid out bowls of tiny, herby lamb chops, diced cucumber, salad, bulgur and stuffed beef tomatoes. We ate in silence for a while. I was hungry. I licked the lamb fat from my fingers, made a small pile of bones at the side of my plate and tried to relax. John talked about his ideas for the new annexe – it was an opportunity to introduce more interactive exhibits, and to bring the museum into the twenty-first century, and I was interested in what he had to say. Everything was going fine until the restaurant door opened and a woman and a man came in together. There was something about the woman, the way her hair was tucked behind her ear and the shape of her eyebrows, which reminded me of Ellen. Suddenly, as if from nowhere, I was battered by the emotional storm I'd been holding back since the afternoon.

I missed Ellen so badly and at the same time I wished I'd never met her. I had loved her and I'd hated her. I'd wanted to help her and I'd wanted to destroy her. I wished, more than anything, that she was alive; at the same time, I was glad she was dead. I couldn't rationalize the conflicts in my mind. My heart seemed to swell until it hurt, pressing against the bones of my ribcage. It was filled with passion – a combination of love and rage – that, since Ellen had died and Jago had gone to live in Canada, had had no outlet and had turned into a hard kernel of repressed emotion. John was saying something about the amulet that I'd dropped in the museum earlier, how he had gone up to the Egyptian Gallery to help search for it and how there had been a panic when it could not be found. I tried to listen, but it was too late. I couldn't help myself. Tears began to fall from my eyes. I tried to hide the crying, but John noticed almost at once.

'Hannah, what is it? What's wrong? Oh Christ, I'm sorry. I didn't mean to upset you . . .'

'You didn't. It wasn't you.'

'It's all right,' he said hastily. 'Somebody had already found the amulet and handed it in as lost property. There's no problem about it.'

'It's not that.'

'No?'

He looked at me anxiously. I tried to compose myself, to swallow my feelings and press them back down inside.

'Sorry,' I said. 'Ignore me. I'm not myself.'

'Bloody migraines!' said John. 'Here, have a drink. Have a napkin. Have another lamb chop.'

I smiled weakly. I dabbed my eyes with the corner of my serviette. The people at the neighbouring tables were trying not to look at me, but we were all sitting so close together it was difficult for them. The conversations around us had dried up.

John cleared his throat. He cut a roast tomato into very small pieces and spread it about his plate. I was mortified to think that I might have embarrassed him. I didn't want him to think that I was like Charlotte, that I enjoyed drawing attention to myself.

'I'm so sorry,' I said again.

'Forget it,' he said. 'Worse things happen at sea.' He smiled and gave my elbow a friendly squeeze. 'You are all right, Hannah, aren't you? You would let me know if there was anything I could do to help?'

I nodded and pretended, just for a moment, that we were a couple and that he would always be there at my side, to pick me up when I fell and brush me down and stand me back on my feet. I imagined the relief of telling the truth, how unburdened I would feel.

I only held onto the fantasy for a moment but that was enough to restore me a little.

In the restaurant, a waiter picked up a small fiddle and began to play, and another sang, his voice like honey and heat. I listened and the grief subsided, ebbed away, fingered its way back into its shell. The other diners began to relax again. Things returned to normal.

'So, how is Charlotte?' I asked brightly.

'She's fine.' John took a drink of wine. 'She's very much into her Music Society practice. It's her latest thing.'

'What are they practising?'

'*Grease*. Charlotte's one of the Pink Ladies.'

'Oh. That's good.'

'It had better be, the amount of rehearsing they're doing. You wouldn't believe how much time it takes.'

I glanced at him, but there was no edge to his voice, no irony. He said, 'They're performing at the Hippodrome at the end of term. I'm sure Charlotte would get you a ticket if you'd like to come.'

'Thanks, but it's not really my cup of tea.'

'Mine neither. I don't suppose I'll be able to get out of it, though.'

We smiled at one another.

'You and Charlotte are very different people,' I said carefully. 'Different from each other.'

'It's true. We don't have much in common.'

'Doesn't that make things . . . difficult?'

John rotated his glass, making patterns of the candlelight flicker through the wine. He smiled at me. 'I know people think Charlotte and I are an unlikely combination. I notice how people look at her, and I know they're thinking she could have done far better than me. She could have had any man she wanted, so why did she end up with the scruffy eccentric? I don't know why, any more than they do. I was just the lucky one.'

'I don't think anyone could be better than you,' I said, but not loudly enough for John to hear.

'Nobody chooses who they love,' he went on. 'That's my good fortune.'

I thought it was the exact opposite.

I looked up and held his eyes for a moment; he smiled a little ruefully and then he looked away.

CHAPTER EIGHT

Ellen and I had known each other for less than five weeks when the school holidays ended and we started together at the comprehensive in Helston, but we were already inseparable by then. I'd never had a best friend before and it was a strange and enchanting experience; for the first time in my life, I was never on my own. Ellen and I rode into school together on the bus, we shared the same table in class, we found a quiet spot to sit together and talk at break-time and we stuck together when we needed partners.

The friendship suited Ellen, who didn't know any other girls, and it suited me, because I'd always been a lonely child. I found friendships difficult. Ellen was not always easy, but I understood what I had to do. When she was happy, I simply admired her and swam in her wake. If she was unhappy – usually because she had been thwarted in some way – my role was to listen to her railing against the unfairnesss of life and to sympathize. Sometimes we sat for hours, hidden in a leafy corner of the Thornfield House garden, her complaining and me agreeing with everything she said. On other occasions, I found myself aiding and abetting Ellen in some scheme that was certain to end badly because I could not talk her out of it. I don't think she would have done half the things she did, if I had not been there. She needed an audience and I was it.

I was no lapdog though. Our friendship worked both ways. Ellen gave to me as much as she took from me, perhaps more. One afternoon, during half-term, Ellen and I were in the garden of the Trethene Arms pushing ourselves backwards and forwards idly on the swings while we waited for Mr Brecht, who had 'popped in' to get a bottle of wine, but had been gone for twenty minutes or more. Two girls who had been in my class at primary school came into the garden clutching glasses of Coke. They sat at a bench, glanced at me, whispered and giggled. I ignored them and their voices grew louder.

'It's Hannah Brown, the weirdest girl in town!' one of them sang out in a stage whisper.

'The *fattest* girl in town!' said the other.

'The *smelliest* girl in town!'

They waved their hands in front of their noses, pulled disgusted faces and collapsed in laughter.

Ellen had been twisting her swing round so the chains had become woven. Now she lifted her feet and let the chains untangle, spinning faster and faster until they were clear. She jumped off the swing, dusted the rust from her hands on the side of her shorts, and sauntered over to the girls. They went quiet under her gaze. They hunched their shoulders.

Ellen stood by their bench.

'You were laughing at Hannah,' she said in a matter-of-fact voice. 'Hannah is my friend and I will never let *anyone* hurt her. Do you understand?'

The girls looked at one another. They smirked, but I could tell they were uncomfortable.

'Understand?' Ellen asked again. They nodded.

'Good,' said Ellen, and she leaned forward over the table

and carefully and precisely spat into each of the girls' drinks. They opened their mouths and stared at her. She smiled at them with her lips, not her eyes, wiped her mouth with the back of her hand, turned around and returned to the swing.

I understood then. That was what it meant to be a friend. It meant standing up for the people you cared about. It meant being brave and not turning a blind eye when the other was in trouble. Ellen showed me the value of loyalty.

I should have learned from her. I didn't.

I have one more important memory from that time. It was a different evening, but soon afterwards. My parents had gone to a church social and I wanted to get away from Cross Hands Lane because volleys of ugly words were pinging like gunshot over the fence that separated our garden from the Cardells'. *'If you don't want a hiding, why d'you talk to me like that, Jago? Why d'you do it, you little shit? Look at you, such a fucking waste of space your mum died and your dad dumped you. Loser, loser, loser!'* The words were interspersed with yelps of fear, or pain, from the dog, a large-headed, bow-legged white Staffie-cross. Covering my ears with my hands didn't stop the words, I had to get far enough away so I couldn't hear them, so I cycled up the hill until the noise of the brook running over the tree roots and rocks in the tunnel of greenery at the side of the lane cancelled out the misery next door. At the crossroads, I decided to ride to Thornfield House. I wanted to be with Ellen.

I heard the music as soon as I reached the house. It was piano music, but not the tinkety-tonk hymn kind the teachers bashed out on the piano at school; no, this was music like moonlight on water, music that ebbed and flowed, rippled and sparkled.

I propped my bike against the wall and walked through the open gates onto the flagstone path. The lower half of one of the front-room sash windows was open. Ivory-coloured voile curtains shimmied in the draught. I walked slowly to the window, taking care not to make a noise, and I looked through.

Ellen was sitting at the piano, with her back to me. She was wearing what appeared to be a sleeveless nightdress, and her feet were bare. Her black hair slid down her back, between her shoulder blades, and her arms were moving in time to the music, backwards and forwards, stretching to get the reach of the keys. Ellen's head occasionally dipped a little. Her feet were tucked under the piano stool. She wasn't using the pedals.

I hadn't known Ellen could play the piano, let alone that she could play so well and so beautifully, as if it were something she had been born to do. Why had she kept this part of her life from me? Why wasn't I allowed to share it? I wanted to knock on the window and interrupt her, so that she would be forced to let me into her world, but then I realized I was enjoying watching her secretly. It gave me a kind of power over her.

It was only when she had finished, when the piece trickled delicately to its end, that I noticed Ellen's parents were also in the room. Her mother was lying on the chaise longue. She was covered by a cashmere throw; just one deformed ankle, one narrow foot with lumpy joints, the white growths stretching the skin, was visible on the pale velvet. Her hair was loose and messy and she too had her back to the window. Beside her, on the floor, was an almost-empty wine bottle and a long-stemmed glass lying on its side.

As Ellen slowly turned on the piano stool, as if she were in a dream, her father raised himself from the chair where he had been sitting, went over to Ellen, and leaned down to kiss her. He held his daughter so tenderly, his hands on her shoulders and his hair falling over his face, and the two of them seemed to be caught in a moment of exquisite intimacy. It was perfect, Mr Brecht looking down at Ellen, she looking back up at him, and smoke from the cigarette pincered between the first two fingers of his left hand curling elegantly around them, wreathing them in a delicate mist.

I felt a pang of loneliness in my heart.

I wanted Mr Brecht to hold me like that.

I wanted to be part of that perfect family so closely bound by their private music. I had thought they included me in everything, but I had not known about this, and if I did not know about this, what else was there? What other secrets?

'Play that piece again, Ellen,' Mr Brecht said, 'for your mother.'

Ellen gave a little smile and a nod. She turned back to the piano, and Mr Brecht stood beside her as the music started up again, just a few notes to begin with, trickling over one another brightly like water running over stone.

A few days later, during our school break-time, I asked Ellen outright if she could play any instruments. I expected her to lie, but she shrugged and said, 'Yeah. Piano.'

'How long have you been learning?' I asked.

Ellen frowned. 'I don't want to talk about it,' she said.

'Why not?'

'I just don't, OK?' She narrowed her eyes and looked at me with an intensity that was a warning to me not to pursue the subject.

'I don't see why it has to be such a big secret,' I said. 'It's only a stupid piano.'

'Shut up!' Ellen hissed. She pushed me, hard, in the chest, so that I stumbled backwards and nearly fell over. 'Shut up, Hannah, you're so stupid. You don't know anything!'

We didn't speak to one another for the rest of the day. Ellen was furious with me and I couldn't work out what I had done wrong.

CHAPTER NINE

By the time John dropped me back at the flat after our meal, the soporific effect of the alcohol was kicking in and I was tired. I made some lemon and ginger tea and took the mug, and Lily, into the living room. The red light on the answering machine was winking at me and the display informed me I had three messages. I pressed the button. Rina had called to see how I was, and there was a confused message from my mother, who obstinately refused to grasp the concept of talking to a machine. I felt a pang of guilt at having missed her, deleted the message and moved on to the third one. A woman's voice said, '*Hannah, it's me . . .*'

Was it Ellen? I stepped away from the telephone with my hands over my mouth and my heart pumping. The cat, alarmed, fled the room. Time seemed to stand still. Panicky thoughts careered through my brain, colliding with one another and shattering into myriad smaller anxieties. I was so terrified, I could not bring myself to reach over and switch the machine off. It crackled and whirred, there was the sound of a cigarette-lighter clicking, an inhalation, and the voice returned. '*It's me, Hannah, Charlotte Lansdown.*'

I sank down into a chair and put my head in my hands. It sounded as if Charlotte were pouring herself a drink. I heard the gurgle of liquid, the chink of ice, and then: '*I just got back from singing and John's not here and the idiot has forgotten his phone.*' She took another drag on the cigarette. '*Would you get him to call me and . . .*' More rustlings, more crackles. '*Oh, it's all right – he's back! Ignore this message, babes. Hope you had a good evening.*' And she hung up.

I exhaled the breath I'd been holding and steadied myself against the wall, pressing my forehead against its cool surface.

I needed help. I couldn't cope with this on my own. This was how it had started before; the beginning of my breakdown had been just like this, only the fear was worse this time. It was a cold fear, like the dead fingers of winter inside me, and it was encroaching faster. Less than twelve hours had passed since I saw Ellen in the museum, and already I felt as if she were standing behind me, breathing her chill, dead breath down my neck, watching, listening, waiting.

I rummaged in a drawer, found my address book and looked up the number of my psychiatrist, Julia. I wrote the number on a piece of paper, and tucked the paper beneath the telephone.

'Eight hours,' I told myself. 'Eight hours from now you can reasonably call her.'

One night, that was all.

I went to bed but I couldn't sleep. I couldn't make myself comfortable – my body seemed to be all bones and awkward angles and trapped nerves. A cat howled outside, in one of the gardens down the street. It sounded like a child in distress, and each time it made its banshee wail, the dogs in the neighbourhood barked in protest. I could hear the drone of traffic on the M32 as a distant background irritation, like a wasp in the room, and emergency sirens repeatedly pierced the night somewhere in the city. Worst-case scenarios chased one another through my mind: I imagined bombs going off, buildings collapsing, madmen with guns, fires, people dying. I was too hot, and then too cold. I was parched, dehydrated, so I drank a glass of water and then felt too full. Whenever I closed my eyes, I saw Ellen's face. Every time I drifted close to sleep, a memory would jump into my mind, a flashback to the earlier nightmare or some part of real life that I had forgotten.

At 5 a.m., in the cool, grey pre-dawn light when the birds began their chorus and the cat finally stopped its yowling, I gave up and climbed out of bed.

I had an idea that if I found a picture of Ellen, if I looked at her face, then the memory of her would lose some of its power. She had only been a girl, after all, a girl who died young. What was so frightening about that? Why had she turned into something so monstrous in my mind? I made some tea and pulled out the shoe-box beneath my bed where I kept the few items from my past that had survived my psychotic purges. I curled up on the white easy chair in the living room, listening to Holst with the cat on my lap, and I opened the box.

I used to have hundreds of pictures of Ellen, but after I came back from Chile, I destroyed most of them. I did not want memories, or to be reminded. I riffled through the items in the box until I found the first of the only two images that remained. I picked it up and looked at it by the light of the reading lamp. I had only kept this particular photograph because Jago had taken it. Because he was out of reach, lost to me now, and because I had so little left of him, I had kept the picture.

It had been taken on my thirteenth birthday outside the comprehensive school while we were waiting for the bus home. The camera had been a present from my parents. I'd taken it to school with me, in my bag.

That November afternoon, Jago had been standing at the bus stop, as usual, with the Williams twins. I was a little afraid of them. They were older boys, and they spent their free time roaring around the lanes on motorbikes that spewed fumes, and shooting foxes. Mum had seen them drinking cider in the field behind the church with some holiday girls. The tone of her voice implied that this was shocking behaviour. Sometimes when Jago was with them, he ignored me, but that day he smiled. I said, 'Hello.' I was wearing a badge on my jumper that said: *Birthday Girl*.

'Is it your birthday, then?' Jago asked.

'He's quick!' Ellen said. We all laughed and he pushed his hair back out of his face from embarrassment and shifted from one foot to another.

'I didn't know,' he said. 'I didn't get you a present.'

I shrugged. 'Doesn't matter.'

Jago jiggled about on his feet.

'I'll give you something better than a present,' he said.

Right there, in front of all the kids queuing for buses, he put his boy-arms around me and leaned down and pressed his lips against mine. Jago gave me a birthday kiss. Cheers rippled round the bus stop. I burned with delight and embarrassment.

And then, flushed and happy, I took the camera out of my bag and asked Jago to take a picture of Ellen and me. We stood together, side by side, in our black tights and winter coats, while Jago bounced about in front of us, trying to find the best angle for the shot. Ellen's head was leaning against mine, my blonde hair tangling with her darker, longer hair. At thirteen, I still had puppy fat, my tummy bulged against the coat waistband. While I looked awkward, Ellen looked coltish. Our postures were different. I was standing face-on to the camera, my feet at 45 degrees to each other, my arms by my sides, smiling shyly from under my fringe, my cheeks dimpled and the metal brace on my teeth just visible. The scarf my mother had knitted was tied in a knot around my neck and the red woolly cuffs of my gloves were sticking out of my coat pockets. Ellen was side-on, next to me, one arm around my shoulder, the other bent at the elbow with the hand on her hip. Her chin was pointed upwards and her lips were pursed in a pretty pout. I'd never noticed before that she was posing, but in the cold light of that morning, as an adult, I understood. Jago had kissed me and now Ellen was flirting with Jago because she could not bear to be left out.

I put the photograph, face down, on the floor. The post-cards Ellen had sent me from Magdeburg were still in the box. I flicked through them. Her handwriting was uneven and messy, there were crossings-out and scribbles. I didn't read the cards, but dropped them on top of the photograph. I tipped out some school reports, Jago's old school tie, a picture of Snoopy he had drawn for me, a metal dog tag in the shape of a bone with *Trixie* inscribed on the front, a discarded watch without a strap, seashells and some dried flowers the origins of which I no longer remembered.

At the bottom of the box was the second photograph of Ellen. It was a small square snap that I had taken with the same camera. I picked the photograph up, turned it over. The colours had faded a little, washed with time, but the image took me back there, to the garden of Thornfield House, on Ellen's eighteenth birthday. She was wearing the silver-grey dress her father had given her the year before and was standing beneath an arch made of wrought iron that Adam Tremlett had erected as part of the garden restoration; it was wound through with climbing roses. Anybody who looked at that picture and didn't know might have thought it was an innocent, commemorative snap, but if they looked closer, they would have seen that something was wrong with the image. It wasn't the tiredness and stress that showed clearly in Ellen's face, the tight smile on her lips. It wasn't that the garden was decorated as if for a party, but she was the only one there. No, the problem was the climbing roses trained to weave through the metalwork arch. The plants had grown well, but they had been neglected, left to run wild. Untamed stems of feral dog-rose wove amongst the cultivars. It wasn't the weedy offshoots that unsettled me. What made my blood run cold was remembering that the photograph had been taken in August. The arch should have been full of flowers, filling the warm evening air with their scent.

Ellen should have been surrounded by roses, flowers about her head and petals at her feet, but there were none.

Not one single bud.

CHAPTER TEN

The best memories of my life were of the times I spent with Jago and Ellen at Bleached Scarp, when we were young teenagers, before everything became complicated and started to go wrong.

Bleached Scarp was a beach that Jago had found and that nobody knew about apart from the three of us. It was our own private heaven, tucked in a horseshoe cove between the cliffs beneath Goonhilly Down. Jago had found a secret way down to the beach via steps hewn through a cleft in the rock. To reach it, we had to climb over the fence that separated the cliff edge from the coastal footpath, and tramp through some marshy ground where the gley-soil was spongey with sedge and black bog-rush. After a few yards, we reached a little scree path winding between rocks leading to the cleft. The first time Jago took us there, he scampered down the dark hole but Ellen and I hesitated, afraid to follow him. The rock walls were wet and black as night, and the sound of the sea echoed up from below, slapping against the cave walls. I didn't like the smell of wet sand and seaweed that blew up through the tunnel.

'Come on! What are you waiting for?' Jago called from the bottom. There was an echo to his voice.

Ellen and I exchanged glances. The wind was blowing in from the sea, whipping our hair across our faces and, 30 feet below, the waves were choppy, the water green-blue. A single seal was bobbing up and down, its head poised above the splashing waves.

'Let's go,' said Ellen. Her eyes were bright. She sat down and took off her shoes. 'Come on, Hannah!' And then she too disappeared. After a while, I followed.

We never told anyone else about the little beach. It was our private place, the place we loved.

It was where we always went, and although I missed going to Thornfield House and being teased and complimented by Mr Brecht, I was happy to be with Jago and Ellen. We weren't three individuals at the beach; we were three parts of one whole. And it wasn't as if I never saw Ellen's parents. Mr Brecht was always there with a smile and a wink when I went round to call for his daughter.

I remember one autumn . . . I was almost fourteen, Ellen nine months younger and Jago sixteen. His body fascinated me. He was growing tall – his feet and hands were huge, but the rest of him hadn't caught up yet. Soft, gingery hair grew under his arms and acne spread over his chest and back. His shoulders were broad and muscular but he was still a boy, still so young.

We had an Indian summer in Cornwall that year. The leaves on the trees had turned red and gold, and the sun shining through them made exquisite colours. We were halfway through the autumn term and it was still warm enough to swim. In my mind's eye, I can see Ellen and Jago standing in their swimsuits on the rocks that slabbed out over the water, counting down, jumping in and emerging, shaking their heads, shouting at the cold and laughing. They were like two muscled, sleek sea-creatures. They raced each other up the rocks, agile as monkeys, and jumped from higher and higher, their arms held out wide as they fell. And when they tired of jumping, they dared one another to swim further out to sea, across the cove from the bottom of one cliff-face to the opposite side. I sat on the rocks on the beach, amongst the spiky little cockle pyramids, and worried about them, hugging my knees and watching the dark shapes of their heads, fearing if I lost sight of either they might drown, and wondering how I would explain that they were gone, and I was still here.

I was never a bold child. I had been spoon-fed caution by my doting parents and I knew people drowned along that coastline every year. I used to beg Jago and Ellen not to take so many risks, but they took no notice. They acted as if they were immortal. They ran, shrieking like banshees, towards the sea. They dived into crashing waves and were pushed and pulled along the pebbles, scraping their knees, their hands, their stomachs. They spent hours together in the sea. When I tired of watching them, I combed the beach for pieces of drift-glass made soft and cloudy by the abrasion of the water and the sand, or collected driftwood to make beach fires on which to cook the small yellow crabs and shellfish that Jago fetched up from the seabed.

I remember it so clearly. Ellen, Jago and me, huddled around the fire, warming ourselves by the little orange flames that blew this way and that, cowering beneath the wind. Jago and Ellen's teeth chattered; they were wrapped in threadbare towels that they tossed up into the gorse when they had finished with them. The smoke was in our eyes and hair, the inside of our mouths tasted of scalding hot cockle-meat and burning wood.

I used to think that, away from the beach, Jago and Ellen would never do more than tolerate each other, and then only for my sake. Each, I believed, thought the other too distant and different. Jago was the rough, uncouth boy from the wrong side of the tracks, Ellen the kooky snob with the wealthy parents. When either Jago or Ellen was alone with me, they made unkind comments about the other. Ellen thought Jago was stupid, Jago thought Ellen was stuck-up. I was the buffer between them.

We all played our parts so diligently, so well that I never realized we were acting. For a long while, none of us did.

CHAPTER ELEVEN

The early hours of the morning dragged on until at last it was eight o'clock, which seemed a reasonable time to call my psychiatrist. Julia Fortes da Cruz had told me, years before, that I could contact her at any time. As the phone rang out I closed my eyes and hoped that she had meant it. I was so relieved when she answered that it took me a moment to compose myself.

'Julia . . .'

'Hello! Who's that?'

I could hear a child in the background, a baby, squawking and laughing. Julia had not had a child last time I spoke to her.

'It's Hannah,' I said. 'Hannah Brown. I was your patient in Chartwell.'

Julia flustered for a moment, but regained her composure quickly.

'Hannah, how lovely to hear from you! Are you all right?'

Her voice had changed. At the mention of the hospital, I imagined her tucking the phone under her chin, signalling her partner to take care of the baby, slipping from the kitchen. Julia was a small, lively, unconventional woman. I was certain she would have a study with plants on the windowledge and coloured glass dream-catchers, crystals and inspirational postcards pinned to the picture rail.

'No,' I said. 'I'm not all right – not really. I'm sorry to call so early, Julia, but something happened yesterday and—'

'It's OK. It's not a problem. I'm glad you called. That's why I'm here.' There was a rustle at the other end of the line and then the familiar elongated electronic note of a computer booting itself up. Julia was looking for my records, reminding herself of my case. I imagined her sitting down at a desk by a window, looking out on an overgrown garden full of children's toys and pots hand-thrown by her arty, eclectic friends. 'What happened, Hannah?' she asked.

'I was at work yesterday,' I said, 'and I saw Ellen Brecht.'

'Right,' said Julia, as if there were nothing unusual in this. I wondered if she remembered the details of my case, or perhaps just the bare bones of memory gave her the shape of my disorder as clearly as I could see the live Tyrannosaurus Rex fleshed out from its skeleton, hanging in the museum. She was probably scanning her computer notes right then, reminding herself. 'Were you on your own, or with other people?'

'There were lots of people there. I was in the museum, in an exhibition area. She – Ellen – was standing amongst the other visitors.'

'And how did this make you feel?'

'For a moment I was happy but then I realized what was happening and I was scared,' I said, and the word was not big enough for the terror I had experienced, and which still lingered, like a hangover, in my mind and in my bones. 'She seemed so real,' I said. 'It was raining outside and her hair was damp. Every detail was real.'

'Or at least it *felt* real, Hannah,' Julia said gently. 'The mind can be very good at self-deception, especially under stress. What happened next?'

'I had a panic attack.'

'OK.'

'And after that I came home but I couldn't stop worrying. I couldn't sleep. I keep thinking about Ellen. What if she's come back, Julia? What if the same thing that happened before happens again and I keep seeing her everywhere? How am I going to manage if she's always there, in my head? What am I going to do? I don't think I could bear to go through it a second time, really I don't.'

Julia's voice was quiet and calm. 'All right, Hannah. That's a lot of "what if"s. We'll jump those fences if we get to them. One shaky moment doesn't make a breakdown any more than one swallow makes a summer.'

'No,' I said, but I was thinking of how real Ellen had seemed to me in the museum, how present she had been.

Julia asked: 'How have you been generally, up until now?'

'Good.'

'Everything's been going along at an even keel? You're eating well? Exercising?'

'Yes.'

'Sleeping OK?'

'Sometimes.'

'Stressed? Anxious?'

'Not really. Not until yesterday.' I took a deep breath and leaned my head back against the wall. Lily was weaving around my ankles.

'OK . . .' I could hear Julia's fingertips tapping on her desktop. 'Listen, Hannah, I don't think there's any need to worry. This event, although I appreciate it was unpleasant and frightening, was most likely a one-off, a flashback. They happen to the best of us.'

I closed my eyes. 'It didn't feel like a flashback. She was so clear and so real and—'

Julia interrupted. 'That's how you described your

hallucinations last time, Hannah. They feel absolutely real to you, of course they do, that's why they're so frightening.'

'Yes.'

'So for now, let's hope this doesn't happen again, but if it does, I want you to stay calm – you remember the breathing exercises?'

'Yes.'

'Do those. And stay in touch. I want to speak to you every few days until things have settled down. Call me any time you need to, day or night.'

I picked up the cat and held her in my arms, up close to my face. I could feel her heart beating beneath my fingers. 'Thank you, Julia,' I said. 'I will.'

CHAPTER TWELVE

While Jago, Ellen and I were growing up, the situation next door at number 10 Cross Hands Lane deteriorated. The Cardells' fights became more frequent and more vicious, until one day Mrs Cardell left the house wearing her slippers and carrying an umbrella and never returned. Mr Cardell responded by bringing home young women he'd picked up at the docks and holding round-the-clock drinking sessions with his mates. Jago missed school more often than he attended. The dog, exhausted by whelping, became stiffer and more cowed until finally my father decided to take matters into his own hands. He put on his best jumper, combed what was left of his hair over the shiny pink dome of his head, went down our garden path and up the Cardells' and knocked on their front door. Caleb opened it. He was wearing a pair of filthy jeans and nothing on his top. He had a can of beer in one hand and a roll-up in the other and he was swaying on his feet, red-eyed and nasty. It was dark inside the Cardells' house because their front-room window had been broken and was boarded. Dad could only see the men in the pit of a living room by the flickering grey-blue light of the television screen reflected on their faces.

He took a deep breath and said, 'I'll give you fifty pounds cash for the dog, Caleb.'

The money was in his hand, where Mr Cardell could see it. Caleb looked at the money and then back at my father. He took a drag on the cigarette.

'I make twenty-five a pup each time she whelps,' he said.

'Yes,' said Dad, 'but she's past it now. You and I both know it. Next pregnancy'll finish her off.'

Caleb Cardell thought about this for a moment.

'Seventy-five and you've got yourself a deal,' he said.

Dad nodded. He had expected this. He took five more notes out of his back pocket and placed them into Mr Cardell's hand.

Caleb put the cigarette in his mouth while he counted the money. Then he leaned over the stair banister and shouted up: 'Jago! Get down here, you lazy bastard, and fetch the friggin' dog.'

Jago came downstairs warily. He didn't look at my father, but dodged past his uncle and went into the kitchen. Dad heard the back door open. He took a couple of steps away, into the fresher air, clasped his hands together behind his back, rocked on his heels and stared into the middle distance. Jago reappeared a few moments later with the dog following timorously, her ears flat and her tail between her legs. She was attached to Jago by a piece of green garden twine. As he reached the front door, Mr Cardell kicked Jago's backside with the flat of his boot. Jago stumbled and fell forward, past Dad, onto his hands and knees on the front path, which was filthy and full of nettles and broken glass.

'Take the fucking kid as well,' Caleb Cardell said to my father. 'You can fucking have him for fucking fuck all,' and he laughed and slammed the door shut.

Back at our house, Mum, who had been listening from

behind the front-room window, buttered some extra bread for tea. Dad came in with Jago and the dog. Nobody said anything about what had happened. Jago and the dog both looked ashamed, as if it were all their fault. Jago sat at the table with us to eat his dinner, though – and he ate plenty. He cleaned his plate in about two minutes flat. He ate un-couthly, scooping food onto his fork and shovelling it into his mouth. If I'd eaten like that I'd have been told off, but my parents merely exchanged knowing glances, and then Mum heaped up Jago's plate again. I had never seen anyone eat so much, so fast, in all my life.

'It's nice to have someone with a good appetite at the table,' Mum said. She smiled at Jago. He wiped his mouth with his hand, burped and said, 'Thanks very much.'

Mum nodded. She was pleased, I could tell.

I kept looking at Jago from under my fringe. I could not think of a single thing to say that would not make me sound like a baby or an idiot.

After a while, we heard raised voices next door. The dog cowered behind one of the living-room chairs and peed on the carpet.

'I'd best be going,' Jago said. He stood up. He looked dirty and scruffy and big, and out of place in our little front room that was neat as a pin.

'Going where?' Mum asked.

Jago shrugged. 'I dunno. Anywhere. I'll find somewhere.'

Dad turned up the telly to mask the sounds from number 10 and said it would be helpful if Jago stayed with us at least until the dog settled down. Mum latched onto what Dad had said as if that had been the plan all along.

'You can't go and leave us to cope with her while she's so unsettled,' she said. 'You just can't.'

Jago looked dubious but did not know how to refuse.

Mum went upstairs to make up the bed in the boxroom.

Dad told Jago to sit down again in the kind of voice that brooked no argument.

I could hardly wait to tell Ellen about all this – she would, I was sure, be mad with curiosity.

For the rest of the evening, Dad and Jago sat together on the settee, awkwardly, with their arms crossed, watching the football, and I sat on the rug and tried to feed cheese to the dog to make her feel more at home. Then Dad said it was getting late and time for bed.

I waited until Jago had used the bathroom, then I tapped on the boxroom door.

'Jago, it's me.'

'What?'

I pushed open the door. The boxroom was a sparse, narrow space in the eaves. It smelled of mothballs and the stinky oil Dad used to clean his fishing rods. Jago was sitting incongruously on the deep pink chenille coverlet on the bed. His face was blotchy where he had been crying. I looked down at my feet so he wouldn't know that I knew.

'What?' he asked again, more aggressively. He wiped his nose with his forefinger.

'What's the dog called?' I asked.

'I dunno. She don't have a name.'

From next door, we heard the sound of glass breaking and Caleb Cardell's roar.

'He's a wanking bastard,' Jago muttered.

'Yes,' I agreed. 'He is.'

Jago sniffed. He made a gobby noise in his throat that both disgusted and excited me, a boy noise.

'Is it all right if I call the dog Trixie?' I asked.

'Suit yourself,' said Jago. 'It don't bother me.'

Jago never returned to number 10 Cross Hands Lane. Caleb was evicted by the council soon after Jago moved in with us, and he never called round to say goodbye. We all acted like that was a good thing. It took a while, but eventually Jago settled into our family as if he should have been part of it all along. He adored both my parents, especially my father, and Dad could not have been more proud, or closer to Jago, if he had been his blood son.

That was how Jago Cardell, my childhood friend and neighbour, the first boy who ever kissed me, became my brother.

My almost-brother.

CHAPTER THIRTEEN

After I'd spoken to Julia, I walked across the city to my work. The sun was low in the sky still but there was a smell of summer in the air and I knew it was going to be a lovely day. I arrived at the museum at the same time as Misty, the intern, only I was on foot and she was climbing out of a snappy little black car.

'Bye, gorgeous, have a good day!' A young man waved at Misty from the driver's window. She sneered at him in a way that wasn't exactly unfriendly, which was about as good as you could hope for with Misty, and raised a hand in greeting when she saw me.

'Who's that?' I asked.

'Some loser.'

'Your boyfriend?'

'In his dreams.'

I smiled at her. I envied her confidence.

Misty and I went into the museum together, via the staff entrance. I hung my jacket on the rack in the corner of the educational-resources room and then checked the calendar pinned to the noticeboard.

'It's going to be a busy morning,' I said. 'Two school parties.'

'Kill me now,' said Misty.

'Make some coffee first, would you, Mist?'

I was determined to keep things light that day. I didn't want my colleagues to realize how out of sorts I was. I didn't want them talking about the previous day's turn, or knowing that I had hardly slept that night or wondering about my mental state. It would be best to pretend that nothing out of the ordinary had happened, and to act casual.

The light was on in John's office. I knocked on the door with my knuckles, and pushed it open.

John was sitting at the desk, rubbing his eyes with his fists. He sat up straight when he saw me and put a smile on his face, but he looked as if he had slept even less than I had.

I smiled as warmly and as normally as I could. 'I just wanted to say thank you for last night.'

'No, no, I should be thanking you.'

'I didn't do anything.'

'You have some great ideas for the annexe. Perhaps you could write them down, Hannah. Email me a few bullet-points . . .'

'Of course.'

He looked up at me then. The whites of his eyes were pink with tiredness but the pupils were grey, almost silvery. I hadn't noticed that before. I wanted to say something to him, to strengthen our connection, but I couldn't think of anything that would not sound insincere or like a platitude.

'Have a good morning, John,' I said. Then I left the office, closing the door gently behind me.

I busied myself with administration work, keeping my head down, shoulders straight, repelling any well-meant enquiries as to my well-being with body language that gave the message I was fine, and had too much to do to indulge in small talk.

I don't think anybody noticed how I kept glancing around, to see if anyone was watching me. I don't think they were aware that I was keeping my back to the wall, avoiding dark corners.

The first tour was a class of eleven-year-olds from Bristol Grammar School. They were cheerful, bright children who looked as if they had been fed plenty of vegetables and orange juice in infanthood, with shiny shoes and clothes that had been bought a little too big, for them to grow into. I remembered Jago when he was their age, how the cuffs of his sleeves never reached his wrists, how his jeans were worn through in places, and the scabby tracksuits he wore, his uncle's cast-offs. I remembered the cracked skin on his lips and his generous, crooked smile, his breath, sour because he never had a toothbrush, and one of his top front teeth was already missing – knocked out by Mr Cardell probably. It gave a rakish look to his grin, although my parents took him to have it fixed after he moved in with us.

Now Jago lived on the other side of the world. God, how I missed him.

He had been working, for several years, as a sustainability adviser with the fishing community in a small Newfoundland port. He stayed in close touch with my parents and had bought them a transatlantic cruise for their Golden Wedding anniversary, meeting them off the ship in New York and treating them to what Mum described as a 'slap-up holiday'. It was Jago's way of making up for living so far away. The last time I saw him had been a couple of years earlier, after my father's heart attack. I'd arrived at the hospital in Truro in the early hours. A nurse showed me to the ward. My father was in a private bay at the end. Mum was asleep in a chair. She had been covered over with a blanket, and a pillow had been placed tenderly beneath her cheek to protect her neck from cricking.

A rugged, broad-shouldered man wearing ill-fitting denim jeans, a scruffy grey T-shirt and a leather string around his thick neck was sitting on a stool on the far side of the bed, with his arms resting on the knees of his splayed legs. The man needed a shave, he looked dog-tired. His hair had been cut very short, his forearms were tattooed and his face was lined. I did not recognize him at first, but as I came into the room he stood up and we held one another's eyes, and it was as if we were children again.

'Jago!' I said, wondering how he, who lived thousands of miles away, had managed to reach my father's bedside before me. I stepped forward to embrace him, but as I did so he stepped back, away. The rejection cut me like a knife.

'How are you?' I asked.

Jago ignored the question. 'Dad's doing all right,' he said. 'They reckon he's going to pull through.'

I looked at my father, who seemed childlike lying, as he was, on his back, in the bed, with an oxygen mask covering his nose and mouth. He was terribly pale, and quiet. I thought he would be appalled if he knew that Jago and I found it painful even being in the same room as one another.

'You don't mind if I sit with you?' I asked, and now my voice was cold.

Jago shrugged. I pulled up a chair and we sat on opposite sides of the bed, with Dad in between us, his gnarled hands resting on either side of the mountain beneath the bedclothes that was his stomach, to the soundtrack of Mum snoring gently on the chair. It was the first time we had all been together in the same place as a family since I was eighteen and Jago twenty, and yet we had nothing to say to one another, Jago and I; nothing at all.

CHAPTER FOURTEEN

It was different when we were young. There was a time, a brief time, when nothing was wrong in our world and we were happy. Jago was living with us, Caleb Cardell was gone, I was losing my puppy fat and my teeth were straight, Ellen's father was still charming and funny and her mother, although poorly, was managing her condition.

Every morning, during that time, I woke up feeling happy and excited because Jago brought an energy into our lives that hadn't been there before. Dad threw himself into being a father to his new son. He encouraged Jago to join the cricket team he coached, he took him fishing and he 'rescued' the rusty old shell of a Ford Escort from a corner of the Williamses' cow barn, brought it home on a borrowed trailer and set it on bricks in the front garden of our house so he and Jago could restore it together. When it was fixed, it would be Jago's car and because he had rebuilt it from scratch, Dad said, he would always know what to do if something went wrong. Restoring the car was a project that lasted years.

Mum cooked Jago a hot meal every night, did his laundry, and he showed his affection for her by moderating his language and doing little jobs, unasked. He fetched in the coal, moved leaves from the gutter, unblocked the drains, cleaned up after Trixie.

It was less straightforward for me to change the foundation of my relationship with Jago from friend to almost-sister. I was fascinated by Jago, but my feelings for him were confused and contradictory. I loved him, but I didn't know why, or how. Even today I'm not sure if I saw him as a brother, a friend, or as a potential lover. It was probably a combination of the three, exacerbated by the hormones of adolescence and combined with a genuine affection for the boy who had always been part of my life and who had suffered so much in the house adjoining ours.

I can't say how he felt about me. How would I know? We weren't the sort of family to talk about feelings.

Not long after he came to live with us, Jago turned sixteen. Dad said it might be a good idea if he left school and did something useful that he enjoyed rather than being stuck in a classroom wasting the teachers' time and his own. Jago had a natural aptitude for mechanics, and was accepted on an apprenticeship in marine engineering. He went to college two days a week; the other days he worked with Bill Haworth, a friend of Dad's who owned a boat, the *Eliza Jane*, which fished out of Polrack. Jago enjoyed the work and Bill said he was good at it.

When he received his first pay packet, Jago bought gifts: a box of After Eights for Mum, a fishing fly for Dad and a necklace made of tiny seashells threaded on a string for me.

After that, he didn't buy presents, but he gave most of his wages to Mum.

Jago didn't mind the weather. He liked the rain as much as he liked the sun. Mum and I sat on the harbour wall to watch the *Eliza Jane* come in and we squealed when we saw Jago standing on the deck, looking like a man, holding the rope between his hands, followed by a cloud of screaming seabirds. He raised his hand to salute us, and I was thrilled to the core. I played out a little fantasy in my head that I was his sweetheart and he was coming home to me. I was always imagining scenarios like that. I don't think I really meant anything by it.

Each morning, when Jago went to work, I knelt on my bed and pulled aside the curtains to watch him leave the house. He perched his mug of tea on the lid of the water butt while he laced his boots. Steam rose in a thin curl from the surface of the tea. I looked down on Jago and I drew a smiling face on the patch of window glass made misty by my breath. Jago always looked up and waved to me. I held up my hand, and touched the tips of my fingers to the glass, bringing them closer together as he grew smaller as he walked away.

After he joined the crew of the *Eliza Jane*, Jago stopped coming to the beach with Ellen and me. He worked long hours and his free time was always taken up with working on the car or helping Dad. He told me he didn't want to waste time playing with silly little spoiled brats like Ellen Brecht. After a while, I stopped asking.

Ellen and I still went to Bleached Scarp. It was still our place.

One day I remember in particular, because it was the day I realized that Ellen's mother was going to die.

When I'd called for Ellen, I'd found Mr Brecht pacing the front garden, striding out and smoking, his shirt hanging loose about his hips. His hair was longer and wilder, and he hadn't shaved for a while; his face was covered in a dark stubble that made him even more beautiful, if such a thing were possible. He was Heathcliff, Mr Rochester, Robert Downey Junior and Kurt Cobain rolled into one.

'Hannah!' he cried, when he saw me. 'You're a sight for sore eyes!'

He put the cigarette in his mouth and held out his arms

and, dreamily, I'd gone to him, expecting to be enclosed and enfolded, held to his chest. He only held me by the shoulders. He only kissed the top of my head.

'Is something wrong?' I asked, and he said: 'Everything is wrong, Hannah. I am losing her. My Anne is leaving me.'

I hadn't known what to say. I looked up at the dark planes of his face. He was staring at the sky, watching the clouds chase one another, and the gulls drifting on the buffeting wind. He seemed noble and heroic, with his hair and his white shirt and the stubble on his chin. I had moved a little closer towards him. Had reached out my hand and touched his forearm with my fingertips. I felt the softness of his skin, its warmth. I felt a clutch in my stomach.

I wanted to tell him that I was there for him, always, and that I would help him and do whatever he wanted me to do. I would be loyal and true and I would never, never leave him. I would have said something, but Mrs Todd came out and she gave me an odd look so I moved away from Mr Brecht and pretended to do up the lace on my trainer.

'The doctor's on his way, Pieter,' Mrs Todd said. 'He'll be ten minutes.' She looked at me. 'It's best you don't go inside, Hannah. I'll tell Ellen you're here.'

I nodded. And Ellen came out and we left to go to Bleached Scarp. The doctor passed us in his Land Rover as we walked along the lane.

The sun was hot that day, but there was a chill wind. Ellen lay on a striped towel close to the cliff-face where there was some shelter. I sat beside her with a sketch pad balanced against my knees. I was trying to draw the sea for a school art project, but it was proving too difficult a challenge. I shaded my eyes with my hand, to watch the progress of a small boat across the horizon. It rose on the swell of a wave, then disappeared.

'Do you think that's the *Eliza Jane*?' I asked.

'I don't know,' Ellen mumbled, without looking up. I sighed, and made a bubble with my gum. Ellen's little transistor radio was balanced on a flat ledge of rock beside us, tinnying out pop tunes. The wind lifted the music, blowing it this way and that. Ellen lay on her front, with her head rested on her folded arms. 'Put some oil on me, would you?' she asked in a lazy voice. I popped the bubble and licked the gum back into my mouth, then I put down the pad and my pencil, picked up the bottle of Ambre Solaire, unclipped the lid, sniffed, and squeezed a small pool of the orange oil into the palm of my left hand. I looked down on Ellen's slim, tapering back. She was wearing a green halter-necked swimsuit, the strings tied in a bow at the nape of her neck.

I hesitated. I was afraid of touching Ellen's skin.

Her back was already tanned a deep honey colour. The tiny hairs that covered it were so fair they were almost invisible. Three moles ran in a straight line from her right shoulder to the tie of the swimsuit.

'Go on,' Ellen said. 'My shoulders are burning.'

I turned over my palm, and let it fall onto her back. Her skin was shockingly hot. I spread the oil over Ellen, feeling the nub of her bones, the parallel lines of her ribs.

Ellen inhaled deeply, and then exhaled with contentment.

With my clean hand, I gently lifted her hair and moved it aside while I oiled her shoulders and the tops of her arms. Then I tapped her in the hollow of her back to let her know I'd finished.

'Thank you,' Ellen said. She smile-squinted up at me. I smiled back.

I could see the shape of her bottom through the tight fabric of the swimsuit. There was something about Ellen's thighs, the long sweep down to the knee, the slope on the inside, that made me want to bite them like I used to bite the plastic hands of my dolls when I was small. Instead, I wiped my hands on my own thighs and lay down beside my friend. Our faces were very close together.

'How is your Mama?' I asked. 'Why did Mrs Todd call for the doctor?'

Ellen wrinkled her nose. 'She was bad today. Worse than normal. She's in pain all the time. All that makes her happy is the garden, but Papa won't let her out there.'

'Why not?'

Ellen shrugged. 'He worries she'll fall. I think she prefers it when Papa is away and she can spend all her time outside. Adam lets her do what she wants, but Papa gets on her nerves. He fusses too much.'

'She's not *really* ill, is she?' I asked.

'You mean is she going to die?'

'That's not what I meant at all,' I said quickly, although it was, of course.

'I don't know. Sometimes she goes sort of . . . weird.'

I moved a little yellow pebble around with the tip of my finger. 'How weird?'

'Far away. Like she's already left and gone somewhere else.'

I looked at Ellen. Her eyes were glassy.

'Sometimes,' Ellen said, 'sometimes I think she . . .'

'What?'

'I think she thinks she would be better off dead.'

'You shouldn't say things like that, Ellen.'

'It's true.'

'No, it's not! You're always saying things like that, making things dramatic, making things up.'

'I'm not! I don't *want* her to die!'

'And I bet she doesn't either! You can't be happy when you're dead. You can't be anything except more dead, so don't say things like that.'

Ellen went quiet then. I thought it was because she knew she had gone too far.

After an awkward few moments, she said, 'You have thousands of freckles. They're very pretty.' She grinned and tickled my nose with a samphire stem. I smiled back and pushed it away. 'Almost as many as Jago,' she went on. 'You really are like brother and sister. You're like twins. Maybe you were separated at birth.'

'He's two years older than me.'

'The hospital made a mistake. They gave him to the wrong family. Or you.'

'We're nothing like one another!'

'You are too.'

'Shut up,' I said, laughing. I propped myself up on my elbows. My shadow fell over Ellen's face.

'You're so lucky,' Ellen said. Then she smiled in the way she sometimes did when she was in a thoughtful mood. Her teeth were very white in her tanned face. Dark strands of hair blew across her blue-grey eyes. I could see myself reflected in the pupils. I liked it that my face was in Ellen's eyes. Suddenly I loved her. I would have liked to put my arms around her and hold her tight. I loved her so much that my eyes became hot and I had to bite the inside of my lip hard to keep myself from crying.

Ellen didn't notice. 'What time is it?' she asked.

'Nearly five.'

'I have to go home. I promised I'd help get Mama ready. We have visitors this evening.'

'Who?'

'People she used to perform with. Russians. A conductor.'

'From an orchestra?'

'Mmm.'

Ellen rolled over, kneeled up and brushed sand from the

front of her legs and her stomach. She began to collect her things together.

'Mama used to be famous,' she said.

'What for?'

'Playing the piano, of course.'

Ellen spoke in a voice that implied I should have known this fact, but since the time we'd argued at school years earlier, neither of us had mentioned the piano and I hadn't heard her play again.

'She used to travel all over the world before she got ill,' Ellen said. 'You know the painting in the front room? That's her in New York.'

I'd seen the picture – it would be impossible to miss it. It was set in an enormous, ornate gold frame, flanked by lights, and it dominated the room. It portrayed a young woman with slender shoulders and a straight spine sitting at a grand piano, her long fingers flexed over the keys. Dark hair tumbled down her bare back; she was wearing a sunshine-coloured silk dress that reflected the lights of the concert hall, its reds, yellows and golds, and the audience, in darkness, were beyond. The pianist had been painted in semi-profile, so her face was not clear, only the curl of one pale ear, a pearl drop earring, the yellow rosebuds woven through her hair, and a ringlet at the jawline. Now I knew, it was obvious the woman in the picture was Anne Brecht, but I'd never made the connection between the healthy young woman at the piano and the real-life one with her poor claw-fingers and her pain.

'That's why Papa started teaching me to play,' Ellen continued as she packed her bag. 'Because it makes Mama happy. It helps her remember what her life used to be like.'

She shook her towel carefully, so the sand didn't blow towards me, and folded it. The love I'd felt for Ellen earlier returned. Now I understood why she did not like to talk about her music. I was filled with a rush of happiness that at last she trusted me enough to confide these things to me.

'When did your mother get ill?' I asked.

Ellen stuffed the towel in her bag. 'When she had me. It's my fault. If I hadn't been born, Mama would be fine. She'd probably be the most famous piano-player in the world by now.'

'That's not your fault. You couldn't help being born.'

'I know.' Ellen leaned over and fastened the straps of the bag. 'But I feel bad about it. You would too, if you were me.'

CHAPTER FIFTEEN

The morning at the museum passed without any problems, but I was tired and spaced-out. I needed some fresh air during my lunch-break. I decided to walk up towards Clifton, where there was a shop that sold excellent home-made pasties. As I passed the university's grand Wills Memorial Building, two women came out of the doors in front of me. They were so engrossed in their conversation, their arms linked at the elbows, that they almost bumped into me and I had to step into the kerb to avoid them. They had their backs to me but I recognized the slimmer and prettier of the two by her voice and her brittle laughter. It was Charlotte Lansdown, John's wife. The pavement was busy with students and shoppers and tourists and I had no option but to stay close to the pair of them. I followed them into the pasty shop. I didn't mean to eavesdrop – I couldn't help it. They were right in front of me and they weren't talking quietly. The plumper woman, the one who wasn't Charlotte, took hold of Charlotte's arm to draw her closer.

'Have you decided what you're going to do?' she asked.

Charlotte tilted her head towards the other woman. 'I'm taking the girls to my parents' this weekend. I need to have space, to – you know – put things in perspective.'

'Hasn't John noticed something's going on?'

Charlotte laughed. 'Him – notice me? You are joking, aren't you? He never pays me any attention. He has no idea how I feel.'

'You have to make up your mind, love. Either tell him it's over or stop carrying on like you are and try to make a go of your marriage. You can't continue like this.'

'Oh, but I want to leave. You have no idea how much I want to leave him.'

'Then do it.'

'But how, Becky? How can I possibly make him understand? He's such a cold fish.' She shuddered for emphasis.

The other woman, the one called Becky, laughed. I was angry, but worse, I felt humiliated for John. How could Charlotte talk about him in that way? How could she?

'It's not like it's all your fault,' said Becky. 'If he made you happy, you wouldn't feel the need to go looking for your fun elsewhere.'

'That's true,' Charlotte said in a voice loaded with self-pity.

'I think you'd be better off apart.'

'But it's not just about me, is it?' Charlotte whined. 'What about the house? The car? The horses?'

Becky sighed. 'Well, you can't have it both ways, can you? You'll have to decide what's more important to you. Your lifestyle or your happiness.' She let go of Charlotte, rummaged in her handbag and took out her purse. 'My treat,' she said. 'What are you having?'

Charlotte turned to look at the chalkboard that hung on the wall beside me. She caught me staring at her; she looked me right in the eye and I looked right back. The colour drained from her face.

'Oh,' she said, struggling to dredge up a smile. 'Hannah. Hello.'

'Hello,' I said.

Charlotte played with the bracelet on her wrist.

'Becky,' she said, 'this is Hannah who works with John at the museum.'

Becky turned and we nodded at one another.

'It's a great little shop this, isn't it?' Charlotte babbled. 'I just adore the spicy spinach and feta pie. Have you tried that, Hannah? You really should.'

I couldn't muster a smile, I was so angry with her. Charlotte blinked nervously. The shock remained on her face. She knew I had overheard the conversation; I knew she knew.

There was only one young man serving behind the counter and several people still in front of us in the queue. The prospect of standing and making small talk with Charlotte for another five minutes or more was unbearable.

'I've got to go,' I said.

I turned to leave and, as I did so, Charlotte reached out and held onto my arm. 'Hannah . . . ?'

'It's none of my business,' I said, shaking her off.

I squeezed and apologized my way out of the little shop and at the door I turned back and walked down the hill, my face burning, wishing I had not overheard the exchange because now I knew John was being deceived, and my complicity made me feel almost as disloyal and culpable as his lying, adulterous wife.

CHAPTER SIXTEEN

As Mrs Brecht's condition worsened, I spent less time at Thornfield House. She needed peace and quiet, and Mrs Todd encouraged Ellen and me to find alternative ways to amuse ourselves during weekends and holidays. I spent as much time as I could with Ellen, but I hardly saw Mr Brecht any more. I didn't stop thinking about him, though; the enforced separation served only to make him consume my daydreams even more. He was never far from my thoughts, and always, when I thought of him, I saw him as he had been when he stood in the garden looking up at the sky, his long hair drifting across his deep, dark eyes, my hand extended, his skin warm beneath my fingertips . . . and the memory rekindled the delicious pang I had felt in my belly.

I pledged always to be there for him.

He would be able to count on me until the end of time.

Ellen and I acted on Mrs Todd's advice and found work in Polrack, a large village close to Trethene that tumbled down the side of a hill to its harbour. It was the closest thing to a town we had in our part of Cornwall. Ellen was employed by an Italian family who made their own Cornish ice cream and sold it from a large kiosk overlooking the ornamental gardens, and I worked as a chambermaid-cum-waitress-cum-kitchen-hand in the town's Seagull Hotel.

Trade came and went with the seasons. During the winter months, the kiosk opened only at weekends and I was needed to help out on the rare occasions when there was a do at the hotel, a birthday party, a wedding or a funeral wake. So it was by chance that Ellen and Jago met in the café at Polrack one winter's day. They hadn't seen one another for a while and we had all changed. We were no longer children.

Ellen and I were in the café eating blisteringly hot cheese and onion pasties and drinking Coke. It was a fierce day. Low, threatening clouds glowered over the peninsula and the waves were smashing into the sea wall, throwing gallons of bitter-cold water onto the walkway. All but the most hardy holidaymakers were long gone; only the coastal-path walkers and the intro-spective people who came alone to spend hours staring out to sea remained. Ellen and I had been helping to clean holiday cottages as a favour to a friend of my mum's. We'd stripped the linen, emptied the cupboards, washed and brushed and tidied and put the cottages to bed for the winter. We'd been paid cash and decided to eat while we waited for the bus back to Trethene because we hadn't had anything except tapwater since breakfast. Our anoraks were hooked over the backs of our chairs to dry off. I had burned my tongue on the hot cheese and was puffing, wafting air into my mouth with my fingers and feeling my cheeks glow. The café windows were misted with condensation, music was playing on the radio, there was a spit and a sizzle to the place, a smell of cigarette smoke and coffee. Ellen was laughing at me and trying to push an ice cube into my mouth, so I didn't see Jago come into the café, although I heard the bell ping. Ellen was sitting facing the door. The expression on her face changed from one of amusement to one of surprise. I turned to see what she was looking at, and there was Jago.

He was huge in his sou'wester, rubber leggings and boots, dripping wet, his hair stuck to his head and his skin pale with cold. Knotted up with the rubber and seawater smell of him was a sweaty man-smell. He was tall by then, more than six feet, and although not well-built, he had stature. His face was turning into a man's face. It was strong, with a slightly crooked nose, dark eyes, and his hair had evolved from the ginger of its youth to a deeper red-brown. He was smiling, holding his hat in his hands. He hadn't noticed me.

I looked at Ellen's face, then I looked at Jago and realized that what she was seeing was not Jago the uncouth boy from Trethene, but Jago, a good-looking young man. Something new was in her eyes too. I didn't recognize it at the time but it made me uneasy. It was only looking back that I realized this was the first time Ellen had seen the possibility of Jago. She was reconsidering him.

Jago held up a hand in recognition and took a step towards us, but Gemma Mills, the café owner, scuttled out from behind the counter flapping a tea-towel at him.

'You keep off my nice clean floor with those wet boots, Jago Cardell!' she scolded, and Jago laughed and scratched behind his ear and blushed a little, and everyone in the café looked at him and admired him. I remembered how he used to be; how he was defensive and nervous and how he hid behind bravado and bad language, and I felt proud of the boy-man who could stand in the café and charm everyone without doing anything at all.

Ellen's hand reached out to mine and squeezed it. She was staring at Jago, smiling up at him through her long, dark fringe, smiling with her blue eyes, looking at him as if he was something desirable; something she wanted. I felt cross with her out of all proportion to what she was doing.

Gemma was all apple cheeks and smiles. She went up to Jago and held him by the arms. 'What have you got for me today then, my lovely?' she asked. 'Have you brought me some crab?'

Jago nodded. 'And a box of mackerel. I put them round the back.'

'You're a good boy,' said Gemma. 'You know just what I like.' And she reached up on tiptoes to kiss Jago's cheek. 'Goodness, you're perishing – let me find something to warm you up.'

She rushed off back to the kitchen and Jago looked over to us.

'Hello, Spanner,' he said.

'Hello, Sadact,' I said.

Ellen said nothing. She was twisting a strand of hair round the finger of her free hand.

'What are you doing here, Han?' Jago went on. 'Aren't you supposed to be at work?'

'We've finished.'

'Not that you can call piddling around like you do working.'

'Actually it was quite intensive.'

'Yeah, right.' Jago rubbed the end of his nose with a knuckle. 'You should try doing a proper job for a change. You wouldn't last five minutes.'

'Messing about on boats? Playing with engines?'

'Children, children!' Gemma returned and pressed a warm paper bag into Jago's hands. 'Something for all of you,' she said. 'Bill and Darren too. It'll put hairs on your chests.'

Ellen giggled prettily, and looked down at her plate. I felt like slapping her.

'Cheers, Gemma,' Jago said. 'Thanks.'

The café was busy with the sound of the kettle boiling in the kitchen beyond and the radio and the murmur of conversation, forks on plates, cups chinking on saucers and the rain beating like little fists against the large windowpane.

'I heard your mother's not been too good,' Jago said to Ellen.

'No.'

'She in the hospice?'

'Not yet. But it's going that way.'

'It's all right there,' Jago said. 'My ma liked it.'

'She *liked* it?'

'Really,' Jago said. 'She didn't mind being there. They know what to do.'

Ellen looked down at the table.

'They're good people,' Jago said.

'But isn't it terribly depressing?'

'No. At least, I don't remember it like that.'

'What do you remember?'

'Laughter. Flowers. The curtains being open. And the dog . . .'

'The dog?'

'There was a therapy dog. Big friendly thing. I bloody loved that dog.'

Ellen looked up again and she was smiling. Her eyes held Jago's and I felt the connection between them and had to look away.

This was something they could share, mothers in the hospice. I could not compete with that and I think I knew then, at that very moment, what was going to happen, the way I sometimes sensed what someone was going to say before they so much as opened their mouth.

I was distracted, temporarily, by light shining through the café window, so bright I had to narrow my eyes. The clouds had blown past and for a moment the sun lit up the sea and the harbour, the boats rocking and rolling like potatoes boiling in a pan, a black dog sniffing at the stacked lobster pots on the jetty. Above the harbour, three gulls flew together in a perfect line. They turned and soared over the café. I shivered. I'd known all my life that three seagulls passing directly overhead was a portent.

It didn't mean anything to me at the time. Only much, much

later, did I realize that the seagulls passed overhead the very moment Ellen took the first step on the path that led in a straight line to her death.

CHAPTER SEVENTEEN

After the encounter with Charlotte and her friend in the pasty shop, I walked downhill to the little bakery that serviced the University of Bristol's Drama Department and staff from the Bristol Royal Infirmary and the Children's Hospital. I turned the conversation I had overheard around in my mind, looking at it every way I could and seeing no vindication for Charlotte's actions or the things she had said. What right did she have to talk about John in that horrible, crude manner and to mock him so cruelly? It was obvious she only stayed with him because of his money. Was she really planning to carry on her affairs behind his back, making him a laughing stock? No doubt it suited her having a husband like John who was so honest he wouldn't doubt his wife for a moment. I wondered how many men she had been with and how many people knew about her infidelities. Hundreds, probably.

Also, Charlotte and her bad behaviour aside, I felt a conflict of emotions: guilt at my eavesdropping on something I wished I hadn't heard, anger that John was being deceived, fear of the potential repercussions, and anxiety. I did not want John to be hurt. I couldn't bear the thought of it.

I didn't know what I could do to make things better, or if I should do anything at all, but I felt I had to show solidarity in some way. At the baker's, I bought two cheese salad baguettes and two cartons of coffee. I returned to the museum and knocked on John's door, but he wasn't in his office.

'Try downstairs,' said Rina.

The museum's main archive, where the thousands of exhibits that weren't on permanent display were stored, covered an area the size of the building's footprint directly beneath it. It was my least favourite place. Huge, long and low-ceilinged, it contained thousands of statues, busts, bones, pictures and other objects, crowded together on shelves haphazardly arranged to make the most of the available space. I had always especially disliked the death masks, dozens of plaster casts taken of eminent Victorian faces as the subjects lay cooling on their deathbeds. Some still had the occasional eyelash or smudge of powder embedded in the white clay.

I unlocked the door to the archive and went down the steep steps, carved out of the rock beneath the museum. The place was brightly but harshly lit by naked lightbulbs.

'John?' I called, but there was no answer.

I hurried past the masks, and the ranks of paintings, the framed ones encased in bubblewrap and blankets, the loose canvases rolled like scrolls, shelves full of bones, teeth, antlers, horns, hooves and tusks, ancient pottery shards and human paraphernalia of the last four millennia. If Ellen was waiting for me, if she was hiding somewhere, it would be here, amongst all the dead objects, all the human remains, those awful Victorian faces. I imagined her shadowing me, moving amongst the exhibits, flitting like a moth. It took all my willpower to keep going, and not to turn and run back up the steps, into the real world, the living world. At last I found John in the section of the archive loosely reserved for medieval human remains. He was wearing his white coat, a magnifying glass over one eye, and his earphones were plugged in. He was so engrossed in his work he had no idea I was there, behind him. I was breathless with relief.

'John . . .' I touched the sleeve of his coat gently so as not to alarm him. He turned and I recognized in his eyes the confusion that comes when a person is interrupted in the middle of a task that requires intense concentration.

'I brought you some lunch,' I said.

He unplugged his iPod and smiled. 'What did I do to deserve this?'

'It was the least I could do to thank you for last night,' I said, and I had to fight back an urge to lean forward and kiss his cheek.

We left the museum and walked up to Brandon Hill Park, where we climbed to the top and sat together on a bench by the path beneath the Cabot Tower, enjoying the views over the River Avon and Bristol's old docks. We ate our lunch and fed little pieces of bread to the squirrels. For a while we talked about work. Then John asked, 'How are you feeling today, Hannah?'

'I'm fine.'

'Migraine all gone?'

'I haven't seen any more ghosts, if that's what you're asking.' I smiled to show I was not offended by his question, and brushed crumbs from my lap.

'What if,' John asked, 'the person you saw yesterday wasn't a figment of your migraine? There are seven billion people on the planet. When you think about it, it's amazing we don't see people who remind us of other people more often.'

He was being kind. He was giving me a logical explanation for what had happened the previous day. That was the sort of man he was. Was this how he coped with Charlotte –

making excuses for her, finding ways to explain and validate her behaviour? Did he act like this out of empathy, or because pretending was easier than facing the truth?

I dug my nails into my hands and stared out over the docks. A memory flashed through my mind. Ellen's hand flat against a glass door, pushing it open. The smell of stocks, a bowl of mints. Ellen, pale as a ghost, hollow-eyed, with the sleeves of her cardigan pulled down over her fingers and her arms wrapped about herself, saying, 'Let's get out of here.'

I shook my head to be rid of it. I didn't want to talk about Ellen, or think about her. I wanted to forget.

'Are you doing anything special this weekend?' I asked John.

He folded his sandwich bag. 'Actually, no. Charlotte's taking the girls to see her mother. They've got tickets for some kids' show.' He smiled. 'So for once I have the house to myself and nobody will mind if I spend the whole weekend reading and listening to music.'

'That sounds good.'

John sighed. 'To be honest, I don't much like it when they're all away. I'm not very good at being on my own.'

'Oh, John . . .'

'Don't look like that! It's not *that* bad. They'll be back Sunday evening. I'll survive. What about you?'

'Me?'

'What are your plans for the weekend?'

'Oh, I was thinking of going down to Cornwall. I haven't seen my parents in a while and Rina said I should get away for a couple of days.'

'She's right. You deserve a break.'

'Mmm.'

I held my head up and brushed the hair out of my face, tucking it behind my left ear. My fingers stayed there, twisting the butterfly at the back of the silver stud. Part of me wanted to ask John if he'd like to come to Cornwall with me, just as a friend, just for the company, so that I could keep an eye on him and look after him, but I couldn't. Not then. Not when I knew, and he did not, that his perfect life was built on such fragile and unreliable foundations.

CHAPTER EIGHTEEN

Mrs Brecht had been dying for ages. It felt like for ever, but that was back then, in the past, when a day's boundaries stretched far further than they do now and a year was a length of time so immense as to be almost incomprehensible. I had known the Brechts for more than six years by the time Mrs Brecht became critically ill. I felt as if I had known them for the whole of my life.

In the months leading up to her death, it was sometimes difficult for me to remember that Mrs Brecht was dying because I had no idea, up to that point, that the process could take so long. In films and books it always happened very quickly, a scene between diagnosis and funeral, an instant between the finger on the trigger and the bullet through the heart. Yet from the time Ellen told me her mother was so ill she sometimes wished for an end to the pain, until her actual death, two years elapsed. Mrs Brecht's dying was slower than the seasons changing, slower than growing up.

And as Mrs Brecht was dying, the garden at Thornfield House was coming back to life. Fruit trees and climbing flowers had been trained against the perimeter wall. A fountain trickled water prettily into the pond during the summer months; there were steps and paths winding amongst the flowerbeds and leading to different parts of the garden: areas for herbs and vegetables, a scented garden, a secret garden and one where all the flowers were yellow. It was full of life, all the time, all year round; in summer butterflies and bees busied themselves around the blooms and blossoms, in winter birds flocked to the feeders. As one group of flowers faded away, another came forward, so the garden changed slightly every day, but each day it seemed to become more beautiful. When Ellen and I returned from work, or from the beach, we sometimes found Mrs Brecht in the garden, leaning on Adam Tremlett's arm, gazing out at what the two of them had created. When she was outside, enjoying the flowers, she seemed happier, as if the pain had receded. Indoors, it only became worse.

Mr Brecht's unhappiness and torment increased in direct proportion to the reduction in his wife's health. I only saw him occasionally – he was often asleep during the day because he spent all night at Anne's bedside, watching over her – but he seemed to grow more gaunt, less groomed, more handsome and tortured with every passing day. He paced through that big old house with a cigarette permanently between his fingers and his hair unkempt, trailing smoke and misery through the rooms. I felt as if my heart was breaking in tandem with his.

On the days when Mrs Brecht was in the hospice, Ellen said it was better if I didn't go into the house.

'Papa can't bear it when she's not there,' she said. 'He has to drink to get through the day.'

'What does that mean?'

Ellen looked at me as if I were stupid. 'Alcohol is an anaesthetic. It numbs the pain.'

'Oh.'

'And he makes me play the piano, all the time, to remind him.'

She picked at her nails and her face clouded over. I remembered how tenderly Mr Brecht had held onto Ellen the time I'd watched her playing piano through the window, and inside I gave a little sigh of sadness at the exquisite tragedy of the situation. This was a terrible time, I thought, and no wonder Mr Brecht was struggling to cope, but after Mrs Brecht was gone, I would step in to comfort him. He would be immersed in grief, no doubt, for a while, but one day the shadows would lift and, when they did, I would be there, waiting. He would see me and he would recognize my devotion and my inherent goodness, and he would reach out for me and hold me to him and whisper: '*Oh Hannah, how could I live without you?*'

Mrs Brecht dying was like leaving school or going to university or having sex, something I knew would most likely occur at some point in the future, but which it was impossible to imagine in the present. Ellen was resigned to her mother's death, though. She knew. During that long, slow time between the knowing and the dying, she hinted at it, always dropping the fact that the day of death was drawing nearer into the conversation as if to ensure nobody ever forgot that she was entangled in the dramatic, climactic scenes of her mother's life.

She told me that her mother had called her to her side while her father was sleeping and told Ellen a secret. Ellen was not supposed to tell a single soul about it, but she told me. Her grandmother, Mrs Withiel, Anne Brecht's mother, had been a very wealthy woman. And she had left everything to Ellen. Ellen would inherit her fortune on her eighteenth birthday. Mrs Brecht was trustee of the money and she had put all the arrangements in place. The rules were very strict: Ellen had to wait until she was eighteen, she couldn't have a penny before then. When Ellen told me this she was wearing the wide-eyed, excited, conspiratorial expression she reserved for special stories, and I was not the slightest bit jealous because I was pretty sure she was making it up.

'Your grandmother didn't seem that rich when we saw her,' I said.

Ellen shrugged. 'Mama says she was. Mama says she didn't spend her money but hoarded it.'

'Why would she leave it to you? She never even met you. Why didn't she leave it to your mama?'

'They fell out. They hadn't spoken to one another in years.'

'And what about your papa?'

'He doesn't know,' Ellen said. 'You mustn't tell him! Promise me on your life you won't tell him!'

I promised. As if I would tell Mr Brecht a tall story like that anyway!

As the time for Mrs Brecht's dying came closer, Ellen became quieter and thinner and more unusual than ever. Our roles, oddly, became reversed. When a palliative nurse was employed to stay overnight at Thornfield House, the impending death became the single most important topic of conversation in Trethene and at school. Other girls whispered about Ellen as we dawdled in the grounds, and now I was the one who turned to glower at them.

'What are you staring at?' I would ask, pushing my face into theirs.

'She don't seem to care,' was what the girls usually said. 'If *my* mum was dying, I'd be crying all the time. But she just gets weirder.'

We would all look over at Ellen, who would be, perhaps, sitting on a bench, holding her knees and staring up at the sky.

'You don't know anything about it,' I would reply. 'You leave her alone.'

Some girls tried to befriend Ellen, because they wanted to be part of the drama, they were fascinated by the proximity of death, but Ellen was not interested in them. She seemed to need only me, and that made me proud to be her friend and I felt more protective of her.

It was true that her grief did not manifest itself conventionally, but I knew it was there. When she wasn't being looked at, and judged, she depended on me for comfort. She bit her nails and shivered inside clothes that were suddenly too big for her. She came as close to me as she possibly could, all the time, as if to share my warmth. She put her hands into my pockets and I covered them with my bigger, warmer hands. Sometimes we squeezed into the same jumper, or we shared a cardigan, me taking one arm, she the other, and our bodies pressed together in between. I felt as if I was growing larger all the time, and Ellen, meanwhile, was disappearing. I was the big, fluffy mother hen, she the scrawny little hatchling.

I liked it that I was the leader and protector now. I enjoyed the changed dynamic. I felt, at last, as if I was truly involved, and not just hovering on the sidelines.

And all the time Ellen's behaviour became stranger.

When she was asked to read out her essay on 'The Nature of Beauty' in English, she stood up and recited a poem about a deer skull she'd found washed up on the beach and now kept on her dressing-table. It was, in fact, a sheep skull, but Ellen insisted it had been a deer. It was not even really a poem, more a random collection of words, like verbal driftwood. She didn't get into trouble for that, nor for all the occasions she sat in class biting off her split ends and taking no notice of the teachers at all. They left her alone, they didn't seem to know what to do with her. Even the sports mistress, Miss Tunnock, said nothing when she sloped off on her own instead of joining in with the cross-country running;

103

rather, to my joy, she sent me off too, to look after Ellen. I particularly enjoyed the expressions of jealousy and outrage on the faces of our classmates as I trotted back to the changing rooms. Ellen and I found a warm place beside a radiator and huddled together, a coat buttoned up around both of us, a single scarf around our necks, so close that our heartbeats aligned themselves and shared the same rhythm.

One afternoon, the school bus dropped us off and I was turning to go home to Cross Hands Lane when Ellen took my arm.

'Walk back with me,' she said. 'I don't know if you'll be able to come in, but walk back with me anyway.'

It was cold and the wind was blowing in our faces. We tucked our chins down into our scarves and linked arms. Our feet shared a rhythm, like our hearts sometimes did.

'What's the matter?' I asked.

She shrugged. 'My fingers hurt.'

'Why?'

'It's Papa. He makes me play the piano.'

'Because your Mama likes to hear it?'

Ellen nodded. I felt a tingle of irritation with her. Was it really too much to ask that she played her mother's favourite pieces of music at such a time?

'It's not just for an hour or two, it's all the time,' she said. 'Yesterday I had to play the *Moonlight Sonata* fifty times.'

'Honestly, fifty times?'

'It felt like fifty times. Now the music's in my head and I keep hearing it. I can't concentrate! I can't think of anything else!'

She pulled her arm free of mine, picked up a stick and whipped it against the leafless hedgerow. Some black-and-white cows on the other side raised their heads. They rotated their jaws and blinked at us.

'He's mad,' she said then. 'Honestly, Hannah, I really think Papa is going mad.'

'Mad with grief?'

'He's obsessed. He won't leave Mama alone, not for a single moment. He sits with her all night; even when she's sleeping he won't leave her. He sleeps beside her.'

I thought that was romantic. I imagined if I were Mrs Brecht, how pleased I would be to wake and find Mr Brecht next to me. I could see myself, my head on the pillow, my hair prettily spread about my pale face, and him, holding my little hand between both of his. I could see a tender smile on his lips as my eyelids flickered open and then he would raise my hand and gently kiss each of the knuckles in turn.

Ellen broke the stick in half and threw it over the hedge.

'I have to play the piano even when Mama is asleep.'

'Why?'

'So she has music for her dreams. Papa said it will help her remember her happiest days, when she was young and healthy.'

I glanced at Ellen to see if she minded that her mother's happiest days were before she was born. I could not tell from her expression.

'If it helped Mama, I'd play the piano all day and all night,' Ellen said. 'I wouldn't care that my fingers were sore or that I hated the music. But she's tired of it too. That's why she keeps asking to go to the hospice. She wants to get away from it . . . from *him*.'

I didn't understand anything back then. I felt sorry for Mrs Brecht, of course, but I couldn't understand why she was being so cruel to her husband. My heart was almost breaking in sympathy with Mr Brecht's. I thought it must be awful to die, but better to be the die-er than the person losing someone they loved as much as Mr Brecht loved his wife. He was the most tragic person I had ever known. Thinking about him made my eyes fill with tears.

*

The last time I talked to Mrs Brecht was the day after my seventeenth birthday in November, a few weeks before she died. She was lying in the downstairs back room at Thornfield House where she could look out into the garden. She was covered with a cashmere shawl, resting. Mr Brecht had taken the car into Truro, and Ellen and Mrs Todd were looking after her.

She had become even more drawn since the last time I had seen her. She was a person going backwards, in reverse, fading like a pencil drawing being erased, bit by bit. Adam Tremlett had brought on some daffodils in his greenhouse for Mrs Brecht, to remind her of the spring she would not see, and Mrs Todd told me to help Ellen carry them into the room. The whole house was full of flowers. My mum had been to Thornfield House once or twice to help Mrs Todd with the cleaning during this difficult time, and she said it was like coming into a botanical garden. Neither of us had ever seen so many flowers in one place.

The daffodils were nothing special, in my eyes. They had small, sunshine-yellow heads bobbing and nodding on weedy green stems hardly strong enough to support them. Ellen walked into the room solemnly, holding her pot to her chest; I followed behind. Ellen placed her pot on the floor, by the French windows, where her mother could see them.

'Aren't they beautiful, Mama?'

'Are they from Adam?'

'Of course.'

Mrs Brecht gave a sigh. 'Who's that?' she asked, raising her tiny, misshapen hand a little. I stepped forward, into her line of vision, and put my pot down beside Ellen's. Mrs Brecht smiled when she saw me. I was so shocked by how little of her was left I had trouble smiling at all.

'Come and give me a kiss goodbye, Hannah,' she said. 'Don't be afraid. This condition of mine is not contagious.'

I leaned down and kissed her forehead. Her skin was cool and waxy.

Ellen perched on the edge of the daybed, and took her mother's hand.

'How are you feeling, Mama?'

'I'm all right, *Schatzi*.'

'Do you want anything?'

'I want you to stay with me a while. Where's your father?'

'He's out. Do you want some music, Mama?'

'Dear God, no,' said Mrs Brecht. 'Let's enjoy the quiet.' Her lips, which used to be so full and juicy-looking, were pale and dry, greyish in colour.

Ellen twisted a strand of hair around her finger. Her cardigan gaped and I noticed bruises on the inside of her upper arm, four small, ugly bruises, sized and spaced like fingertips. Ellen let her arm drop. I meant to ask her what had happened and how she came by the bruises, but I never did. I forgot them.

Mrs Brecht spoke softly. 'The daffodils remind me of my birthday. I used to have beautiful parties in the garden here when I was a child,' she said. 'My mother filled it with decorations, paper lanterns, bunting . . . and the daffodils. Thousands of daffodils. I always thought they were my flowers, grown specially for me.'

She rested her head back against the cushion. 'I wish you had known your grandmother,' she said to Ellen. 'She had a good heart and she would have loved you very much.'

'Yes, Mama.'

Ellen shot me a significant look that I ignored. Nothing her mother had said had hinted at an inheritance. I remembered Mrs Withiel and how all the Trethene children called her 'witch' and how she lay dead for three weeks in Thornfield House before anyone found her. I twisted a strand of hair around my own finger and sucked the end of

107

it. The clock on the mantelpiece was ticking, and Mrs Todd was vacuuming somewhere inside the house.

'I'm so tired of this waiting,' Mrs Brecht said quietly. 'Really, I've had enough.'

'The nurse will be here soon,' Ellen said. 'Do you want anything in the meantime, Mama?'

'Pull the curtains back, would you, Ellen. Tie them back so I can see the whole garden.'

Outside, Adam was digging over one of the beds, wrapped in a donkey jacket and boots. It was so cold that his breath was fogging around him. Frost on the trees made them sparkly and white. It was like looking through a window into a Christmas globe.

'I've known him all my life,' Mrs Brecht whispered. 'I was friends with Adam long before I knew your father.'

Ellen stroked her mother's hand.

Mrs Brecht smiled. 'When we were children we danced together at the Helston Flower Festival. He always used to say . . .'

'What, Mama?'

Ellen's mother closed her eyes slowly and turned her head to one side as if trying to catch hold of the words from the past.

'That's where I wish I was,' she murmured, 'out in the garden with Adam.'

'But it's so cold out there, Mama.'

'I wouldn't feel it,' Mrs Brecht said. 'The cold wouldn't bother me at all.'

CHAPTER NINETEEN

I was up early on Saturday morning, feeling less edgy. I'd slept better and was glad to have something planned for the weekend, so it did not stretch out in front of me like a straight road going nowhere except towards another Monday morning. It would make me feel good to see my parents; they'd be pleased to see me and I would be less concerned about the fragility of my mental state if I was with other people. It was solitude I dreaded.

I caught a taxi from Montpelier to Bristol's Temple Meads station and the train, fortunately, was on time. I found a window seat, drank coffee and ate an almond pastry for breakfast as the train rumbled southwards through Somerset. It was altogether a pleasant journey. I had a book to read, the sun was shining, the countryside beyond was glorious. I even dozed for a while, and by the time I alighted at Helston, I was feeling better than I had for a while.

At the station, I caught another cab, one that took me through the tiny, winding country lanes that led to Trethene. I felt like an adult in a toy world. Everything in South Cornwall seemed too green, too pretty, too small. The car rolled through little fords, and wildflowers dipped through steep-sided lanes – all foxgloves, campions and oxeye daisies.

Sweet, whitewashed cottages sat amongst their gardens, and the leaves of the trees dappled the air.

As the car pulled up outside number 8 Cross Hands Lane I pushed my sunglasses up onto my forehead and studied the cottage. There was nothing of the chocolate box about my parents' home. It was a small, plain council house, but Mum and Dad had always been happy there. It had been their home since they married. They had tried to prettify it. White and pink sea breeze had self-seeded in the garden wall, and little red roses scrambled around the door. The front garden was tiny – a toy garden. How had Dad managed to fit Jago's old car in there? How had they managed to restore it in that pocket-handkerchief space?

I let myself into the house with the key that was always hidden under the plastic milk-bottle tidy by the front door. Mum was, predictably, in the kitchen wiping down the surfaces with a damp J-cloth and, through the window, I could see my father in the back garden watering his vegetables. The kitchen, as always, had been bleached to within an inch of its life and was neat as a pin. I called, 'Hell-o-o! It's me!' and Mum's face lit up as she turned to see me.

'Hannah! What a lovely surprise,' she said, drying her hands on a tea-towel, and then reaching her face towards mine for a kiss. She put the kettle on and asked, 'We weren't expecting you, were we?'

'No, I just came over on a whim. I was missing you and Cornwall.'

'That's lovely! Can you stay?'

'For the night, but I'll have to go back to Bristol tomorrow.'

'Oh.' The single syllable was loaded with disappointment. I tried not to resent being made to feel guilty, turned my back on Mum so she wouldn't see my face, and took some cups and saucers from the cupboard.

Mum fussed about with a packet of biscuits and a knife, waiting for the kettle to boil before she risked antagonizing me again by saying, 'You're looking a bit peaky, dear.'

'I'm fine.'

'You look tired.'

I opened my mouth to reassure her, but suddenly I did feel tired. I wished I was thirteen again and that I could run upstairs and put on my pyjamas and snuggle beneath the coverlet of my single bed. I wished Trixie was still alive to lie across my legs, and my life was full of sparkly nail varnish and hair-crimpers, magazine problem pages, a passion for animals and Saturdays spent in Falmouth town trying on all the items on the sales rails and sitting on the sea wall dipping chips in ketchup with Ellen. I wished Jago was there, bringing his energy into the house and making us all laugh. I wished my mother was younger and less frail so that I could tell her everything, ask her what I needed to know, and trust her to take care of things without burdening her with the fear that I might be slipping back to the dark place she and Dad had had to pull me from before.

'I've been working hard, that's all,' I said with a brittle cheerfulness.

'You mustn't overdo it, Hannah.'

'I know.'

'Remember what the doctor said about stress and—'

'Mum, I *know*. Please don't go on.'

I filled the teapot, laid a tray, and then me and my mother, she slightly chastened, went out through the little lean-to conservatory that Dad and Jago had put up years back so that Mum had somewhere nice to sit and read, and out into the back garden. Dad greeted me effusively, found mismatched deck chairs in the shed, dusted off the cobwebs, and set them up for us. He continued with his work, listening to the cricket on the radio, while we sat in the shade of the cherry tree and chatted. For a while, the conversation was innocuous. I began to relax. I watched the bees busy about the honeysuckle flowers that grew through the hedge. And then . . . I don't know what came over me – I truly did not mean to talk about the past – but for some reason I found myself saying, 'Mum, you remember Ellen Brecht, don't you?'

At that very moment, Dad dropped his hose and it twirled around him like a snake, soaking the washing on the line. Mum looked up at the bedlinen that had been almost dry and was now spattered with dark wet patches. She gave a little sigh but, uncharacteristically, did not scold Dad for his clumsiness.

'Yes, I remember Ellen, and her parents. I cleaned at Thornfield House for a while when Mrs Brecht was ill.'

'Of course you did. I'd forgotten.'

'It's been turned into a pub now, Thornfield House. Did you know?'

'Last time I was here, you told me it was going to be knocked down.'

'I think they wanted to demolish it and build holiday flats, but they couldn't get permission.'

'It would have been the best thing for it,' said Dad. 'Good riddance. They should have bulldozed that place years ago.'

'It had been on the market for a while,' Mum continued. 'Nobody wanted to take it on. But now it's a gastric pub. Sally Next-door-but-one went for lunch there the other week. She said it's quite tasteful, if you like that kind of thing. Olives and you-know-what. It's popular with the tourists. They've turned that lovely front room into a bar.'

I blinked and for a moment I recalled every detail of the room with its tall twin sash windows and the piano taking pride of place, and the chaise longue where Ellen's mother used to rest. I remembered how the sunlight fell on the beautiful chestnut-coloured wooden floor, the gently billowing curtains and the fancy plaster rose-work above the chandelier, the ornate marble fireplace full of candles, the smell of lavender and candle-wax, the sound of *Clair de lune*.

I remembered the bloodstain soaked into the floorboards that no amount of scrubbing would lift, the broken mirror, glass on the windowledge. I remembered Ellen screaming as if her heart was broken – oh God, the sound of her! I covered my face with my hands, trying to block out the memory.

'Hannah?'

I blinked again and I was back in my parents' small garden, sitting awkwardly in the orange-and-green-striped deck chair with the sound of the water splashing from the hose and the birdsong and children's television coming over the hedges together with the smell of frying onions from the open kitchen window of the neighbouring house. I felt a little dizzy. I tipped the dregs of my tea onto the grass.

'Were Ellen's parents nice to you, Mum?' I asked.

My mother frowned. 'Oh, I don't know. They were generous enough but I didn't really get to know either of them. They weren't the kind of people you could talk to. They weren't like us.'

'No. I suppose they weren't.'

'Mrs Todd kept herself to herself. And of course they were Catholics so we never socialized at church.'

Mum fiddled with her earlobe. Then she said, 'I never used to like going into that house after Mrs Brecht was gone. It changed. Everything changed.'

'I know what you mean.'

I glanced at my father. He had turned off the tap and was draining the hose, winding it around his shoulder. Water pooled on the concrete patio stones at his feet. He didn't like looking back at bad times. He didn't like Mum thinking about them either.

I reached over and took my mother's hand. It was large and dry, knobbly with knuckle, the skin age-spotted. My parents had always been old. I had never known them young.

'Look at you, both sitting there with long faces,' Dad said briskly. 'It's a beautiful day. Why don't we walk into Trethene and get ourselves a sandwich and a bun. My treat, eh?'

'That's a good idea, Malcolm,' said Mum, and she manoeuvred herself awkwardly out of the chair, picked up the teacups, and disappeared into the dark of the house.

My father rubbed his beard. 'Your mum don't like talking about that Brecht business,' he said.

'I know, Dad, I'm sorry. But—'

'Leave the past alone,' said my father. 'No good can come of picking the scabs off old wounds. None at all.'

CHAPTER TWENTY

It was December, the month after my seventeenth birthday. The peninsula was fogbound. The air was chill, even in my bedroom, and an all-pervading damp crept into everything – clothing, the walls, dreams, bones. For days there was no end to the fog and I hated it. I felt choked, strangled by it. I wanted to claw my way out, to keep walking until I found a place where I could step through its curtains out into daylight. At Goonhilly, the satellite dishes, smudged and indistinct, turned their huge faces to the skies, seeing through the persistent greyness as clearly as if it were not there, but on the ground the people struggled. The fog disorientated me. I found myself lost, more than once, close to home on lanes I'd known all my life. I didn't know which way to turn, which path led home, which to the cliff edge. It was easy to imagine murderers in the mist, men with knives and cudgels, slit-throats and vagabonds, and the icy-cold touch of ghost-fingers on my cheeks, lifting my hair, whispering fog-breath secrets in my ear.

Rather than walking up the hill in the early-morning dark, I waited each morning at the bus stop at the far end of Cross Hands Lane for the school bus and heard the clattering rumble of its engine long before the twin yellow circles of its

115

headlamps materialized out of the gloom. Ellen was always on the bus already, sitting in the seat by the window, second row from the back, saving the space beside her for me. Until the morning when she was not there.

The day before, Mr Brecht came to the school early to pick up Ellen and take her home.

'You go too, Hannah,' said our teacher, when she read the message delivered by a younger child. 'Look after her,' she said, folding the piece of paper neatly into four, as if it were too important to be screwed up and thrown into the waste-paper basket. Everyone, the rest of the class, looked down, embarrassed, as Ellen and I packed up our things, picked up our coats, and left the room.

'See you,' Ellen said quietly. There was a murmur of farewells.

Ellen's father was waiting outside the main entrance, smoking a cigarette in the fog. He was wearing a long coat and a scarf. He looked like an actor in a film. His breath was clouding around him together with the wreath of smoke, giving him a ghostly shroud. The planes of his face had sunk over the last months. Dark shadows cloaked his eyes, and his demeanour was that of a man on the brink of losing everything. I wished I had some way of letting him know that he was not alone; that I understood how he was suffering and admired him for it. Perhaps he *did* know. Perhaps one day in the future he would tell me that my unspoken devotion was what had seen him through those terrible days.

He looked up when the movement of the door caught his eye, and Ellen ran into his arms. He embraced her, hugged her close, and I held back and picked at my nail varnish.

'You have to be brave, *Schatzi*,' Mr Brecht was saying. 'I need you to be strong for the next few hours because God knows how we're going to get through them.' He said something else to her, in German. Ellen nodded and stepped back, holding her head high.

Mr Brecht's car was parked by the main school entrance, beneath a sign which said *Strictly No Parking*. Ellen got into the front seat, beside her father. None of the Brechts ever used a seat belt. I sat behind Ellen and strapped myself in. The car was low-slung with leather seats and a hi-fi system that filled the interior with weird, windy classical music I did not recognize but it pulled at the strings of my heart.

Half a dozen twiggy stems of red carnations wrapped in florist's paper lay on the back seat of the car beside me. They had a sickly, peppery scent and seemed sad, desperate flowers. I picked them up and held them on my lap, for something to do.

Mr Brecht drove fast through the fog but I was not afraid. I would have trusted him to drive me anywhere. Ellen sat still in front of me, with her hands folded together, staring straight ahead.

'Will it be soon?' she asked her father and Mr Brecht nodded and said, 'Yes.'

'I hope it's not today,' Ellen said. 'Mama doesn't like the fog.' She began to cry, silently. This was not like her. I could see the tears running down her cheeks and falling into her lap. I put a hand on her shoulder and squeezed through the thick material of her padded coat, but Ellen did not react at all.

It was strange driving along the roads that I knew so well, and everything grey and blurred or altogether disappeared. I couldn't see beyond the wire fence that enclosed Culdrose but I knew the aircraft hangars and the helicopters and the fuel tankers would still be in there, doing their work. Somewhere behind that fence my father would be sitting in his plain office with the notices squared up and pinned to the board, his uniform shirt straining at the buttons; a functional desk lamp, a metal waste-paper basket, a telephone. He would be organizing the movement of personnel and equipment, ticking off tasks on the schedule in front of him, being jolly and bossy. He wouldn't know that his daughter was driving by on the road beyond on the back seat of a low-slung German car. He didn't know that Ellen's mother was about to die, any time now.

At the traffic-lights we were caught in a jam and that felt even more strange, all the other people in all the other cars going about their business as if this were just another normal day and not the day when Anne Brecht would die. We drove very slowly past an accident – a car shunted into the back of a milk-float. People were standing around, blowing on their hands, shaking their heads. Shards of glass lay amongst the milk-pools. The milkman was still wearing his cap over a woolly balaclava. A tiny little Christmas tree with tiny little twinkling electric lights stood on the dashboard of the milk-float. I wondered what Mrs Brecht was thinking and what it felt like to know that, in a few hours, there would be no more life. Was she afraid? Was she praying, right now, for grace – hoping to live long enough to see Christmas, or the swallows returning for one last time and the primroses opening up their little yellow faces in the banks at the side of the road? Was she thinking about the things she would never see, or those she had seen already? Was she thinking at all?

I thought that if I were in her position, I would not allow myself to die. I would keep myself alive through willpower. I would make myself take one more breath, and then another. I would not let go of life, not give it up, never. Surreptitiously I unwrapped a fruit gum from the packet in my pocket, prised it loose from its partner with my thumbnail and put it into my mouth. It tasted dry and acid, a taste I always associated afterwards with that long car journey.

Mr Brecht must have forgotten I was in the car, or else he wanted to keep me there, because he didn't take the road through Trethene, but the one that led directly to Thornfield House. He pulled the car into the drive. Mrs Todd's small black car was parked outside, along with Adam Tremlett's Ford van and another green hatchback.

Mr Brecht stopped the car aggressively, dragging on the handbrake before the wheels had stopped turning. He said something under his breath, climbed out, slammed the door and strode towards the front door.

I got out of the car and passed the flowers to Ellen, who looked pale and scared.

'I'd better go,' I said, and Ellen asked, 'Don't you want to come in and say goodbye to Mama?'

No, I did not want to go into Thornfield House, and no, I did not want to see Mrs Brecht again – it had been bad enough last time. I wanted to go home and curl up in front of the fire and read *Flowers in the Attic*, which was inside my school bag, and chat to Jago, but Ellen's face was so expectant, so pleading, begging me not to leave her to go into that house alone, that I did my best to smile and I said, 'Yes, of course.'

A pair of large, muddy boots was lined up square on the step outside the front door. Mr Brecht, on his way in, kicked them viciously.

I'll never forget the atmosphere inside the house that afternoon. It felt as if it were waiting for the death. It was eerily quiet, so quiet that as we took off our shoes in the hall I could hear the ticking of the clock on the landing. Mr Brecht had already gone upstairs and there was some commotion, hushed voices, banging. Ellen looked up, and then took my hand and led me into the kitchen.

'What's going on?' I asked.

Ellen shrugged. 'I expect Adam's brought more flowers for Mama. Papa doesn't like it.'

Mrs Todd was in the kitchen, sitting in a chair by the window, knitting. Her face was pinched with fatigue and anxiety. She greeted us and put the kettle on to boil. A tray was already laid with teacups and saucers.

'You'd best wait here for a few moments,' she said. The voices upstairs grew louder, two angry, subdued male voices – Mr Brecht cursing in German – and then there was banging, the sound of something rolling down the stairs. Ellen and I opened the kitchen door and looked out. Flowers were scattered all over the stairs and hallway. Mr Brecht was gathering armfuls of them from the room where his wife lay dying and throwing them down the stairs. They bounced off the portraits on the wall, leaving wet smears. Loose petals stuck to the frames and floated in the warm air. Vases and jars littered the carpets; there was more broken glass. Adam Tremlett galloped down the stairs in his thick, grey gardener's socks. His face was racked with anger. He gathered up the flowers as best he could, and walked through the hall and out of the front door, which he slammed shut behind him. Ellen and I looked at one another.

'Do you think it's all right to go up now?' Ellen asked Mrs Todd.

'I should give it a few more minutes,' said Mrs Todd. She opened the door to the cupboard under the sink, took out a dustpan and brush and a cloth, and went wearily into the hall to clean up the mess.

Time slowed down. The air seemed heavier, more condensed, every action assumed a significance. After for ever, Mrs Todd reappeared in the kitchen and nodded to us. We left the red carnations in their paper on the kitchen table. I followed Ellen up the stairs. The carpet was damp beneath my feet. Mrs Brecht was being nursed in the bedroom beside

Ellen's, at the front of the house. It was a large room but it felt like a cave, illuminated only by a standard lamp in one corner, and a small bedside lamp that had been covered with a red scarf to mute the light. A recording of piano music was playing, softly; it wove through the room like the fog outside, insinuating its way into me until it was integral to me as drawing breath. Flowers would have softened the room, brought some life into it; without them it felt bleak. Emptied of adornment, the room resembled a bridal suite, only reversed.

Death's bride, Mrs Brecht was tiny in the bed, her body so wasted that it barely made an impression beneath the bedclothes. In death she maintained her glamour. Her hair was still shiny, her nails polished, and the lovely face that had been distorted by pain the last time I saw her was now relaxed, the skin smooth. She seemed childlike, not quite human. A drip that fed a tube connected to the back of Mrs Brecht's hand clicked behind the bed. She lay on white pillows, dressed in oyster silk pyjamas, a patchwork coverlet pulled up to her chest. Her eyelids flickered when Ellen and I came into the room. The heater had been turned up high; the air was cloyingly warm. Mr Brecht sat on a chair close to the bed, holding his wife's hand and staring into her face. Ellen sat carefully on the bed. I went to stand by the window. I pulled the curtain back a fraction. Outside I saw Adam Tremlett standing by the gate in the fog. His hands were cupped around a match. He was trying to light a cigarette but his eyes caught mine. He was looking straight up at the window and I noticed that his boots were unlaced. I let the curtain fall back and turned to watch the bedside tableau.

'Not long now, my love,' Mr Brecht said softly to his wife. 'Soon it will all be over, the end of pain, the end of everything.' He leaned over Mrs Brecht, her hand clasped between his, his lips so close to hers that they must have been sharing the same breaths. It seemed, to me, a shockingly brave and wonderful thing to say. If my parents had been in the same situation, the one who wasn't dying would have tried to re-assure the other that everything was really all right. They'd have said something positive about getting better or made a joke or talked about something trivial and inconsequential like the weather or a programme they'd watched on TV. My heartbeat quickened for Mr Brecht.

'Shall I change the music?' asked Ellen.

'No.' Mr Brecht shook his head. 'It's not time for that yet.'

I knew the music Ellen meant. Chopin's *Raindrop Prelude* was to be the soundtrack to Mrs Brecht's death. Ellen's father had told her the brain remains in a state of almost-consciousness for a while after physical death. When Mrs Brecht stopped breathing, when her heart no longer beat, she would not be able to open her eyes, or talk or feel or taste or smell, but her ears required no physiological stimulus to function. She could still listen to music. Her husband wanted Chopin to be the last thing she heard before her final synapse expired. Chopin was the music with which he had wooed her; Chopin would take her into death. That was his wish.

I couldn't help wondering if, given the choice, Mrs Brecht mightn't have preferred something a little more cheerful, but I was sure Mr Brecht knew best.

Mrs Brecht moved her head slightly, turning towards Ellen. Her lips parted.

'She wants to stop the music, Papa,' Ellen said.

'Put something else on then. The Debussy. She loves the Debussy.'

'No, not the Debussy. She doesn't want that.'

'I said, put the Debussy on,' Mr Brecht demanded in a tone of voice that brooked no argument. Ellen frowned, but she stood up and obeyed him. I was watching Mrs Brecht's face. I saw an emotion cross it – it wasn't sadness, it was more like fury. Death seemed to make everyone angry. Mrs Brecht closed her eyes again. I lifted the curtain the tiniest fraction. Mr Tremlett was still outside, scowling and staring up at the room. I wondered how long he would stand there.

Her cleaning finished, Mrs Todd came in and took her place in an upright chair in the far corner of the room. She sat straight-backed in the pool of light cast by the standard lamp, knitting, her needles clicking. The wool was in a bag beside the chair. I wondered if she stayed in that room the whole time, guarding Mrs Brecht. Not the whole time. She hadn't been there when we arrived back in the car, when Adam Tremlett was in the bedroom.

We remained there silently in the room, for an hour maybe, perhaps a little longer, with the piano notes winding amongst us, settling on our skin, slipping through our hair, skimming the dry lips of the dying woman, moving on again. I began to feel sleepy. I went to sit beside Ellen and she put her head on my shoulder. I stroked her hair. Then the nurse, who had been resting, came into the room. She looked at us all, the man draped on the pillows beside his dying wife, Mrs Todd, still knitting, the dark, slim schoolgirl and the larger, fair one both still in the black tights, pleated skirts and jumpers we wore to school in the winter months, holding one another, and she said, 'Take a break. Get changed, have something to eat, rest for a while.'

'I'm not leaving my wife,' said Mr Brecht. 'Not now. I'm not leaving her for another second.'

'She's sleeping. I'll be here with her. You need to prepare yourselves. This will be a long night.'

'No,' said Mr Brecht. 'I'm not leaving.'

My heart almost broke with the tragedy and romance of it all. Still, *I* was glad to be told to leave the room. I didn't want to stay there for another moment. There was something bad about the room where Mrs Brecht lay dying. Something was wrong and it wasn't just the dying.

I kissed Ellen goodbye at the front door, and she stood there, a slight, mournful figure, one hand on the frame, waving to me as I left Thornfield House and made my way back home. Adam Tremlett's van was parked outside the church. The light was all but gone now, everywhere prematurely darkened by the winter evening and the heavy fog. It was easy to imagine the wraiths of dead people weaving through the gloom, the sea fret thick with the spirits of the drowned.

Afterwards, always, I remembered every detail of that evening. I remembered Jago being rough and boyish with me, trying to cheer me up or at least distract me, but I couldn't forget what was happening in that room in Thornfield House, I couldn't stop thinking about Ellen and wishing I was with her, at the same time as being relieved and glad that I wasn't. Waiting for someone to die, I thought, is a terrible thing. In the end, Mum told Jago to leave me alone and sent me upstairs for a bath. I came downstairs in my pyjamas and dressing-gown and Mum dried my hair for me with the dryer and a brush. She was very gentle. After that, we ate supper. Nobody spoke much at the table. Dad said something about putting the Christmas decorations up but nobody was interested. After we'd eaten, Jago wrapped up and took the dog for a walk, Dad watched television in the living room, and Mum and I prepared meals that Mrs Todd could warm up during the coming week.

When Jago returned, he and I played cards for a while.

'Do you remember what it was like when your mother died?' I asked.

'You don't forget stuff like that.'

'Was it like this? Was everyone waiting for it to happen?'

Jago shook his head.

'It was over before I knew it. One minute everything was normal and the next the nurses were reading me stories in the hospice. They had a book called *The Great Big Bullfrog* that I liked. I'd learned all the words by the time Mum passed. The nurses said that was clever for a boy of six.' He smiled at the memory. 'I thought I was the dog's doo-dahs,' he said.

I smiled with him.

'What about your dad?'

Jago shrugged. 'The last time I saw him was the day Mum died. When we got back from the hospice he dropped me off next door with my uncle and aunt, told me to behave myself, said he'd be back in a bit and disappeared.'

'He never even said goodbye?'

'No. You can see why they were pissed off. I was literally dumped on them.'

I stopped smiling then. Jago punched my arm.

'It turned out all right though, didn't it, Spanner? I ended up here, with you.'

'Yeah.'

Jago hugged me awkwardly.

'You'll be all right,' he said. 'You need to keep your chin up. Be brave, Han. Everything will be bad for a while, but it'll get better.'

Later, I took Trixie upstairs with me and lifted her up onto my bed. Trixie lay beside me with her chin on my chest, snoring comfortingly. I thought of poor Mr Brecht, about to be widowed in his prime, the only woman he had ever loved torn away from him so cruelly and so young. I thought of him there, in the bedroom, sitting beside his dying wife, and the poignancy made my eyes fill with tears.

I didn't mean to, but I must have fallen asleep, for when I woke it was the middle of the night, and an owl was hooting outside. I took this to be a sign that it was over, that Mrs

Brecht was gone, and I sobbed, quietly, therapeutically and pleasingly into the comforting bulk of the dog's muscly old body.

The next morning was the morning when Ellen was not on the school bus.

CHAPTER TWENTY-ONE

My parents and I did go into the village for our lunch and we spent a pleasant afternoon together. We had tea back at the cottage, and afterwards, I told Mum to sit down and put her feet up while I washed and dried the cups and saucers and put them away. I knew she would check afterwards to make sure everything had been cleaned to her exacting standards, and more than likely repeat the whole process herself. As I hung the tea-towels out to dry, I could see Mum was tired with the effort of having me there. Since my breakdown, we'd found it difficult to spend time together. We loved one another still, but I exhausted her and she irritated me. She was always on high alert, looking for signs of imminent mental collapse, which meant I had to take particular care to reassure her I was fine. Normally this wasn't so difficult, but because I was feeling out of sorts, the tension in the little house was high that day.

'It's such a lovely evening, I think I'll go for a walk, Mum,' I said. She was sitting in the living room. The television was turned on but the sound was muted. I could tell from her face that she had been on the point of nodding off.

'Stay here and watch television with me,' she said. 'There's a history programme on in a minute that you'd like.' It was a half-hearted request. I went over to her chair and kissed her forehead.

'Really, Mum, I could do with some fresh air,' I said. 'I've been stuck so long in the city and you know I'm still a country girl at heart. I miss the sea.'

Mum smiled then. She lived under the impression that Bristol was a terrible place full of drugs, sin and pollution. Anything I said to reinforce this prejudice pleased her no end.

'I'll be back before it's dark,' I promised, and I picked up my jacket and went out.

I walked for a while along the lane, then climbed over a stile and crossed into a field. The summer air was warm and balmy, the field full of butterflies. My mind slowed down, and I relaxed as I walked through grass that was waist-high, watching the rabbits scuttering at the field's perimeter, and the little birds darting in and out of the hedgerows.

I didn't set out with any destination in mind, and it was a while before I realized I was heading for Bleached Scarp.

It was further than I remembered, and a more demanding walk. The farmers had removed most of the footpath signs to deter holidaymakers from traipsing across their fields, and stiles I remembered climbing as a child were no longer there. I was charmed anew by the red-brown cattle grazing in the meadows, by the wildflowers, the profusion of yellow, white and purple amongst the blowing grass, and the old wall steps, flat stones built into the ancient field boundary walls, to assist walkers. I was less enamoured of the electric fences that seemed to have been wrapped around almost every field.

Eventually I reached the crest of the hill which rolled down on the other side towards the coastal footpath, and beyond that the cliffs leading down to the sea. Puffy, white flat-bottomed clouds scudded across a perfectly eggshell-blue sky, and the sea beneath was dark aquamarine, the waves tipped with foamy white horses. I was proud of the view. I stood there for a few moments and summoned up the past. I could almost see us, the three children, Ellen, Jago and me, with our scabby knees and our dirty hands and our pockets full of pebbles and sweets. I could see us scrambling down the hill, running, falling, chasing, Ellen and Jago always ahead of me, calling to me to hurry up, to keep up, not to be such a scaredy-cat.

And then I blinked, and they were gone, and it was just me, all grown up and alone and enjoying the view for what it was – a beautiful view, one of the best in the world. Our view.

I took the traditional route, through the field, across the path and over the fence beside the sign that read *Danger of Death, Eroding Cliff Face*, trying not to smile with pleasure at my own daring. I used to be so frightened of this place, but the cliff was not so high, the path not so slippery. Was I braver now? Was I more confident because I was an adult, or had I merely imagined the dangers when I was a child? It took me a few moments to find the hole in the cliff that opened into the tunnel down to the beach. It was a smaller gap than I remembered, but the tunnel inside was less steep and dark; it was not the dizzyingly dangerous drop I recalled. The rough steps inside were manmade, hewn out of the rock to make getting to and from the beach easier and safer. It was likely, obvious even, that the passage had been used by smugglers. I scrambled down into the hole, listening to the sea slapping the cliff wall below, using my elbows and knees to keep my descent steady until I could climb onto the rocks and jump into the cave that opened onto the beach. The dank darkness, wet sand, the seaweed smell, the echoing of the sea in the cave felt like coming home to me. It was exactly as I remembered.

Other children had found the beach and claimed it. Empty

cans had been burned in a fire and old towels had been stashed in the shrubs at the cliff-foot. Yet it was still as it always had been: the sand marked with bird-prints and the tide rattling the pebbles, the wind and the light and the taste of the ocean. I looked up to the rocks where Jago and Ellen used to jump. If I squinted, I could almost make them out, those friends from my childhood, daring one another to leap into the sea. The memory made me smile. Coming back, I thought, had been the right thing to do. There was nothing to fear about this place. The memories I had of our times on the beach were good ones.

I followed the cliff wall to the place where the rock had cracked, forming a little cave where we used to hide things. I reached inside, searching with my fingers until they found a cockle-shell, and the ancient plastic cigarette lighter that Jago used to light fires. My drift-glass was gone. Somebody had found our hiding place and they'd taken my glass. I was glad if somebody else had it. I didn't even care if it had been thrown back into the sea. It was a sign that life goes on. Places stay the same but children grow up and move on, and other children come to take their place.

After that, I took off my boots and my socks and paddled into the sea, not caring that the legs of my jeans would be soaked. The sand was grainy beneath my feet and the water was icy cold. I knew if I waited a few moments my feet would become used to the chill and I wouldn't feel the burn of the water any longer. I looked down at my feet. The water around them was stained red, streaks of red that dissipated with every wave. I pulled one foot, then the other, out of the water. Neither was cut. I looked again but the stain was gone.

It had only been momentary, but this made me uneasy. My heart began to pump with some urgency. A cloud passed over the sun and I glanced up, over the cliff, to see what was blocking the light . . . and at exactly the same moment the cloud withdrew and the sunlight burned my eyes; it pierced into my brain. I took a step forward, stumbled and scrabbled back to my feet. My eyes were still sun-dazzled and half-blinded, but I noticed a movement on the clifftop above. I shielded my eyes with my hand and looked again. Someone was there, on the cliff edge. I blinked. There was a dark retinal spot in the centre of my vision. I looked away and when I looked back again I could tell by the silhouette of the person standing on the cliff that it was a woman. She was standing at the edge of the cliff, perfectly still, looking down, watching.

It was her, I was sure of it.

Who else could it have been?

It was Ellen.

CHAPTER TWENTY-TWO

In January, four weeks after Mrs Brecht's funeral, the rain came. It pattered against the glass of the tall French doors that opened out onto the terrace at the back of Thornfield House. It was raining so hard that the black compost Adam Tremlett had spent hours scooping into the pots that lined the terrace was spitting out over the pale paving slabs. The water in the pond was dancing in the twilight and flat grey puddles were forming in the newly laid turf.

I was sitting in the back room waiting for Ellen, who hadn't finished her piano practice. She'd been practising when I called round that morning, and she was still practising at four o'clock in the afternoon. She was trying to master a particularly difficult passage and her father was with her, instructing her. I could hear Mr Brecht's voice, low and persuasive, and I could also hear Ellen's voice, frustrated and angry.

Her fingers were voicing her despair. I heard it, anyone could hear it in the notes of the tricky, twisty tune. It wasn't even pretty music, nor the kind her mother preferred, not the moonlight music or the sea music or the heartbreak music or the love music or the music that reminded me of lying on the beach at Bleached Scarp with the sun on my face and the wind breathing over the waves. It wasn't Mozart or Grieg or the Saint-Saëns Concerto that Anne had loved, but something discordant and clangy, like the sound of pain.

Ellen's father was trying to teach his daughter how to translate their grief into music. That's what was going on and it was torture for Ellen because her grief was quite eloquent enough: it needed no translation.

They buried Anne Brecht in the graveyard of the Church of Our Lady Star of the Sea, out on the moors. It was a bleak winter's day and a strange and lonely ceremony, the casket being lowered into the family plot beneath the wide arms of the ancient churchyard yew. Only a few local people were there – my family, Mrs Todd, of course, and Adam Tremlett, who was not in the church but stood at the edge of the churchyard, after the service, watching the interment from a distance. Most of the people attending were Germans, Mr Brecht's family come over for the occasion, together with a handful of mourners from the world of classical music who were strangers even to Ellen; men in long coats and women with slender waists and high heels, their grief expensively and exquisitely accessorized. People whispered that they had come from London, from Germany, from Russia even. They were rumoured to have sat at the bar in the Seagull Hotel talking animatedly and drinking vodka into the early hours.

Ellen wore a simple black dress of her mother's, a black coat, black tights, and she draped a lace mantilla she had found in her mother's wardrobe over her head and face so that people should not see her tears. Her father was dressed in black from head to toe. His hair, uncut for weeks, hung about his shoulders, damp in the drizzle. He was thinner, more angular than he had been before, and this, together with the long hair and the dark stubble around his face and neck, made him seem younger; far too young to be a widower. He and Ellen stood beside one another, wretched, but strangely dignified.

I had nothing black to wear to the funeral, so had to resort to the only formal clothes I had, my school uniform. I stood between my parents, feeling childlike and ridiculous, watching Mr Brecht and Ellen. When it came to sprinkling the earth onto the coffin, he turned away. He then strode away from the grave, and disappeared behind the church. Ellen followed. I wondered if I should run after them, but Mum looked down at me and whispered, 'Leave them be.' A little later, I heard a wail of abject despair in the distance, from beyond the church, and I knew it was him.

Jago was at the funeral too, standing beside my father. He listened to the graveside words, and then he crossed himself and walked away. I saw him crouched beside a different grave, not a proper one, just a grassy spot beside the far wall. Mum said that was where the ashes of people who couldn't afford a proper memorial were scattered.

'Do you think that's where Jago's mother was laid to rest?' I whispered.

Mum nodded. 'Probably.' She glanced at my father. 'We never thought to ask him, did we, Malcolm?'

Dad shook his head. 'He'll be all right,' he said. 'Don't worry about the lad. It's what's in his head and his heart that counts. Not a spot of turf.'

Now, more than a month later, the Brecht household was still deeply in mourning. Mr Brecht paced the house, refusing to let anyone touch anything of Anne's, insisting everything was left where it had been as if he really believed that one day she would come home. The room in which she had died was locked and he had the key. He wouldn't even let Mrs Todd in to air it, but went in there himself and stayed for hours sometimes. The room was next to Ellen's and some nights she heard him through the wall, walking up and down, listening to recordings of her mother playing the piano.

The cashmere blanket that used to keep Mrs Brecht warm was still folded neatly at the head of the chaise longue in the front room, and the hot-water bottle she used to soothe the pain in her heels still lay, unemptied, at its foot. In the back room, where I was waiting for Ellen, her mother's books were lined up on the shelves of the bookcase. They were new books, mostly unread, because in the last months her fingers had been too sore to turn the pages. She used to ask Ellen to read to her sometimes, as an alternative to listening to music. Her sunglasses had been left on the fireplace; her walking stick lay across the armrests of the wheelchair that stood beside the French windows; the ribboned straw hat she wore in the garden in summer was hooked over the handle. A pair of flip-flops sat side by side next to the French windows, as if they were waiting for Anne to return and slip her small, deformed feet into them. Her rings, all her beautiful rings, were in a glass dish on the fireplace.

All the light, all the energy seemed to have seeped out of the house, under the doors and through the keyholes. Where it had been airy and elegant and full of life, now it felt cavernous, empty and looming.

Ellen was having nightmares. She told me she could feel something lurking in the shadows of her dreams, not the fragile presence of her mother, but something big and threatening, something violent. She said, in her dreams, she knew whatever it was that threatened her was watching her, waiting for her to do something that would trigger it to kill. Only she didn't know what it was that she must not do. She believed the essence of the dreams. She said she knew she was going to be hunted down, and that she would die, only she did not know where, or when, or how. During her waking hours, she worried about setting the curse in motion, like the Lady of Shallott. What she said disturbed me. The shadow of her nightmares began to infiltrate my dreams too. I worried when I was awake – not about me, but about Ellen.

I felt uncomfortable sitting alone, waiting for Ellen, in the back room where Anne Brecht so often sat. The fancy German clock on the mantelpiece ticked loudly and the rain beat against the window, and the off-key piano music was like the soundtrack to a horror film. I was torn between sympathy for Ellen, and sympathy for her father. How could he expect her to play well so soon after her mother's death? And how could she play so badly when all he asked of her was a little concentration?

I looked down at the newspaper on my lap. Mrs Todd had given it to me, opened out and flattened at the page she wanted me to read. The article was an obituary. The author had clearly been an admirer of Anne Brecht. He had written at length about her talent, and how her youth and beauty and vibrancy combined to make her one of the most popular and famous female pianists ever. The accompanying photographs showed Anne at work and at leisure during her celebrated visits to New York and Rome, and she looked beautiful and happy, posing in the sunshine like someone who knew they had been gifted the luckiest of lives.

When I'd finished reading, I put the newspaper down and wandered over to the window. I looked out at the rain, watching the drops chase one another down the glass. The night was drawing in now, the garden was darkening. I could see no further than the pond.

I went to the bookcase and pulled out an old copy of the *Tatler* that had been tucked in next to the marble bookend. I took it back to my chair and flicked through the pages. The Debutante of the Month interested me – a willowy blonde reliably dressed in a pale twinset and pearls. I was not entirely sure what a debutante was – the posh people's equivalent of a Page Three girl, I supposed. I turned a few more pages and the magazine folded open at a double-page spread, which had obviously been looked at many times before. The main photograph, taking up most of the first page, was of a woman holding a baby in her arms. The woman was Anne, Mrs Brecht, but younger than I'd ever known her. The baby had to be Ellen.

In the picture, Anne was wearing a white, scoop-necked dress and sitting in an upright antique chair beside a tall window. A heavily brocaded curtain had been tied back, and the window looked out over a formal terrace and landscaped parkland. The caption said the photograph had been taken inside the *Schloss Marien, the exquisite country home of Anne's mother-in-law, Countess Friederike von Schontiede, in the glorious countryside beyond Magdeburg, overlooking the River Elbe.* Ellen had told me on many occasions about the castle where she used to live, and about how her father's grandparents were related to minor German royalty. I had never believed her. Now I realized that some of what she had said, at least, was true.

It was only after reading the caption that I looked at the photograph again, more closely, and noticed Mr Brecht, standing beyond the open window, on the terrace. He was breathtakingly handsome, dressed in casual trousers and an open-necked shirt, leaning in a rather louche and completely adorable way against the base of a reclining stone hart, a cigarette between the fingers of his free hand.

I gazed at him for a while, touched his face with my fingertips, and read on.

The article gave a brief list of Anne's musical accomplishments. Her last public performance had been in St Petersburg, eight weeks before Ellen was born. Anne was only twenty-one at the time but the article quoted several sources proclaiming her to be an important, prodigious talent – her rendition of *Liebeslied* by Fritz Kreisler being regarded as the definitive version of the work, and so forth. *And,* the writer gushed, *the birth of Ellen Louisa is the icing on the cake of happiness for Anne and for her charming husband, Pieter, who has been her musical teacher and mentor since she was twelve years old.*

I didn't read any further because a door slammed in the hallway and I heard Ellen's footsteps running up the stairs. Mr Brecht came into the room where I was sitting and Mrs Todd followed behind. She poured a glass of whisky and passed it to him. He took it and drank. Neither of them had noticed me.

'How was she today?' Mrs Todd asked. Her hands were folded in front of her and her eyes were downcast.

'Hopeless,' Mr Brecht said. 'She was deliberately sabotaging the piece. She won't listen to me, she won't do what I tell her, she won't try. I don't know what to do with her, Mrs Todd. I am at my wits' end.'

He put his hands on the back of Mrs Brecht's chair and dropped his head between his arms.

I cleared my throat. Mr Brecht straightened up and pushed back his hair.

'Hello, Hanchen,' he said, with a tired smile. I smiled back, hoping he would understand the exquisite depth of my sympathy.

'Go upstairs and talk to Ellen,' Mrs Todd said to me. 'Dinner will be ready in half an hour.'

I nodded, laid the magazine down on the arm of the chair, and made my escape.

CHAPTER TWENTY-THREE

On the way back to my parents' house, I stopped at the Smuggler's Rest, a small roadside pub, charming in its decrepitude. I didn't make a habit of going to pubs on my own, but I needed a drink after seeing the woman on the clifftop. Either my mind was playing its terrible games again or Ellen really had returned from the dead. Or, and this was a thought that had been forming in my mind over the past few days, perhaps she had never died. Perhaps everything I had been told, everything I had believed, was wrong.

Maybe there had been some conspiracy and Ellen Brecht was still alive and was trying to reach out to me.

I did not know what to think, what to believe.

What I did know was that I could not let my mother see me as I was. I had to calm myself. Alcohol, I reasoned, might do the trick. Also, it would be reassuring to sit in the pub's messy little beer garden amongst the lacy cow parsley and the tiny brown pollinating moths while the sun was going down, with people around me talking and relaxing as if everything was all right in the world.

The last time I had been in that particular pub was when I was eighteen. I used to go there with Ricky, my first boyfriend. I still remembered what we did in the car park. As

I walked into the gloom of the bar, I looked across the garden, to the place where Ricky used to park his car all those years ago, and in spite of everything, I wrapped my arms about myself, and I smiled.

Only a handful of people were inside the bar, which was poky and dark and smelled of dishwasher steam. I ordered a pint of cider and the barman was filling the glass when I realized I had no money with me. This was enough to bring tears to my eyes. I felt like a child denied the one thing I really wanted. Everything was going wrong and it always seemed to come back to Ellen. She was always at the root of my unhappiness. Embarrassed, I apologized to the barman and turned to go when a slight, grizzled man stepped in front of me, pulled off the woollen beanie he was wearing, peered into my face and said, 'It's little Hannah Brown, isn't it?'

I took the tissue he was holding out to me and used it to wipe away my tears.

'Yes,' I said, and stepped to the left to move past him, but he moved with me.

'You don't remember me, do you? It's Bill – Bill Haworth. Your brother, Jago, used to work on my boat.'

'Oh yes, Bill! How nice to see you.' I tried to squeeze past, but he took my arm.

'I'll get your drink,' he said. 'You look like you could use it. Go and find a seat outside where we can talk. I'll be with you in a moment.'

'It's kind of you, Bill, but—'

'Go on,' he said.

I wound my way around the bar to the garden, found a free bench, sat down and picked apart a beer mat until Bill arrived with my cider and a second pint for him. He put the glasses on the wooden table slats and sat on the opposite side of the bench, which rocked and creaked, all its joints going out of kilter. I put my feet square on the ground to balance it.

'All right then,' said Bill. 'Now you've got your drink, you can tell me what you're doing here and what it is that's upset you.'

I held the glass in my hands and drank several gulps. The cider was sweet and cold and delicious.

'I'm down visiting my parents for the weekend,' I said. 'And nothing's wrong. I just . . .' I looked into my drink and watched the bubbles climbing the inside of the glass. It was too complicated to explain, even to Bill, who knew some of it already. 'It's difficult being back,' I said. 'I feel like a stranger, as if I don't belong here any more and at the same time it's as if I never went away.'

'My opinion,' said Bill slowly, 'for what it's worth, which ain't much, is that when a person goes back to a place they left, they also goes back to the age they was when they left it.'

I thought about that for a moment. 'Yes,' I said. 'That's exactly how I feel.'

Bill looked pleased. He took a long drink. I watched his throat move as he swallowed. Then he solemnly put the glass back on the bench.

'You heard from that brother of yours lately?' he asked.

I shook my head. 'No. I haven't spoken to Jago since Dad's heart attack.'

'That was years back.'

'I know.'

'Why don't you talk to each other? You used to be thick as thieves, you two.'

'We just don't. We don't have any reason to talk.'

Bill snorted. 'That's the daftest thing I ever heard. You're living on opposite sides of the world, living different lives, you must have plenty to say to one another.'

I nodded, hoping he would change tack if I agreed with him. I brushed a ladybird from my forearm.

'He's all right though, is he – Jago?' Bill asked.

'He's doing fine. He's got a good job.'

'And a good woman to go with it?'

'No,' I told Bill. 'He can't seem to find the right person.'

I looked down again. Somebody had folded a crisp packet very small and stuffed it between the slats in the bench.

'Jago's one of the good 'uns,' said Bill. 'He's one of the best. Any one of us would've helped him. Whatever trouble it was he was running from – women, money, whatever – we'd have seen him right if the daft sod, excuse my language, hadn't buggered off like he did.'

He drank again, licked his lips and put the almost-empty glass down. He had a tattoo of his grandchildren's names on his forearm. *Shoni* and *Jude*.

'You couldn't have done anything to stop Jago leaving,' I said. 'Nobody could.'

'Ah well,' Bill said. He tapped a cigarette out of a packet and rolled it along the table. 'Next time you speak to him, tell him I asked after him.'

'I will.'

'And tell him to get his arse back here. Tell him there's still work for him. Tell him . . .'

I waited.

'Tell the bugger that we still miss him.'

Bill stood up then, put the cigarette behind his ear, picked up his empty glass, patted me on the shoulder, and went back inside the pub.

I pulled the sleeves of my cardigan tighter around me and gazed out into the distance, across the flat bogland where a summer mist was forming, wreathing itself around the great satellite dishes of Goonhilly.

I closed my eyes for a moment. When I shut them, I could see the figure on the clifftop clearly silhouetted against the sun's glare. It was Ellen. Always Ellen.

CHAPTER TWENTY-FOUR

I went upstairs to find Ellen, as Mrs Todd had told me to; she was in her bedroom, sullenly collecting her towel, shampoo, conditioner. She went into the bathroom, and I followed. She locked the door and turned on the hot tap as far as it would go. I waited for her to speak. I couldn't help but notice that Anne Brecht's toothbrush was still in its mug, the flannel embroidered with her initials still folded on the windowledge; the mat she used to prevent her from slipping in the bath was still there too, along with her cosmetics, her lotions and creams and oils.

'He's a bastard,' Ellen said without looking at me. 'He's a fucking evil lying bastard.'

I was used to this kind of outburst. I folded down the lavatory lid and sat on it, my hands clasped between my knees, while Ellen took off her clothes and dropped them on the floor. I could smell the warm, private scent of her skin, her armpits, her sweat as she undressed. She continued to rant, half-sobbing.

'What happened exactly?' I asked.

'I said some things to him.'

'You swore?'

Ellen shrugged. I sighed. If she didn't want to make her father angry, why did she behave like this?

'It was his fault!' she said. 'I *had* to swear to shut him up. He said some horrible things.'

'What things?'

'He said Mama didn't love us, that she was a liar, that she was seeing other men behind his back right up until the day she died. He said . . .' Ellen paused and looked at me '. . . that she was a whore.'

I gasped. I could not imagine Mr Brecht saying such a horrible word, and especially not about his wife. He had worshipped the ground Anne walked on and the air she breathed. This had to be another of Ellen's lies, or at the very least an exaggeration.

'Why would he say that?'

'I think he's mad. Do you know, Hannah, sometimes when I've been playing the piano, he's called me "Anne". He's spoken to me as if I were her. He's— Oh, I don't want to tell you! But I have to remind him. I have to say: "Papa, it's me, Ellen!" And even then, sometimes, it takes a while for him to recognize me. That's not normal, is it? That would freak anyone out.'

She picked up her clothes and stuffed them into the tall linen basket in the corner of the room. I bit a fingernail nervously. I wasn't sure how much of this to believe, or how to react.

'Perhaps he needs more time to get over losing your mother,' I suggested.

Ellen snorted. 'He needs a lobotomy,' she said. She was a little calmer now. This was almost a joke.

She wrapped a green towel around herself, leaned over and tested the water with her hand, half-disappearing in a mist of apple-scented steam. She topped the bath up from the cold tap, water gushing like a geyser.

'Don't look,' she said. I turned my head slightly to the left and lowered my eyes, but still I watched beneath my lashes as Ellen wriggled out of her pants, dropped the towel, stepped into the big, old-fashioned bathtub and sank beneath the water. Her hair stuck to the back of the bath. She held her hands up in front of her, stretching and clenching her fingers, trying to ease the soreness in her joints. The skin on her face and shoulders gradually pinkened. Then she closed her eyes and slid under the water and most of her disappeared Her knees stuck up, glistening wet. I wanted to do something to help Ellen. I knelt at the side of the bath, poured shampoo into the palm of my hand, and when she resurfaced, I reached over and washed her hair. Ellen didn't protest. She kept her eyes closed while my fingers explored the shape of her head, wiped suds from the curve of her little ears, worked the shampoo through the skein of wet hair. I tried to wipe away a mark on her neck, but it wouldn't wash off and I realized it was a bruise.

'What happened to your neck?'

'Papa did it.'

'Oh Ellen, don't say things like that.'

'He did,' she insisted. 'I don't think he means to hurt me – at least, I don't think it's me he wants to hurt. I think it's Mama.'

Now I knew she was lying. Mr Brecht was moody, he was passionate, but I knew he would never, ever put his hands around anyone's neck, least of all Ellen's, and never Anne's. I remembered the absolute love in his voice when he said he would never let anything, or anyone, hurt his wife or daughter.

Downstairs, one end of the long cherrywood table in the dining room had been laid for three people, with silver cutlery, candles in candlesticks, linen serviettes. A record played on the hi-fi in the corner. The record was slightly warped; I could tell by the way the light reflected from its rim as it spun on the turntable. It was a crackly live recording of Anne Brecht in performance. At the end of each movement the applause coming through the speakers was rapturous.

Outside the rain was still falling and the sky was dark. It was late and I hadn't eaten in hours. I was hungry.

I sat opposite Ellen. Her father came into the room. He ground out his cigarette in the cut-glass ashtray on the sideboard, and came towards me. He smelled of Gitanes and vetiver and glamour.

'You're looking very beautiful tonight, Hannah,' he said. He put his hand on my shoulder, and gave a little squeeze. The feeling travelled all the way through my body. I held my hands tight together in my lap and smiled up at him as elegantly and as eloquently as I could.

He pulled up a chair and sat beside Ellen, unfolded his napkin and spread it over his knees.

'Are you talking to me yet, Ellen?' he asked.

'If I don't have to, I'd rather not,' she said. I winced at her rudeness. Mr Brecht took a deep breath.

'I'm sorry, sweetheart, that we ended up fighting, but you bring it on yourself,' he said. 'I don't want to be angry with you, but you make me angry. You don't listen to me. You remind me of your mother and how she didn't listen to me, and I can't deal with that right now.'

'That's your excuse, is it?' Ellen asked.

'Oh, Ellen,' Mr Brecht said. 'We have a guest. Let's at least be civil in front of Hannah.'

He opened the wine bottle on the table, and half-filled three glasses. I took a sip. We never had wine at home. I liked the sensation of holding the glass in my hand. I liked the way the light shone through the wine. I enjoyed feeling so grown-up. While we sat there, formally, like three people in a painting, Mrs Todd came in with a tray – three bowls of steaming pea and dumpling soup, three small, home-made bread rolls and butter scooped into curls on a small dish. She served the soup and we ate in silence, listening to the music. After that, there was meat in an oniony sauce with herb-roast potatoes and tiny fresh vegetables. It was delicious. Mr Brecht wasn't eating much, but drinking wine, topping up his own glass. When the bottle was empty, Mrs Todd brought another. Ellen picked at her food, moving it around the plate. She did not touch her wine.

After the main course was finished, she asked her father if the two of us could be excused.

'Just a moment,' Mr Brecht said, and he came around the table and took something out of his pocket. It was the little gold chain with the treble clef charm that Ellen's mother used to wear round her neck. Ellen sat still as a statue while Mr Brecht fastened it around her neck. Then he leaned over and kissed the top of his daughter's head.

'I'm being hard on you for your own good, *Schatzi*,' he said. 'It is because I love you. If I did not love you so very much, I would not get so angry. You understand, don't you?'

Ellen nodded.

'Good girl,' said Mr Brecht.

He was standing behind her. He couldn't see her face. Only I, sitting opposite, saw the anger in her eyes. It scared me.

CHAPTER TWENTY-FIVE

I walked in the gloaming from the pub back to Cross Hands Lane. Mum and Dad were already in bed. They'd left a ham sandwich covered in clingfilm on a plate for my supper. I made some tea, ate the sandwich, watched a little television, then went upstairs and slept like a baby in the single bed on which I'd slept through my childhood and my teenage years. I had forgotten, until I slipped between the clean sheets, how soft the mattress was, how familiar and comforting. All that was missing was Trixie. She'd died at home, under my bed, while I was in Chile. Dad had wrapped her in a blanket and dug a hole in the garden to bury her.

I had found it easy to grieve for Trixie. The tears had come unforced, the pain in my heart was genuine and oddly comforting. I remembered the dog's big, ugly face, her timidity, her predisposition to drool, her bloodshot, trusting eyes, and I ached with love. I missed her, pure and simple. But it had been so difficult to grieve for Ellen. I had not cried when I read the letter that told me Ellen had died; I had not cried when I returned to Trethene years after that. I had done my best not to think about Ellen, or her death, at all. Deep in my heart, I did not accept that she was gone. I never articulated my feelings, but I convinced myself that 'dying' at a tragically young age was simply another way for Ellen to put herself in the limelight.

I had never, truly, believed she was dead.

I couldn't talk to anyone about this. It was too complicated. Even when I was at my most messed-up, I managed to hide how I really felt.

In the hospital, after the breakdown, I was told to acknowledge my feelings for Ellen, and let them go. They made it sound so easy, those soft-voiced counsellors with their long silences, their: *'How do you feel?*'s, their: *'Tell me what you're thinking*'s. Julia told me to go deep inside myself and dredge out the darkest memories, those that had buried themselves so far within my psyche that I was fearful of uprooting them. *'Dig them out,'* she had said, as if she were talking about potatoes. *'Take a good look at them, then move away!'* I never did as she suggested. If I had pulled out those memories and examined them too closely, I would have risked poisoning the present with the toxicity of the past.

Only now, after all those years had gone by, I wondered if I had been right all along to deny Ellen's death. And if she was still alive, if I could talk to her, then I could explain. I could make things better.

Mum had placed a jug of garden lilies on the little windowledge in my room, and in the morning I knelt on the bed and looked past the flowers that were already shedding pollen on the sill, out of the window. They reminded me of Ellen's eighteenth birthday – the spilled pollen on the white tablecloth, the sense of dread. I shook my head to chase away the memory. That was the past. This was now. The garden of the house that used to belong to the Cardells was tidy now, and ordered. The concrete had been dug up, the old rabbit hutch and clothesline were gone. Instead there was a tidy, pocket-handkerchief-sized lawn, a herb garden, bird feeders. A couple of foldaway chairs sat side by side on the patio. It looked like a pleasant place to sit and enjoy the sun and pass the time.

It was true, I thought, that time made some things better. Bad neighbours were replaced by good ones, disorder by harmony. Only it worked the other way around too.

I slid off the bed and picked up my towel and toiletry bag. I went into the bathroom, tiny and cramped, still with an old-fashioned chain-pull flush on the lavatory, old-fashioned white ceramic tiles and big old taps above the enamel bath. It was poorly ventilated and icy cold in winter. Black mould grew in the corners of the windows, and the grouting of the tiles. I'd tried to persuade my parents many times to upgrade and modernize the bathroom, I'd offered to organize and pay for a refurbishment myself, but they refused. They didn't see the point. They said: '*Why fix what's not broken?*' They liked the bathroom how it was.

I lay in the bath and remembered the day I received the letter from my mother, in which she told me that Ellen had died. It had been a big-sky, clouds-painted-on, bright South American day; handsome, long-maned horses stamping and blowing, kicking up red dust, the call of the cowhands, the answering bellow of young bulls. One of the Japanese students working in our group had taken the pick-up into town to fetch supplies, and had returned with a handful of mail along with the bags of rice and sugar, boxes of cereal, tins of meat and vegetables. She had handed out the letters – it was rare for post from England to reach us at all. There was only one letter for me. It had been posted, in Cornwall, more than two months earlier and had taken that long to reach me. I'd recognized my mother's writing and gone into the barn we were using as a dormitory to read it in private.

I'd sat on the top bunk, opened the envelope with my thumb and taken out the letter inside – just one folded piece of blue paper from the gift set I had given my mother for

Christmas years before. She had written, without preamble:

Dearest Hannah,

I have some terrible news for you. I am sorry to tell you this in a letter, but of course I cannot reach you by telephone and I feel the news cannot wait until you return home as I don't know how long that will be. Ellen Brecht has passed away. She has gone to join her mother in Heaven. It was a drowning accident and pray God she did not suffer. Her father has gone away back to Germany, so I have heard, and the house is closed up.

I know you will be very sad and I'm so sorry I can't be with you, my darling girl, to comfort you but I pray your good friends in South America will look after you in this difficult time

I remembered each word exactly and the way my mother's old-fashioned handwriting looped across the page, so the letter must have made a deep impression, but at the time, it hadn't made sense to me. Was it because I was so far away from home? Because I felt so removed? Or had I just not been capable of facing up to the truth? My mother's words seemed false and artificial. There was so little information in the letter, it was ridiculously brief given the news it contained. I didn't believe it.

I had folded the letter, put it back in its envelope and kept it in the pocket of my shorts, meaning to find a shady spot where I could take it out and read it again later, to compose questions in my mind, to understand it – but sometime during the morning it had fallen out of my pocket. The letter was lost and I did not search for it. That made it easier for me to put it from my mind. I didn't say anything to anyone. I didn't talk about its contents, not even to Ricky. I simply pretended I didn't know that Ellen was dead. I did not allow myself to think about her death, or why she had died, or how. It was easier for me to carry on as if the letter had never existed. That way, I did not have to think about the last time I saw Ellen, or what I had said to her and the way we had parted.

That way, I could pretend that one day there would still be a chance for me to put things right between Ellen and me.

CHAPTER TWENTY-SIX

Spring came, and with it came the daffodils that had been Anne Brecht's favourite flowers. Her birthday would have been in April. It was an especially lovely month that year. The wildflowers were prolific and joyful, the blossom on the trees in the garden of Thornfield House gloriously showy in its pinks and whites, but rather than enjoying the natural beauty, Mr Brecht avoided it. Ellen told me he spent the whole of the anniversary of Anne's birthday in the room where she had died, on his own, with only the music to keep him company.

Since Mrs Brecht's death, I had taken to spending more time at Thornfield House again. Ellen and I drifted through rooms that still seemed to be full of the presence of her mother, as if she had not managed to escape the place, even in death. I watched Mr Brecht carefully, from a distance, because I did not know what I should say to him, and because his torment was so biblical in its depth. Mrs Todd did her best to keep the household running on an even keel but it was a Sisyphean task.

One morning, Ellen and I came upstairs to find her father standing on the landing, holding Mrs Brecht's white cotton bedsheets in his arms, pressing his face into them. He was

154

not looking after himself. He seemed thin and ill. His determination to suffer, his self-imposed martyrdom, almost broke my heart.

A few days later, Ellen and I were sitting on the bench overlooking the fields at the back of the church, enjoying the spring sunshine, when she told me her father had been trying to summon Anne's spirit.

'What do you mean?' I asked.

'He wanted to contact her in the spirit world. He asked me to go into the room next door to mine and help him. He'd got a ouija board.'

Ellen said this in a matter-of-fact way, not in one of her dramatic voices. I glanced at her, looking for signs she was making the tale up, but I couldn't see any.

'You didn't use the ouija board, did you?'

'I didn't want to, but he made me.'

'But, Ellen, those things are really dangerous! You might have ended up summoning the devil or something!'

'I know. But Papa insisted.' Ellen picked at the hem of her skirt. 'He said what if Mama was trapped in some dark place surrounded by souls in torment, drifting through purgatory trying to get back to us. What if she was icy cold and lonely and everything was black, and the wind was howling around her and the souls were screaming and wailing . . . I didn't want to touch the ouija board but I couldn't leave her there, on her own, in that dark, lonely place.'

'What happened?' I asked. My voice was little more than a whisper.

'Papa turned off the light. There was just a candle on the bedside table. We were sitting on the bed.'

I shivered.

'We put our fingers on the glass, and Papa called for Mama.' Ellen was speaking very softly now.

'Did she come?'

Ellen pulled her coat tighter around herself.

'Ellen?'

'Something came. Something made the glass move. It moved across the board all on its own, not slowly but fast, like this.' She scissored the air with her hand. 'And at the same time, the candle was flickering and there was a strange smell in the room.'

'What kind of smell?'

'It was sweet, like lavender.'

'Oh my God!'

'Papa asked the spirit to prove it was Mama.'

My heart was beating so hard I could feel the pulse in my neck. Our faces were close together. I could taste the spearmint from Ellen's gum in her exhaled breath.

'And then the glass began to move again, all by itself – and the candle blew out! There was a kind of misty glow floating above the bed, like a cloud. It almost looked like a person, it almost had a face and arms, but not quite. It hovered there, shape-shifting as the letters were spelled out on the board.'

'What did the spirit say?' I asked.

'First it moved the glass to the letter S, then the U . . .'

'Su? What does that mean?'

'Wait, there's more! There's the C, the K, the E and the R.' Ellen sighed. Then she sat back on the bench and looked at me, her eyes big and round and innocent.

'Ellen?' I was confused. 'What did the spirit say?'

'SUCKER! It said SUCKER!'

'Why did it say that?'

'Oh, you're so thick sometimes, Hannah!' Ellen stood up and began to run across the field, scattering birds that had been feeding in the long grass and screaming with laughter, calling, 'Sucker! Sucker! Sucker!'

'Ellen!' I called. I picked up her bag as well as my own. I

was furious. '*Ellen!*' I shouted as I ran after her. 'Ellen Brecht, *I hate* you!'

Ellen turned round. 'There are no spirits!' she shouted. 'There are no ghosts! Once you're dead, you're dead for ever and ever and ever! Amen!' And she laughed and ran some more.

That was what she was like.

Only not all of her stories were lies.

One evening, when we were sitting in the back room playing gin rummy with Mrs Todd, Mr Brecht, who had fallen asleep in his chair, lifted his head. He looked across the room towards us. His eyes were unfocused.

'She never loved you, you know,' he said to Ellen. Ellen bit her lip, picked up the queen of diamonds and put down the two of clubs. Mrs Todd took a card from the pile and put down the ace of spades.

Mr Brecht raised his finger and pointed it at Ellen. 'She blamed you. It was you who made her ill.'

'Your turn, Hannah,' said Mrs Todd. I already had two aces in my hand, but I was afraid to finish the game there and then. I took a card from the pile, and put down the ace of hearts.

'She used to say—' said Mr Brecht.

'That's enough now, Pieter,' said Mrs Todd. She pushed back her chair.

'She used to say,' he repeated in a louder voice, still jabbing his finger towards Ellen, 'that she should have had you drowned at birth!'

'Go upstairs, girls,' Mrs Todd said quietly. 'He doesn't know what he's saying.'

Afterwards, Mrs Todd came up to Ellen's bedroom with a tray of Horlicks and biscuits. She put the tray on the dressing-table and her hand on Ellen's shoulder. 'Your father had too much to drink,' she said. 'He didn't mean any of that.'

Ellen shrugged her hand away. 'I don't care,' she said.

'Your mother loved you,' said Mrs Todd. 'You know she did, Ellen.'

'*I don't care!*' Ellen repeated.

Some of what happened at Thornfield House was awful, but all of it was exciting. Everything there seemed more important and more intense; emotions were heightened, everything was significant. Ellen and her father burned more brightly than ordinary people. They were dazzling. And of course I couldn't help comparing my life with Ellen's. While hers was gloriously poetic and extreme, mine was stagnant and plain as ditchwater. My parents were unemotional and predictable; they were the grey embers to Mr Brecht's dancing flames. At home, I felt constricted and claustrophobic. Jago was working most evenings, or out with his friends, but I was expected to sit with my parents in front of the little old telly even though the reception was dreadful and Dad insisted on voicing a running commentary on every single programme. One or the other, or sometimes both, of my parents would fall asleep in their chairs and the snoring, interrupted every now and then by Trixie's flatulence, was a soundtrack to those evenings. Our rented cottage was not even a quarter the size of Thornfield House; it smelled of Fairy Liquid and cabbage, and, worst of all, after supper every evening Dad went upstairs whistling 'Whistle While You Work' with the *Daily Mirror* tucked under his arm and locked himself in the bathroom for twenty minutes. It was so mundane, so boring, so crushingly, achingly dull.

April ran into May, and May into June. Ellen was not looking forward to her seventeenth birthday, her first without her mother. We took our exams, school broke up for the summer, and we returned to our respective jobs.

One evening after work, when Ellen and I were sunbathing in the garden at Thornfield House, Mr Brecht came back from a trip to Truro with a largish, flattish cardboard box. It was coloured silver and was tied with a duck-egg-blue ribbon. He strode out into the garden, crouched down beside us, and passed the box to Ellen.

'It's a present,' he said.

'What for?'

'For you, Ellen. Does there have to be a reason for a father to treat his daughter?'

Ellen sighed and knelt up. We were both wearing bikinis, and I knew that Ellen was aware of how good she looked in hers. She sat high on her heels, with her back straight and her hair falling down behind her ears. I didn't want Mr Brecht to notice the ripples of puppy fat about my waist, or my breasts, which were bigger than Ellen's but white and heavy. I shook out the T-shirt I'd been using to pillow my head, and wriggled into it. Mr Brecht looked at Ellen, and smiled. He took his cigarettes out of his jacket pocket, shook one from the box, put it between his lips, lit it and blew smoke out through his nose.

The skin on Ellen's thighs was grass-patterned, criss-crossed by thousands of small indentations. She lifted the lid of the box.

Inside was a silver-grey evening dress made of beautiful, slippy material with tiny crystals sewn around the neckline. She held it up.

'Oh, that's the most beautiful dress I've ever seen!' I cried. I reached out to feel the fabric. 'It's gorgeous.'

Ellen folded the dress back into the box.

'Aren't you going to try it on?' I asked.

'Later,' Ellen said. She was sullen; for the thousandth time her surliness towards her father embarrassed me.

'You do like the dress, don't you?' he asked.

'It's lovely.'

'Put it on then.'

'Papa . . .'

'Go on!' he said. 'I want to see you wear it.'

I couldn't understand Ellen's reluctance to please him. If Mr Brecht had given me a dress like that, I'd have worn it all the time. I'd never have taken it off.

'Go on, Ellen,' I said. 'Make sure it fits.'

Ellen scowled, but she stood and slipped the dress over her head. It slithered over her shoulders and ran down her body like water. It fitted like a dream, and it shimmered in the sunshine, the crystals catching the light. Her mother's necklace glinted where the little clef sat in the hollow at the base of her throat. She looked so lovely, in the dress, and it must have felt so good on her skin that it should have made her happy, but it didn't. Her shoulders were hunched, and her eyes downcast.

Mr Brecht smiled and flicked the ash from the end of his cigarette. 'You're so like your mother,' he said. 'Turn around. Let me look at you.'

Ellen sucked in her lower lip. She looked as if she were close to tears. Reluctantly she turned.

'Beautiful,' Mr Brecht sighed. He took another drag on the cigarette, then dropped it onto the lawn and ground it out with his heel. 'Shame it's only skin-deep, eh, Ellen?'

Ellen shot her father a look. It was almost hatred.

I glanced from one to the other.

'What about you, Hannah?' he asked. 'Do you think Ellen's boyfriend will like the dress?'

I laughed awkwardly. 'Ellen doesn't have a boyfriend.'

Mr Brecht laughed too. He reached out to me and pulled me close to him. I fitted into the crook of his shoulder, felt the rough cotton of his trousers against the skin of my bare leg. He smelled of cigarette smoke and leather and something spicy and masculine. He squeezed the top of my arm.

'She does,' he whispered into my hair.

I looked up at him. He nodded with a teasing twinkle in his eye.

'Don't you know about Ellen's secret romance, Hannah?' he asked.

I shook my head.

He raised his eyebrows in surprise. 'She hasn't told you? And you're supposed to be her best friend? That's not very nice, is it, Ellen?'

Ellen's face had gone pale. She stared down at the grass. Her hair was hanging forwards, over her face. She looked ghost-like in the silvery dress with her bare feet and her long, hanging hair, like the mad heroine of some Gothic novel.

'She sneaks out of the house to meet someone,' Mr Brecht said, holding me even closer. 'She says she's going to see you, but I don't think that's always the case. She tells me that you're always asking favours of her, begging her to go to your house. She says you've had your heart broken and that you need her. She says that you, Hannah, can be very demanding.'

I flushed now. I had never demanded anything of Ellen. It was the other way around. And how could she tell her father those lies about me? How could she make him think that I was weak and helpless and that I had been dumped? Ellen continued not to look at me.

'It's not true,' I said quietly enough for him to hear. His fingers tightened on my arm.

'I think,' said Mr Brecht, 'my daughter has been using you, Hannah, as an alibi.'

'Stop it!' Ellen cried. 'Shut up!' She lifted up the hem of the dress and turned and ran from the garden, the soles of her bare feet flashing beneath the hem. Mr Brecht and I watched her go.

Mr Brecht sighed. He moved away from me and scratched his head with both hands.

'I didn't know,' I said.

'Ellen has been corrupted by her mother,' said Mr Brecht. 'She has learned the art of deceit and manipulation from an expert.'

I gazed up at him. He smiled at me, then he took hold of my face in his hands and he leaned down and kissed the top of my head, very gently.

'You're a good friend to Ellen,' he said.

It was one of the best moments of my life.

I didn't see much of Ellen for a while after that, but I found out the truth soon enough. I was at work in the Seagull Hotel. From the top bedroom window, a duster in one hand and the handle of the vacuum cleaner in the other, I saw Ellen and Jago sitting, side by side, on the harbour wall, swinging their legs, their heads close together, looking into the water and laughing. As I watched, Jago leaned his head down towards Ellen's and he kissed her; she kissed him back, and the kiss seemed to last for ever.

Ellen's father was right.

She had been deceiving us both.

CHAPTER TWENTY-SEVEN

After I'd bathed at my parents' house, I dressed, went downstairs and ate a 'proper' cooked breakfast – the like of which I hadn't enjoyed in a while – with my mother and father. Then, while they went to the morning service at Trethene church, I walked across the moors to the Catholic Church of Our Lady Star of the Sea.

In all the years since her death, I had never been to Ellen's grave. I wasn't sure why not, but not going had been a choice, not an accident. I supposed I hadn't wanted the memory of it in my mind. When I thought of Ellen, I didn't want to think of a headstone, a graveyard. That morning, though, I thought it would be the right thing to do, for Ellen and for me. I hoped it might bring me some kind of closure. A grave would be irrefutable evidence that Ellen was dead. It might stop my mind creeping away on its wild flights of fancy that Ellen might still be alive. I hoped it would make her leave me alone.

The church was far larger than the squat little seafarers' church in Trethene. It was more than a mile from the village, standing on its own, at one of the highest points in the area, where it could be seen by those living all around. The grave-yard was weatherworn, spread haphazardly inside the boundary wall. I stood just inside the gate, looking around me, pulling my jacket close. There were hundreds of graves. I supposed Ellen must have been buried with her mother.

My legs felt weak as I stepped into the churchyard. I hadn't been this close to Ellen in decades. I had a feeling she knew I was there, as if she were watching me from a hiding place somewhere in the leaves of the tree, or the mouth of one of the church gargoyles, a wraith in the tatters of that silvery-grey dress. It was ridiculous, of course. I put the thought from my mind but I couldn't help the icy feeling at the back of my neck, the cold fingers creeping up my spine.

It was the graveyard, I told myself. It was the preconceptions most of us have about death, a culmination of the books I'd read and the stories I'd heard about ghosts and retribution. I'd been conditioned to be afraid of the dead by superstitions and legends.

I knew I should have visited Ellen's grave before, not just for my sake, but hers too. With her father gone, and Jago in Canada, there had been nobody else. Now I'd finally made it to the church, I hadn't even brought flowers. It had never crossed my mind to bring something for Ellen. What kind of friend was I? How could I be so thoughtless?

I walked around the perimeter of the churchyard, negotiating, with some difficulty, the uneven ground, trying to remember where Mrs Brecht had been buried. The older, overgrown, untended graves were scattered amongst the newer ones with their posies and photographs and wreaths. Some of the headstones were so worn that it was difficult to make out any of the inscriptions. *Sacred Heart of Jesus have mercy on my soul*, I read. I trailed my fingers along the gritty edge of the tops of the headstones, tilted as if they had been windblown. I had walked all the way around to the back of the church when I saw the yew tree clearly for the first time. It was enormous, squat – more than a thousand years old. Its dark green branches spread out like arms sheltering the graves beneath, and I remembered then. I remembered standing beneath the branches of that tree at Mrs Brecht's funeral, how some of the little poisonous berries had fallen and lay like dull rubies amongst the grass. I recalled the priest talking and how my toes were squeezed by the black shoes I'd grown out of but which my mother had insisted I wear for the occasion, and how I had wished I wasn't wearing school uniform, how I'd felt too old for it, awkward, embarrassed. I remembered turning my head to look at Jago and how he had reassured me with his eyes. I remembered Adam Tremlett standing apart, the look on his face.

I walked slowly forwards. The last time I saw the grave, it had been a hole in the ground. Now it was headed by a memorial stone, made of black granite fashioned into a curved, upward sweep on the top, that reminded me of a musical clef. A gold border followed the line of the stone, a few inches from the outer edge, and inside, beautifully and deeply engraved, were the words:

Anne Isobel Brecht

You were the music, while the music lasted.

The words had been interwoven with a musical score in the background. I knew what it was, although I could not read music. It was the *Raindrop Prelude*. I could hear the notes in my mind as I looked at the gravestone.

Beneath that inscription were three blunt words cut more crudely, as if their commission had been a necessary but unwelcome afterthought.

Also Ellen Louisa Brecht.

The grass that covered the grave was overgrown, but somebody had tidied the area by the headstone and a bunch of wildflowers had been placed in a jar beside it. I crouched down and picked up the jar. It was half-full of water. Whoever had left the flowers must have been there recently. I stood again and then I saw the glass – and my blood ran cold.

The drift-glass that I had collected as a girl and hidden in the rocky crack at Bleached Scarp had been placed on top of the headstone.

It was my drift-glass, I was sure of it. There were about thirty tiny pieces, the sharp edges softened by the rub of the waves and the sand, until they were like curiously shaped gemstones; all about the same size, all milky shades of green, clear, brown, and one single piece, about an inch in size, that was blue.

I picked up the blue piece and held it in my hands, turning it over, feeling its smoothness between my palms. It was the same temperature as my skin and as familiar as my heartbeat.

Only three people had known where the glass was hidden. One of us was, supposedly, buried in this grave, one was on the other side of the world, and I hadn't moved it.

Clouds blew across the face of the sun.

I put the blue glass in my pocket and turned and then I ran out of the graveyard. I didn't look back to see if anyone was watching and I didn't stop running until I was back inside my parents' cottage.

CHAPTER TWENTY-EIGHT

After I saw Ellen kissing Jago on the harbour wall, I made even more of an effort to avoid her, at the same time ignoring Jago as best I could. I thought they wouldn't last long – not without me. I was the one who had brought them together, I was the link between them. I knew them both, individually, better than anyone else.

Mr Brecht was right – they had betrayed me, and they continued to do so. They had both lied to me and used me. If they had confided in me, if they had been honest, perhaps I would have felt differently, but they had not. It did not take much effort to convert my hurt into anger, anger that I suppressed, but which simmered inside me.

Now I knew what to look for, their deceptions were obvious. Jago was nineteen, he came and went as he pleased, but I knew when he was lying. He got home from work late, he said he was going up to the farm when I'd already seen the Williams twins driving away from it, and he was often 'running errands' for Bill.

When he was home, he spent more time in his room, on his own, and less with me. He had used to enjoy my company, but now he seemed to find me tiresome. He could no longer be bothered with me.

It must have been much harder for Ellen, who was only sixteen and whose father was clever and alert and watching. He did not know who she was seeing, of course, not then. He cannot even have been certain that his suspicions were correct, although I believe he trusted his instincts. Now she could no longer use me as an alibi, Ellen used her work, although Mr Brecht had taken to following her into Polrack and sitting in his car, watching the kiosk where she sold ice cream, trying to catch her out. We were all playing the game. From the hotel, I watched Mr Brecht watching Ellen, and I saw how Jago would walk past the kiosk – sometimes he went past a dozen times – waiting for a signal that it was safe to go in. Knowing I was the only one who knew everything was a seductive kind of power.

I saw Jago and Ellen sitting together in the harbour. I saw them kissing down one of the town's tiny alleyways, Jago pressed against Ellen and her arms tight around his neck. I noticed how buoyant Jago was, how happy and handsome, and jealousy ate into me. It made me sour and sullen. It made me lonely. I watched even though the watching hurt me. At the same time, when one or other of them lied to me, or I glimpsed them together without me, I had a surge of pleasure that my anger with Ellen had been justified. Now I knew how Mr Brecht felt. Now I knew why he was sometimes cruel: it was because Ellen *was* a manipulative liar. She didn't care about either of us, Mr Brecht or me. All she cared about was herself.

Ellen tried to wheedle her way back into my affections, but although I did not snub her directly, I would not sit beside her on the bus, and I took circuitous routes to avoid having to pass Thornfield House. If she came to call for me, at Cross Hands Lane or at the hotel, I made excuses or got other people to make them for me. I never gave Ellen the chance to talk to me alone. I didn't want to hear what she had to say. I was not ready to forgive her.

Then one day, Jago came into my bedroom and suggested we go back to Bleached Scarp, the three of us, as we used to in the old days.

We hadn't been to the beach at all that summer, and angry as I was with Ellen and Jago, I missed the times we used to spend there together. Something inside me, some longing for the past combined with a desire for Jago to pay some attention to me, made me agree to go.

When I saw Ellen on the Polrack bus the next morning, I sat in the seat beside her. She smiled but looked a little wary. I told her Jago had spoken to me about going to Bleached Scarp, and asked how she would manage to get away from her father for the whole day.

She smiled. 'He's going to London to meet some people from the music industry. They're taking him out to dinner and putting him up in a hotel. He's looking forward to it. I think he wants to sleep with one of the women.'

I had to bite my lip so as not to protest at this. Mr Brecht was not the sort of man to go and sleep with someone just because he could! Trust Ellen to think up such a nasty lie.

She smiled and touched my forearm with her hand.

'It'll be lovely to have a day together, Han,' she said. 'I've missed you.'

I managed to smile back. 'I've missed you too,' I said.

When the day came, a taxi picked Mr Brecht up very early; the morning light was still damp and yellow. Ellen told us how she waved goodbye at the door, pretending she was sleepy although her heart was beating like a drum. Mrs Todd had laid out her breakfast in the dining room and sat by the window, knitting, while Ellen ate her croissant and jam and drank her coffee. She was careful to behave exactly as if she was going to work, but she was wearing her swimsuit beneath her clothes. She left the house at ten past eight, as though she were going to catch the usual bus into Polrack. Instead, as soon as she was over the brow of the hill and out of sight of every window in Thornfield House, she ran down the lane to our house, where Jago and I were waiting.

I saw the smiles they exchanged, but they did not touch one another, not in front of me. I almost pitied them for not realizing how obvious they were but I wanted to forget about the truth, that day. I wanted us to be back to how we used to be, when everything was easy and everything was fun. I wanted to feel happy again. I wanted the sour anger inside me to go away.

I rode my bike up the hill and along the lanes to the beach, and Ellen sat on the back of Jago's. We left the bikes hidden behind an old caravan in the Kynance Cove car park and walked back to the spot where we climbed over the fence and went down to the beach. The sea was calm that day, so calm that we could see the fish deep in the blue-green water, the seaweed waving like hair, the crabs scuttling along the seabed. Waves splished softly at the foot of the cliff. Ellen was half-crazy, thrilled to be back at the beach. She climbed the rockface as deftly as she used to, and jumped into the water with a loud scream of joy, making a great splash. She resurfaced laughing, shaking her head, calling Jago to come on in, and then she dived beneath the water again, just her narrow ankles and her feet breaking into the air. Jago ran in after her and they played together like children.

They had forgotten me already.

And then: 'Come on, Spanner!' Jago called, water falling sparkling from his arm as he waved. 'It's not cold at all.'

'Liar!'

'Please, Han, please come and play!'

'Yes, come on, Hannah,' Ellen begged. 'It's spoiling our fun, seeing you sitting there on the beach like a sad old woman.'

And then they both set to chanting, 'Hannah! Hannah! Hannah!' and clapping their hands in time to the chant.

It felt good to hear them both calling me like that.

It was enchanting to have both of them focusing all their attention on me.

I took off my sweatshirt and shorts and left them on the rocks. I walked into the sea a few steps at a time, hobbling on the shells and pebbles, letting my body get used to the water's chill inch by inch, squealing as it touched the sensitive skin of my belly. When I was too far in to retreat quickly, Jago chased after me, splashing, and pushing me down into the water. I screamed abuse at him, but I loved being teased by him and I gloried in his attention. I fought him back more roughly than I normally would, and for a while we tussled in the sea and I felt exhilarated and free and alive. Ellen held back. She let me have my time with Jago. We spent the whole day going in and out of the sea, warming up on the beach, and then cooling off in the water. In between, we drank the cider Jago had brought from the flagon and lay on our backs and laughed. Ellen stretched out, with her arms above her head, regardless of the sand in her wet hair, and she laughed up at the sky. Jago leaned on one elbow, watching her. He laughed too. He was a little drunk.

'You crazy, beautiful girl,' he said. This made Ellen laugh even more and then she stopped laughing because he forgot himself and leaned down and kissed her. She pushed him away but she knew I had seen. Jago rolled over, wiped his lips, looked at me.

'It's OK,' I said with a shrug. 'I know about you two. I've seen you kissing before.'

Ellen and Jago glanced at one another. This intimacy hurt me again. Tears of self-pity rose in my eyes.

Ellen reached out and touched my arm. 'Do you mind?' she asked.

'Will it change anything if I do?'

'Hannah, we never meant to . . .' Jago put his hand on my shoulder. A teardrop fell from my cheek onto the back of his fingers.

'We were going to tell you,' Ellen said. 'We just didn't want you to have to go round telling lies for us. To my father.'

'Don't be stupid, of course I don't mind,' I said, trying to sound as if I meant it. I didn't want to hear their apologies or their excuses. I didn't want to know the details. Most of all, I did not want them to pity me. I shrugged off Jago's hand, sat up and wiped my face with my T-shirt.

There was a silence. Ellen funnelled sand through her fingers and I could feel Jago's discomfort. I wasn't going to help them out by saying something kind.

'You won't tell anyone?' Jago asked. 'You won't say anything to Mum and Dad or Ellen's . . .'

'Of course I won't,' I said. 'What do you think I am?'

'I think you're a spanner,' Jago said. He grinned at me. I tried not to smile but I couldn't help myself. I pushed him and he pushed me back.

'Loser!' he said. 'Sadact!'

'Shut up, Cardell, or I'll have you!'

'I'd like to see you try!'

And after that I jumped on Jago and tried to fill his shirt with sand and Ellen joined in and we wrestled and tumbled and messed around just like we used to. They tried to make it up to me. For the rest of that day, I was the centre of Ellen and Jago's attention. They showed their gratitude for my loyalty by giving me all the affection I could have wanted. Ellen backed away from Jago and he played with me, and between them, they made me feel happy again.

But time ran on. The morning turned into afternoon, the sun moved across the sky, half of the beach was shadowed and the air cooled. The batteries on the tinny little radio ran flat and I started to worry about Ellen's wet hair. I held hanks of it in my hand, trying to wring out the water, but I knew it would take ages to dry.

'How will you explain it to Mrs Todd?' I asked.

'Oh, I'll say I took a dip in the sea at Polrack after work.'

'Do you think she'll believe that?'

'I'll say I was hot.'

'I think we ought to go,' I said.

'Just a little longer,' Ellen pleaded. 'Just a few minutes more. I don't know when I'll be able to do this again. It might not be for years. You know what my father is like.'

'As long as we go now, there won't be any trouble.'

Ellen shrugged. 'I don't want to go yet,' she said.

I frowned at her. Was she doing this on purpose, trying to make us late so there would be a problem?

She was sitting cross-legged, like a wild creature, a mermaid, with her long hair about her shoulders, and her nose and cheeks a bit burned, picking pebbles from the sand and throwing them into the sea. Jago had gone quiet now. He was collecting driftwood, but there wasn't time for a fire. We needed to be going. He came over to me and dropped something in my lap.

'Blue glass,' he said. I'd never seen that colour drift-glass before. The piece was about an inch in size, its edges completely rounded by the sand. I held it in my hand.

'That's lovely,' I said. 'But it's gone six, we have to go.'

'Not yet. In a moment,' Ellen said. She drew a line in the sand with her finger, then rubbed it out with her palm. 'I'd like to stay here, on the beach, for ever,' she said. 'I could live in the cave.'

'You'd be scared on your own.'

'No, I wouldn't. I'd be happy. I'd have the birds and the seals for company, and nobody would ever know I was here.'

'I'd stay with you,' said Jago. 'We could live here together, just you and me.'

And me! I wanted to shout. *What about me?*

Ellen smiled, dropped her head right down and pulled the sleeves of her sweatshirt over her hands.

'Would you live with me, Jago?' she asked. 'Really?' Her words were muffled by her knees.

'You know I would.'

'We have to go,' I said. 'Jago, honestly. We have to go right now.'

Neither of them took any notice. They were looking at one another.

'Oh please!' I cried. 'Please let's go before there's any trouble!'

They took for ever packing up. They kept smiling although they were both quiet. I felt excluded again. I kept telling them to hurry up but they wouldn't listen.

What happened next was their fault, not mine.

We cycled back along the tiny lanes that wound through the fields, lanes that only the cows and tractors used, taking the back route to Trethene, the sunburn stretching the skin on our legs. When we turned the corner into Cross Hands Lane we saw the car parked outside the cottage.

'Oh fuck!' said Jago. 'Whose is that?'

'It's Papa's,' Ellen said.

I felt as if I had always known the car would be there. I looked towards Ellen: her eyes were wide although her skin had paled. I wondered if a public confrontation with her father was what she had wanted all along. I wondered if she had planned this to make everyone feel sorry for her.

'Perhaps you should just go home, Ellen,' I suggested. 'I'll make up some story . . .'

'I don't want to face him on my own,' she said.

'You're not on your own,' said Jago. 'I'm here.'

174

Ellen made one of her overdramatic faces. 'Jago, he can't know I've been with *you*! That'll make things a thousand times worse.'

'Why? We haven't done anything wrong.'

'That's not the point. If Papa finds out I was with you, he'll think we've been . . .' she tailed off. 'You know.'

Jago let out a sigh of frustration.

I tried to breathe slowly. I'd told them this was going to happen, they should have listened to me.

I took Ellen's hand. 'Come with me,' I said. 'Jago, don't say anything.'

We walked round to the back door. Jago followed a few paces behind.

My parents and Mr Brecht were together in the front room, which seemed too small and cluttered and pedestrian for the drama playing out inside. Mr Brecht was standing by the window, looking out. He must have been watching us. His hands were clasped behind his back.

'Oh Hannah!' Mum exclaimed, and I could tell from her voice that she was relieved and angry in equal measures. 'There was a tree on the railway line and Mr Brecht's train was cancelled so he came straight back home. He's been so worried. Where have you been all day? It's half past seven!'

'We went to the beach. It was such a nice day and—'

'You told me you were working, Ellen,' Mr Brecht said, without turning round.

'When I got there, they said they didn't need me.'

'I went to the kiosk, and they told me they hadn't seen you all day. Where were you?'

'We were honestly at the beach,' I said.

'Which beach?'

'Polrack.'

'You were not at Polrack.'

'Well, never mind the details. All's well that ends well, eh?'

said Dad. He stood up and rubbed his hands together. 'How about a beer, Mr Brecht?'

Mr Brecht seemed not to hear him.

'You lied, Ellen,' he said. 'I try to trust you, I try to believe you, but you lie and lie and lie. You're just like your mother.'

'I haven't done anything wrong.'

'Then why do you lie?' Mr Brecht took hold of Ellen and led her out of the house. She stumbled after him passively, doll-like. Jago made to follow her, but Dad grabbed his arm.

'Leave it, son,' he said.

Jago shook off Dad's arm. For a moment I feared he would do or say something terrible. Instead he went into the kitchen and, moments later, we heard the back door slam.

For the rest of the evening, our family was subdued. Mum put the supper on, Jago stayed out and Dad turned up the volume on the television as if that would make everything better.

I curled up on the settee and bit my fingernails.

'Do you think I should go up to Thornfield House and make sure everything's OK?' I asked.

Dad shook his head. 'Leave it be, Hannah. Everything will be fine. You'll see Ellen at work in the morning.'

But I didn't. Ellen wasn't on the Polrack bus the next day or the next or the next.

She never served another ice cream from the kiosk by the harbour. She never so much as set foot in there again.

CHAPTER TWENTY-NINE

Cornwall had been beautiful but I was a stranger there now. I was glad to get back to the city. Bristol's Montpelier district was about as different to Trethene as it's possible to be. My road was busy with its usual eclectic mix of characters; street music and cooking smells, veiled women pushing buggies, older men with bellies straining the buttons on their shirts, swaggering young men and girls with their trousers low on their hips. People were spilling out of the pubs, drinking their drinks at the kerbside, and boys cycled round on bicycles, weaving in and out of the cars.

I bought a few supplies, then hurried up into the flat. Lily, who had been fed by the lady who lived upstairs, was nonetheless peeved at being abandoned all weekend, and demanded attention. I fussed her, drew the curtains and turned on the lamps. I switched on the television for company.

The light on the telephone answering machine was flashing. I switched it on, but no message had been recorded. I pressed 1471 to find out who the last caller had been, and found that John Lansdown had called about half an hour before I'd arrived home. I called straight back, but he did not pick up the phone. Anxiety about him loaded itself on top of my worries about Ellen. I had known secrets about Ellen and now I knew secrets about John and his marriage. In Ellen's case, no good had come of the truth, but that didn't necessarily mean it would be wrong in the current situation. I wished I knew what to do for the best. I wished there was somebody I could talk to, somebody impartial who would be able to tell me what to do.

Dad always used to tell Jago and me, 'If in doubt, do nowt.'

Sometimes doing nothing was the hardest thing in the world.

I ran a bath, and as I undressed, the piece of blue glass fell out of my pocket and rolled along the carpet. I picked it up and put it on the dressing-table. I wondered what exactly it was that had happened over the past forty-eight hours.

I reminded myself that I did not believe in ghosts. I was a scientist and a pragmatist. I worked in a museum, surrounded by the detritus of death. I understood corporeal processes. I also knew something about the mind, and the physiology of the brain, how chemical imbalances can be exacerbated by stress, how easy it is for people to convince themselves of the reality of something that may have been nothing more than a couple of neurological malfunctions

I knew many things, but I could not, for the life of me, work out how my drift-glass had made its way from the beach to the gravestone.

It made no sense to me.

The thought that had been niggling away at the back of my mind was still trying to attract my attention. I did my best to ignore it, but it would not go away.

The glass on the gravestone made no sense – unless Ellen had put it there.

CHAPTER THIRTY

After the day on the beach, Ellen was grounded, so I travelled to my hotel job on the bus by myself for the last two weeks of the summer. In the Seagull, I cleaned the bathrooms and stripped the beds, restocked the linen cupboards, emptied the dishwasher, set the tables for breakfast and prepared clotted-cream teas for the residents. I looked out of the top bedroom windows and saw Jago repairing the lobster pots on the harbour wall, or standing with his feet apart, balancing on the deck of the *Eliza May*. He didn't joke and laugh with his crew-mates any more, not like he used to. I watched him walk up and down the hill, looking for Ellen, hoping she'd come, although he knew she wouldn't. She couldn't. Sometimes he sat on the wall, staring into the water. At home, he was withdrawn and introverted. He was no fun any more. I didn't know what to do, or say to him.

Ellen was stuck in Thornfield House until she promised to abide by her father's rules and stop lying to him. There were no celebrations for her seventeenth birthday. I called for her once or twice but was secretly relieved when I was not allowed to see her. I knew if I did, I would have to listen to her raging against her father's tyranny and the unfairness of her life. I looked up from the gateway and Ellen was at her bedroom window, gazing out, standing in the same place her grandmother used to stand. I wondered if all the unhappiness that took place there was something to do with the house itself; if it was cursed. When I suggested this at home, Mum told me not to be ridiculous. She said what was happening in Thornfield House was just a consequence of circumstance.

'Teenage daughters and widowed fathers don't mix,' she said. 'They're like oil and water. Ellen's at the age where she's bound to rebel, and he's bound to be a bit on the protective side. Don't worry, Hannah, Mr Brecht can't keep her locked up for ever. She'll be back at school next week.'

The following Saturday, we met Mrs Todd in the post office.

'How is Ellen?' Mum asked.

'She's not helping herself,' Mrs Todd said. 'There's a terrible atmosphere in the house. Neither of them will give an inch. They're both as stubborn as each other.'

Mum sucked in the corners of her mouth and shook her head.

'Perhaps you could come round, Hannah, and try to talk some sense into Ellen,' said Mrs Todd. 'Come over after lunch tomorrow. I'm going to visit my friend in Exeter. I'll let Ellen know you're coming and perhaps she'll try to be civil.'

At home, we ate a big lunch after church the next day and, when the dishes had been washed and dried and put away, Jago and my father went to the sports-ground to practise in the cricket nets. Mum sat at the kitchen table with her sewing basket, listening to the radio.

I leaned down to kiss her cheek.

'I'm off to Thornfield House,' I said. 'Wish me luck.'

'Good luck,' said Mum. She squeezed my hand.

I put Trixie on the lead. I thought perhaps if I turned up

with the dog, Mr Brecht would let Ellen come out for a walk. What harm could possibly come of that? Two girls and a dog. Probably the most innocent combination possible, and I would smile at him and be charming to make up for all Ellen's surliness.

Trixie and I squeezed past the Escort in the front garden. Its restoration was a task that, my mother often opined, like the painting of the Forth Road Bridge, would never be completed. No matter how many scrapyards Jago and Dad visited, they never seemed to have exactly the component they needed, when they needed it. Several rusting pieces of engine were lined up neatly by the front wall of our house.

Trixie and I meandered slowly up the lane, enjoying the dappling shade, the birdsong, the peaceful sound of the burbling water of the hidden brook. At the gate to Thornfield House, I paused. The house looked different. The wisteria that used to climb up the front of the house had been pulled down – a great heap of twisty stems was piled on the lawn. I didn't notice, not immediately, what else had changed. I walked up the drive to the front door, Trixie panting behind. The door looked as if it was closed, but was very slightly ajar. I tied Trixie's lead to the ornamental boot-scraper in the porch, told her to sit and wait, kissed her snout, then gently, I pushed the door open and went inside, into the hall.

Nobody was in the front room, or the dining room, but I could see the French windows were open at the back. I crept through and looked out into the garden.

Adam Tremlett had not been back and nobody had taken care of the garden in the months since Mrs Brecht had died. Mrs Todd had done her best but even the vegetable plot was too big for her to cope with on her own. I was used to the encroaching disorder but there was something odd about the garden that afternoon. I couldn't work out what it was, but something was wrong. I stood for a moment, my eyes wandering amongst the shrubs and the flowerbeds, and a single, small red poppy bobbing like a flag made me realize. All the flowers were gone.

I stepped through the French windows into the warmer, outside air. The fountain was not working. The pond was clogged with vegetation. Some of the fish had already died; they were floating on their sides, dull-eyed. Others were at the surface, gasping for oxygen, their little round mouths helpless and desperate. I pulled handfuls of sodden flower-heads out of the pond. Petals floated forlornly on the black water as I heaped dripping armfuls of stocks, geraniums, delphiniums and countless other flowers on to the terrace. When I felt there was enough clear water for the surviving fish, I shook the water off my arms and tried to work out what had happened.

Mr Brecht was lying beneath the shade of the copper beech tree with its almost-black leaves. He was curled on one side on one of two padded sun-loungers. A small, ornate metal table stood beside the lounger and on it was a vodka bottle, a glass and a pair of long-handled secateurs. The bottle was almost empty. I crept forward, hoping Trixie would not bark.

Mr Brecht stank of vodka. His sunglasses had slipped awkwardly up his face, they were skew-whiff on his fore-head. His eyes were closed, his mouth open. He was snoring. There was a dark, damp patch on the cushion beneath his head where he had dribbled in his sleep. His shirt-sleeves were rolled up to the elbows, and his hands and forearms were covered in scratches and small, black scabs. He had been working hard. He had cut down every flower in the garden.

Ellen's denim jacket lay on the lawn, as if it had been dropped and abandoned. I pictured the two of them having a terrible fight. I couldn't imagine what it had been about, or what they had said to one another. I couldn't imagine the despair that had driven him to this. I reached down and picked up the jacket. My shadow fell over Mr Brecht's face, and I held my breath for a moment, but he did not stir. I crept out of the garden, going back through the house the same way I had come in. I ran upstairs to check, but Ellen's room was empty. The house was silent. She was not there.

I crossed the landing and pushed open the door to Mr Brecht's bedroom, the one that he used to share with his wife. It was a large, light room at the back of the house, overlooking the garden. Sunlight fell in slabs across a wide, unmade bed, the sheets crumpled into white peaks, the pillows gathered together in the middle of the bed. I walked over to the bed, picked up a sheet, and cradled it in my arms. I took it down, out into the garden and gently I covered Mr Brecht to protect him from insects and from the sun. It was all I could do for him and he did not stir.

By the front door, Trixie wagged her stubby tail from side to side and grinned up at me, panting with pleasure.

'What a good girl,' I said, leaning down to *shhh* the dog as she made her funny grunty noises of welcome. 'What a good, clever girl you are!'

I walked back along the lane, Ellen's denim jacket hooked over my shoulders. I wondered where she had gone. If she'd been heading for our house, I'd have passed her on the way. Perhaps she was at the beach. Trixie and I reached the church and the dog looked up at me expectantly – this was one of our routes. We could walk through the churchyard and out into the fields, over to the cliffs and maybe we'd find Ellen. Pink, yellow and green confetti, left over from the previous day's wedding, was dotted on the pavement outside the lychgate like late-summer blossom. We followed the footpath through the churchyard, Trixie trotting behind me, her claws clicking on the flagstone path. The stone was sun-warmed, giving off its own heat. At the back of the church the graves were less well-kept. Some of the headstones were tilted and the plastic bin was full of old wreaths and faded flowers. The air was thick with the smell of rotting plants. I let Trixie off the lead and climbed across the graves, weaving my bare legs carefully around the stinging nettles, wafting at the midges. I went through the gate that opened out into the fields and Trixie came after me.

I saw Ellen before she saw me. She was sitting on the old bench, on the far side of the churchyard wall. She was sitting like a statue, with her legs crossed at the ankles and her hands folded in her lap. She was wearing her green sundress, the one patterned with daisies that had been her mother's favourite. Her black hair fell down her back, over her shoulders. It was tangled, messy, stuck with leaves and bits of grass. The skin on the back of her arms was dirty.

I went towards her quietly, stepping carefully. I didn't want to scare Ellen, who sat so still that the birds had come down to hunt insects by her feet and a single brilliant blue-black dragonfly was stretching its wings on the arm of the bench beside her. It was cool in the little overgrown corner of the field. Ellen glanced up as I approached, and smiled. I sat beside her and slipped the jacket over her shoulders. She was sitting rigidly. She looked dazed. Trixie came over, sighed, turned round three times and lay at my feet.

'Are you all right?' I asked.

Ellen nodded.

'I saw what your father did, to the garden.'

Ellen looked at me. Her eyes were dark and shiny.

'He's mad. I told you, he's mad. I asked him to stop but he wouldn't listen.'

'Did you fight him?' I asked.

She shook her head.

'What happened then, Ellen? How did you get so dirty?'

'I locked myself in the bathroom while he was tearing up the garden. And then I looked out of the window and I could see he was asleep and he'd drunk so much I knew he'd sleep for ages. I was going to come to your house. I was going down the lane when Jago came by on his bike.'

Ellen hesitated and then took a deep breath and said, 'We talked a bit, but I was afraid someone would see us so we came here, to be private.'

'You just talked?'

'No, Hannah, we didn't just talk. Can't you guess what we did? Can't you work out how I got dirty?'

My heart was pounding.

Ellen smiled shyly.

'I wanted to kiss him,' she said. 'I asked him to kiss me. He kissed my eyelids and I said, "No, kiss my mouth, kiss me properly, kiss me like we're dying and it's our last kiss ever." And then . . .'

Ellen looked up at the sky. The jacket slid off her shoulders.

I held my breath. I was afraid of what she would say next, and at the same time I knew.

'It wasn't Jago, Hannah, it was me. I made it happen. I took off my dress and I wasn't even embarrassed. The sun was all warm on me and he was looking at me like I was amazing. I felt so happy, Hannah. I wanted to do it. I made him.' She laughed.

'Oh God,' I whispered, because I knew this meant a line had been crossed. There would be no going back now, for Jago and Ellen. I felt as if I were falling down into a hole, tumbling head over heels, disappearing, because now Jago and Ellen had united themselves there would be no room for me at all any more. I might as well no longer exist.

'There's blood on the grass,' Ellen said. 'It's a sacred spot. Somebody will put a statue there one day. People will come to look. It will be world-famous as the place where Ellen Brecht lost her virginity to Jago Cardell.'

She didn't seem to realize what she was saying. She had no idea. This was just another part of the game to her, another act in the ongoing drama of her life. But I looked at her, and I noticed she was crying, silently; her face was wet with tears. My heart softened. I reached out and she leaned against me, like she used to; she twined her arm in mine and she rested her damp cheek against my shoulder.

'He said he loves me,' Ellen whispered. 'He said he's always loved me. He said he will find a way for us to be together.'

I watched a dragonfly settle on a leaf and stretch its wings in the sunshine. I followed the tracery of the lace pattern in the wing with my eye. I thought how easy it would be to hurt that dragonfly. Just one move of my hand, and it would be dead.

'You need to be careful, Ellen,' I said. 'You must be very careful. What you're doing, all of this . . . it's dangerous.'

Ellen was still smiling to herself. She wasn't listening. She thought nothing could hurt her now. She had no idea.

CHAPTER THIRTY-ONE

The run of fine, balmy days ended that night with a literal bang as a massive thunderstorm thirty miles long pounded the south-west of England. The power in Montpelier went down almost immediately. Nobody was out in the dark streets, in the rain that lashed the roads and pavements, setting off car alarms, flooding the storm drains, causing water to bubble back up through the covers. I lay on my bed. Lily inveigled her way under the duvet and settled beside me. From time to time, lightning lit up the room, bleaching the walls and the dressing-gown hanging on the hook on the wardrobe door, the chest of drawers. I remembered how Trixie used to be terrified of thunder. When the storms came, she would shuffle under my bed and nothing would tempt her out until the noise and the lightning stopped. I used to turn up the radio, to try to drown out the noise, but it didn't help.

I turned the piece of blue glass over in my hand. Lily lay, vibrating with purrs, on my chest. She liked the feel of my heartbeat. I liked her warmth.

I thought of Trixie, hiding from the thunder under the bed. I remembered Jago when he was still young, crawling under the bed to comfort the dog, his long, skinny legs sticking out across the bedroom carpet, a dirty grey sock with a hole at the toe wrinkled around one foot, the other bare apart from a verucca plaster, and me, hanging over the other side of the bed to laugh at the boy and the ugly white dog snuggled together beneath it. I missed them so badly that I didn't know if I could last another night without them.

I opened my eyes and stared up at the ceiling. The rain-drops running down the window were reflected on its surface, illuminated by car headlights as they drove by, slowed to a crawl by the density of the rain.

I wondered if I was, unconsciously, somehow responsible for moving the drift-glass. I remembered reading some scientific evidence pointing towards the existence of polter-geists. Weren't they the physical manifestation of a psychological disturbance? There were credible, well-documented cases of poltergeists moving, or causing the movement of, physical objects. Only usually it was some-thing minor: a lightbulb swinging on its wire or a cup falling from a shelf. It seemed unlikely in the extreme that the glass could have been transported all the way from the beach to the gravestone by my own mind, no matter how badly dis-turbed that mind had been.

'You're tired,' I told myself. 'In the morning everything will make more sense.' And then lightning filled up the room and I saw a shadow in the mirror – only it was not a shadow, but a face – Ellen's face, looking out at me from behind the glass with a desperate expression in her eyes, wet hair streaming down her head and one hand reaching out towards me, the palm turned upwards in a gesture that said, *Help me!* For a moment, I thought she was trapped in the mirror – I thought I heard her scream, and her hands seem to scratch and scrabble at the other side of the glass – and

then the light dimmed, and all that was left was the glare of
the negative image of Ellen's face burned on the back of my
eyes.

CHAPTER THIRTY-TWO

Ellen did not return to school the following week. She was not on the bus for the first three days of term, and when I cycled up to Thornfield House on the fourth day to find out why, Mrs Todd answered the door and told me Ellen would be studying at home from now on.

'But what about her A-levels?'

'She can study at home,' said Mrs Todd.

'Can I see her, please?'

Mrs Todd shook her head. 'Not today, Hannah.'

I felt a kind of panic in my stomach. I looked into the older woman's face and was sure I discerned sympathy deep in her eyes.

'Please, Mrs Todd, just for five minutes.'

'I'm sorry. Not today. Come again tomorrow – things might be better then.' Mrs Todd pushed the door shut, literally closing it in my face.

I backed down the drive, looking up towards Ellen's window. She was there, staring out. I held up my hand, waved. My eyes were stinging with the sun. Ellen bent down and lifted the lower window sash. She leaned out, holding one finger to her lips, and threw something out – a paper aeroplane. I chased it, caught it, held it up to show Ellen I had it safe, and then I waved again and walked backwards out of the drive.

It was strange how things had changed. Everything had been so different a few years earlier; I remembered Ellen and me doing cartwheels on the front lawn at Thornfield House when we were thirteen or fourteen. The world spinning past us, the sky, the grass, the house. Standing up, panting, a little dizzy with our hair in our mouths and feeling happy from the exertion. Mrs Brecht, in her wheelchair, laughing, the sun catching the gold of the necklace around her pretty throat and Mr Brecht, the contest judge, stroking his chin saying, '*Hmmm. A very difficult decision,*' and then awarding both of us the joint first prize of a 50p coin, even though we all knew that Ellen's cartwheels had been better than mine. I remembered Mr Brecht pushing his wife, tipping the wheelchair back by its handles, making car-revving noises and then leaning over to kiss her face and her, still laughing, turning her lips towards his. And later, Mr Brecht sitting beside Anne on the chaise longue, her eyes closed to hide her pain and he massaging lavender oil into her hands, treating each sore knuckle with such tenderness and affection. Gentle, kind, good Mr Brecht, his poor wife, the two of them so much in love, and Ellen the spoiled, precocious, but still compliant daughter.

I unfolded the paper aeroplane as I picked up the bike that I'd left propped beside the wall. The message was brief, roughly scribbled in felt pen, done in the few moments while I had stood at the door talking to Mrs Todd.

Tell Jago come at midnight, stay close to the garden wall, hoot like an owl three times xxx

I had hoped it would be a message for me. I was the one who had bothered to come up to see Ellen and my reward was to be used as a go-between. It didn't seem fair. I put the letter in my pocket, climbed on the bike, and rode it slowly along the lane.

Back home, I sat at the table in the kitchen, struggling with an essay about the similarities between theropod dinosaurs in the Mesozoic Era and the birds of today.

If I gave the letter to Jago, then I would be instigating a chain of events over which I would have no control. Jago and Ellen were natural risk-takers. Ellen would enjoy the thrill of whatever she was planning and Jago, I was sure, would do whatever she asked of him. It would be better not to give him the note. He wouldn't know any different and I would be able to sleep sound in my bed knowing he wasn't going to get into any trouble. In fact, not giving Jago the note would definitely be the right thing to do. I considered, for a moment, leaving it somewhere where one of my parents would find it. They would ask what it meant, and I would be obliged to tell them what I knew. That would put a stop to Jago and Ellen's secrets and lies. I was enjoying this idea and playing out its various consequences in my mind, when my conscience intervened. It reminded me that Ellen was my friend and Jago my brother. Both trusted me. They both thought I was on their side. We were the Three Musketeers, all for one and one for all. I could not let them down.

I shouldn't have done it. I should have trusted my instincts and kept quiet, but in the end I gave Jago the message, and that night, Ellen and Jago's love affair moved into a new phase, one that only the three of us would ever know about. From the beginning, I knew it would lead to disaster – I *knew* – but once it had started there was nothing I could do to stop it.

From that night on, almost every night, Jago crept like a thief out of number 8 Cross Hands Lane and walked up the hill to Thornfield House. Sometimes, he returned almost immediately. Those were the nights when the lights were still on downstairs, or when Mr Brecht was pacing the room next to Ellen's, the room where his wife died, his shadow on the curtains that hung at the window alerting Jago, and forcing him to turn away. Other times Mr Brecht drank himself to sleep, and slept so deeply that nothing would disturb him. Those nights it was safe for Jago and Ellen to meet, to be together. They were like a force of nature, like water or air or gravity. Nothing could stop them. Mr Brecht could put all the obstacles he liked in their way. He could try to contain Ellen in the house, in her room, but it was like trying to hold back the wind or the tide.

My parents got up early and went to bed early. By the time Jago was ready to leave our house, they were already fast asleep, the door to the bedroom slightly ajar, as it always was, so the landing light could guide them to the bathroom should they need it in the night. While Jago prepared to go to his lover, my father snored enthusiastically and my mother huddled beneath the blankets, curled towards him. The noises Dad made far exceeded the little creaks and clicks that Jago made as he left. The central heating in our house had switched itself off and the house was cosy, the air thick with the smell of washing powder and whatever Mum had cooked for dinner. Trixie was beneath my bed, or on it, dreaming of rabbits she would never catch, her paws and eyeballs skittering harmlessly. She stirred but did not make a sound when she heard Jago leave.

I heard him. Every night I heard.

I knew what happened. I knew what they did. Jago told me some of it, and Ellen some of it, and though I tried not to think about it, my mind filled in the gaps. I lay in bed, listening to the dog's sleepy little snuffles and grunts while Jago jogged through the darkness up the winding lane to Ellen's house. He saw the cats and the owls and the foxes, and they saw him. The lights of the fishing boats far out to sea pierced the night's blackness; they twinkled and bobbed above the waves. Jago recognized some of the boats by their lights and he felt less alone. As he ran to Ellen, his breath streamed away into the night behind him, disappeared. He did not think of anything as he ran but he knew this was what he must do. He had to go to her.

At Thornfield House, he stopped and waited at the gates, checking for any signs of activity downstairs, watching the window of the room beside Ellen's carefully. The curtains to that room had been drawn since the night Mrs Brecht died, and the light inside was always muted but, if Mr Brecht was there, sooner or later a shadow would fall across the window. If, after a few minutes, Jago was confident the coast was clear, he stepped into the garden. He had to be careful not to trigger the porch light, which was motion-sensitive. He kept close to the garden wall, avoiding the gravel on the drive, looping around until he came to the far corner at the front of the house. There he stopped and looked up. Ellen had been watching, always. She had already pushed up the lower sash of her window. Her father believed that when he turned the key that locked her bedroom door, his daughter was inviolate. He didn't know that Ellen and Jago were making a mockery of his precautions.

The night garden at Thornfield House used to smell sweetly of the stocks and wallflowers Adam Tremlett had planted in the beds that lined the drive. There used to be other scents, daphne, honeysuckle, rose. The flowers were long gone, and although the bees and butterflies didn't come to the garden in daylight, the moths continued their night-time pollination of the grass and the flowers that were safe from Mr Brecht's secateurs because they did not look like flowers. Jago was like a moth, purposeful but silent. He knew the front of Thornfield House like the back of his hand; he knew the brickwork, where he could put his feet and where he couldn't; he knew how far he had to climb before he could pull himself up into Ellen's room.

He had to be careful. The light in Mrs Todd's window, at the top of the house, sometimes burned on into the early hours. She liked to knit and read in her room. She was a light sleeper and easily disturbed. Years of caring for Anne Brecht had imprinted in her an ability to listen out, always, for the slightest untoward noise or signal that something was amiss. Jago had worked out what he must do if Mrs Todd's light was still on. He waited until she went into the small bathroom beside her room. Any sounds he made climbing into the house were masked by the tapwater Mrs Todd ran while she brushed her teeth.

Ellen waited for Jago, barefoot and ready for bed on the other side of the window. She had already barricaded the door, moving her dressing-table up against it. She helped him through the window, smiling. Jago could not be too gentle with her although she was solid, strong. He was so afraid of damaging her, of hurting her in some way. All Jago wanted to do was rescue Ellen and make her happy. He wanted to set her free. Ellen saw herself as a real-life storybook princess, locked in a tower by her cruel father. She made Jago take on the role of knight in shining armour and it was a role that appealed to him, he who had been the underdog for so many years. Ellen had not chosen to be imprisoned by her father, but she did nothing to help herself. All she had to do was concede a little, humour him, be kind to him, empathize with him, but she preferred to dig in her heels and fight. The drama of the situation appealed to her. She liked the excitement of it. She believed there would be a happy ending for Jago and her, no matter how far the situation between herself and her father escalated, because stories always had happy endings. The characters in dramas always lived happily ever after.

I didn't know what happened, exactly, when Jago was in the room with Ellen, but I used to torment myself wonderfully by imagining it. In my vicarious scenarios, they didn't talk. They never talked. I imagined them kissing, Ellen tasting of toothpaste, her mouth receiving his. She would be hungry for him. Jago touched Ellen in the dark. He touched her hair, her shoulders, slid his hands down her smooth arms. He brought the fresh air in with him, the moon and the breeze, the sea wind, the tide and the wildflowers. They moved over to the bed. Ellen slipped between the covers. Jago stood beside her, and took off his clothes. His jacket first, and then his T-shirt that he pulled over the top of his head so Ellen could half-see in the star- and moonlight coming through the window the stretch of his chest, the muscles of his arm, the dark underarm hair, two pale nipples. She smelled him in the warmth of the abandoned shirt and she watched as he unbuttoned his jeans, let them fall, stepped out of them. And lastly he took off his shorts and Ellen felt a pleasure inside that was deeper and more exquisite than any pleasure she had experienced before. She was ready for him. She could not wait for him. She could not get enough of him.

Jago and Ellen made love. That was why Jago went to Ellen in the night; that was why she summoned him.

Later, when happiness had softened Ellen, when she had moderated her behaviour and I was allowed back into Thornfield House, she told me some of it. She touched her throat as she told me; her eyes shone and her voice was husky with excitement. I didn't see it, but I could imagine her head thrown back and her shoulders, her small breasts, the chain around her neck and the catching of air in her lungs, her black hair spread about the white pillow, Jago's pushing into her, her slender feet hooked around his back, so much incredible, mutual pleasure, such obligation, so much that was so right.

She described the breathless moments of the sexual act

itself, she feeling the fill of him, he always rushed with the pleasure of her, her glorious shivering. And afterwards, she told me how they suppressed their laughter and how Jago said, '*I love you,*' into her ear, how his lips and his fingers were in her hair. '*I love you, Ellen Brecht,*' he said. '*Let's be together always, for ever, let's be lovers until we die. I love you so much it kills me to leave you. I think about you every moment of every day. I want to tell everyone about you. I want them to know.*' And she said in return, '*You can't! You mustn't! Don't breathe a word to anyone, not anyone.*'

'*I know,*' he said. '*I know.*'

He always fell asleep first; he had been working all day and was exhausted by the physical act, worn out by the nervous energy he had used in the subterfuge of climbing into the house, and by the anticipation that had dogged him all day. Ellen stayed awake. She was on guard, protecting her lover from the dangers of the night. She turned over, spooned her back into his warmth, stared at the panes of glass in the window, listened out for footsteps on the landing, a give-away cough. Outside, the night was brighter than inside. She watched the moon move slowly from one windowpane into the next. Her eyes were tired, but she did not sleep, not when Jago was with her. She knew that soon, before dawn, he would have to leave, and she did not know how, night after night, she found the strength to wake him, to send him away, to say '*Goodbye.*'

Hers was the best drama, the most exciting life, the most thrilling and dangerous and liberating. Ellen lived and loved and she burned and burned, bright as a star, believing she would live and love for ever.

CHAPTER THIRTY-THREE

Eventually, after hours of crashing and booming, the thunder moved away from Bristol and I skimmed the surface of sleep. I dipped in and out of dreams and almost drifted off, but each time was pricked into wakefulness by the memory of the woman standing on the clifftop and the glass on the gravestone. I kept hearing Ellen's voice. In my half-sleep she beckoned me into the mirror and I followed her. Behind were the Trethene moors, and she and I moved across the marshland. We were both in our nightgowns, barefoot, our hair blowing behind us as we stumbled through the mist, tripping on marshy hillocks as the moon drifted in and out of fast-moving, shape-shifting white clouds.

I called out to her, '*Ellen, wait! Let me see you!*' but she ran on, snatches of her voice on the wind, and, although I was compelled to keep her in my sight, I did not want her to turn. I did not want to see her face.

In the early hours, an alarm went off down the street somewhere. It shrieked, splintering the dark, for ten minutes or so at a time, and then it went quiet again, before restarting. I couldn't get used to the noise, or the intervening silences. I was too hot in my bed. I tried lying on top of the covers, but I was still too hot. Sweat prickled the skin that wasn't exposed to the cooling air. I got up and opened the bedroom window, but no draught was coming through. I needed to open the living-room window at the front of the flat to create a through-draught.

The power had been restored. That was probably what had triggered the alarm. In the orange glow of the street-lamp, I could see two men talking on the pavement below. It was clear from their body language that they were in some kind of trouble, or were expecting it. One was well-built and good-looking, holding a cigarette and shifting his weight nervously from one foot to the other, like a boxer. The other was scrawnier, with yellow dreadlocks and a face that looked as if it had recently been in a fight. I wanted to open the window, but if I did, the men might hear the noise – they might look up and see me and think I'd been eavesdropping. I imagined them scampering up the wall like spiders, climbing in the window, prowling through the flat, hunting me down. I didn't dare turn on the light.

I walked to the kitchen at the back and slid open the window. Lily paced the sill, backwards and forwards, rubbing her head against my wrist. Outside, a cat was prowling the wall that separated the garden of my building from its neighbour. The rabbit that belonged to the children in our garden flat was crouching in its hutch; I could see it clearly through the wire mesh, which meant the lights downstairs must have been switched on. Perhaps the family who lived there had been disturbed by the alarm too. Perhaps they wanted the men outside to know they were awake. Lily jumped onto the floor and wound herself around my ankles. I reached down to stroke her.

I had a longing to be outside, in the cooler air. I imagined myself stretched out flat on the scrubby patch of rain-drenched lawn in the garden, in front of the rabbit hutch, amongst the discarded plastic toys, beneath the moon. But I had no access to the back garden, and I could not go out of the front door, not with the two men standing there, by the streetlamp, waiting for something or someone.

I went into the living room but did not switch on the light, not even a lamp. I turned on the television with the remote, kept the sound to silent. The TV was tuned to a news channel; there were riots, people throwing petrol bombs, people being beaten with batons, people lying dead on the streets, blood making wet black shadows around them. I switched over. A different channel. Young men were sitting around a table, playing poker. I neither understood nor cared about poker. I turned the television off, feeling enervated. And outside, the alarm was blaring: *naah, naah, naah* – like a wounded animal with an electronic bleat.

I went back into the kitchen, took a bottle of whisky out of the fridge and half-filled a tumbler. There was ice in the freezer. I took my drink into the living room and sat curled in my white armchair in the almost-dark with Lily on my lap. I didn't feel like music or reading or candles, any of my usual distractions. I didn't feel like anything. I was numb and cold, despite the heat, and terribly alone, as if I were the only person in the world, the last person alive, the one to witness the fading of the sun.

It was a long night, but at last the morning came. I mopped up a leak on the kitchen windowsill with a cloth and listened to the early news on Radio 4. I ate yoghurt and muesli for breakfast, fed the cat, wrote a note to remind myself to buy some more litter for her box and was just about to leave for work when the phone rang. It was Julia, my therapist.

'Hi, Hannah,' she said in her positive but not overly chirpy counselling voice. 'Just thought I'd give you a quick call to see how things are going.'

'OK,' I said. 'OK-ish.' I tucked the phone under my chin and leaned down to find the umbrella in the hall cupboard.

'Has something happened?'

I took the umbrella from the cupboard, and returned to the living room.

'I'm not sure.'

'Would you like to tell me about it?'

I took a deep breath. 'I went down to Cornwall at the weekend,' I said. 'I wanted to see my parents, but also . . . I don't know why exactly, but I felt drawn to the beach where I used to go with Ellen. I was thinking about her and I saw something – someone was watching me.'

I heard Julia's little intake of breath, like a small sigh in reverse.

'I don't know who it was,' I continued quickly. 'The sun was behind her so I couldn't see clearly, but it was a woman and she was standing on the clifftop in a place only Ellen would know.'

'It could have been anyone, Hannah.'

'I know.'

I didn't say it but I was thinking that it could also have been no one.

I sat down on the white chair. 'And there was something else, something weird. I went to Ellen's grave. I'd never been there before – I know you told me to go years ago, but I hadn't. Anyway, I went and I found something there – something from our childhood.'

'What did you find?'

I was feeling a little dizzy. 'Some pieces of glass. We used to call it drift-glass. Glass that had been in the sea. I used to collect it. I'd left it hidden somewhere secret, somewhere only Ellen would know. And somebody had moved it and put it on Ellen's gravestone. Don't you think that's strange?'

'How could you be sure they were the same pieces of glass? You can't have seen them for years.'

'Because . . .' I stopped. I couldn't explain about the single blue piece and I didn't think I should tell Julia about my growing feeling that Ellen was still alive. She would think I really had lost my mind. 'I don't know,' I said. 'But I'm certain they were.'

There was a silence at the other end of the line for a moment or two. It made me feel vulnerable.

Then Julia said, 'I'd like to see you, Hannah, just to catch up for a coffee. It would be good, I think, to have a talk face to face. How would you feel about that?'

I felt relieved. Julia would know if I was all right or if I was falling apart. She was a professional. She'd be able to tell. And perhaps she could prescribe me some drugs or some therapy; something to help me sleep. Perhaps, if we were together, I could be honest with her and she would be able to make things clear in my mind.

'It would be lovely to see you again, Julia,' I said. 'I think it would be really helpful for me.'

'Good,' she said.

We arranged to meet in Bristol the following day.

CHAPTER THIRTY-FOUR

I was eighteen in November. Mum and Dad took Jago and me into Exeter. We ate pizzas in a lively Italian restaurant complete with a real pizza oven and a waiter with a huge, comedy pepperpot. The waiter kept kissing his fingers to indicate that something was delicious. Dad said you could tell the restaurant was authentic by the little dishes full of grated Parmesan on every table. I enjoyed it and Jago did his best, but he was fidgety. Dad had made him wear a shirt and tie. They didn't suit him. My parents gave me fifty pounds for my birthday and Jago gave me a charm bracelet. I put it on my wrist and he promised to buy me a new charm every year.

My best gift was from Ellen and Mr Brecht. Ellen presented it to me the next time I went to Thornfield House while Mr Brecht opened a bottle of champagne. Mrs Todd was looking on. The gift had been beautifully wrapped. It was an encyclopaedia of Natural History, a huge tome full of beautiful colour pictures. Inside the front of the book, Ellen had written: *To my best friend always* and her father had simply written: *with love*. I traced over those two words with the tip of my finger so many times that they began to fade.

The pages of the book were heavy and silky. They smelled divine. I never tired of looking at them and imagining what it must be like to be on an ice-floe, or in a jungle, or a desert at sunset with the polar bears and the monkeys and the snakes. The book was what made me decide for certain what I wanted to do with my life. I wanted to be an explorer. I wanted to visit remote parts of the world and discover new species. There were so many places to go, so much to see. Most of all, I decided I wanted to be away from Trethene.

The gift also confirmed my suspicions that things couldn't be so bad between Ellen and her father if they could still collaborate when it came to choosing a present for me. After I'd unwrapped the book, they stood together, both delighting in my pleasure, Mr Brecht's hand on Ellen's shoulder and she leaning slightly towards him, each raising a glass to me. I went to thank them, and they both kissed me. They were, in many ways, so alike. They had, by mutual consent, called a truce in my honour. If only, I thought, Ellen didn't always make life so difficult for herself and for everyone else, then maybe everything would be fine.

Except, I couldn't see Mr Brecht ever forgiving her for what she was doing with Jago. Not now. Not when the deception had gone on for so long in his house, under his nose. Not when they were effectively making a fool of him.

My heart ached for Mr Brecht.

The winter rolled in, cold and grey and sullen. Time moved so slowly back then, as if the world were spinning at a different speed. In any day, there would be hours when I had nothing to do except wander around the countryside, or lie on my bed with my eyes closed thinking about how boring my life was and how I wished it was more exciting. I planned out my future: A-levels would start in the new year, and then I'd work in the Seagull during the summer and go off to university in September. I'd study the sciences and then go to work for the BBC's Natural History Department, or for a wildlife charity, and I'd make films or write books. I would be famous. I'd change the world.

Without Ellen, I was lonely at school and often bored. I wasn't interested in the boys who were my contemporaries. They were like cattle, I thought, slow and heavy and smelly, in comparison to Mr Brecht. They would not know how to charm or seduce or love or suffer. Their interests were mundane, their conversations inane. I couldn't bear the thought of them near me yet they seemed to be all the other girls thought about.

Home, too, seemed ever more constricting. My parents were settling comfortably into late-middle age; they had their routines, their favourite programmes, their regular menus. And Jago, who could have brought some fun into my life, had no time for me.

I was walking the dog along the river estuary one afternoon, when I found him sitting hunched on the rocks, watching the tide come in, spilling along the mudflats where the wading birds with their long, thin legs and arced bills strutted and fed. I sat beside him, not touching him, not saying anything. I wrapped Trixie in my coat. The three of us sat on the rocks and stared out at the gunmetal-grey water and the sky and the birds.

Jago picked up a pebble and skimmed it across the surface of the water. It bounced twice. Dad always used to say that meant bad luck.

'Throw another one,' I said. 'You need three bounces.'

Jago tried again. The pebble jumped off the water once, as if struck by electricity, but the second time it dropped into the water and disappeared.

'Again,' I said, but Jago shook his head.

'What are you thinking about?' I asked.

'I have to take Ellen away from here,' he said. 'I need to

205

get her away from her father, far away, somewhere he can't find her.'

'Why?'

He frowned at me. 'Why do you think? So we can be together without all this sneaking around.'

'Where will you go?'

'I don't know. Abroad. Anywhere. It doesn't matter.'

Jago put his head in his hands. I let my head fall to the side so that my cheek rested against his shoulder. I hugged the dog close to me.

'If you just waited a while,' I said, 'until Ellen's a bit older, then her father won't be able to stop you seeing her. He'd probably be fine if you just—'

'No,' Jago said. 'He'll never let her be free. He'll never let us be together. I'll have to take her away, and you'll have to help us.'

I sighed. This was Ellen's lament. She had taught it to Jago, and now he was following the script too.

'What can I do?' I asked.

'I don't know. I don't know how we'll do it, but I'll think of a way. We'll have to decide where we're going, as far away as possible, and I'll have to find a job. We'll need money. Especially if we're living abroad. We'll need the cash to tide us over.'

A pair of mute swans circled overhead. Their necks were extended impossibly long and their wings rippled through the air, stately but loud as gunshot. Trixie looked up and growled.

'Ellen's going to get an inheritance when she's eighteen,' I said quietly. 'At least, she told me she was. A fortune, she said. Hundreds of thousands of pounds. I don't know if it's true, but—'

'It is true.'

I moved away a little to look at Jago's face.

'How do you know?'

'Ellen told me,' he said. Inside, another little bit of me curled up in pain. I had thought I was Ellen's confidante. All those secrets she'd told me that I thought were private, just for the two of us – had she told Jago too? 'She doesn't know how much the inheritance will be,' Jago said. 'And that's not the point. I don't want to be scrounging off her. I want to look after her. I want her to be proud of me.'

I said nothing. I was trying to contain my hurt.

'The money will help, of course,' said Jago. 'It's not like it won't be useful. It means we'll be able to go wherever we want, anywhere in the world. Do you think the witch would be pleased to know we were using her money to escape Trethene?'

'You shouldn't call Mrs Withiel a witch,' I said crossly. 'It's unkind.'

Jago laughed. 'When did you get so up yourself?'

'Shut up!'

He put his arm around me and said, 'Don't be such a spanner.' And because he had used my childhood nickname, I burrowed into his warmth and forgave him.

'I don't want you to go away,' I said. 'What will I do without you? What will happen to me? What about Mum and Dad?'

'They'll be fine and you've got your own life to lead. You don't need me. You're going to be a famous explorer.'

'I don't want to be anything without you.'

'You won't be without us. You'll be our accomplice. You're the key to everything. In fact,' Jago said, 'there's something you can do now. You can start collecting supplies and putting them in the cave at Bleached Scarp so that Ellen has somewhere to go to if things get too bad with her father.'

'What supplies?'

'A tent, matches, blankets. You'll have to wrap everything up in plastic, to make it waterproof.'

'Ellen can't stay on the beach . . .'

'No, but if she has to get away in a hurry, there needs to be enough there to keep her warm and dry for a few hours,' Jago said. 'If she can't get to me or I can't reach her.'

He frowned and looked out at the water. I watched as the swans extended their feet and braced their wings to land in the water. I never tired of watching the birds.

'And you must promise not to say anything about this to Mum and Dad. Not a word.'

'Of course I won't. I never tell them anything.'

The swans touched down, meeting their reflections, flapping to a stop.

'He's getting worse,' Jago said.

'Who?'

'Mr Brecht.'

'You only ever hear Ellen's side of the story, Jago.'

He looked at me. 'What do you mean?'

I shrugged. 'He's all right when I'm there. I mean, he's still mourning his wife, obviously, but he doesn't seem that bad to me. He bought me a nice birthday present. And sometimes . . . sometimes Ellen makes things up.'

Jago snorted. 'He's mental! Ellen didn't make up him cutting down all the flowers in the garden. She didn't make up being locked in her room. She didn't make up him hitting her.'

He picked up another pebble and threw it into the water. One of the swans turned a haughty face towards him. Trixie tensed in my arms.

'Yes, but Ellen . . .'

'Ellen what?'

Jago looked at me. I couldn't say it to him. I couldn't say: 'Ellen *does make it up about him hitting her*' or '*Ellen winds him up so badly he can't help himself'* or *'If Ellen didn't tell so many lies then he wouldn't be so angry.'*

So all I said was, 'It's not as if Ellen's father *doesn't* love her, Jago. If anything, he loves her too much.'

CHAPTER THIRTY-FIVE

I thought about the earlier telephone conversation with Julia as I walked through Bristol in the rain up to Stokes Croft and Jamaica Streeet, and I used her techniques to keep my mind occupied, describing the city to myself, filling my mind with it so there was no room for Ellen. I was coming close to that state of tiredness when it's difficult to distinguish between being awake and being asleep, between conscious thought and dreams. I knew it was a dangerous place to be. I had to keep hold of reality. I had to be clear about where life began and nightmares ended, but even during the walk I drifted once or twice.

I was not the first to arrive at the museum. The lights had been switched on in the staff rooms and somebody had already boiled the kettle. I had a quick look round to see who was there. The blue glow of a computer screen permeated the opaque glass in the window of the door to John's office. It was ajar. I stepped quietly through. John didn't notice me, he was too involved in what he was doing. The blinds were drawn over the window and he was hunched over his computer, the light from the screen reflected in the lenses of his glasses.

'John?' I said quietly. He jumped and turned. He looked

terrible. His hair was sticking up, and he was unshaven. His disarray made me feel a little stronger, less aware of my own fragility. Mentally, I took a step away from the cliff edge on which I had been balancing.

'Are you all right?' I asked, moving a coffee mug that said *My career lies in ruins* to make room for me to perch on the corner of the desk.

'Yes, yes,' John said. 'I'm fine. I came in early to finish a paper.'

'You look like you've been here all night.'

John flinched a little at that, and I had an awful feeling that I had inadvertently arrived at the truth. I remembered his wife's words three days previously, how she was thinking about ending their relationship, and wondered if she had, for once, been honest with him and if he had, as a result, left home. Was that why he had tried to contact me? Had he been looking for a shoulder to cry on, or a place to stay? Had I let him down at the time when he had most needed a friend?

I couldn't be sure. I was surmising. The picture of Charlotte and the girls was still pinned to the corkboard on the wall, where it always had been. Charlotte was still smiling down at her husband, with a carefree look in her eyes, just as she always had.

'Is everything OK, John?' I asked. 'You really don't look right.'

'It's Charlotte . . .' he said.

'I thought it must be. Oh John, I should have been there for you this weekend, I'm so sorry!'

He frowned. 'Why? Why should you have been? Why are you sorry?'

I swallowed. 'I thought . . . Didn't she . . . Haven't you . . . I don't know.'

John took off his glasses, breathed on them, then cleaned them with the tail of his shirt.

'She's staying on at her mother's for another couple of days.'

'Oh.'

I made myself nod as if this was good news while the wheels of my mind realigned to make sense of the information. So Charlotte was procrastinating still. Was she using the extra time away to make practical arrangements? Finding temporary accommodation, changing her bank account? Or was she whiling it away with one of her lovers?

John yawned. Then he leaned back in his chair and stretched his arms above his head.

'I was fed up of being at home on my own and thought I might as well do something constructive,' he said, 'so I came in here last night. I only meant to work for an hour or two, but I must have been engrossed because next thing I knew, it was dawn and I had a crease on my cheek from sleeping on the desk.'

'Oh.' I smiled as best I could. 'Poor you. Would you like a coffee?'

'I think I need one.'

'White, two sugars?'

'You're an angel.'

I turned and went into the kitchenette. While the kettle boiled I saw John, through the open door to his office, standing by the window and combing his hair with his fingers.

CHAPTER THIRTY-SIX

Another Christmas came. It was to be the last one at home for any of us, although we didn't know it. I remember feeling itchy that December, and constrained, like an insect that's ready to shed its nymph-shell and emerge an adult. Almost everything my parents did irritated me and, rather than conspiring with me, Jago was more remote than ever.

I may have changed, but the rituals did not. Dad fetched the ancient tree down from the loft, just as he did every year, and I helped decorate its spindly, tinsel-and-wire branches with Woolworths' glass baubles and fairy-lights that tinkled out a medley of festive tunes. Mum made mince pies for the elderly. Trixie walked around the tree, which took up a big part of the living room, knocking it over at least twice a day. Mum, Dad, Jago and I took turns marking off the programmes we wanted to watch over the festive period from the lists in the *Radio Times* and *TV Times* magazines, although I am certain that Jago, at least, had little intention of spending the whole holiday sitting in the living room at number 8 Cross Hands Lane.

On the anniversary of Mrs Brecht's death, a few days before Christmas, I spent the day with Ellen and her father.

Mr Brecht seemed to be back on form. Planning an outing in memory of his wife gave him a purpose. He wanted us to do something that she would have enjoyed, and that we would enjoy also.

Mr Brecht looked as handsome as ever when I arrived at Thornfield House. He had trimmed his beard, and his hair, although still shoulder-length, was clean and silky. He wore a long coat over his black shirt and trousers. He kissed me on both cheeks, told me I looked beautiful and helped me into the front seat of the car. Ellen was already sitting in the back. The front seat was her gift to me. I turned to smile at her and she reached over and took hold of my hand. Hers was cold and gentle and I knew from her touch that she was in a good mood.

Mr Brecht drove us all the way to St Ives, playing Joan Armatrading on the car stereo and encouraging us to sing along to the words. The heater blasted warm air at my legs. I rested my forehead against the side windowpane and had a little fantasy that I was married to Mr Brecht. It would be possible, perhaps, in another year or two, when he had recovered fully from Anne's death. Every month that passed, the age difference between us would be less significant. I closed my eyes and imagined myself lying across his bed while he slowly undressed me. In my mind, I hitched up my hips so he could pull off my jeans. I shivered as I felt his lips on my belly. And then he said, 'What are you thinking about, Hannah?' and I lurched back into the real world and hid my embarrassment behind a gushing rush of memories of his wife.

We had lunch in a lovely little restaurant, shared a fresh seafood platter and drank white wine. I felt elegant, adult, sophisticated. Mr Brecht showed me how to take the shell off a prawn, he taught me to use the cracker to reach the crab meat but I refused to drink an oyster from its shell, no matter how he tried to persuade me. We washed our fingers in a bowl of lemony water. After that, we walked the steep narrow streets of the town together, browsing the art and craftwork in the shop windows, wrapped in coats and hats against the wind and the three of us linked by our arms.

In the evening Mr Brecht took us to a candlelight concert in a big house set high on the hill, not piano but a string quartet. At the reception afterwards, he talked to people he knew from the classical music business and Ellen and I ate canapés and drank glass after glass of champagne as we drifted amongst the guests. The rooms were decorated with tiny, sparkling lights and everything was clean and open and spacious. I loved the colours of the pictures hung on the walls, I loved how the building had been designed to make the most of every gleam of light and every shadow. My country accent, my rosy, Cornish cheeks were not a disadvantage in that environment; instead they made me appear different to the people who had come from the city to spend Christmas by the sea. Everyone seemed interested in me, everyone laughed and asked questions, and touched my arm and told me I was 'sweet' and 'charming' and 'real'. I wondered if some of them thought I *was* Mr Brecht's girlfriend. My head was light, my mind fizzed, it was all so pretty and lovely and so different from my normal life.

It was cold outside, but I stood on the balcony and gazed out across the harbour to the hill where a little chapel stood, illuminated. Mr Brecht followed. He stood behind me, so close that I could feel the heat of him. He blew smoke around my face and I leaned my hands on the railing.

He put his hands inside my coat, on my waist. I breathed in to make myself slimmer.

'Hannah,' he said, his voice in my ear. 'Have you enjoyed yourself today?'

I nodded.

'Good,' he said. 'I knew you'd like it here. I love St Ives and there's something in you that reminds me of me.'

And I thought that was a signal, I thought he meant it as a sign that he was ready for me, so I turned to him and reached up to kiss him, but as I pressed towards him, he pulled backwards, away.

'Oh Hannah!' he said, and he laughed, and held me firmly around the waist. 'You are wonderful.' And he leaned down and kissed my cheek, just beside my ear. Then he gently moved my hair out of my eyes and said, 'Don't ever change.'

He only kissed me once, and it was a chaste kiss, an honourable kiss; nobody could have said that he took advantage of me – in fact, it was the opposite. I would have been happy to give him far more than he took, but the kiss marked me for life.

At the time, I played the scene over and over in my mind. I elaborated and adorned it, imbued it with significance and romance until thinking about Mr Brecht and what he had said consumed me. He thought I was perfect the way I was, so he must have been thinking about me just as I thought about him. Had he been waiting for an opportunity to kiss me and tell me that he loved me? Because that had been what he meant to say, I was certain of it.

Now I'm not so sure what happened. I was drunk. I was giddy on life. I had been fantasizing about Mr Brecht all day. I thought about that evening so often, tweaking the memory, making little changes here and there until it was as perfect as it could be, that I can no longer be sure of the exact sequence of events, or what they meant. All I know is that even now, Mr Brecht's kiss feels like one of the most precious things that ever happened to me.

Back at home, afterwards, the clutter of our cottage irritated me more than ever. Everything was old and shabby and fussy, the patterns on the carpets and curtains clashing and fighting one another, the knick-knacks on the shelves and in the cabinets crowding every little space. It made me want to scream and break things. It made me desperate to get away.

Every day, during Christmas week, I found an excuse to walk up to Thornfield House. I sat with Ellen and Mrs Todd, while Mr Brecht drank and told us stories about him and Anne. In my mind, I substituted myself for Anne in every scene. I was certain Mr Brecht was looking at me in a different way. I thought he was preparing me.

On New Year's Eve, the pubs were licensed to stay open until midnight and there was to be a firework display at Polrack. My parents could not be doing with the noise, and anyway, they said, they needed to stay in to look after Trixie. Jago said he was spending the night at the Williamses' farm. Ellen badgered her father into taking us into town.

Polrack was packed full of revellers, drinking on the streets, despite the cold, and sustaining themselves with hot dogs and doughnuts. Mr Brecht gave Ellen a ten-pound note, said he'd meet us on the harbour at midnight and disappeared off to the pub. Ellen and I bought cartons of warm cider and made our way down to the harbour. We sat on the wall, dangling our legs over the black water, waiting for the fireworks. Within moments, Jago appeared, and he sat beside Ellen – and I realized they had arranged it, the two of them. They wanted to spend New Year's Eve together so they'd devised a plan. Once again, I was an alibi. They spoke quietly together for a few moments, then Jago reached around Ellen to tug at my sleeve.

'Go and keep an eye on the Baudelaire, Han,' he said to me. 'Watch the door and come and tell us if Psycho comes out.'

'No,' I said. 'I'm staying here. I want to watch the fireworks.'

'You can watch the fireworks from outside the pub.'

'Oh yeah? On my own? It's my New Year too, you know.'

'Oh Hannah, don't be so selfish,' said Ellen.

I felt like pushing her into the water. Really I would have liked to have shoved her in, hard, and listened to her screams because it would have been absolutely freezing.

Instead, I climbed to my feet and walked slowly through the crowd, my hands in my pockets, my shoulders hunched. People were grouped noisily around the pub, pressed together for warmth and companionship. The atmosphere was convivial. There was plenty of laughter and music and cigarette smoke and the smells of beer and fried onion and the fish smell that always pervaded Polrack, but the jollity only made me feel more lonely. I was the only person on her own. Everywhere else, people were holding hands, or they had their arms around one another, or they were in groups or couples. They were all laughing and hugging and having a happy time. They would always look back on this New Year with pleasure, and all I would remember was being on my own amongst the crowds.

I shuffled around for an hour or so, spending the last of my money on hot cider, feeling tearful and lonely. I kept checking the church clock, but time was moving painfully slowly. I was cold. I wished I was at home with Mum and Dad and Trixie. At least they wouldn't use me. At least they wanted me for myself. I toyed with the idea of going into the pub to seduce Mr Brecht, but I didn't dare go quite that far.

Eventually, after for ever, there was a sound like gunshot. Everyone looked towards the illuminated clock on the church-tower. The minute hand showed a fraction before midnight and somebody with a loudspeaker counted us back from ten to one. At midnight, the clock chimed and everyone embraced everyone else. I was by myself, beside the entrance to the Baudelaire, when Mr Brecht came out. He was wearing his hat, and his long coat, and was tucking his scarf in at the neck. He paused, put a cigarette between his lips, and cupped his hands around it to light it. Then he began to excuse his way through the crowds, looking for Ellen.

I could have reached Ellen and Jago before he did.

I could have done, but I did not. Instead I followed behind, walking in the space created by his wake.

I was standing almost at Mr Brecht's shoulder when he saw them, Jago and Ellen, together, he holding her head between both his big hands, her arms inside his coat, wrapped around his waist, and the two of them kissing, their bodies so close you could not have put a cigarette paper between them. The boats that bobbed in the harbour were blowing their horns to welcome in the New Year, the church was ringing its bells, the harbourside rang out with the sound of 'Auld Lang Syne' and the sky was lit up by fireworks. Everyone was cheering except me and Mr Brecht.

We just stood still and watched.

I thought he would do something at once to humiliate Ellen and Jago in front of all those people, but he did nothing. After a few moments, he dropped his cigarette onto the ground, then turned and walked away, disappearing into the crowds.

This frightened me more than if he had exploded with anger immediately. I knew he would neither forgive nor forget. Sooner or later, he would punish Ellen and Jago. He would find a way.

CHAPTER THIRTY-SEVEN

The next day, in Bristol, everything went wrong. Everything.

It had started going wrong during the night.

I had another nightmare, one that began as a glorious, technicolour dream. Jago and I were children again, and he loved me again, and I was so happy that we were together that I could hardly contain my joy. It was Ellen's birthday, we were taking presents to her, and somehow I knew Thornfield House would be festooned with balloons and bunting. The lane was pink and white with blossom-laden trees; the birds were singing and rabbits were hopping about on the verges – it was like some surreal Disney-esque version of childhood. In my dream, I realized that all the bad things that had happened – Ellen dying, Jago leaving – were lies. I held Jago's hand, and he smiled at me as we walked through the sunlight . . . and then a mirror-image version of me jumped out in front of us. She was wearing a mauve frilly dress and matching ankle socks, and she was holding a shotgun.

'I'm not going to hurt you,' she said to Jago. 'I'm going to kill you!' And she raised the gun to her shoulder and fired – and the bang was so loud it woke me, but not before I had felt, in my dream, Jago's blood raining down on me.

I was weeping in my sleep. I got out of bed, went into the living room, pulled out a chair, stood on it and felt for the emergency stash of sleeping pills I kept on top of the bookcase. I had no dreams with the pills but had to ration them carefully because the doctors did not like prescribing them, and I was too afraid of poisoning myself to order extra supplies from the internet. Lily padded around the apartment shadowing me, miaowing at me to stroke her. I picked her up and held her to me like a baby. I soaked up every morsel of the comfort she gave.

I normally only took half a pill, but because it was already gone 2 a.m. and I was desperate, I swallowed one whole with a gulp of water. I went back to bed and felt the delicious waves of drug-induced calmness creep through my body inch by inch until I drifted into blissful oblivion.

I slept, of course, but I missed the alarm a few hours later or, more likely, switched it off in my sleep.

It was after 9 a.m. when I woke with a headache and a narcotic hangover. I was flustered and my mind was woolly. I checked my diary as I dressed. A school party was due at the museum for a tour starting at 9.15 a.m. I called Misty who said she'd stand in until I arrived. In a hurry, I washed, dressed and put on a little make-up. I went out without eating or drinking anything, not so much as a glass of tapwater.

I waited, hopefully, at the bus stop on Ashley Road for ten minutes, and when no bus came decided to walk, only to be overtaken by a number 13 two minutes later. Worse, I happened upon a road-traffic accident at the Jamaica Street traffic-lights. A white-faced woman was pacing forwards and backwards on the pavement while the young man she had knocked off his motorbike was tended by paramedics. He was wearing leathers but they had been ripped to shreds. There was blood on the tarmac; blood on the broken glass that was scattered around the junction, blood on the shards of glass embedded in the motorcyclist's grazed skin. Both the front of the car and the Yamaha were mangled.

'I didn't see him,' the woman kept saying. 'He came from nowhere. I didn't see him.'

People were ignoring her. They were taking diversions to avoid her.

I remembered Ellen then. I remembered the dazed expression on her face the day I found her on the bench at the back of the church, and I was filled with a rush of shame. She was little more than a child and she was almost certainly in shock that afternoon after she'd watched her father destroy her mother's garden. Why hadn't I acted? Why didn't I at least tell my parents what was going on? I'd convinced myself that things were not as bad as Ellen made out. I told other people that too. But I'd seen Mr Brecht's handiwork with my own eyes. I knew. *I knew even then* and still I did nothing – no, worse than nothing, I sympathized with him. I had dreams of a future with him. I thought I loved him.

At work, things went from bad to worse. Misty asked me to call the Educational Services customer-care team. Normally, messages like this denoted imminent good news: a booking from a partner organization, or perhaps the BBC's Natural History team were requesting access to an exhibit. I returned the call straight away and was told, gently and sympathetically, but nonetheless officially, that the parent of one of the children on a recent *Life on Earth* tour had complained about the scientific explanation of evolution being given greater prominence than the creationist version.

'The thing is,' the woman said, 'the child's mother is a city councillor. She's always banging on about the erosion of good old-fashioned religious morals. This is bound to generate sympathy and media interest.'

'What should I do?' I asked.

'Be careful who you talk to. If anyone identifies themselves to you as a journalist, they have a right to reproduce what you say, so don't say anything. The PR Department is working on an official statement.'

'Oh God.'

'Exactly!' Then: 'Try not to worry,' the woman finished lamely. 'We get this kind of thing all the time.'

I tried to swallow my humiliation but it was a bitter pill. Already, I felt as if I were being publicly criticized. I wondered if journalists were prying into my background. What if they found out about my breakdown? What if they found out about Ellen? What if they did an exposé on me, plastered me across the front pages?

My heart was racing with fear, and by mid-morning I was light-headed and spacey with too much adrenaline in my system.

I didn't stop for lunch in order to make up the time for being late that morning. Instead, I moved a collection of Thecodontosaurus fossils back down into the archive. As I wrote down the description and location of the bones, I was almost certain I was being watched in that underground space, crowded with objects. I sensed movement in the shadows; something seemed to flit between the racks, hiding from me, but observing me. A shadow fluttered in a way that reminded me of bats' wings and, distantly, I heard a noise. It sounded like Ellen's sobbing. I peered around the racks and gazed at the ranks of death masks. I made myself look at them, to convince myself that they weren't moving, and as I did so there was a crash as something fell from one of the shelves behind me.

'Who's there?' I called. 'Who is it?'

But there was no answer, and I could find nothing broken or damaged on the floor.

Shakily, I returned upstairs to the office with fifteen minutes to spare until the afternoon's Women's Institute tour. I'd seen the group assembling in the foyer as I came up from the archive. There were about forty women of all ages in summer suits and cardigans, chattering animatedly, waiting for me. They had been oddly oblivious to the Tyrannosaurus Rex, too involved in their conversations to pay it proper heed. Perhaps they'd all been to the museum before. Perhaps a 42-foot-long monster with teeth the size of carving knives was nothing to these women.

In the office, Misty was standing by the photocopier studiously stapling fact-sheets together. I sat down on a plastic chair by the table. The WI were connected to the Church. Were they expecting me to give equal weight to both versions of evolution? What if the complainant was amongst them? What if she'd come along to take notes? Once the thought was in my mind, it began to expand, twisting and turning, inveigling its way to the front of my brain. I closed my eyes and I saw Ellen's face. It zoomed towards me, and then receded to a pinprick. I was having trouble breathing. I didn't feel right. Thoughts careered through my mind. There was a buzzing in my brain and the floor began to tilt and I realized, too late, what was happening.

'Misty!' I called as I slipped from the chair, tipping it and falling awkwardly against the table leg. I lay with my cheek pressed against the rough material of the carpet, conscious but frozen by paralysis. This had happened before, once or twice in the bad old days preceding the breakdown. I just had to remember to breathe slowly, to control the panic, to breathe in and hold it and . . .

Misty's face appeared in front of mine, her eyes wide open with shock. She shook me, gently, by the shoulders.

'Hannah? *Hannah!* What is it? What's wrong? Oh my God! Rina! Help! It's Hannah – I think she's dead!'

CHAPTER THIRTY-EIGHT

I waited for Mr Brecht to inflict some punishment on Ellen, or to come round to our house to complain to my parents about Jago kissing her at the harbour, but he did nothing.

The longer that nothing happened, the more anxious I became. Mr Brecht would have his revenge, his pound of flesh, I was sure of it. He would make Jago and Ellen suffer for their deceit, but I did not know how, or when, and every day I became a little more afraid. I wondered if I should warn Jago – but how could I without admitting what I had done?

So I did nothing either. I waited.

The first time in the new year when Jago slipped out at night to be with Ellen, I could not sleep until he returned because I was convinced Mr Brecht would have been lying in wait for him . . . but Jago came home, as normal, went back to bed for an hour or so and was his customary semi-comatose self when Mum took in a cup of tea to wake him for work at seven.

After a couple of weeks had elapsed, with no dramas and no repercussions, I began to let down my guard – just a little.

I shouldn't have. Mr Brecht was clever. He was biding his time and waiting for the right moment to get his own back.

One day, early in March, when I was at Thornfield House after school, Mrs Todd came up to Ellen's bedroom with drinks for us and a plate of sandwiches. As she closed the door quietly behind her, she said, 'Ellen, your father thinks somebody has been inside the house. An intruder.'

Ellen immediately blushed. She dropped her head so that her hair fell forward to hide her face. I felt empathetically hot and guilty too.

'Why does he think that?' she asked.

'He's found footsteps in the flowerbeds by the front windows. And somebody has been disturbing things inside the house.'

'I'm sure it's just his imagination, Mrs Todd. You know what he can be like.'

'Your mother's things,' Mrs Todd said. 'He thinks somebody has been going through your mother's things.' She stood beside Ellen, reached out her hand, and touched her cheek gently. 'If it was you, or if you know who it was, tell me now.'

'It wasn't me,' Ellen said. 'And I don't know anything about anybody searching Mama's things. Really I don't.'

As I left to return home, she whispered to me to warn Jago to stay away. I told her, sharply, that I was no fool. I understood the danger.

Jago blanched when I related the evening's events to him.

'They were *your* footprints in the flowerbeds,' I said. 'You should have been more careful. You could have been blamed for everything.'

'It wasn't me inside the house,' said Jago. '*I* haven't been through Mrs Brecht's things. I only ever go to Ellen's bedroom.'

'I know – but if Mr Brecht finds you lurking outside his house in the middle of the night, he'll think it was you, you idiot, especially when your shoes match the footprints in the flowerbeds.'

'Fuck,' Jago said under his breath.

'You can't go round there again, Jago. Not until this is sorted.'

'But how will I see Ellen?'

'You can't. Not for now. Wait and see what happens.'

It wasn't much of a strategy, but it was all we had.

Dad came in the next night, washed his hands under the tap in the kitchen and said, 'Funny peculiar thing happened in the Smuggler's Rest.'

'Oh yes?' said Mum, who was stirring onion gravy at the cooker.

'I was having a quiet pint with Bill Haworth when Mr Brecht came in.'

'There's no law against it.'

'No, but I've not seen him in the Smuggler's before. He reckoned somebody's been snooping round their house.'

'How terrible,' said Mum. 'Did you know about this, Hannah?'

I was sitting at the table doing my homework. I nodded.

'Anyway,' Dad continued, 'he wants to know where he can buy a shotgun.'

I knocked over my mug. Tea spilled all over the old exam papers I'd spread out. I grabbed a kitchen towel and dabbed at the liquid.

Mum looked at me.

'Well, it's fair enough. A man has a right to defend his property,' said Dad.

Most people in Trethene would have agreed with that sentiment, but nobody was prepared for what happened next.

The first we heard of it was when there was a knocking on the door at our house. Mum answered. It was the woman from the village shop with a message for her. Mrs Todd had phoned, apparently 'sounding flustered', and asked Mum to go round to Thornfield House urgently. Mum didn't know what the problem was, but she picked up her coat and left straight away. I wanted to go with her, but she told me to stay put and finish my essay. She went out and returned, several hours later, ashen-faced, and immediately poured herself an Advocaat. I knew something was wrong then because I'd only ever seen my mother drink alcohol at Christmas and funerals. She didn't even like the taste of it. Dad came in from the garden, took one look at Mum, put his hand on the small of her back and steered her into the living room. He shut the door. I crept up to it and listened. Mum was not crying – she never cried – but there was a tremble in her voice.

'You should have seen the blood, Malcolm,' she said. 'I scrubbed the floorboards, poured bleach on them, but the stain wouldn't lift. It's soaked in too deep. It'll be there for ever.'

'What about Tremlett?' Dad asked in a low voice. 'Where is he now?'

'In hospital. They say he's going to lose an eye.'

I put my hand over my mouth.

'Ellen saw it all,' Mum said tremulously. 'Mr Brecht found Tremlett inside the house going through Mrs Brecht's jewellery and hit him on the back of the head with the fire poker. Mrs Todd said he'd have killed him if Ellen hadn't got between the two of them.'

'Good God.'

'The poor girl was covered in Adam's blood, Malcolm. Imagine!'

My mother's voice dropped to a whisper. I picked out the odd word: *broken, smashed, mirror, shattered, upturned, ripped*. Then I heard the click of the back-door latch, and Jago called, 'Hello!'

I stood up and went into the kitchen. He had his back to me and was looking inside the fridge. He turned round with a bottle of milk in one hand and a plate of ham with the mustard pot balanced on its rim in the other.

'Hannah?' he asked. 'What is it?'

I shook my head. I could not speak. I did not know how to begin to tell him.

'Is it Ellen?' he asked.

I nodded yes.

'Christ, what's happened now? What's the Psycho done?'

'It wasn't his fault! He came in and caught Adam Tremlett robbing the place!'

Jago put the bottle and plate down and took a step towards me.

'What about Ellen?'

I stamped my foot in distress. Trixie whimpered and hid as far as she could under the kitchen table.

'Is she all right?' cried Jago. 'Is Ellen OK? Oh fucking hell, what's happened?'

He opened the back door. I grabbed onto his arm, held onto him. 'No! No, Jago!' I screamed. 'Don't go there, stay here!' But he shook me off and went back out into the night.

My father, hearing the commotion and finding me crying in the kitchen, went off after him. They returned soon enough, both of them. Thornfield House was already empty. Mrs Todd, Ellen and her father were gone.

CHAPTER THIRTY-NINE

At the museum, Rina helped me back up on to the chair. 'Take your time,' she said. 'Take it easy.'

'I'm sorry.'

'It's all right. No harm done. I bet you didn't eat any lunch.'

'There wasn't time . . .'

'So you fainted. Is low blood sugar the only problem?'

I shook my head. 'I had a sleeping tablet last night. I think it must still be in my system.'

'Was this prescribed medication?'

I felt ashamed of myself. Worse, I felt dreadfully sick. 'No, it was an old pill from when I had a bad patch before.'

'Oh Hannah!' Rina said. 'What's got into you? You're worrying me.'

'Sorry,' I said again.

She pushed a packet of biscuits towards me and I took them, unwound the packaging and nibbled at the edge of a digestive. My mouth was dry, but the sugar helped with the nausea.

'What happened before?' Rina asked.

'What do you mean?'

'You said the sleeping pill was from a bad patch before.'

'Oh, nothing. Stress.'

'Is that all?'

I nodded.

'It's nothing to be ashamed of,' said Rina. 'Do you know, I'm almost relieved to find out that you're not perfect, Hannah. You seem to sail so smoothly through life.'

I almost laughed. Rina, you do not know the half of it, I thought.

Rina clasped both of my hands in hers and rubbed them. After a few moments, she took a deep breath – which was a signal that she was about to embark on a speech she had prepared earlier.

'I think, Hannah, you should get away from here. Not just a night with your parents – I mean proper getting away. Out of the country.'

'I know. I think you're right.'

'And,' Rina said, her voice rising to denote that this was positive news, 'as luck would have it, an opportunity has arisen which would be absolutely perfect.'

'Oh yes?'

'John is going to Berlin for the Trans-European curatorial conference on Wednesday. I was going to go with him but I've so much on my plate at the moment that I've been looking for a way out. And you're it!'

'Me?'

'Yes. You could take my place. It would be perfect for all three of us. I can get on with my research. You'd be in a different place, away from all this. You'd meet people from the international museum community, and you need to network, Hannah, if you're going to further your career. John will be in his element. You know what he's like, he'll get carried away with enthusiasm for various projects we can't afford and he'll need someone there to point out the im-practicalities, the financial implications, the impossibility of

231

staging anything progressive in our poor old building. Dear Hannah, if I can't be there, Bristol *needs* you to go with him and be the big black cloud of rationality raining on his parade.'

She didn't say it but I knew she was also thinking that a foreign excursion would conveniently keep me out of the way while the councillor's complaint was investigated too.

I smiled at her. 'Don't you think John would mind me tagging along?'

'He said he'd love to take you. Charlotte can't go because of the girls.'

'So you've talked about this already?'

'We're concerned about you.'

'Of course you are. If *you* started seeing dead people in the museum I'd be concerned about you too!'

Rina opened her mouth and closed it again.

'I know you've been talking about me,' I said. 'Everyone's walking on eggshells. Everyone's treating me like I'm losing my mind.'

Rina winced.

'I'm sorry,' I said at once. 'Sorry, Rina, that was rude and unkind.' I covered my face with my hands. 'I'm so sorry.'

Rina stood quietly for a moment and then she said, 'Hannah, we're your friends. We aren't judging you, we're not interfering – we're trying to help.'

'I know.'

'You don't have to cope with this thing, whatever it is you're going through, on your own.'

'Thank you.'

'Oh, don't be grateful. We're being selfish. There will come a time when we'll need you to look after us.'

I thought of John. I thought of Charlotte.

Rina realized she was making progress. 'And, Hannah,

dear, it's not as if we're asking you to do something . . . objectionable.'

'No.'

'I'm sure you mentioned that you'd always wanted to go to Berlin.'

I smiled up at Rina. 'You're right.'

'I'm always right,' she said.

CHAPTER FORTY

Adam Tremlett needed five pints of blood and was in intensive care for three days.

Trethene was buzzing with rumour and speculation. To start with, everybody believed the version of the story that my mother had told my father: that Mr Brecht had found Adam Tremlett inside his house, pocketing Mrs Brecht's jewellery. For Mr Brecht to react as he did, in such circumstances, was understandable.

But then a second version of events began to do the rounds. Someone in the Smuggler's Rest had spoken to Adam Tremlett when Adam was in his cups one evening – as happened quite regularly before he was attacked. Adam said he'd been invited to Thornfield House to quote for some landscaping work on the garden. Mr Brecht wanted to turn a small piece of land into a memorial to his wife. He'd asked Adam not to mention this to anyone, as it was to be a surprise for his daughter, but Adam had been so enthusiastic about the project that, after he'd had more than a few, he'd talked. If this was true, then Pieter Brecht had planned the whole thing. He'd lured Adam into the house, planning to kill him and make it look as if he'd been acting in self-defence. If Ellen hadn't intervened, it would have been cold-blooded murder.

The village was divided in opinion. Sympathies were mixed. At school, people kept asking me what was true and what was lies. I didn't enjoy this kind of attention, and I knew no more than anyone else. All I could do was insist, always, that Mr Brecht was a good man at heart, that he would never do anything terrible unless he had been provoked beyond reason, but I wondered.

If he was capable of plotting to kill Adam, and if he had been prepared to wait so long to take his revenge, what might he still be planning to do to Jago?

I was relieved that Mr Brecht had gone away.

The police went to the hospital every day, and when Adam Tremlett was well enough to be interviewed, he said he didn't remember anything about what had happened in Thornfield House or how he came to be injured. When this news filtered through to our family it promoted a heated discussion. Jago said Mum should go to the police and tell them what she knew, but Mum pointed out that it was all hearsay. She never saw Adam Tremlett, Mr Brecht or Ellen. By the time she arrived at Thornfield House, Adam had been taken away in an ambulance and Ellen and her father were not present. All Mum knew was what Mrs Todd told her as the two women cleaned the front room – which was that Adam Tremlett had broken in and Pieter Brecht had hit him with the poker. She didn't know if Tremlett had threatened Mr Brecht, or lashed out at him. She didn't know if what Mr Brecht had done had been an act of justifiable self-defence. There were plenty of regulars in the Smuggler's Rest willing to testify that Mr Brecht was worried about intruders, and there was a surprising amount of sympathy for him. People were fed up with rising crime rates. They thought it was about time somebody made a stand to protect their own property. Adam was a drunk and a hothead. He wasn't saying anything to defend himself, and now the Brechts and Mrs Todd were gone, there was nobody to corroborate the story one way or the other.

Mum didn't want to be involved any more than she already was.

'It's not our business, Malcolm,' she said to Dad. 'It's water under the bridge now, best let it be.' And Dad nodded and told Jago to stop mithering his mum.

Nobody knew where the Brechts and Mrs Todd had gone. It was as if they'd vanished off the face of the earth. Jago was almost out of his mind with worry for Ellen and frustration at not knowing where she was. I spent hours sitting with him, listening to his conjecture, reassuring him, but I was sick with anxiety too. I couldn't eat and I couldn't sleep.

'Ellen's tougher than you think,' I told Jago. 'She'll be all right.'

'But what if her psycho-dad has really flipped this time?' he asked. 'What if he's murdered Ellen and Mrs Todd and killed himself?'

'He wouldn't do that,' I said. 'He *loves* Ellen! And he's not mad. She makes most of it up.'

Jago looked at me as if I were an idiot. 'Hannah, he nearly killed a man.'

'Not just any old man, Jago. Someone who had broken into his house to steal his dead wife's things!'

Once the thought that Mr Brecht might have killed himself was in my head, though, I could not get rid of it. It was a worm of worry that niggled away in my mind until I was as uneasy as Jago about the whole disappearance. We decided to go to Thornfield House ourselves to see if we could find any clue as to where they might have gone, or what Mr Brecht might have done.

We chose a quiet evening, when both our parents were out. We walked up the lane together, and although I was afraid of returning to that big, looming house, I was happy to be doing something with Jago, just him and me, as it used to be. The house, when we reached it, was in complete darkness. There was no sound from inside, no movement. Still we were careful. I stood guard at the gate, while Jago climbed up to Ellen's bedroom window as he had done so many times before. The window was closed, but not locked. Jago managed to work the lower sash open. He climbed inside, came downstairs, opened the front door and let me in. We pushed the door to, but did not lock it.

'Remember the very first time we came here?' Jago asked in a whisper.

'With the witch?'

'No, not then. The first time we came into the house, when the Brechts were moving in.'

I nodded.

'I think I fell in love with Ellen then,' he said.

'You did not! We were just kids. You didn't even like Ellen at first!'

'I did. I thought about her all the time.'

'Shhh . . .' I said. 'What was that?'

'Nothing. Don't be such a baby.'

'There's someone upstairs!'

'No, there isn't. There can't be.'

I felt sick with nerves.

'Come on,' whispered Jago. He stepped forward and put his hand on the door to the front room.

'No,' I said, remembering what Mum had said about the blood. 'Don't go in there, please, Jago.'

Jago dropped his hand, saying, 'If we look separately, we'll be twice as fast.'

'I'm not going anywhere on my own.'

'All right,' Jago said. 'We'll stay together.'

We were hoping we would find a piece of paper lying around with a forwarding address on it, or a luggage label or something. We went into all the downstairs rooms except the front room, looked on all the tables and counters, and opened the drawers that weren't locked, but we didn't find anything. The rooms were spotlessly neat, just as they always had been. Only there was something cold and nasty about Thornfield House, something that had not been there before. It did not feel right. The atmosphere crawled under my skin and unsettled me. I could not wait to be out of the place.

Still I followed Jago up the stairs, exactly as I had done the first time. We didn't switch on any lights even though dusk was falling outside. The landing was in near-darkness. I wrapped my arms around myself.

'Let's just go, Jago,' I whispered.

'I need to know where Ellen is,' he whispered back. 'I need to know she's OK.'

He went up the narrow stairs to the attic, where Mrs Todd's room used to be. I used the first-floor bathroom, not daring to lock, or even close the door, flushing the lavatory and washing my hands under the basin tap – noticing, with horror, that a clump of bloodied hair was still stuck in the plughole in the bath. I dried my hands on the lemon-coloured towel hung over the rail. The towel was damp.

I dropped it and jumped back.

My instinct was to shut the bathroom door, lock myself inside and scream. But the bathroom was at the back of the house; only woodland lay behind, so nobody would hear me. And I couldn't leave Jago in the house on his own, not when he didn't even know someone else was there.

I opened the door a fraction and looked around. I couldn't see anyone but the landing was dark. I tiptoed forward, one tiny step at a time, my feet sinking into the thick carpet. I could smell fear on myself. At the bottom of the attic steps I paused and looked up.

'Jago!' I called as softly as I could. '*Jago!*'

When I felt the hand on my shoulder, I jumped and gasped.

'Jago!'

'Shhh.' He held a finger to his lips.

'Someone's here!' I whispered.

He nodded and pointed to the door to the room next to Ellen's, the room where Mrs Brecht had died.

In the darkness, we could see a lighter strip beneath the door. The light was faint and flickering, candlelight. As I listened I heard, above the pounding of my heart, the faintest sound of sobbing.

We crept towards the door. We had already walked right past it. Whoever was in that room must surely have heard us coming in. They must have heard the toilet flush. They may even have seen us outside, in the garden, looking up. They might have been following us around the house, hiding in the dark shadows, waiting their opportunity . . .

Jago and I looked at one another.

'What if it's Mr Brecht?' I mouthed.

Jago shook his head. He reached out to the door handle.

'No!' I cried. 'Jago, don't!' But Jago had already turned the handle. He pushed open the door.

The man sitting on the bed was wearing a donkey jacket. He had his back to us. His shoulders were hunched, and his posture was of defeat and despair. His head was wrapped in bandages. As Jago and I stood and stared at him in horror, Adam Tremlett slowly turned. The side of his face that we could see was swollen and bruised; the skin was mottled black and yellow, and ugly black stitches train-tracked across his forehead, disappearing beneath a bandage that crossed his face diagonally, covering his right eye. He slowly raised himself up from the bed to his full height.

'Come on!' said Jago. He grabbed me by the hand and pulled me towards the stairs. We galloped down, not caring how much noise we made, not caring about anything but escaping. At the bottom, Jago threw open the front door and we ran out of the house, out into the lane, and although my lungs felt like they were bursting in the cold night air, we didn't stop running until we were home.

A few days later, we received a postcard showing a picturesque Saxony town. It had a German postmark and was covered with Ellen's trademark small, neat handwriting.

We are with Mrs Todd in Magdeburg staying with my grandparents, she wrote. *They are looking after us very well. My aunt is going to bring us back to Cornwall as soon as Papa is better. I'll see you soon, love Ellen.*

'Is Mr Brecht ill?' I asked my mother.

'I don't know,' she said.

Two more postcards arrived in quick succession, together with a letter from Mrs Todd to my mother. Inside was a cheque, made out to my parents. Mum passed it to Dad. He looked at the cheque, whistled, folded it and put it into his wallet.

'What's that for?' I asked.

'It's my payment for helping Mrs Todd clean up,' said Mum.

'Blood money,' muttered Jago.

'Enough to treat us all,' said Dad. 'We can get that car of yours on the road at last, son!'

Mum said Mrs Todd's letter was reassuring. The Brecht family were rallying round Ellen and her father. They had employed a physician to help Mr Brecht deal with his demons. They had sent a 'generous' sum to Adam Tremlett as compensation and Adam Tremlett had agreed to drop all charges against Mr Brecht. Ellen was recovered from her ordeal. She was 'quiet, but calm'.

'What do you think that actually means?' I asked.

'Never mind Ellen Brecht, you worry about yourself,' Dad said, with a nod towards the kitchen table where my books and papers were laid out. 'You've got the rest of your life to worry about other people.'

Soon enough the A-level exams started. They were an ordeal to me. I felt out of my depth, and helpless. It dawned on me that maybe I was not, after all, clever enough to go to university and become an explorer. But if I didn't do that, what else could I do? Natural History was the only subject that had ever interested me.

The other students congregated at the bus stop and in the cafeteria for post mortems after each exam. I stood at the fringes of the groups, feeling isolated and wishing Ellen were with me so we could, together, laugh at the false agonizing. Ellen had never been able to tolerate any form of hypocrisy.

Now she was no longer in Cornwall, I missed her desperately. Several times I became Ellen in my dreams. I saw her father through her eyes. I walked into the front room and saw him raising the iron poker above his head. I saw Adam Tremlett's blood, black and wet on the floorboards, and I imagined running to get between Mr Brecht and Mr Tremlett and slipping on the blood – and the stickiness of it on my hands, how it would not wipe away.

The nightmares woke me and I lay on my bed, staring at the patterns of the Artex on the ceiling and thinking of Mr Brecht. I told myself he had only been defending what was his. He had a right to defend his property. *Anyone would have done the same.*

I walked up to Thornfield House once or twice a week with the dog, in the evenings, but nobody was ever there. The front door that Jago and I had left wide open the night we broke in had been padlocked, and the ground-floor windows boarded over. The garden was reverting to wilderness but at least some of the flowers had returned, the self-seeding varieties of stocks and poppies and verbena. The lavender bushes that were amongst Mrs Brecht's favourites had grown new heads, along with one or two of the roses.

'What if they decide to stay in Germany?' Jago asked over and over again. 'What if they've left for good and I never see Ellen again?'

We were sitting at the kitchen table, close together, Jago and I. I had one more exam to go and was trying to revise. Jago was tapping his fingers on the table and chewing his lip, both habits irritating me. Trixie lay solid on my feet. I could feel her heartbeat through my socks.

'Jago, can you stop doing that?'

'What?'

'Drumming with your fingers. It's annoying.'

Mum looked over from the sink where she was peeling potatoes.

'Let Hannah get on with her revision, Jago.'

'I don't know how any of you can get on with anything while Ellen's in Germany with the Psycho,' said Jago.

Mum sighed. 'They'll be back at the end of the month,' she said, without looking up. 'Mr Brecht's better now, by all accounts. His sister's coming back with them, to keep an eye on things.'

'How do you know?'

'Mrs Todd sent another letter,' said Mum. 'She asked me to open up the house.'

CHAPTER FORTY-ONE

It was Rina's birthday so we all went to the Hope and Anchor after work, as was the tradition. Most of us were crowded round a couple of tables in the small, steeply terraced garden, standing close together drinking cider and dipping into communal packets of crisps that had been torn open and left on the tables. I had been cornered by Betty Tralisk, an earnest young historian who was writing a history of the Raja Ram Mohun Roy, the so-called Father of Modern India who, due to an incongruous twist of fate and an ill-timed bout of meningitis, had died in Bristol and was buried in the city's Arnos Vale Cemetery. Betty wanted to stage an exhibition at the museum in honour of the Raja, and suggested it could be financed via the education budget. She wanted my opinion on this. I was finding it hard to concentrate. I sipped my cider and nodded in the appropriate places but my mind was elsewhere. I noticed Betty staring at me in a way which suggested she was waiting for a response.

'Yes,' I ventured tentatively. 'I absolutely agree.'

'Thank you,' said Betty. 'So you'll raise the matter with the trustees?'

I nodded, and apropos of nothing, John caught my eye

across the garden and smiled. Charlotte was standing close to him, laughing at something someone had said to her. Her head was tipped back so I could see her face in profile, the line of her throat silhouetted against the bright sky behind her.

So she hadn't said anything to John yet. She hadn't told the truth. She hadn't left him. She was chronically unfaithful – she didn't have a kind word to say about her husband, she was planning to leave him – and yet she was happy to stand behind him in the pub garden and act the part of the good wife. John still had no idea what she was really like.

I couldn't look at Charlotte. I had to turn away.

Somebody tapped my shoulder. I turned. It was Rina.

'Cheers!' she said, raising her glass.

Dutifully I chinked with her. 'Happy birthday!'

'Now then,' she said, 'I meant to tell you earlier but it slipped my mind. After you'd gone home yesterday you had a visitor. A nice woman – dreadlocks, multi-coloured clothes. Pierced lip. You were supposed to meet her for lunch.'

'Julia! Oh Rina, I completely forgot!'

'That was evident. She was very charming about it.'

'Did you . . .' I took a deep breath. 'Did you tell her what had happened?'

'Some of it. She seemed concerned.'

'Shit. Sorry, Rina, but shit.' I couldn't believe the arrangement had slipped my mind, and was furious with myself. I had been looking forward to meeting Julia. I needed to talk to her, and I had completely forgotten what we had agreed. Confusion was one of the four main symptoms of psychosis, along with hallucination, delusion and lack of insight. Oh well done, Hannah, I thought. That's three of the four boxes ticked. Or maybe even a full house.

I picked the phone out of my bag. It was switched off. I couldn't remember when I'd switched it off, but when I turned it on, it beeped as several new messages and missed-call alerts came in, one after the other, most from Julia. I felt helpless. I felt useless. I was adrift.

There was no doubt in my mind now, I was losing my grip. I was usually so organized. My colleagues teased me all the time about my obsessive punctuality, my insistence on ordering and cataloguing and making sure everything was noted and in its place and done in the right way, at the right time. Now I couldn't even remember a simple meeting.

Before I had a chance to text Julia an apology, I felt a gentle hand on my arm.

It was Charlotte.

'Hello, Hannah,' she said.

'Oh hi,' I replied, as coldly as possible.

She held up a glass. 'I bought you a drink. Misty said you're a white-wine lady.'

'Actually I'm drinking cider.'

'Oh.' She put the wine glass on the table. 'You could always have it later,' she said.

I thought I would rather tip it into the flowerbed than drink it.

Charlotte played with her hair and fidgeted for a moment. There was a sheen of sweat between her breasts and she was wearing shiny, tangerine-coloured false nails. For the thousandth time I couldn't believe that somebody like John had chosen to marry somebody like Charlotte and not somebody like me. I could have made him happy. I would have done anything to make him happy – and yet here I was again, incapable of anything apart from waiting on the sidelines to pick up the pieces when his life fell apart.

'Is there something else, Charlotte?' I asked rudely. 'Only there are people here I'd like to talk to.'

Charlotte sighed. 'Yes, there is. God, this is awkward. I don't know how to say this, but Hannah, the other day, in the pasty shop . . .'

'I haven't said anything to John.'

'I know, thank you. I just . . . Well, he . . . He told me you were going to Berlin together. To this conference.'

'Yes.'

'Hannah, I know what you must think of me – only please don't say anything about me to John while you're in Berlin.'

'John's my friend, Charlotte. I respect him.'

'I know you do, and that's why I'm asking you not to say anything.'

'Everyone else seems to know what you're up to. Don't you think he has a right to know?'

'He does, yes, only I'm asking you to let me talk to him. It will be better coming from me.'

'But you won't say anything!'

'I will when the time is right.'

'When will the time be right, Charlotte? When you win the lottery and can manage without John's money? Or when you find someone richer than him to seduce?' I was angry, but I kept my voice low.

Charlotte frowned. She seemed upset but I was certain she was play-acting.

'It's just . . .' She looked up at the sky. She was wringing her pretty little hands with those garish nails. 'I know what these conferences are like, Hannah, I've been to enough of them. They're terribly boring, full of pretentious old duffers – not you, of course – and the temptation, always, is to drink too much because there's nothing else to do and— Oh please, Hannah, please don't say anything to John. I don't want him to hear this second hand. It has to come from me and—'

She stopped in mid-flow and smiled frantically at some-body behind me. I turned, and it was John. He squeezed past me, and stood beside Charlotte. I saw the fingers of his hand reach out and take hold of hers. Charlotte smiled at me helplessly. John raised his wife's hand to his lips, and kissed it. Charlotte looked close to tears. I had no sympathy.

'Are you talking about Berlin?' he asked. 'Charlotte's so pleased you're coming with me, Hannah. It lets her off the hook.'

Charlotte nodded miserably.

'But it won't all be work,' John continued. 'We'll be put up in rooms in a mediocre hotel, not in the city centre, granted, but we'll have coffee-making facilities and a trouser press, all mod cons. We'll have to sit through a couple of boring presentations and make small talk with a lot of intellectuals – although really you don't even have to do that. I could be the official face of the Brunel Memorial Museum and you could do exactly what you wanted. Stay in bed, watch movies, drink gin . . .'

I could not smile.

'Don't you mind your husband going away with another woman?' I asked Charlotte pointedly. 'Won't you be lonely?'

Charlotte swallowed. Her face was rigid with tension. 'I'm used to it,' she said. 'I'll keep myself busy.'

'What's not to like, Hannah?' asked John. He was a little drunk. He waved his glass around with enthusiasm. 'This trip is basically a free, short cultural break with a stimulating talk on the dialectical relationship between curators and spectators thrown in.'

'But—'

'Good. Anyway, I must circulate. My beautiful wife and I are off to talk to Misty and her boyfriend about popular culture and street art. I'll see you later.'

As he moved on, Charlotte turned to look at me over her shoulder. 'Thank you,' she said. She bit her lip. 'I'm sorry . . .' she began, but I turned away before she could finish the sentence.

CHAPTER FORTY-TWO

My last A-level exam was the worst. I struggled to fill the allotted white space, finished forty-five minutes before the end and sat at my desk, doodling. When the invigilator finally said, 'Put down your pens!' I couldn't wait to escape. I picked up my bag, went into the cloakroom to wash my hands and, while I was there, overheard a conversation between two of my classmates that made me realize I'd completely misinterpreted one of the questions. The last little part of me that was holding on to the hope that I might secure a place at a good university crumpled up and died.

Mired in self-pity, I wandered up the High Street, went into Bottoms Up and bought a four-pack of cider and a quarter-bottle of gin. I caught the bus as usual, but didn't get off at the Trethene junction, riding on past the petrol garage until I was the only passenger left. I walked back to the church, the carrier bag of alcohol weighing heavy on my arm, and went through the churchyard and out of the gate on the other side, to sit on the bench beside the spot where Ellen and Jago first made love. Once sat down, I opened the first can of cider.

As the sun set, I lay on the bench with my knees hooked over the armrest, watching the sky change colour, the undersides of the clouds illuminated and changing from white to yellow to apricot, orange, gold, pink and scarlet before the sky eventually faded to nothing. I sat up then and watched the night roll in over the sea, and I saw the cows grazing, swishing their tails, their shadows growing longer and longer until they merged with the hedge shadows and all the shadows were one, and a tractor, in the distance, made lines in a crop-field as the day died away. I felt a great emotional affinity with all of life, and at the same time was as lonely as the moon. I emptied all four cans of cider, weed behind a bush, which was difficult because my balance wasn't very good, had a bout of hiccups, which I managed to stop by knocking back several mouthfuls of neat gin, and then fell asleep on the bench, with my head cushioned by my bag.

I was woken, some time later, by Jago. He had been driving round the lanes in the Escort, which had finally been restored thanks to Mr Brecht's money, looking for me. He helped me up off the bench, held my hair out of my face as I threw up into the hedgerow, and put his arm around me to stop me staggering and falling as we walked back through the churchyard to the lane where the car was parked.

'I really, really love you,' I told him, holding onto his waist, as we stumbled together between the graves. The night was Cornwall-black, pitch-black, dark as a wrecker's soul.

'Thanks, Spanner,' Jago said.

'But I really *really* don't want you to keep sneaking around Thornfield House when Ellen comes back because it's far too dangerous.'

This struck me as a deep and meaningful statement and one that demonstrated what a caring and thoughtful person I was. I began to cry the loud, self-pitying sobs of the young and inebriated.

'Shut up,' said Jago. 'And there won't be any more

sneaking around. I'm going to take Ellen away. We're going to America.'

'America!' I repeated. My head was too thick with drink to take this in.

Back at number 8, Mum took one look at me and said, 'We'd better sort you out before your father gets back or you really will be in trouble. Go and run her a bath, Jago.'

She sat me down at the kitchen table, put a blanket around my shoulders, and made me drink some cold water. I was sick again. There was a pain inside my skull as if someone was hammering in my brain.

'What on earth brought this on?' Mum asked.

'She messed up her exams,' said Jago. 'She's worried she won't get into university.'

'Is that all? That's not worth getting all het up about, Hannah.'

I nodded miserably.

'I never went to university, nor did your father, and we've done all right for ourselves.'

I sniffed. I felt the walls of the cottage close in around me until I could hardly breathe. I was like Alice in Wonderland after she'd drunk the growing potion.

'But I want to be an explorer,' I said. 'And you have to go to university to be an explorer, it's the only way.'

'There's always another way,' said Mum. 'You could open a shop or write a book. Or you could volunteer to go and work on a fossil dig.'

I looked at her. 'How do you know about fossil digs?'

'Someone mentioned it at church. Their grandson's spending a gap year somewhere – South America, I think – helping get the dinosaur bones out of a tar pit or something.'

I sat up a little straighter.

Mum smoothed my hair. 'Although I don't want you doing that, Hannah. I didn't carry you for nine months and

250

raise you all these years for you to go off to the other side of the world.'

I snuggled into her.

'There must be places closer to home,' Mum said. 'Do they have fossils in England?'

'Mmm.' I nodded. 'Charmouth.'

'Charmouth,' Mum repeated. 'Charmouth wouldn't be so bad.'

CHAPTER FORTY-THREE

The Berlin curatorial conference partner hotel was in Schönhauser Strasse, a pretty, five-storey building that looked, to me, exactly as a German hotel should look – all shutters and windowboxes, tall windows and steep gable-ends. The taxi John and I had caught at Tegel airport dropped us on the pavement outside, and we went through a revolving door into a small, carpeted foyer. The porter took our bags while John checked us in, and then we followed the porter up a narrow staircase to the second floor. Our rooms both faced the street, but were at opposite ends of the corridor.

'You wanted rooms together?' asked the porter.

'No, we didn't,' I said quickly.

I had found the experience of travelling with John a little awkward. He had been polite and attentive, letting me take the window seat on the plane, lifting my bag from the carousel and so on. He was the perfect companion, but every time he mentioned Charlotte or his daughters or even his plans for the future, the weight of the truth I was hiding from him grew a little heavier on my shoulders. I had been quiet during our journey and resolved to spend as little time alone with John as possible. I was looking forward to being at the conference, where the conversation would be more general, less specific.

There was to be a black-tie gala Willkommen dinner for attendees that evening, at the Haus der Kulturen der Welt venue in the city centre. John and I agreed to meet in the hotel bar at 6.30 p.m., and we parted to go into our separate rooms. Mine was exactly as I had expected it to be – small, clean, impersonal, but pleasant and comfortable. I enjoyed a small frisson of pleasure from being in a different city, doing something different, being somewhere else. I opened the window wide and looked out. The street below was busy with traffic and pedestrians. I liked looking at the different signage, the German words with their Gothic fonts, and inhaling the spicy, mouth-watering smells of Bratwurst, onions and sweet fried pastries rising up from the pavement vendors. Even the texture of the air felt different.

My phone beeped to alert me to a text. It was from Rina. *Lily-cat is fine. Don't work too hard.*

I bathed, unpacked my small case, and sat on the bed while I read through the conference itinerary. A couple of the lectures sounded interesting and I wrote down their times and venues. On the little desk beneath the window was a faux-leather folder full of leaflets and tourist information about things to do and see in Berlin. I picked it up and read about the city bus tours, a brief history of the Brandenburg Gate, Schloss Charlottenburg and Potsdamer Platz. I opened out a small, folded map and laid it on the desk, scanning the names of the bigger cities nearby: Szczecin, Hamburg, Hannover, Leipzig, writing down places I'd particularly like to visit. Then I saw it: *Magdeburg.*

Just one word, and yet it brought so many memories back to me. Magdeburg, the seat of the Brecht family home. Magdeburg was where Ellen had been born, where she had lived for the first ten years of her life, where Mrs Todd had taken her to recuperate after her father had tried to kill

Adam Tremlett. Magdeburg was where the family had rallied round Ellen. It was where nobody noticed quite how badly she had been damaged by what she had witnessed.

With my fingernail, I traced the line of the A2 road that linked the two cities of Berlin and Magdeburg. It wasn't that far away. I picked up the map, folded it, and tucked it into my handbag. Then I opened the notebook that I'd bought specifically for the purpose of making notes about this trip, so I wouldn't forget anything that might be useful in the future. I stared at the blank page. I wrote the word *Magdeburg* and underlined it. Then, although it was whimsical and silly, I wrote *Ellen Brecht* in large, ornate letters, and I drew a curly, ornamental border around the letters, a border full of hearts and flowers.

Ellen always liked to be the centre of attention.

After that I changed into the only cocktail dress I owned. I'd bought it for the museum's 150th anniversary the previous year. It was dusty pink, and seemed a little loose on me now. I shifted it over my shoulders until it fell straight. It was a demure dress by the standards of somebody like Charlotte, but I felt awkward in it. I was not used to having bare shoulders. I preferred to be more hidden. It was strange how I, who had been such a podgy child, had grown into such a bony, angular adult. Even though I was alone in the room, I slipped a cardigan over my shoulders and immediately felt more covered and comfortable. I stood in front of the mirror to put on lipstick, eyeliner, mascara, fastened my hair with a clip, slipped into my only pair of heels and, hoping I looked presentable but not flashy, went down the stairs.

John was already in the bar, but I didn't recognize him at first.

I scanned the room: it was long and narrow, tastefully decorated in classic shades of maroon and gold. There were a few couples, a group of businessmen, a beautiful girl sitting on her own, and an attractive, long-legged man in evening dress sitting at the bar drinking beer and reading a newspaper. The man turned and smiled at me. I looked away, and then looked back.

'John?'

He slipped off the stool, took my hand, leaned over to kiss my cheek.

'I didn't recognize you without your glasses,' I said. 'You look so . . .'

'Handsome?'

'Tidy. I was going to say tidy. It's not just the glasses . . .'

John shrugged. 'Yeah, well, I thought I'd better have a shave.'

'The clothes. You look . . . Well, it suits you.'

'Thank you,' said John.

I allowed him to help me up onto the neighbouring stool. I was unsettled and hot. I wished I'd made a little more effort with my appearance. I wanted to keep looking at him, to work out why he seemed so very different this evening, but I didn't want him to notice me looking. I imagined, for a moment, how he must have been as a student, young and tall and rangy. He would have had something of the film star about him. No wonder Charlotte had been attracted to him. No wonder she had chosen him. I only wished I had known him then. I wished he'd met me before he met Charlotte. It was all such a mess, so wrong, and so unfair. He should have been with me.

I pulled myself together.

'I don't think I've ever seen you in a shirt that's been ironed before,' I said. 'No offence.'

He laughed. 'None taken. I don't think I've ever seen you in a dress before, either. You look very nice, Hannah. I ordered you a kir royale – presumptuous, I know. I hope that's OK.'

'It is.' I liked kir royale very much, but would never have thought of ordering one myself.

'So have you decided what you'd like to do in the morning?' John asked.

I took a sip of my drink. 'I'd like to go to Magdeburg.'

John raised his eyebrows.

'A friend of mine – Ellen, the one who died – she lived there for a while. I didn't realize how close it was to Berlin.'

'It's not far. Magdeburg is still a big place, though.'

'I know. But they – Ellen's family – lived in a grand house overlooking the river. It was called Schloss Marien. I'm sure it can't be that hard to find. I'd just like to see it. We're so close . . .'

'It would be a shame not to,' John agreed. 'How are you going to get there?'

'I don't know. I haven't worked that out yet.'

John ate a pretzel from a little glass bowl on top of the bar and checked his watch.

'My laptop's in my room. We could look the Schloss up when we get back, see if there's a bus or something.'

'That'd be brilliant.'

John's phone beeped then. He took it out of his pocket, looked at the screen, and smiled. He turned the phone towards me. Charlotte had sent a photograph of their two little daughters in their pyjamas, waving into the screen. The message was: *Night night Daddy.*

'Sweet,' I said.

'Sorry.' John put the phone back in his pocket. 'Before I had kids of my own I couldn't stand people who were always going on about theirs. Charlotte knew I'd be thinking about them.'

'They're pretty girls,' I said, but there was a feeling like lead in my stomach.

We finished our drinks and went outside to find a taxi to

take us to the Haus der Kulturen der Welt. The street was still busy. There were two lanes of traffic travelling in each direction, buses, cars and taxis mostly, their engines making a thunderous noise, and horns sounding every now and then. The air retained the day's warmth but I held the cardigan tight over my shoulders and felt self-conscious in my make-up and heels. The heads of people in the passing cars were turning to stare at John and me in our formal clothes. John kept stepping out into the road, trying to hail a taxi. They were all busy and rushed by in a wind of exhaust fumes.

I looked down at my feet, which seemed oddly naked in the strappy little shoes. I remembered how I used to sit on Ellen's bed, leaning back on my hands, while Ellen held my foot on her lap and glossed the nails for me, how Ellen's dark hair fell down over her face, how she tucked it behind her ears. I remembered Ellen's gentleness, her crossed legs, her concentration as she slowly painted a line down each nail, the chill of the brush on each of my toes in turn and the sweet, chemical smell of the polish. I felt a shiver of sorrow.

I looked up, across the busy street, and I saw her.

For the third time in as many weeks, I saw Ellen.

CHAPTER FORTY-FOUR

Dad came into the kitchen and said, 'The Brechts are back. Just saw Ellen getting out of a cab.'

I put down the pasty I was eating and looked up at him.

'Ellen's back?'

'Yep.'

'Is her father there?'

'He stayed in the taxi.'

I ignored Trixie's hopeful face, put on my trainers, grabbed my bike and cycled up the lane to Thornfield House. The flowers that had bloomed in the garden while the Brechts were away were still attached to their stems. Ellen's bedroom window was open, and Nirvana was blasting out. It was the first time I had ever heard any music that was not classical or piano coming from the house. I dropped the bike on the drive, scooped up a handful of gravel and threw it at the window. Ellen's head appeared. She waved, disappeared, and emerged seconds later through the front door, throwing herself at me. We swung round together, hugging and kissing. We were both laughing. I was genuinely happy to see her, from the bottom of my heart. I felt as if I had come home, as much as she.

As we embraced, I remembered how Ellen was, the

solidity of her and the fresh apple smell of her, the slipperiness of her hair against my cheek. My love for her was pure, for once untainted by jealousy and resentment. And relief rushed through my veins, because she was fine, Ellen seemed perfectly fine. I hadn't seen her looking so happy and healthy and untroubled for years – not since before her mother died. Nothing terrible had happened to her; she had not been hurt, she was going to be all right. I was thinking, This is the beginning of the future. Everything will be good from now on. And at exactly the same moment as I thought those things, a rush of fear hurtled through my bloodstream, finding every tiny capillary, tingling my fingertips, making my hair stand on end. It was a premonition, like the three seagulls overhead, but of what, I did not know.

'Is your father out? Are you on your own?' I asked, stepping back and looping my arm through Ellen's. 'Are things better? Are you really OK?'

Ellen was still smiling. She shook her head to toss her hair back over her shoulders. It was longer than it had been the last time I saw her, and glossier. She was wearing a jade bracelet and new clothes, a short skirt and a cotton shirt with a vest underneath. Her skin looked healthier, her cheeks were fuller, she had put on weight and she looked far better for it.

'Everything is fine,' she said. 'I've been treated like a princess by my grandparents and Papa's had lots of therapy.' She sucked in her cheeks, crossed her eyes and spun a forefinger at her temple. 'My Tante Karla has come back with us to keep an eye on him. She says she'll keep him in line! And you're here and they're out – so I'm free to do as I please! What shall we do? Shall we go to the beach?'

'Won't your father mind?'

'He and Karla have taken the taxi on into town to buy groceries. Give me two seconds . . .'

'Don't go back inside! What if your father—'

'It'll be fine.'

Ellen ran indoors and I stepped backwards, closer to the wall, into the shadows cast by the roses, in full bloom now, growing up the trellis. The garden was full of flowers. It was overgrown and wild, but it looked like a normal garden again. I gnawed my thumbnail. Two white butterflies danced past and a robin hopped around on a patch of formerly manicured lawn that was now sending up long grassy spikes. I watched a spider slowly sink down a thread suspended from the highest part of the porch over the door. It was small and brown, purposeful. When it reached a point about four feet below the porch roof, it stopped and spun on its thread.

I heard a car engine on the road; it slowed as it approached Thornfield House.

I pressed myself closer against the wall, but the car sped up again and drove by.

Ellen returned with a bag slung over one shoulder. She pulled the door gently shut behind her. 'Come on,' she said, grabbing my arm. 'Let's go.'

'What were you doing? You were ages.'

'I had to tell Mrs Todd I was going out,' Ellen said happily. 'She's in such a tizz about Tante Karla being here she said she was glad I was spending some time with you.'

'I can't imagine Mrs Todd in a tizz.'

'She doesn't want my aunt in her kitchen. She's banging stuff around.' Ellen frowned and pursed her lips, and did such a wickedly accurate impression of Mrs Todd angrily rearranging her implements that it reminded me how much fun she used to be.

'I'm so glad you're back,' I said, swinging on Ellen's arm.

'So am I!'

We walked through the churchyard and out into the fields. It was a warm, oppressive day, and as we crossed a field full of cornflowers and poppies, Ellen said she wanted to rest.

'Are you all right?' I asked.

'Just tired.'

We dropped into the long, feathery grass. Myriad small butterflies and moths were busy about us. Ellen took a plastic bottle out of her bag and offered me a drink. I stripped seeds from different kinds of grass, while she lay on her back for a few moments, and closed her eyes. The skin on her face had gone very pale. I thought it must be the sunlight bleaching it. I brushed a fly off her cheek. She was wearing new studs in her ears. Her mother's necklace was tucked beneath the neck of her shirt. Her legs and arms were tanned; only her face was pale.

'It's nice to lie here,' she said sleepily, covering her face with her arms. 'It's a different kind of grass in Germany. It's greener and not so soft.'

'You had grass-homesickness,' I said.

She laughed and then she yawned. She stretched her arms above her head.

'How's Jago?'

'He's fine. He's out fishing.'

'Has he missed me?'

'No.'

Ellen opened her eyes wide.

'Of course he has.' I sprinkled seed into the little cups made by Ellen's clavicles. 'We both have. We missed you like anything. He'll be over the moon that you're back.'

Ellen smiled. She pushed herself to her feet, brushed away the grass seeds and then reached out her hands to pull me up.

'Come on,' she said. 'Our beach is waiting for us.'

The coastal path was busy with walkers in their boots, their maps strung in plastic around their necks, their dogs and canvas hats. Ellen and I waited patiently for the opportunity to climb the fence. She sat down on the bank, amongst the torn-petalled pale purple knapweed, and put her head on her knees while we were waiting.

'You OK?' I asked again, and Ellen said she was fine.

'It's just that the flight and the long car journey back from London drained me of my energy,' she said. 'And I've got so fat. *Oma* kept giving me food whether I wanted it or not. I need some Cornish sea air to make me feel like myself again.'

Eventually we made it down to the beach. Ellen was astounded by the supplies that I had, under Jago's instruction, stashed in the cave.

'What's all that?' she asked.

I shrugged with self-deprecatory pride. 'A little tent,' I said. 'A sleeping bag. Blankets. A primus stove. Candles. Water. Food. So if ever you need to get away, you can.'

Ellen jumped on me, wrapped her arms around my shoulders and her legs around my waist, and she held on to me, shouting, 'You did this for me?'

And I yelled back: 'It's all for you, Ellen, all of it!'

That day, the sea was green and frilly at the edges, little splashy waves frothing as they broke over the pebbles like egg-white in a frying pan. We took off our shoes and paddled. I stopped when the water reached my ankles, giving my feet time to adjust to the cold. Ellen walked past me, she walked until the hem of her skirt was darkened by the water soaking into it, and then she stood, looking out towards the horizon. I felt a clutch of something inside me, something nasty. It was the same fear I'd felt before, the anticipation of trouble. I shook the feeling away, swung my leg and kicked up a spray of water, soaking Ellen's back. She raised her hands to the side of her head in a parody of an old-fashioned screen star, squealed and turned, kicking water back at me. Within seconds we were having a proper water-fight. We were laughing and shouting, messing around, having fun.

When we were both as wet as it was possible to be, we went back onto the sand, stripped down to our underwear and laid our clothes out on the rocks to dry. Ellen's make-up had run. She knelt, with her hands in her lap, holding her face up to me like a child while I wiped away her mascara with a corner of my T-shirt. Her skin shimmered in the sun. It was smooth, covered in a million tiny goose pimples. Tiny white salt crystals were forming at the bases of the little hairs on her arms.

'Why is your face so pale when your legs and arms are so brown?' I asked, and Ellen shrugged and said, '*Oma* made me wear a straw hat to save my complexion.'

Something was different about Ellen. I couldn't work out what it was. I had expected her to have been changed by the trauma she'd witnessed, but if anything, she was calmer now. She was less nervy, more passive. The time with her family had, I reasoned, done her the world of good.

We lay together, dozing, until the sun dropped below the cliff-line, shadows were creeping over the sand and the sky was lined with pink fish-scale clouds.

'Won't your father be worried about you?' I asked Ellen.

'He can't make a fuss. Not in front of Tante Karla.' Ellen propped herself on one elbow, pulled a comedy face and wagged her finger. In the voice of an admonishing woman, she said, '*Um Gottes willen, Pieter, das Mädchen ist jetzt fast erwachsen!*'

I giggled. 'What does that mean?'

' "The girl is practically an adult, stop treating her like a child!" My aunt's really nice,' Ellen said, lying down again. 'In Germany, we walked in the gardens and fed the ducks in the pond, and when it was raining we listened to the Rolling Stones and had a *Kaffeeklatsch* – that's coffee and cake and chat, just for female people. She made me tell her everything.'

'Everything?'

'Well, almost everything. I didn't tell her about Jago. Well, I did – I mean, I told her there was someone I liked but not his name or any more than that. I didn't tell her, you know, that . . '

I nodded.

'She made Papa see sense. She sorted him out. She won't put up with his moods. As long as she stays with us, every-thing's going to be fine,' said Ellen. 'I'll probably have to play the piano tonight, because she loves listening to it, but even that's OK because she likes happy stuff. She's given me some new music to learn. She told Papa that listening to requiems and dirges all the time was counter-productive and not healthy for a young woman of my age.'

'She sounds really nice.'

'She is. You'll have to come and meet her.'

When the sun was altogether gone, we dressed in our damp clothes, cold now against our skin that was prickly with sunburn, climbed the tunnel steps and headed back to Trethene. It was too dark to go across the fields and the lanes were busy with holiday traffic. We kept having to press our-selves against hedges to make way for big, shiny cars weighed down with bicycle racks, surfboards and roof carriers. Lobster-faced children stared at us through the windows. The car park outside the pub was full and the garden benches were packed. The waiting staff scuttled amongst the tables with trays of condiments and soiled plates. At Thornfield House, the garden lights had been switched on for the first time since Anne Brecht died. A tall, short-haired woman wearing sandals and spectacles was watering the plants in the front garden, which already looked a little tidier than before.

'Tante Karla – we're back!' Ellen called.

'Hello, Ellen,' the woman said warmly. 'And you must

be Hannah. Let me come and give you kisses!'

I laughed and allowed myself to be embraced.

'You are a beauty,' she proclaimed, holding me at arm's length in order to take a good look at me. 'Isn't she beautiful, Ellen? *Ja?*'

Ellen grinned and toed the gravel on the drive.

Over Karla's shoulder, I could see Mrs Todd, standing beyond the open door, just inside the hallway of Thornfield House. She was in the shadows, watching us.

Aunt Karla told Ellen to go and shower and make herself presentable for dinner. Ellen hugged me and whispered, 'Tell Jago I can't see him tonight, but I'll try and come down to Polrack tomorrow or the day after. Tell him not to come here until he's heard from me.'

'All right.'

'Thank you.' Ellen gave me another hug. 'You're my best friend, Hannah,' she said. She kissed my cheek. 'I'll always love you.'

CHAPTER FORTY-FIVE

And she was there – Ellen was there – in the centre of Berlin, standing on the other side of the street, talking to someone. She wasn't looking at me, but there was no doubt in my mind that it was her, wearing a dark-coloured summer dress and dark shoes, with sunglasses holding back her hair.

Pedestrians on the opposite pavement blocked my view for a moment. I blinked and held my breath as the crowds drifted away, but Ellen was still there. She had turned her back to me and was looking in a shop window.

This did not feel like a hallucination. This felt real. Tricks of the mind didn't look at shop displays. They didn't!

I looked from John, to the road, and back again.

The traffic was roaring, hurtling towards me, but there was a break behind it where the next tranche of vehicles had been stopped at the lights. I waited for the break, then, clutching my cardigan and my bag, I took a deep breath, stepped off the kerb and began to run.

I heard John's shout behind me, but I didn't stop to look back. It was difficult running in my high heels, and I had to stop to take them off. By the time I'd done that, the lights had changed. The traffic was coming again, bearing down on me. I made a dash for the centre of the road, where there was a small pedestrian island. I heard the horns blaring – I'd looked the wrong way. There was a third stream of traffic, some kind of contraflow. I was confused. I couldn't tell which direction the cars were coming from. I stood still for a moment, my head spinning, trying to work out which was the safe way to run, when I felt myself pulled clear, into the island in the centre of the carriageway. All around me, horns bleeped. I heard angry shouting.

'For fuck's sake!' said John, holding tightly onto me, restraining me by the arms. 'What are you doing, Hannah? Are you trying to get yourself killed?'

I ignored him and looked back across the road. Ellen was gone.

He was still ranting.

'You just tried to run across four lanes of traffic! You stopped in the middle of the bloody carriageway to take off your shoes! What were you thinking, Hannah? Are you mad?'

'I didn't – I—' I looked over his shoulder. Where had she gone?

'I need to get over there,' I said.

'Where? Why?'

I turned to look at John. His shirt had come untucked from his trousers and his bow tie had unknotted itself; the dash across the road had messed up his hair. The most striking thing about him was the concern in his eyes. I looked down.

'I saw her again.'

'Who, Hannah? Who did you see?'

I picked my cardigan up off the ground. It was dusty and one cuff was torn. My feet were dirty too.

'I saw my friend Ellen,' I said. 'Ellen Brecht.'

CHAPTER FORTY-SIX

Tante Karla treated her brother, Pieter, Ellen's father, to a trip to the Colston Hall in Bristol to see *Fidelio*, which was her favourite opera. They were due to return in the early hours. Mrs Todd stayed behind in Thornfield House with Ellen. The housekeeper was getting on by then, and the events of the past weeks had exhausted her. When Ellen said she was going out for a few hours, Mrs Todd didn't even ask where she was going.

'Be back before your father,' was all she said, and then she probably looked forward to a few hours' peace and quiet on her own with her knitting and the radio.

Jago met Ellen at the top of the lane. It was the first time they'd been alone together since Ellen returned from Germany. I don't know what happened that night, but I have imagined how it must have been for them. When Jago saw her that night, emotion rose in him like the sun rising in the sky. She smiled at him, shyly. He wanted to run to her. He wanted to envelop her and be next to her, with her, for ever. In that moment, when he saw Ellen in her dark green miniskirt, her mother's bracelets jangling at her wrists, and her arms long and smooth and brown, Jago decided to marry her. As soon as possible, as soon as she was eighteen, as soon

as they could get away from her father. He didn't say this to
Ellen because he didn't want to overwhelm her. He had lived
long enough with his uncle and aunt to learn that too much
emotion can be a frightening thing.

First they went to the pub – the big one, the Trethene
Arms – where nobody noticed them amongst the crowds of
tourists. Jago drank cider and Ellen sipped iced lemonade,
sucked the flesh from the slice of lemon and wrinkled her
nose at the bitterness. Jago told her that he'd been for an
interview with a marine-engineering company that had
branches in America. He said he was thinking of New York.
If he could get a work permit, they could go there, together.
The work was hard, but the money was good. They'd be able
to rent an apartment, nothing fancy, but it would be a start.
He promised Ellen that whatever part of her inheritance they
had to spend to set themselves up, he would pay back. That
money would be hers.

Ellen said, 'It's not my money, Jago. It's ours. Whatever we
do, we do it together.' She sipped her drink, then went on,
'That money will pay for our freedom. That's what my
grandmother wanted.'

'What about your father?' Jago asked, and Ellen shrugged.

'What about him? What can he do? There's no way he can
keep the inheritance from me. It's mine. And it'll come to me
in less than eight weeks.'

When they had finished their drinks, Jago and Ellen
walked back down the lane, across the churchyard, and sat
on the bench behind the wall. It was June, close to the
solstice, and there was still a little light in the sky at 10 p.m.
Jago was tongue-tied: there was so much he wanted to say to
Ellen. He did not have the words to tell her how he felt about
her, how strongly he had missed her, how incomplete he felt
without her. She, lost in her own thoughts, seemed, to him,
uncharacteristically remote. He mirrored her quietness.

Close as they were, and despite their mutual affection, neither had the slightest understanding of what was going through the mind of the other that evening.

I was out on a date of my own that night. My mother, true to her word, had put me in touch with the grandson of her friend from church, the one who'd been gaining archaeological work experience in South America. His name was Ricky Wendon and he was a short, stocky young man with a mop of dark hair, an easy smile, dirty nails and unending enthusiasm for the Chilean excavation. He had deferred his university place for another year, so he could return to the dig in September, and saw no reason why I should not join him there. He said the dig team had been short-staffed for the last couple of months, since a couple of Swedish volunteers had returned to Stockholm. We went to the Smuggler's Rest and on the back of a beer mat Ricky wrote the names and addresses I'd need to make the relevant enquiries about joining the dig . He was good company. He bought me one glass of cider and then another – refusing to allow me to reciprocate in a manner which I found attractive, masculine and exciting. I wondered if he was expecting me to kiss him.

Ellen and Jago lay in the grass in almost exactly the same spot where they first made love. A gentle midsummer moon was in the sky, its silver-blue light falling on their bodies. Ellen, more wide awake than she had ever been before, felt like a character in a painting. She could see the picture in her mind's eye: the long grass almost black but dotted with pink, yellow and white flowers, the stars in the night sky, the full moon casting its light, the church in the background with its gravestones, the two pale, naked young people in the foreground like Adam and Eve. She shivered and Jago put his arm around her and pulled her close. She felt her body pressed against his larger one. She put her hand on his thigh.

'I'm pregnant,' she whispered.

'Richard Wendon is a very good name to have if you're going to have something named after you,' I said.

Ricky, a rather intense young man, and not quite as drunk as I was, nodded, although I don't think he had a clue what I was talking about. His cheeks were flushed.

'Ricardosaurus. It sounds a lot better than Hannahsaurus. That just sounds like the punchline to a very bad joke.' I laughed rather too much.

'Nothing has been named after me. I didn't actually find anything new that needed a name,' Ricky pointed out with unnecessary pedantry. 'All I did mostly was sieve and wash the dirt off stuff that came out of the dig. It was mainly bits of rock. And I made a lot of coffee.'

'But you were still there. You still saw an actual dinosaur in the place where it died. The last time anyone saw that creature . . . what was it again?'

'Some kind of saurischian iguanodont.'

'Exactly. Imagine, nobody's seen it for all those millions of years and now you're looking at it again and—'

'Actually, Hannah, no people were around in the Late Jurassic.'

'I know! But if they *had* been, they would have seen it. And nobody else would have seen it in the meantime until you did.' I shook my head in awe.

'You still can't see much of it,' Ricky said. 'If you didn't know about it, you wouldn't even realize it was there. It's not that impressive.'

I wasn't really listening. I was lost in wonderment, running with the dinosaurs through a leafy Jurassic wonderland inside my mind.

'If only I'd known you three weeks ago, Ricky, I could have written all about your work in Chile in my biology exam, and instead of failing I'd have got an A.' I thought about this for a moment. 'Or at least a B – or a C. At least I'd have passed.'

The pub was dark and smoky. Nothing seemed to sit straight. The floorboards were buckled, the walls were at a tilt, the narrow bench seat where Ricky perched was poised at such a severe angle that he had to lean the other way to compensate. The small wooden table rocked on its legs. Ricky shook a few peanuts out of the packet into the palm of his hand. He tipped them into his mouth. The underside of his chin was dark with stubble. I thought it was sexy. I liked the lumberjack shirt he was wearing and the dark hairs on his arms and the little white scar on the back of his hand. I had a brief, pornographic thought that had nothing at all to do with palaeontology and which I pushed aside rapidly, shocked at the filthiness of my own mind. Instead I reached out my hand and touched the fabric of Ricky's shirt. It was warm and fuzzy and reminded me of a pair of Scooby Doo pyjamas I used to have when I was ten.

Ricky smiled at me in a reassuring way. 'Don't worry about your results. They don't count for so much in South America,' he said. 'The professor cares more about enthusiasm and having the right attitude than qualifications.'

'I definitely have the right attitude,' I said. My chin slipped off the palm of my hand. 'Oops,' I said, and I giggled.

Jago knelt reverently beside Ellen with his hand on her belly and stared at her in the moonlight. She smiled up at him bravely although she felt like crying.

'We're going to have a baby?' he asked.

'Mmm.'

'Oh God, that's wonderful. That's the most wonderful

thing that has ever happened to me. Apart from you, of course, Ellen. Apart from you.'

He leaned over and kissed Ellen's stomach just below her belly button. Ellen turned her face to one side and squeezed her eyes tight shut.

In the car park of the Smuggler's Rest, Ricky kissed me. His lips pressed against mine so hard it hurt, our teeth clicked, his tongue, persistent and muscular, was in my mouth. It was my first real, passionate kiss and it turned me on like a light. Ricky tugged at the waistband of my jeans. He slipped his warm hand between my shirt and my skin. Through the kissing, I tightened the muscles in my belly. His fingers found my breast beneath my bra and I gave a gasp of surprise and delight as he squeezed it gently. I hoped he wouldn't stop there.

Ellen and Jago were dressed. They walked back through the churchyard, past the graves of the sailors and their sweethearts. Jago was so happy, so completely suffused with joy that he felt as if his feet were floating above the ground. He was conscious of the little bats that dived from the church-tower and the calls of the night-birds; he could even hear, from far away, the sea as it pounded into the land. He wished he were out there now, on the deck of the *Eliza Jane*, because only the sea was big enough to measure his happiness. Ellen, slightly ahead of him, walked with her head bowed.

'Don't worry,' said Jago. He leaned forward and put a hand on her shoulder. 'I'll look after you. Both of you. I won't let anything bad happen. It'll be all right.'

'You're sure?'

'How can it not be? We have one another, we're having a baby, we're going to be a family. We'll go away together. We can go tomorrow . . .'

'After my birthday.'

'After your birthday then – whenever, as soon as you like.'

'If my father finds out I'm pregnant . . .'

'Shhh, shhh, honey.' Jago pulled on Ellen's shoulder to make her stand still. He turned her towards him. He took her beloved face in his hands.

'How will he find out?' he asked. 'Who will tell him? Does anyone else know?'

Ellen shook her head. 'I haven't even told Hannah.'

'That's OK then,' said Jago. 'We'll be careful. We'll be all right. It's only a few weeks to your birthday. We'll be fine.'

In Ricky's little car, I put my head back and laughed. I felt flushed, exhilarated, happy – as if I'd been for a run or won a prize. Ricky kissed me once more, then climbed off me, back into the driver's seat, and fastened his fly.

'Wow!' he said, pushing the hair out of his eyes. 'Hannah, that was something else.'

I sighed contentedly. I could feel my hair spread out on the back of the seat, I knew my clothes were in disarray and the windows of the car were steamed up and it must have been rocking away in the pub car park, in its corner space by the wall, like something out of a comedy sketch. Anyone might have seen. They probably did. I didn't care. I didn't feel used or sleazy or anything at all except happy, happy, happy.

From somewhere, Ricky produced the johnny and tied a knot in the end, pinging the rubber.

I found this funny too.

'Can't I keep it?' I asked. 'As a souvenir?'

'You're crazy-amazing!' said Ricky, and he wound down the window and threw it expertly into the bin by the wall.

CHAPTER FORTY-SEVEN

Because I had almost got us both killed, and because after that we both needed a drink, John and I never made it to the dinner at the Haus der Kulturen der Welt.

Instead, we ended up in a small back street bar. John took off his bow tie and stowed it in his pocket, and I put on my cardigan and unclipped my hair, letting it fall loose around my shoulders. I found a table by the wall while he went to the bar and returned with two bottles of beer, which he banged down. He scraped back the chair and sat opposite me, his knees wide apart, one on either side of the table.

'Right,' he said. 'Hannah, please will you explain what's going on.'

'I don't know,' I said.

'You thought you saw your friend, but you know your friend is dead. So why did you run across the road? You knew it couldn't be her. You *knew*! And, Hannah, that was pretty damn scary!'

'I'm sorry. We'd just been talking about going to Magdeburg, hadn't we, you and I. Ellen was in my mind. And when I saw her – when I *thought* I saw her – I forgot about everything. I just wanted to reach her. I've been think- ing . . . Lately I've been wondering if she might still be alive.'

I looked up at him. 'Maybe there was some kind of mix-up. Perhaps Ellen never died.'

'Christ,' said John. He exhaled and ran a hand through his hair.

'I know it sounds a bit . . . unlikely.'

'Just a bit.'

'You don't understand – Ellen's life was complicated.'

'Even so, Hannah, what are you suggesting? That she faked her own death?'

'I don't know.'

I picked at the label on the beer bottle.

'Ellen and I were so close.' I held two fingers pressed together up to demonstrate. 'This close, perhaps almost *too* close. I don't think I've ever really believed she was dead. I couldn't understand how she could leave me; how she could not *be* any more. It has never made sense to me.'

John sighed. He took a drink from the bottle. 'Is that why you want to go to Magdeburg? To look for answers there?'

'Something like that, yes.'

John stared at his beer.

I picked up my bottle. The little paper doily was stuck to the bottom. I peeled it off, drank. The bar was jolly, like an advert for Germany, with big mirrors on the walls and scores of lights with red-and-gold glass shades. The bar staff were wearing long green aprons tied at the waist, white shirts and black trousers, and everything was shiny. The fancy gold lettering on the large plate-glass windows cast shadows across the table, and John's shirt.

'Hannah,' he said gently, 'it seems all this is really getting to you. I'm worried about you.'

I twisted my ring around my finger.

'I'll be OK,' I said, but inside I was quietly pleased that he cared enough to be worried.

We drank a couple more beers, then wandered into the

city. Darkness had fallen. I carried my shoes by the ankle straps. The pavements were dusty and warm beneath the soles of my feet. We bought hot battered apple rings from a street stall and leaned on a wall by the river to eat them, dipping them in warm honey, watching the boats go by and the reflections of their lights in the purplish water. There was a warm, summer-city, brackish smell to the air.

'Do any of Ellen's family still live in Magdeburg?' John asked as we looked out over the water. A solitary gull sculled through the late-evening sky.

'I don't know.'

'Would it help you to find them, to talk to them?'

'Perhaps. I wouldn't want to see Ellen's father again, but there was an aunt – Tante Karla. She might remember me.'

'You liked her?'

'Yes. And the family used to have a housekeeper, Mrs Todd. She'd been with them for ever.'

'Did she come back to Germany?'

'I think so. The Brechts were all she had in her life.'

I screwed up my paper bag and looked at John in his dinner suit, the wind ruffling the hair that had reverted to its usual untidy state. A five o'clock shadow played across his chin. I wouldn't let myself think about how much I cared for him.

'I used to be frightened of Mrs Todd,' I said. 'But she was only ever doing her best for Ellen. She even paid for her to—'

'To what?'

'Oh, nothing,' I said.

CHAPTER FORTY-EIGHT

I was happy – the happiest I'd ever been in my whole life. I felt as if I was peeling away from my old life, the life that had so constrained me. None of the things that had happened in the past seemed to matter to me any more. I was eighteen, I had a boyfriend who picked me up in his car and took me into Falmouth to drink cider and eat chips and watch films. I'd finished school and I had a plan – a good plan – and everything in my life was, for once, pretty much perfect.

I still thought about Mr Brecht, of course, but he was not so important to me now. Dreams of marrying him and soothing him back to happiness seemed tiresome compared to the exhilaration and excitement of my life in the here and now, the fun I was having with Ricky. To be honest, I was a little embarrassed about how I used to idolize Mr Brecht. Thinking about him too much, recalling the night he kissed me, for example, made me feel uncomfortable; even a bit ashamed. Now I was involved in a real relationship, I felt far more mature and rational.

I composed a careful letter which I sent to the professor in charge of the Chilean excavation to ask if there were any volunteer vacancies, enclosing my CV and a long, illustrated explanation about why I was so keen to participate, in order to convince him of my enthusiasm. I hadn't told my parents, not yet, but they must have had an inkling as to what was going on. I knew Mum would act as if she were pleased, but would be quietly heartbroken if I went to South America. She had sown the seed of the idea in my head, but had never dreamed I would go through with it. Why would I? I was the timid, unadventurous child. If only she knew how bored I was of vacuuming the bedrooms in the Seagull Hotel, emptying the waste-paper baskets and wiping the sticky breakfast-tables. I got through these chores by thinking about how it would feel to board a jumbo jet and cross the Atlantic. My tentative plans filled me with anticipation so thrilling it made me catch my breath. I had to hold tight to my stomach, press on it with my fists to calm the butterflies of excitement inside.

Ricky called for me almost every evening. I sat beside him in his car and he told me every detail of his day, and I told him every detail of mine, and he always told me some stupid jokes which I found funnier and cleverer than they really were. He teased me relentlessly, was sweet and a little pompous, and he made me feel better than I was. I'd had no idea it was possible to be so happy. I had never had so much energy or felt such potential within me, as if I could achieve anything I wanted to – as if the world really was my oyster.

Ricky took me into the travel agent's in Falmouth and we asked the assistant about cheap ways to fly to Chile. She asked questions and we told her about the dig and she said, ooh, she wished she'd done something like that when she was younger. She said, 'You always think you'll have time to do these things, and then one day you wake up and you're married with three kids and a mortgage and you're exhausted and you realize it's too late.' Ricky and I smiled at one another. We were quietly proud that we hadn't left it too late. The assistant printed out a list of flights and prices and gave it to me. Even the cheapest and least convenient option was more expensive than I'd anticipated, and it was clear I was going to have to save every penny I could earn until September if I was going to join Ricky on the dig.

After the travel agency, Ricky and I drove out into the countryside, found a secluded lane, pulled in at the gated entrance to a fallow field, wriggled out of our jeans and had breathless, gleeful sex. We did this at every opportunity. Our private joke was that the little Fiat would soon need new springs. I walked around with a permanent sore feeling between my legs that I bore with pride because it reminded me of Ricky every time I sat or stood or simply moved about in my chair. Ricky came for tea at my house often. He charmed and perhaps ever so slightly bored my parents with his earnest enthusiasm and his detailed descriptions of South America. I was invited to Sunday lunch at Ricky's and was intimidated and impressed by his tall, well-spoken mother and high-ranking Royal Navy father. After a huge meal I played Monopoly with Ricky's younger sisters in a living room the size of a tennis court and hung an imaginary photograph of myself and Ricky on our wedding day amongst the scores of family portraits on the walls.

Every Friday afternoon, I went into the Post Office and paid the money I'd earned that week into my savings account. It was adding up.

I was so tied up with Ricky and my own newfound happiness that, in the little spare time I had when I was not working, I was not paying any attention to Ellen. Tante Karla was still at Thornfield House and I excused the neglect of my friend by rationalizing that, as long as Karla was there keeping an eye on things, I didn't have to worry about Ellen. Jago was working extra shifts wherever he could get them, saving up his money too. Because of this he wasn't seeing much of Ellen either. She was, for a while, pretty much on her own.

She tried to see me. She walked down to Cross Hands Lane to call for me, but each time I was out. If I'd been there for her then . . . if I'd been more observant . . .

But I wasn't paying attention. I didn't notice.

The morning when things started to go badly wrong again started auspiciously enough. I was alone at home, eating toast and honey in the kitchen, listening to the radio, when Trixie set up her daily routine of barking at the postman. On the hessian mat by the front door that said *Welcome* was a blue airmail letter. I pulled an astonished face at Trixie – who grinned and panted back – picked up the letter, and Trixie and I ran upstairs. I shut the bedroom door behind us and sat on the floor with my back against the wall, holding the letter to my chest. I could feel my heart beating through my shirt.

I opened the envelope with my thumb, unfolded the letter, read. It was brief and to the point. There *was* a vacancy for another volunteer on the dig and the team would be happy to welcome me among their number.

'I *can* go. I'm going!' I cried. Trixie thumped her stubby little tail as I knelt beside her and covered the side of her big, ugly head with kisses.

I read the letter about twenty times, until I'd memorized every word, then I folded it carefully, tucked it into the pocket of my shorts and went downstairs. At last, something amazing had happened to me. At last, I had something exciting to tell Ellen! I put on my trainers in a hurry, hopping on first one leg, then the other, got the bike out of the shed and pedalled up the hill, my legs powered by excitement. I stood on the pedals, leaning forward over the handlebars and pushing down as I rode through the dappling tree shadows. I knew my days in Trethene were numbered, days of going up this hill, of listening to the brook rushing down over its stones, of collecting wildflowers from the hedgerows, and waiting for the Williamses' prize-winning dairy herd to lumber in their docile manner from the grazing pasture to the milking sheds while covering the lane in manure.

When I reached Thornfield House, I propped my bike against the wall and skipped over to the front door. I rang the bell, expecting Tante Karla to open the door. I couldn't wait to see her – I knew she'd be thrilled by my news – but instead Mrs Todd was there and my heart sank, because I knew, as soon as I saw her face, that something bad had happened. It wasn't only Mrs Todd. The inside of the house seemed darker. There was no music playing, no windows open, no sound of Tante Karla cheerfully going about her business.

'Good morning, Mrs Todd,' I said. 'Is Ellen in?'

Mrs Todd opened her mouth as if she were about to send me away, and then she changed her mind and closed it again. Behind her, I saw Ellen standing in the gloom of the hallway. She was wearing a long white nightgown and she looked like a wraith, her hair all lank around her shoulders, her long feet bare, her shoulders hunched and her eyes like hollows in her face, as if she had been crying for a hundred years. Her arms were wrapped around herself as if she were cold and her head was held low, like a prisoner in a war photograph.

'What's happened?' I whispered. 'Oh God, what now?'

I pushed past Mrs Todd and she moved her body slightly to let me by. I heard the front door closing quietly behind me as I rushed forward and clasped Ellen in my arms. She was resistant, doll-like, and she smelled strange – unwashed, but there was another smell to her, slightly metallic, slightly milky. Her hair was greasy against my cheek. I took her hand, led her into the kitchen. She was limping oddly. I pulled a chair out from the table and helped Ellen into it; I almost had to fold her at the waist and knees to make her sit. Then, because it was what my mother would have done, I filled the kettle from the sink tap and put it on the stove. An undrunk cup of tea was already cold on the table, a skin on top of the liquid. The kitchen was dark and cool, full of the salty, meaty smell of boiling ham. A large saucepan rattled on the hob. A blue glass vase full of dying knapweed, oxeye daisies and yellow ragwort stood on the windowledge. Tante Karla must have put the flowers there – they weren't Mrs Todd's style at all – but already there was a smell of slime and decay about the vase.

Is Pieter Brecht dead? I wondered for a moment. Has he killed himself or been mortally injured in an accident? No, that was not possible. Mrs Todd would have said something at once. It couldn't be Jago. Jago was fine when he left for work at the crack of dawn that morning. He had been whistling when he left the house. I'd heard him slam the door of his Escort and start up the engine. If anything had happened to him, I would have heard before Ellen.

'Where's Karla?' I asked. 'Has something happened to her?'

'She's gone back to Germany,' said Mrs Todd.

Ellen looked up. 'Papa sent her away.'

'Oh.'

'Mr Brecht's mother is unwell,' Mrs Todd said. 'She's been unwell for some time. Karla has returned to Magdeburg to look after her.'

'Papa insisted,' said Ellen. 'He told her we'd be fine. We were fine. We were right as rain until she left.'

I unhooked three mugs from the rack and glanced over my shoulder at Ellen. She was sitting, leaning forward with her hands between her legs, her back hunched, her hair falling over her face. Her feet were dirty. Mrs Todd stood at the entrance to the kitchen. Time seemed to have slowed down awfully. I put a spoonful of coffee granules into the bottom of each mug and, when the kettle whistled, filled them with boiling water. I took a bottle of milk from the fridge door, and poured milk into each mug. I put the bottle back, stirred three heaped teaspoons of sugar into Ellen's mug and put it in front of her. Ellen did not move.

'What's happened?' I asked Mrs Todd again.

Ellen looked up, for the first time, and held a thin finger to her lips.

'Papa's upstairs,' she breathed.

Because the light was behind Mrs Todd as she stood in the doorway, she was a silhouette to me, odd wisps of hair caught by the golden sunshine coming through the hall window, and I couldn't see the nuances of her expression, only the line of her lips.

'Ellen has got herself into trouble,' she said quietly.

'What kind of trouble?' I asked, sitting down in front of Ellen, taking hold of her hands. I squeezed them for re-assurance but she did not respond. They were icy cold in mine and limp as a dead girl's hands.

'The baby kind,' Ellen whispered.

CHAPTER FORTY-NINE

That night, in Berlin, in my hotel room, I thought about Mrs Todd. I remembered how loyal she had been to the Brechts, how she had stayed on for Ellen's sake after Mrs Brecht's death, how she had always tried to protect Ellen. I had been so scared of her when I was young, and now I could see the situation from an adult perspective, I was ashamed of the way I'd treated her.

I was not haunted by nightmares, but by regret. I thought of all the times when Mrs Todd had quietly intervened at Thornfield House; how, sometimes by simply walking into a room, she had caused a subtle shift in tension; how she had protected both Anne Brecht and her daughter. It had to be more than loyalty that kept her there after Anne's death. She must have loved Ellen. It was something neither of us realized or recognized at the time.

The next morning, I went downstairs for an early breakfast of bread and fruit, then I returned to my room and telephoned my mother. She was surprised and flustered to hear my voice, assuming immediately that something had gone wrong, that I was in trouble, that I was ill. I reassured her that everything was absolutely fine, and made some small talk about the frustrations of airport security checks and the friendliness of the German people, then I took a deep breath and asked, 'Mum, you don't happen to know what became of Mrs Todd, do you?'

She paused before replying. 'She stayed with her sister for a while and then she went to Germany. The Brecht family gave her a cottage in the grounds of their house. They looked after her in her old age.'

'Do you mean Schloss Marien? Was that where her cottage was?'

'That's it! She liked it there. She used to write to me every Christmas, just a few lines inside the card, and once she sent me a photograph of the Christmas Market; it looked very nice. Your father and I were thinking maybe of going one year and meeting up with her, but we never got round to it.'

'She *used* to write?'

'Before her stroke. She lives in a nursing home now.'

'Do you have the name of the home, Mum? Or the address? I thought I might pop in to see her, seeing as I'm so close.'

Mum wasn't sure this was a good idea, but I assured her that all I wanted to do was take some flowers to the old lady. I didn't tell Mum, but I also needed to let Mrs Todd know that I finally understood how brave she had been, how loyal and how helpful. I wanted, in some small way, to atone for not understanding or appreciating Mrs Todd when I was younger.

My mother obligingly went off to find her address book and her reading glasses, and returned a few moments later. She dictated the name and address of the nursing home to me, taking great care of the spelling. I thanked her, promised I'd be in touch when I was back in Bristol, and then I trotted along the hotel corridor to John's room and knocked.

'Come in!' he called.

He was sitting at the desk by the window, drinking coffee

and looking at his emails. He smiled when he saw me and jumped up to move his suit from where it lay over the back of a second chair. I sat down.

'Did you sleep well?' he asked.

'Great, thanks. You?'

'Like a log.'

I felt shy being with John in a hotel room. It seemed intimate. I tried not to look at the unmade bed, the crumpled white sheets, the boxer shorts balled up beside the bedside table.

I cleared my throat. 'I just wondered if I could borrow your laptop to find out about getting to Magdeburg, like you mentioned yesterday.'

'Help yourself.'

He passed the computer to me and I Google-mapped firstly Schloss Marien, and then Mrs Todd's nursing home. Both were outside the city, although the nursing home was closer to Berlin than Magdeburg. While John made more coffee, I researched the options for using public transport, and realized it was not going to be easy.

'Any luck?' he asked.

'It's going to have to be taxis,' I said.

John looked over my shoulder. 'What's that place?'

'You remember I was telling you about the housekeeper, Mrs Todd? She's had a stroke and that's where she lives now. I'd like to go and visit her. Just to say hello, and take her some flowers.'

'That's going to be awkward to get to.'

'I know. But . . .'

'I could take you,' John said. He smiled and scratched his head. 'We could hire a car. That'd be the easiest thing to do.'

'What about the conference?'

'All that's on this morning is a workshop on Interactive Interpretive Tourism. I'm not that interested.'

I exhaled. 'I don't want to ruin your trip, John.'

'You won't,' he said. 'If we drive, we can go and see your Mrs Todd, have lunch in Magdeburg, take a look at the Schloss Marien and still be back in time for the evening session.'

'But why would you want to come with me?'

'I'll get to see a bit of the countryside. Let's face it, once you've seen the inside of one conference facility, you've seen them all.'

I had a feeling he was being gracious to make it easy for me. Still, I was overwhelmed with gratitude and relief. Whatever happened, I knew I would cope with it better, and in a more reasoned way, if John were with me. I would be able to share some of my history with him. And always, afterwards, this would be something we would have between us.

'Thank you,' I said.

CHAPTER FIFTY

The shock of Ellen's words left me breathless. Ellen did not look up but she must have felt the tension in my hands. I wondered why she hadn't said anything to me sooner, then I realized that she probably hadn't confided in anyone. Mrs Todd did Ellen's laundry, she watched over her, she must have guessed that Ellen was pregnant, and when I thought back, it seemed obvious to me too. Ellen's pallor, her tiredness, her weight gain, her recent quietness were all signs. I hadn't been with her much, or I would surely have realized. I forgot entirely about my own good news. It was nothing compared to this.

'Ellen has been seeing your brother in secret,' said Mrs Todd in a quiet voice. 'Clearly they haven't been very careful.'

I looked up at her. Her face was still in shadow. She was hovering like a spectre.

'Please can I talk to Ellen on my own, Mrs Todd?'

'There isn't much time,' The woman replied. 'Pieter might come downstairs any minute. He mustn't—'

'He mustn't know,' Ellen hissed. 'He'll kill Jago if he finds out.'

I thought back to New Year's Eve and I felt sick.

'Ellen needs your help,' said Mrs Todd.

'What are we going to do?' I asked. I could see no way out of this situation, and for a moment I was furious with Ellen for allowing this to happen. Jago too. How could they have been so irresponsible? So stupid! How could they have mired themselves in this mess when everything in my life had been going so well? I'd never have allowed Mr Brecht to see them kissing if I'd known *this* was going to happen!

Mrs Todd sighed. She stepped forward into the room, standing behind Ellen. Her hands were twisting, the fingers working away at themselves. I'd never seen Mrs Todd so unsettled before and it made me uneasy.

'It's not too late.' Mrs Todd hesitated over her choice of words. 'What I mean to say is, the situation can be sorted out.'

'The trouble can be got rid of,' Ellen whispered, keeping her head low but raising her eyes to meet mine. She had the look of a zombie about her, she was so pale and her eyes were so shadowed and tormented.

'Mr Brecht must not know,' said Mrs Todd. 'For your brother's sake, Hannah, as much as Ellen's.' She made a little gagging sound and I remembered that it was Mrs Todd who had found Ellen cowered over Adam Tremlett's battered body on the wooden floor of the smashed-up front room; Mrs Todd who had pressed clean tea-towels against Mr Tremlett's wound to stem the bloodflow while she waited for the ambulance; Mrs Todd who, with my mother, had swept up the broken glass and china and tried to scrub the stains from the floorboards. She knew and understood Mr Brecht's potential for violence. She knew what he was capable of.

A shiver ran across my scalp and down the back of my neck. I looked from Mrs Todd to Ellen. I thought of Jago.

'Mrs Todd is right,' Ellen said, almost robotically. 'We have to get rid of the baby.'

I wished Ellen would not use words like that. I remembered a film we had been shown at school about the consequences of unprotected sex and closed my eyes to get rid of the image.

'There's a private place outside Truro where they won't ask questions,' said Mrs Todd. 'I can find the money.'

'There must be another way,' I said.

Ellen looked up. She shook her head. 'There isn't.'

'What about Jago? Does he know about the baby?'

'It's not a baby yet,' said Mrs Todd.

'Yes, he knows,' said Ellen.

'That's all right,' said Mrs Todd. 'You can tell him you lost it. Miscarried. It's not much of a lie.'

'No, no!' I felt agitated now, as if Mrs Todd and Ellen were pushing a huge boulder towards me and it was gaining momentum. 'You can't do what you're saying without telling him. You can't lie to him! You can't, Ellen – it's not fair. It's his baby as much as it is yours!'

'Shhh!' Mrs Todd snapped, glancing up towards the ceiling. 'If *he* hears you . . .'

'Why can't you just go away?' I asked Ellen.

'You know I can't,' she said. She pulled up the hem of her nightdress. Beneath it, her ankle was horribly swollen, and coloured purple; the skin was spread so thinly over the swelling that it looked as if it might split at any point, like an overripe plum.

'He did that to you?' I gasped.

She let the nightdress drop again. There was a tiredness in her eyes, a resignation that I had never seen before.

'I was standing at the door waving goodbye to Tante Karla,' she said dully. 'She was in the taxi and I said something about how much I would miss her, and . . .' She exhaled slowly.

'And what?'

'He said he was glad she was gone. He said "good riddance". He called her an interfering old witch. And so I knew.' She looked up at me and gave a little shrug. 'I knew he hadn't changed at all. He just wanted her out of the way. The taxi was at the gates and I thought I could run after it, that I could get in and go with Karla – but he was too quick.'

'What did he do?'

'He closed the door on my ankle,' Ellen said. Her voice was calm, matter-of-fact. 'He did this to me and he loves me. Think, Hannah. Think what he'll do to Jago.'

I scratched the inside of my elbow. 'Did Tante Karla see what happened?'

Ellen shook her head. 'Papa was different when she was here. He's clever at making people believe everything is all right. She doesn't know anything.'

I didn't want to believe Ellen. I wanted this to be another one of her stories, an exaggeration of the truth, a melo-dramatization of a mundane sequence of events, but this time Mrs Todd was there, endorsing Ellen's version. This time, even I could not convince myself that Ellen was lying.

'I know it's difficult, Hannah,' Mrs Todd murmured, 'but what we're doing is for the best. It's the only way.'

CHAPTER FIFTY-ONE

Weis Kloster was a nursing home for retired gentle-women, run by nuns and located in former convent buildings on the outskirts of Magdeburg. The surroundings were beautiful, like the grounds of a country estate – all lawns and lovely, wide-limbed trees – and the sunshine showed the place off to its best advantage.

John and I had stopped on the way to buy a bouquet of blowsy orange-pink roses and baby's breath for Mrs Todd, and I held the flowers, tastefully wrapped in recycled paper, on my lap.

I knew, as soon as I saw it, that Mrs Todd would approve of the nursing home. The large, arch-shaped front door was open wide, and inside was a sparse but elegant reception area. We rang a little hand-bell and a sweet-faced nun wearing thick-rimmed spectacles materialized behind us. John had telephoned ahead to let the nuns know we were coming to see Mrs Todd, and when we wrote our names in the visitor book, the nun smiled and gestured for us to follow her.

The heels of our shoes tapped on the tiled floors of corridors with arched ceilings. The walls were whitewashed and inset with narrow windows that filled the place with light. At the centre of the Kloster was a large chapel, coloured light falling through the stained-glass windows and making spangles on the floor, where a nun sat praying beside a veiled woman.

The nun led us into a separate wing. She stopped at one of a number of identical doors and knocked with her knuckles, although she did not wait for a reply but turned the handle to open the door. A tiny old woman was sitting in a chair by the window. It took me a moment to recognize her as Mrs Todd. She was wizened and shrunken, like an apple that's been left too long in the bowl, her hands flickering in her lap with the tremor of Parkinson's. Still she wore black, still her white hair was in a bun, still her spectacles hung around her neck although she had no need of them any longer.

The room, clearly a former nun's cell, was light and airy and clean. Apart from the chair, all it contained was a single bed, high enough to be practical for use by an elderly woman, and a narrow chest of drawers. A framed picture of a dark-haired child wearing a white dress was propped on the chest, together with a few trinkets, and a plain wooden cross had been nailed to the wall.

The chair had been positioned so that Mrs Todd could look out of the window. She was too old and frail now for reading, or knitting, or any of the other pursuits she used to enjoy. All she could do to pass the time was watch the world through the four small square panes of glass in the leaded window. I wondered if that was what became of all of us in the end, if we lived to be old. Watching the world through window glass.

A different nun, the one who had taken the flowers from us, brought them back in a glass vase which she placed on the shelf beside the door, next to the picture of the child, so that Mrs Todd could look at the roses while she was in bed. The nun, who seemed to speak no English, sniffed the roses and smiled broadly.

'*Schön!*' she said. '*Frau Todd, sind sie nicht wünder-schön?*'

'*Ich brauche keine Blumen,*' said Mrs Todd. I did not know what she meant, but the nun made a kindly if apologetic face. She mimed that Mrs Todd tired easily, and that we should not stay too long. '*Maximal zehn Minuten!*' she said, holding up the fingers of both hands, before she left the room in a bustle of skirts and soft footsteps.

There was nowhere for John or me to sit, apart from the bed. I sat on the edge of it, close to Mrs Todd. John stood by the door, looking for and failing to find something he could pick up and read.

I shuffled a little closer to the old lady, leaning towards her, resting my elbows on my knees. From there, I too could look out of the window.

'Mrs Todd,' I said, 'I'm Hannah Brown. I used to be friends with Ellen.'

The old lady blinked.

I cleared my throat. 'I've been thinking about Ellen a lot lately,' I continued. 'And you. When I think of Ellen, I think of you too.'

'I should have stood up for her,' Mrs Todd said. 'She wanted the flowers but he threw them away.'

'Who wanted the flowers, Mrs Todd?'

'Anne.'

I remembered Mr Brecht throwing the flowers down the stairs and Adam Tremlett gathering them in his arms.

'I promised her mother that I would look after her,' said Mrs Todd, 'but I failed her. I let him have his way and it wasn't what she wanted, not at all.'

A tear made its way over the rim of one of her watery eyes and slid slowly down her cheek. I reached over and gently wiped it away with the tissue I kept up my sleeve.

'Mrs Todd, nobody could ever accuse you of being less

than diligent. That's why I wanted to come and see you, to tell you how much I— *they* appreciated you,' I said. 'You could not have done any more for the Brechts. Nobody could have asked more of you.'

From the doorway, John asked gently, 'When did you start working for the family, Mrs Todd?'

'When Mrs Withiel was expecting.'

'Mrs Withiel was Ellen's mother's mother,' I explained. I turned back to Mrs Todd. 'So you looked after Anne from the day she was born?'

'Before she was born.'

Without turning her head, Mrs Todd raised her hand in the direction of the photograph on the shelf. 'That's her,' she said. 'That's my Anne.'

John picked the photograph up and passed it to me. I held it carefully on my lap. Anne looked like a happy child, leggy and skinny with two of her front teeth missing. She was standing in the back garden at Thornfield House.

'She was a lovely little girl,' I said.

'And no trouble. Never any trouble, she was good as gold,' said Mrs Todd.

'I always knew you were close.'

'The Withiels were good people. They loved that child more than life itself. And then she started to play the piano . . .' Mrs Todd's voice fell.

'You didn't like her playing the piano, Mrs Todd?'

'She played like an angel. They didn't want to send her away so they had tutors come to her. There was room to put them up – plenty of room in Thornfield House. One came after another, but Anne was better than all of them.'

'And when she was twelve, they sent for Pieter Brecht?' I asked.

Mrs Todd nodded. Her hands were trembling and she had slumped a little in the chair. It seemed disrespectful to touch her, to lift her straight. At the sound of Pieter Brecht's name she became visibly agitated. She licked her lips and her eyes moved forwards and backwards.

'He'd already made a name for himself in Europe. They said he was a genius. He had a charisma . . .'

Mrs Todd looked at me as if she were trying to make me understand something without having to articulate it. Her lips opened and closed as she tried to find the words she needed. Then she gave up, closed her eyes and rested her head back on the pillow that had been placed at the top of her chair.

'I'm sorry,' I said. 'I didn't mean to upset you. Would you like a drink, Mrs Todd? A cup of tea?'

'Water.'

'I'll go,' said John. He left the room, closing the door quietly behind him. I heard his footsteps receding down the corridor.

I moved a little closer to Mrs Todd, so close that our knees were almost touching and I could see the white hairs growing downy on the skin of her face, and the beat of her pulse through the vein on her neck. I thought, God forgive me, but I asked the next question anyway.

'You never liked Pieter Brecht, did you?'

The old lady moved her head a fraction. 'He corrupted her.'

'But he loved Anne! Surely he would never have done anything to hurt her?'

There was silence in response. I waited, but Mrs Todd said nothing. Her eyes flickered open and although her face did not change, her hands were wrung together as if in grief.

'He was twenty-seven and she was fourteen,' she said, at last. 'Fourteen years old.'

There was no ambiguity as to her meaning.

I said: 'Oh. I see.'

'And Anne was so innocent, such a child. Some girls are so knowing but she wasn't. She didn't know anything. She was so precious to her parents that they'd wrapped her in cotton wool. She didn't know – she had no idea.'

I too turned my face towards the window then, and looked through the four small panes of glass out into the gardens, where two nuns were weeding a flowerbed and a third was walking very slowly, her arm linked through that of an elderly woman. All the nuns were smiling. This was such a good place, I thought. So open and light and beautiful. It was the antithesis of Thornfield House with its secrets and sins.

Questions lined themselves up in my mind, one after the other. I had thought I understood the Brecht family, I had thought I knew almost everything there was to know about them, but I knew nothing.

I remembered waving to the old lady who stood at the front window of Thornfield House, looking out. Anne's lonely mother. I remembered what she had said about the devil stealing her daughter away.

'Mr and Mrs Withiel realized too late,' said Mrs Todd. 'Far too late. By then Anne thought she was in love with him.'

I blushed then. I remembered how I had felt about Pieter Brecht. How I had been seduced by him, how I had believed in him, how I had wanted him. I looked down at my hands, the bitten-down fingernails, the ringless fingers.

'So he brought her back here, to Magdeburg?' I asked quietly.

'Yes.'

'And you came with them?'

'I promised Mrs Withiel I'd look after Anne. I promised her.'

'Oh Mrs Todd, you did!' I took one of her hands in mine,

and held it. It was light as a feather, and about as substantial. 'You were wonderful with all of them.'

'When Anne's daughter was born, she insisted on naming her after her mother,' Mrs Todd said. 'She persuaded Pieter's parents to side with her on this. He hated the name. He was drunk at the baptism. He . . .'

The door swung open. I hadn't heard the footsteps on the tiles of the corridor beyond. I uncurled my spine and turned to see John carrying a tray, a jug of water and a glass, a tiny dish containing three tablets and a plate of bread, cold meat and pickle. With him was the young nun.

'*Fünfzehn Minuten!*' she said, tapping her watch and then shaking her head and wagging her finger in a parody of scolding.

'I'm sorry,' I said.

I wanted a little more time. I looked back to Mrs Todd. She was gazing out of the window. I leaned over and kissed her, very gently, on the cheek. She reached up her hand and touched my face.

'You did everything you could,' I said. 'You were like a guardian angel to Anne and to Ellen. You were wonderful.'

'I never told anyone about the baby,' she whispered. 'No one.'

'I know you didn't.'

'Nobody found out it was your brother's.'

'I know.'

'You were a good girl, Hannah,' Mrs Todd murmured, softly enough for neither John nor the nun to hear. 'You were a good friend to Ellen.'

I wasn't though. The truth was, I could not have been a worse one.

CHAPTER FIFTY-TWO

My father was returning from a night shift when he saw me cycling up the lane. It was early, half past six in the morning, and still cool; my breath streamed behind me like my hair. I was so tied up in my thoughts that I didn't recognize his old Ford van. He parked the van outside our house and then followed me up the lane on foot. I stopped at the church, propped the bike up against the wall, and went through the gate. Dad followed.

He found me sitting in the cool gloom at the back of the church. I'd never been one for religion, despite the best efforts of both my parents, so he knew something was wrong. He sat beside me for a while in silence then he cleared his throat and awkwardly patted my shoulder. He was as he always was: all beard and navy-blue jersey and the smell of menthol.

'I'm going to Chile, Dad,' I said. 'I'm going to help with a fossil dig.'

'Good,' he said.

'Good?'

'Yes. It'll do you good to get away from here.'

'Don't you mind?'

'Of course I mind, but I wouldn't be much of a father if I didn't let you do what you wanted to do, would I?'

I would have liked to have hugged my father then, but we weren't that kind of family, so I sat still and stared at my knees and the dust on the back of the pew in front.

'Are you worried about telling Mum?' he asked.

'A bit.'

'She'll be all right. Probably go a bit misty-eyed at first, but she's so proud of you, Hannah. You should hear her at the church socials. It's "Hannah this" and "Hannah that". The congregation is sick and tired of hearing how wonderful you are.'

I managed a smile.

'Come on,' said my dad. 'Come back home and I'll cook you a proper breakfast. Two eggs. Black pudding.'

I shook my head. 'Thanks, Dad, but I'm going to have breakfast with Ellen.'

Dad didn't ask any questions. He just smiled. 'Good for you,' he said.

He patted my back, gave me a fruit pastille from the top of the packet he kept in his trouser pocket, and even though it was warm and a little hairy, I put it in my mouth. I still had a little glob of orange jelly stuck to my back molar when I arrived at Ellen's house.

The clinic was a big, double-fronted, brick-built house, set in landscaped gardens. Nobody would have guessed by looking at it what went on inside. We had taken risks just to get there. We invented a story to persuade Mr Brecht to allow Ellen out for a few hours. We told him that I had been unwell and had been referred to the hospital for a check-up, hinting at unspeakable feminine problems. Mrs Todd had agreed to drive me because my father was on night shift. I had wheedled around Mr Brecht, telling him I was scared to go alone and begging him to allow Ellen to come with me, and he had, eventually, agreed. I'd been terrified he would follow

Mrs Todd's car and spent the journey looking behind me, panicking if any vehicle took the same route as us for more than a mile or two. But we arrived without incident and everything seemed calm and normal. As normal as anything can be, in an abortion clinic.

Mrs Todd led the way, looking painfully old-fashioned and out of place in her headscarf and coat. We followed behind, holding hands. Ellen had dressed smartly for the occasion. She was wearing one of her mother's linen dresses and ballet pumps. She was also wearing sunglasses 'to hide the tears later', she explained, and I'd had to swallow the irritation I felt that even in this situation she was playing the drama queen, acting out her role.

I carried a bag that Mrs Todd had prepared for Ellen and hidden in the boot of her car. Mrs Todd went over to the reception desk clutching her old-fashioned handbag by its handles with her chin held high. A big glass vase full of stocks stood on the desk next to a bowl of mints wrapped in paper.

The woman behind the desk was reassuringly middle-aged and broad of beam. She smiled in a professional way at Mrs Todd, and then at Ellen and me.

'Ellen Brecht,' Mrs Todd said. 'She's here for . . . to . . .'

'Ah yes, Ellen. I've got you here on the list.' The woman smiled over Mrs Todd's shoulder. 'Which one of you two—'

'Me,' Ellen said.

'All right, dear. We'll just take a few details and then the doctor will come and have a chat with you. Nothing to worry about. You've got your overnight bag?'

'I'm picking her up this afternoon,' Mrs Todd said.

'No, I'm afraid after a procedure we insist on an overnight stay, so that we can make sure everything's all right.'

'I've been through all this with someone already,' Mrs Todd said. 'It's been agreed.'

'Well, we'll see what Doctor says, shall we?' the receptionist replied, never for a moment losing her crocodile smile.

The doctor was another woman. She took Ellen off to be examined while Mrs Todd and I sat awkwardly together in the reception area. A pile of expensive, glossy magazines was arranged on a small glass table in the corner of the room, but I felt it would be inappropriate to read about celebrity gossip, given the gravity of the situation. Instead I watched pretty little electric-coloured fish darting in and out of the plants in a large aquarium set into one of the walls.

Ellen returned, looking pale and tearful. The doctor took the three of us into a private room with a hospital bed. Ellen sat on the bed. She looked about twelve years old. I sat next to her, feeling, once again, like a mother to her, and Mrs Todd remained standing.

The doctor explained that Ellen was fourteen weeks pregnant. She would be given a general anaesthetic and then a dilation and curettage procedure to remove the pregnancy. Providing there was no haemorrhaging or any other problems, Ellen would be allowed home, but a good eye must be kept on her and she would need to be regularly checked for signs of infection. I felt very hot and uncomfortable listening to the words the doctor used. I squeezed Ellen's cool little hand. She did not squeeze back.

The doctor told Ellen to get undressed and into bed. She said a nurse would come to give her her pre-op shortly. She asked Mrs Todd if she would like a cup of tea and Mrs Todd said no thank you.

When the doctor had left the room, Mrs Todd unpacked Ellen's bag. Ellen pulled off the dress and slipped the nightdress over her head. Mrs Todd hung the dress in the cupboard.

'I'll have to get back to your father, Ellen,' she said.

Ellen looked at me. 'I'll be here,' I said. 'I promise I won't leave you.'

Mrs Todd asked if we would be all right; we said we would, and she left. A nurse came and picked up Ellen's notes.

'It'll all be over and done with before you know it,' said the nurse. 'Nothing to worry about. Only next time, young lady, be a bit more careful.'

Ellen turned her face towards the window.

'The doctor will be here in a minute,' the nurse said, more gently.

The doctor came, and she and Ellen left together, Ellen walking behind like a condemned woman, and I was left on my own in the room, waiting.

An hour or so passed. I gazed out of the window. The room was peaceful but I was hungry. I didn't know how long Ellen would be. I thought it would be best to find something to eat before she returned, so I hurried to the café. I bought a cup of tea and a bun, which I ate on the way back. When I reached the room, Ellen was lying in the bed with the sheet pulled up so it almost covered her face.

'I'm sorry!' I cried, rushing over to her. 'I just went for a drink and . . . Is it over?'

'It's all sorted,' she said quietly. She did not open her eyes.

'Are you all right?' I smoothed her hair.

'I will be,' she said. 'I just need to sleep.'

She slept almost greedily, as if she could not have enough of it, and I realized that she probably hadn't slept much over the past few days. I lay beside her and put my arm around her. I didn't mean to, but I too drifted off. The room was warm, and the sound of birdsong coming in from outside and the rhythm of Ellen's breathing had a pleasant, soporific effect.

A little later a woman came in with a heated metal trolley

and gave us each a plate of chicken stew, peas and mashed potato. Ellen's face was still sleep-crumpled.

'Are you feeling better now?' I asked and Ellen rubbed her eyes and yawned and nodded. 'What about Jago?' I asked. 'When are you going to tell him?'

'I don't know.'

She wriggled up on to her elbows and looked at me. 'Please, Hannah, please don't say anything to him. Promise me you won't. I have to explain this myself.'

'You are going to tell him the truth?'

She nodded. 'I will, I promise, as soon as the time is right.'

In the afternoon, we lay on the bed watching television until the doctor returned to examine Ellen. I went back to Reception, and was relieved to see Mrs Todd, waiting.

'It's all right,' I said. 'It's all over. She's fine.'

Mrs Todd closed her eyes and mouthed a little prayer. I heard her say, 'God forgive me.' And then I looked towards the glass door and there was Ellen, pale as a ghost, walking towards us. The sleeves of her cardigan were pulled down over her fingers. She reached out her hand and pushed the door open.

'Let's get out of here,' she said.

CHAPTER FIFTY THREE

After we left Mrs Todd in her nursing home, John and I went for coffee and cake at a little café on the outskirts of the shopping area. I told John everything she had told me.

'Did you know about Ellen's parents?' John asked, stirring sugar into his cappuccino. 'How they got together?'

'Some of it. Do you know, for years I thought her father was the perfect man. He seemed so devoted to his wife.' I laughed to myself. 'I had a crush on him. I used to want him for myself.'

'He obviously had that effect on younger women.'

'No, it wasn't that.' I remembered Mr Brecht's hand on my waist. I remembered how it had made me feel. I remembered trying to kiss him in St Ives, how I had distorted the memory until I was no longer sure of the truth. I felt a pang of frustration for my ridiculous, besotted teenage self. 'He wasn't – you know ... he didn't go after young girls. He wasn't interested in anyone but Anne. He was completely obsessed with her. Ellen used to say he was mad, but I didn't believe her. I didn't see it.'

'What do you think now?'

'I think she was right. It was there all the time but I wouldn't acknowledge what was going on. I didn't want to think of Mr Brecht in a bad light, but . . . he was jealous, insecure, possessive, paranoid. He could be so manipulative . . . And Anne consumed him to the brink of insanity. He must have been a nightmare to live with. He probably liked it that Anne was so ill, because when she was incapacitated she was easier to control.'

I felt sad and also guilty, ashamed that I had been too naive, and too short-sighted, to understand. It wasn't only that I was seeing the situation now with an adult perspective. I had deliberately misunderstood when I was younger. I was culpable.

'At least, he *thought* Anne was malleable,' I said. 'She and Ellen were experts in outmanoeuvring him. Anne was running rings round him right up to the day she died.'

'I have never understood,' said John, 'why some people feel they must control the ones they profess to love.'

I looked at him. He was frowning and staring down at his cream cake. He had cut it, with the side of his fork, into small pieces.

'I suppose it comes down to trust,' I said carefully. I watched his face. He flinched very slightly at the word.

'Isn't it true though, Hannah, that those who hold on too hard are the ones who drive the people they love away? If a person wants to stay with you, they will stay.'

I nodded.

'So long as everyone is honest.' John speared a piece of cake with the prongs of his little fork and held it in front of him, examining it. I thought that if I was going to say anything to John about Charlotte, now would be the time. I took a deep breath.

'John, the other day, in Bristol, I saw Charlotte and—'

'Tell me more about the Brechts.'

He put the cake in his mouth. During this whole exchange he had not once looked at me.

I exhaled slowly and said, as if I were reciting something at school: 'Mr Brecht loved his wife. He loved her to death. She was everything in the world to him and he wanted her to feel the same. But she didn't. He put so much pressure on her, all the time. I can see that now. The only way she could get away from him was to die.'

'And he was the same with Ellen?'

'It was more complicated with her. More distorted.' I took a sip of my coffee. 'What pushed him over the brink,' I said, 'was that he believed Anne was in love with the gardener, Adam Tremlett.'

'Was she?'

'Probably. They'd known one another all their lives; they were friends before Pieter Brecht came to Cornwall. I think Adam understood her. He knew what was going on. Even on the day she died, they found a way to be together.'

I put down the cup and remembered the flowers that Mr Brecht had thrown down the stairs at Thornfield House; I remembered looking out of the window and seeing Adam, standing by the gates, looking up at the room, and I recalled how Pieter Brecht would not let Ellen change the music. Sadness and comprehension rushed through my veins with the very next heartbeat.

I scooped the last froth from my coffee cup with a little spoon and put it in my mouth.

'After Anne died,' I said, 'Mr Brecht cut the heads off all the flowers in the garden. That's what he was like. He couldn't contain his jealousy. It was bigger than him. It was toxic.'

There was silence for a few moments. The sun had come out and was illuminating the busy square beyond. People rushed this way and that, crossing the square, stopping to look in shop windows or to chat, or to buy flowers and sweets from the stalls. Somewhere, not far away, somebody began playing the violin.

'Ellen was in love with my brother,' I said. 'Did I tell you that?'

John shook his head.

'She was. Despite how her parents were, she still managed to love Jago.'

'You love your brother too, don't you?'

'I thought so,' I said. 'I thought I loved him very much, but I was jealous of him and Ellen. Oh John, I was so selfish.'

'You were very young.'

'That's not always an excuse,' I said.

CHAPTER FIFTY-FOUR

I went into Jago's room while he was at work and looked through his drawers. I found a brown paper bag. Inside was a packet of three tiny bodysuits, and a pair of scratch mittens. I held the little clothes to my heart and gazed out of the window. I had to tell him that the baby was no more, but how could I, when I wasn't supposed to know it had ever existed?

I was angrier with Ellen than I'd ever been before. I hated her for putting me in a situation where I had to lie to Jago – not lie, exactly, but not tell the truth. I dragged the burden of my knowledge and his ignorance around with me every day. I was angry with him too, angry that he had been so stupid as to make Ellen pregnant, angry that he had kept it from me so that I could not talk to him about what she had done, and angry that because he had not been honest with me, I had to lie to him.

I felt unfairly trapped inside the huge lie, a lie that was not of my making, a terrible thing; one of the three of us believing he had created a life, one knowing she had ended it, and the third all-knowing and entirely powerless.

And also, I was angry that the lie was spoiling what should have been a perfect time for me. Once again, a drama of

Ellen's had spilled over into my life. I should have been carefree, happy, planning my escape from Trethene and having fun with Ricky. It wasn't right that I was burdened with the guilt of knowing about the abortion. Even Jago's innocence annoyed me because it made me feel bad. I could hardly wait to get away from both of them. I was glad I was going to Chile, somewhere so distant that Ellen wouldn't be able to reach me.

I sometimes thought about how much she would miss me when I was gone. Who would she involve in her dramas when I wasn't there, I wondered.

In the meantime, my relationship with Jago soured. I avoided being at home when he was there so that I did not have to look at his face, did not have to pretend I did not know.

When he was not at work, Jago spent his time in the shed in the back garden, making things from the offcuts of wood he had begged from the yard in St Keverne. Curls of lathed wood littered the lawn, shining in the sunlight like barbered hair. I picked them up and crunched them between my fingers. One morning, I went into the shed. Hidden beneath the tarpaulin was a crib, sanded and polished to a fine shine. I ran my finger along the wood. No baby laid in there would ever have a splinter. I rocked the cradle to and fro. It didn't squeak or creak. It was beautifully made, with love, for Jago's son or daughter. I thought then that I had to tell him the truth. He couldn't go on believing in something that didn't exist. It was not right.

Later, I sat with my back to the wall of the shed and looked out across my father's small, neat garden. Trixie, old now and stiff, hobbled over and lay beside me with a sigh. The sun made her fur hot beneath my fingers. And behind me, in the shed, I could hear Jago planing, chipping, sharpening, polishing. I practised the words I intended to say in my head, and when I was well-rehearsed, I fetched a glass of squash for Jago from the house and took it into the shed. Jago removed his goggles and wiped sweat from his eyes. He took the glass from me and drank the squash in one go, his Adam's apple moving as he glugged. He chinked the ice at the bottom of the glass, and then took a piece out and rubbed it over his face.

'Jago,' I said.

'Yep?'

'Ellen told me . . .'

'Told you what?' He blinked. A gingery stubble was growing around his jawline and he still had a few acne spots on his neck. The ice water dripped onto his shirt. I was filled with tenderness.

'Oh, nothing,' I said.

I went up to Thornfield House, hoping to persuade Ellen to tell the truth to Jago, but we weren't alone for five minutes. Mr Brecht wanted to talk about the preparations for Ellen's eighteenth birthday party. She did not want a party, but the idea of it had become her father's latest obsession. He was manic, asking Ellen what she wanted the theme of the party to be, how she would like the house to look, what food she would prefer. Ellen didn't care. She made a half-hearted effort to appear interested, but she didn't fool me so I couldn't see how her father could be fooled either. He tried to make me join in with him, but I didn't want to play that game any more. I didn't want to be on his side. I looked at him as he stood frowning at Ellen, and I couldn't remember what it was that I used to find so glorious in him. Compared to Ricky, Mr Brecht was old. His hair was receding a little, the beard was stupid, the long hair ridiculous on a man his age. The first two fingers of his right hand had been yellowed by nicotine at the tips, and he was too thin, too persistent, too odd.

Despite all his talk, none of the party arrangements were concrete. No parcels had arrived, no invitations, as far as Ellen knew, had been posted. There was none of the excitement and activity she remembered there being when her parents threw parties together back in the old days. Ellen felt foreboding, but no pleasure. She was aware of a tension in her father that, she believed, would only be released when the birthday was over and done with.

Also, she was anxious about her inheritance. It was a long time since her mother had told her about it; more than two years had passed and Ellen was fretting about the details. Her mother had assured her that no action was necessary on her part; the arrangements had been put in place, the documents she needed would be sent, or delivered directly to her, but Ellen had no point of reference – no name, no telephone number, nobody to ask for advice or reassurance. She had never met a lawyer about an inheritance. She did not know what to expect.

Whenever I saw her, all Ellen wanted to talk about was the inheritance, but I closed off. I was determined not to be interested. It was one of the things about Ellen that made me cross and jealous. What had *she* ever done to deserve coming into a fortune? Why did such things only ever happen to people like Ellen, not to people like me? I read stories in magazines and books but I had never heard of anyone in real life coming into money on that scale before.

The baby was on Jago's mind that summer, and the inheritance was on Ellen's, but I did my very best not to dwell on either subject. I had a life of my own at last, a life that was separate from theirs, less complicated. At last I had plans and relationships that didn't involve either Jago or Ellen. Now I knew that the time to leave was imminent, I could hardly wait for it to arrive. Away from Trethene, I thought I would open up like a flower, and people would see the person I had always meant to be: not Ellen's sidekick or Jago's adoring younger sister, but Hannah Brown, trainee explorer and lover of Ricky Wendon.

I no longer wanted to be at home, with Jago rubbing me up the wrong way and my parents shuffling round worrying about the crime in Chile and the drugs and the heat and the water. Neither did I wish to be at Thornfield House, tiptoeing on eggshells through the myriad things Ellen and I couldn't talk about, or having to deal with Mr Brecht's birthday-party weirdness. I was happiest with Ricky, planning the next year of our lives, having fun, not needing to worry about things.

Because I was no longer available to act as a convenient go-between, communication became a problem for Jago and Ellen. One evening in early August, as the sun sank behind the neatly trimmed Leylandii hedge that separated our back garden from the farmland beyond, I heard Jago's footsteps on the stairs and he pushed open the door to my bedroom. I was sitting on the bed, with Trixie, reading. Jago came in, sat heavily on the end of the bed, bouncing me up, put his head in his hands and said, 'I'm going round to Thornfield House.'

'You can't.'

'I have to see Ellen.'

I put down the book. 'Jago, you can't. Really, you mustn't. What if her father hears you? What if he attacks you with the poker like he attacked Adam Tremlett?'

'He can't hurt me for no reason.'

'If he finds you in his house at night that's a perfectly good reason, and anyway . . .' I looked at my feet '. . . I think he knows about you and Ellen.'

'No, he doesn't.'

'He might do.'

'How could he?'

I shrugged. 'Perhaps he's seen you together.'

Jago shook his head. 'No. It's impossible.'

'You don't *know* that he's never seen you.'

Jago ignored me. 'I have to go to Thornfield tonight. I need to talk to Ellen about leaving.'

I sat up straight. 'What about leaving?'

'I've thought it through. Her birthday party is the perfect time to go. She'll have her legal documents by then. Her father will be busy with the other guests. He won't be able to watch Ellen all the time, not with so many people there. All she needs to do is walk out of the house while he's entertaining and I'll meet her on the lane. We can drive straight to London, to the airport.'

He smiled bashfully. 'I've booked two tickets to New York on the early-morning flight.'

I could see this was a good plan but I did not like it.

'What about me?' I asked.

'Good point,' said Jago. 'You could be our back-up at the party. You could keep an eye on the Psycho and distract him if he looks like he's going after Ellen.'

That had not been what I meant at all. My eyes filled with tears and I chewed at a nail, but Jago didn't notice.

'I must make sure Ellen understands what she needs to do,' he said. 'I have to see her and talk about the plans with her. She won't be able to pack or anything. It would be too risky. But she can have some of your things, can't she, Hannah? You don't mind?'

I turned my head away.

Jago noticed something was wrong then. He leaned over and punched me gently.

'Oh come on, Spanner, don't be sad. I'll make it up to you one day,' he said. 'I promise I will. We both will.'

Jago washed noisily that evening in the bathroom, leaving splashes of water all over the windowledge and the floor. He washed his face and under his arms with a flannel. He rinsed his beautiful copper-red hair under the cold tap, and shook his head like a dog. He went into his room with a towel around his shoulders, shut the door and put on some music, and stayed there until our parents were asleep. But I heard him go out at midnight. I heard and I ached with worry, because I knew it would only take one small thing to go against them, one glance from a window, one cough, one creaking floorboard – and they would be caught and that would be the end of everything.

I couldn't sleep.

I was still awake when I heard Jago opening the back door less than two hours after he had left. I slipped out of bed, tiptoed past the half-open door to my parents' bedroom, and went downstairs as quickly and as quietly as I could. Jago was in the kitchen, naked apart from his jeans, examining cuts and grazes on his left arm and shoulder. He looked terrible, as if he had been dragged through a hedge of thorns. There were leaves in his hair, and his jeans and hands and feet were bloody and filthy.

'What's happened?' I gasped. 'Where's your shirt? And your shoes?'

He didn't look up as he answered, 'The Psycho heard us.'

'Oh God!'

'I got out the window but I couldn't hold on. I fell. I think . . .' Jago winced as his fingers touched a deep cut on his back '. . . I think he saw me in the garden.'

'Did he recognize you?'

'I don't know.'

'Ellen,' I whispered. 'What about her?'

'She'll be OK. He thought I was trying to break in. He didn't realize I was on the way out.'

'What if he calls the police? Here, let me do that.' I took a wad of damp cotton wool from Jago and washed the grit from a wound at the back of his shoulder.

Jago winced again. 'He already did. As I came home through the woods, I saw the patrol car go by on the lane.'

Jago groaned. I gave him a gentle slap to make him turn his shoulder.

'What will you say if the police come knocking on our door?'

'I don't know. I'll think of something.'

'Mum and Dad will go mental.'

'I'll just deny I ever left the house. You'll back me up, won't you, Hannah? You'll say I was here all the time?'

Of course I would. I'd give him an alibi just like I always did. I had a pang of longing to be away, somewhere else, somewhere big and hot and different where people didn't have to lie.

'God, you're a mess, Jago Cardell,' I said as my brother's blood turned the wet tissue a sickly pale pink.

'It could have been worse,' said Jago.

'How could it have been worse?'

'The Psycho was pointing a shotgun at me through the window.'

CHAPTER FIFTY-FIVE

It was a beautiful drive from Berlin to Magdeburg, the road following the wide river, and the city, with its mixture of old and new architecture, slowly unspreading itself before us. John told me that it had been heavily bombed in the war. He said the city and its people had suffered terribly. He talked about the reunification of Germany, and a colleague of his who worked at Magdeburg University, and I half-listened . . . but I wasn't really interested. I was fizzing with excitement and nerves at the prospect of seeing Schloss Marien, the place that had been so central to Ellen's life.

We found the entrance to the grounds easily enough, but it was a private road, protected by large, wrought-iron security gates. Stone pillars stood on either side, and two Gothic wild boar lying on top frowning at us rather comically over their tusks. Trees in full leaf completely hid the view. John got out of the car and opened the map out on its roof.

'We might be able to see something from up there,' he said, indicating a vantage-point. I couldn't follow the map, but I trusted him. He turned the car round and looped back along the main road, parking in a picnic area at the bottom of the hill on whose slopes the house was built.

We walked together up a wide and well-trodden footpath, beneath a canopy of broad-leaved branches. Squirrels ran above our heads and there was birdsong, and sunlight dappling our way. It was very lovely. The air was fresh and although I was still nervous, I felt peaceful, as if I had been meant to come to this place.

John strode out ahead of me. 'I have to say, this is better than being stuck in a conference room,' he said.

I suspected he was worrying about what he was missing and how he would justify his absence to his colleagues, but didn't want me to feel bad about it.

After that, he didn't say much, and I too was lost in my thoughts. The path grew narrower, the climb steeper. I took off my jumper and tied it around my waist. My scalp was hot and I wished I'd brought something to fasten my hair back with. I wondered if Ellen had played in these woods as a little girl. Probably she had. Anne Brecht loved nature. She would have brought Ellen here for walks and picnics. Had Ellen come back to the forest when she was a teenager, knowing she was already pregnant? Had she walked up this path on her own? God, she must have been so lonely here, motherless and cut off from Jago, with her little secret growing inside her.

We had reached the top of the hill. I leaned over, panting, my hands on my knees. My legs were aching with the exertion but it was a good sensation.

'Hannah!' John called. 'Come and look at this!'

I followed him over to a gap in the trees where a bench hewn from a fallen trunk overlooked the valley below. We could see for miles. There, on the slopes, was Schloss Marien, a rambling set of buildings set in well-ordered gardens that gave way to fields and meadows. The river curled in a u-shape around the estate like a giant, green-grey ribbon.

'Wow,' I said. 'It's beautiful.'

'It's some place.'

'Ellen always said . . .' I began, but I trailed off. I had never entirely believed the stories of her life in Magdeburg. The Schloss had sounded too much like the setting for a fairy tale.

There was no moat or drawbridge, and no dungeon. It certainly wasn't the turreted, fairy-tale castle that Ellen had described to me as a child, but the main house was three storeys high, with the top set of windows looking out from amongst the red roof tiles. It was grand, but it had a friendly, haphazard look to it, as if buildings had been added on over the years without too much thought for aesthetics. Standing on the hill, looking down, I had a strong sense of déjà vu. It was Ellen, I thought, standing at my shoulder, looking with me. I held onto the trunk of a tree, rested against it and gazed down, taking it all in. I was certain, absolutely certain, that Ellen had stood where I was standing now, in this exact same spot, beside the same tree. The feeling was so strong that I thought if I reached out my hand behind me, Ellen would take it in hers, and hold on to me. I missed her. I missed her with all my heart. For a moment the grief was unbearable.

'Hannah?' John said. 'Are you OK?'

'Yes, yes, I'm fine. Do you think the Brecht family might still live there?'

'I don't see why they shouldn't,' John replied. 'Not unless they had some financial misfortune and had to sell. These kinds of places tend to stay in the family.'

I sat down on the bench, trying to take it all in. Below, in the grounds of the house, somebody was sitting on a ride-on mower, making stripes in the grass on the lawned areas to either side of the drive. The drone of the machine's engine drifted up to us through the air. It was indistinct, but I thought I could also hear music coming from inside the house, just snatches of it every now and then when the wind was coming in our direction. I could have been mistaken.

Several cars were parked in the courtyard beside the house.

'Someone's coming out,' said John.

'Where?'

'Down there, at the side. Someone's coming out into the garden.'

I craned forward to look, and he was right. We were too far away to see clearly, but it was obvious that the person was a woman. She was slender, with dark, shoulder-length hair. Everything about her was absolutely familiar to me.

I reached out and took hold of John's arm.

'What is it?' he asked.

'You can see that woman, can't you?'

'Of course I can.'

'Then she's real, she's not in my mind?'

'I'd say she's definitely real.'

I turned to look at him.

'That's her, John,' I said. 'That's Ellen Brecht.'

CHAPTER FIFTY-SIX

I hardly slept and was up at dawn the next morning, anxiously waiting for it to be late enough for me to go to Thornfield House to make sure that Ellen was all right and to collect Jago's clothes.

'What on earth's the matter with you two this morning?' Mum asked as she scrambled eggs, clattering away at the side of the pan with her fork. 'Jago was out of the house before the birds were up and now you're jumping about like you've got ants in your pants.'

'I just want to see Ellen,' I said. 'I want to check she's all ready for her party.'

'When is it?'

'Friday.'

'Ahh,' said Mum. She scraped the eggs onto toast and passed me the plate. 'Who's going to this party then?'

'Family mainly, I think. I expect the German relatives will be coming over.'

'I dare say that'll be it,' Mum nodded.

I had no appetite but I ate to stop Mum from nagging, and as soon as I'd finished my breakfast, I walked up to Thornfield House. My heart was pounding in my chest as I rang the doorbell. Mrs Todd answered. Her face was pinched and tense.

'Ellen is in the garden,' she said, standing aside to let me pass. Since the day at the clinic, Mrs Todd and I had been awkward with one another. It was the burden of sharing a guilty secret; but I knew something else was wrong that day, something extra.

I walked through the house into the back room, through the French windows and into the garden. It was early, and not warm, but Ellen was sitting on a chair beneath the frondy branches of the willow tree, reading. I could tell by her posture that nothing was right. Her back was straight, her shoulders rigid, all her angles were sharp. Her father sat beside her, cleaning his gun. I baulked at the sight of it, then stepped forward again.

'Hello!'

Mr Brecht looked up at me, then, without acknowledgement, looked down and continued his work.

I sat on the chair beside Ellen. She was breathing strangely, panting almost.

'OK?' I asked. She gave the tiniest of nods and turned a page of her book.

'Somebody tried to break into our house last night, Hannah,' said Mr Brecht. 'Isn't that strange? Aren't we unlucky to have attracted the attention of yet another intruder?'

'How awful,' I said. The words sounded all wrong; artificial, not convincing. 'Was it a burglar?'

'I don't know,' said Mr Brecht. 'But he was trying to take something, that's for sure.'

'Papa called the police,' Ellen said in a loud, brittle voice. 'They think it was unpremeditated. Just some lad walking by who thought he'd take his chance.'

'What do you think of that, Hannah?' Mr Brecht asked, smiling at me as if he could see right into my soul. I was afraid to say anything. He would know if I was telling the truth or a lie, I was certain of it.

'I . . . I don't know.'

'Strangest thing was,' said Mr Brecht, sticking a long, thin brush down the barrel of the gun and pumping it up and down viciously, 'this opportunist wasn't wearing a shirt. Don't you think that's odd, Hannah?'

'It was warm last night, Papa,' Ellen said.

Mr Brecht raised a disbelieving eyebrow as if he thought his daughter could hardly have come up with a less likely explanation. If the situation wasn't so terrible, I thought, it would be funny.

'Or shoes,' he said.

Now I was afflicted with a terrible urge to laugh. The feeling came over me all at once and the more I fought it, the stronger it was. I wrapped my arms around my waist and leaned over, trying to suppress the feeling.

'Are you all right, Hannah?' Mr Brecht asked. 'Ellen, take her inside and get her a drink.'

We went upstairs, and I threw myself face down on the bed, laughing uncontrollably. I couldn't stop. Tears were streaming down my face, and it was only when I heard an enormous bang that I managed to swallow the hysteria. I sat up straight then, wiping my face with my sleeves.

'What was that?' I asked, as gunshots boomed through the early-morning air, shattering the quiet, rousing every nerve in my body. The ugly noise ricocheted around the room, bouncing off the walls.

'Oh God, Ellen, is that your father? What's he doing?'

'Shooting rabbits.'

'Killing them?'

She nodded. 'Target practice.'

We stared at one another. I sniffed.

'You need to go,' Ellen said. 'Go now while he's out in the field.' She dived under her bed and emerged with a large carrier bag. 'It's Jago's things,' she said. 'Get them out of here.'

I took the bag, saying, 'Did Jago have a chance to tell you last night about his plan? Do you know what you have to do at the party?'

Ellen nodded.

'Then what's wrong?'

Ellen pulled a face, hugged herself and shivered. 'He knows something, Papa does. He keeps saying stuff.'

'What sort of stuff?'

'Sly little remarks and comments.'

'But he's always been like that. He's always trying to catch you out.'

'I know – but this is different. Even before last night . . . I don't know what he knows, but he knows something.'

'Do you think he recognized Jago last night?'

'I don't know.' Ellen bit her lower lip. Her arms were wrapped around herself and she jiggled up and down. 'What if he did, Hannah? What if he was watching and waiting? What if he saw Jago climb out of my window? What if he saw him climb in?'

'He probably didn't,' I said without much conviction.

But he might have done. Ellen was right. He might have done anything. I stood up and put my arms around her, pulling her to me. She rested her head on my shoulder. We looked out through the window and in the field over the road we saw Mr Brecht raise the gun to eye-level and take aim.

'I hate him,' Ellen whispered.

'It'll soon be over,' I said, stroking her head. 'Just a couple more days and you'll be away from here for ever. You'll be free. Everything will be fine. You'll see.'

CHAPTER FIFTY-SEVEN

The moment I saw Ellen, a little breeze blew up on top of the hill and wafted my hair across my face. It was soothing and soft – it made me feel as if I was where I had always been supposed to be.

'Are you all right, Hannah?' John asked.

I nodded.

John sat on the bench beside me. He rested his elbows on his knees and turned a twig between his fingers.

'I can't believe it,' I said, 'but she's there. That's her. What should we do?'

'Perhaps we should sit here a minute and think about this.'

The sweet breeze cooled my face on the hilltop, and down below, the same breeze lifted her hair. John and I watched as she pulled up a chair on the terrace, by the fountain, and then another. She went back inside the house and returned shortly with a straw hat on her head, and a book in her hand. Another woman followed behind, a tall, short-haired woman. I couldn't be certain, but she looked to me like Tante Karla. The two women appeared to be laughing. After a few moments, a third person came out to join them and they all sat down together.

'She looks happy,' I whispered. 'She looks all right.'

I looked to John for confirmation and he smiled at me. He brushed his fringe out of his eyes.

'Hannah, you know that can't be Ellen.'

'It's her. My hunch was right. She never died.'

I gazed down again. I felt as if I were looking into a different world, a world where a dead girl could be alive again, where she could be happy, where her life could play out in safety, away from anything that could hurt her. I had the feeling that, if I took my eyes from her, Ellen would disappear. She would be gone from me, for ever this time.

Perhaps, I thought, we didn't need to do anything more. We had come to Magdeburg, I had seen Ellen. God knows how, or why, but she was there and now I knew she was there, maybe the best thing would be to leave her in peace, and go back to my life and forget her.

Only I could not do that.

'Oh John,' I said. 'I don't know if I could bear to lose her again.'

I stood up, and I knew what I had to do. I turned back to the path and began to walk downhill; after a moment, my footsteps quickened and I broke into a run.

'Slow down!' John called. 'Wait for me!'

But I didn't want to wait for him, or anyone. As I ran, my feet skittering on the dry soil, sending pebbles racing down the path before me, I felt the weight of grief and loneliness slip away from me. They disappeared, were gone, like magic; it was as if they had never existed. All the time that spanned the distance between the moment when I read my mother's letter, sitting on the top bunk in the barn in Chile, to now, contracted to nothing. Ellen was just a few hundred yards away from me. The impossible was going to happen. I was going to see her again.

I had been given a chance to make things right.

CHAPTER FIFTY-EIGHT

It was the day of Ellen's party. Mum and I went to Thornfield House early. Mum had been enlisted to help clean the house in preparation. When we arrived, the house was a hive of activity. Men were outside erecting a marquee in the garden, caterers were laying out equipment in the kitchen and Mrs Todd was going around the house conscientiously moving anything of value to a safe place.

Ellen was as jumpy as a prawn on a skillet. She was dreading the party, dreading the thought of taking her mother's place, standing by her father's side and welcoming the guests, but at the same time she was racked with excitement about her impending elopement and claiming her inheritance. It was an exhausting combination and she looked terrible, her eyes wide with anxiety, her face a mask. She looked far older than her years. She worried me. She was so nervy that I thought she was almost bound to fight with her father or say something that would jeopardize the escape plan. She might do anything.

The postman came, but there was no large envelope, no papers for Ellen, nothing from any firm of solicitors.

'That must mean the documents are going to be delivered

by hand,' she said. 'Somebody will come and give them to me. Perhaps I'll have to sign for them.'

'Perhaps,' I said.

Mr Brecht prowled around the house, smoking and rubbing his hands together.

'What exactly is going to happen this evening?' Ellen asked him, and he laughed.

'That would be telling! All you need to know, *Schatzi*, is that there will be plenty of surprises for you. Oh yes!'

Ellen frowned. 'I don't like surprises, Papa.'

'But life is full of surprises, Ellen. You, for instance, surprise me every day. Your capacity for creativity never ceases to amaze me.'

Ellen glanced at me from under her fringe. Her eyes were saying: *See what I mean?* And she was right, her father was behaving as if he knew something she didn't. He was unsettling me too.

We went into the front room where Mum was polishing the grand piano to a gleam. Silver candelabras had been positioned around the room and a new rug lay on the floor, covering Adam Tremlett's bloodstains.

'I think your father must be planning for you to give your guests a recital tonight,' Mum said to Ellen with a smile.

'I expect so,' Ellen said. She lifted the piano lid and trickled her fingers along the keys. Then she sighed and replaced the lid. 'Have you heard anyone mention anything about my German family, Mrs Brown? Do you know if they've arrived yet? I thought my grandparents would have come to see me this morning. I hoped Tante Karla, at least, would have come.'

Mum straightened and stretched, pressing her two hands into the small of her back.

'Nobody's said anything to me,' she said. 'But perhaps they've been told not to. Perhaps that's all part of the surprise.'

'Perhaps,' said Ellen. She didn't sound convinced.

For the thousandth time she went outside to see if anyone had arrived with her legal papers. Each time a vehicle passed along the lane her face brightened with anticipation, but each time she was disappointed. No cars pulled into the drive.

Mr Brecht, meanwhile, strode around the house directing the tradespeople in a loud and unnaturally jolly voice, making everyone feel uncomfortable.

'He's not being normal,' Ellen said as we pinned bunting in the front garden, which gave us an opportunity to keep an eye out for the solicitor. 'Something's wrong.'

'Ellen, your father is never normal. He's actually trying to do something nice for you for a change. That's probably all it is.'

'No,' Ellen shook her head. 'He keeps looking at me. He knows something. He's planning something – I know he is.'

She stood on the step-ladder and peered over the wall. 'Oh, where is this lawyer?' she cried. 'Where is he? Why doesn't he come?'

I turned to see Mr Brecht standing behind us. I wondered if he'd overheard and my cheeks flushed. He caught my eye and winked. I looked away again quickly.

'Who are you waiting for, Ellen?' he asked.

'Nobody, Papa.'

He was holding a large white envelope. He tapped it against his thigh.

'I think you're lying, *Schatzi*. I think you're lying to me again.'

Ellen climbed down the step-ladder. She was trying to look relaxed, but failing. Mr Brecht fanned his face with the envelope.

'Is that for me?' she asked, holding out her hand. Mr Brecht moved the envelope out of her reach.

'It has your name on it.'

'Please, Papa. Please give it to me.'

'Hmm,' said Mr Brecht. He looked at the envelope and then back at his daughter. 'You were expecting some papers today, weren't you, Ellen? But you didn't say anything to me. Why not?'

Ellen made a grab for the envelope. He moved it again. He laughed.

'Why didn't you talk to me about your inheritance, *Schatzi*? Why didn't you confide in me? Did you think I didn't know? Of course I knew! I've known you were the beneficiary of your grandmother's will ever since we returned to England! Your mother and I met the solicitor and he explained everything. It was one of the first things we did.' He laughed nastily. 'The silly old woman had tried to arrange things so that I couldn't get my hands on her money. She should have tried harder.'

A knot of worry began to tie itself in my guts.

Ellen stiffened. 'I didn't talk to you, Papa, because Mama told me not to. She told me not to trust you.'

'Ellen . . .' I said, reaching out for her. She shrugged me off.

Mr Brecht's face had tightened and his eyes had narrowed. He and Ellen stared at one another.

'Your mother was the sole trustee of your grandmother's will, Ellen,' he said. 'And before she died, she signed the trusteeship over to me.'

Ellen was leaning forward, trembling.

'Mama would never have done that. She told me! She said she'd never let you get your hands on my fortune!'

Mr Brecht smiled and shook his head. 'She shouldn't have cheated on me,' he said. 'I was loyal to her, I loved her, I looked after her and she . . . she lied and cheated and made a mockery of our marriage. She was the one who broke the trust between us, *Schatzi*. My crime was nothing compared to hers. I didn't even *want* the money.'

'What did you do to her?'

'Nothing. I gave her the pen and showed her where to sign her name. She thought she was giving her consent for you to go on a school trip, but in fact she was making me trustee of your fortune. She should have been more careful, Ellen. Those who deceive can't afford to be complacent.' He sighed. 'It's such a pity,' he said. 'I didn't want you to suffer, *Schatzi*, but I had to make her pay for her infidelity, one way or another.'

'You're a fool,' Ellen said. 'How was that making her pay? She didn't even know you'd tricked her into making you a trustee. It didn't hurt her!'

Mr Brecht took a deep breath. He rubbed his chin.

'She did know,' he said. 'I told her when it was too late for her to do anything about it.'

I remembered him sitting by the bed where Anne Brecht lay dying. I remembered how he held her hand in his, how close his face had been to hers, so close she must have breathed in his exhaled breath, how he had whispered to her and how I thought he had been comforting her. I remembered how she had turned her face from him. She had been too weak to speak but I had seen the look in her eyes.

'Oh God!' I cried, in horror.

Mr Brecht looked at me, surprised, as if he had forgotten I was there.

'I had to tell her what I'd done, Hannah,' he said. 'Because if she didn't know, if she didn't spend the last hours of her life thinking about what *she*'d done, what was the point?'

Beside me, I could feel Ellen's distress pricking through the air like electricity. I willed her to stay composed.

Mr Brecht reached out his hand and Ellen took the envelope from him.

'It's all in there,' he said. 'You're eighteen now. It's all yours. Have a good read.'

He turned and walked back into the house. His step was light and easy.

Ellen waited until he had disappeared inside Thornfield House before she started shaking. She was in shock. She was beyond tears. I put my arms round her and I kept whispering to her, reassuring her, telling her that everything would be all right, that she would be fine.

We went into the corner of the garden where we could hide beneath the willow tree. We sat together in the long grass and she ripped open the envelope, tearing into it with her teeth and fingers, scattering papers around the grass.

She took out a letter, read it quickly and passed it to me. It was from a Falmouth-based firm of solicitors, just a covering letter that said all the documents pertaining to Ellen's inheritance were enclosed and asking her to confirm receipt by return.

'Is there a cheque?' I asked. She shook her head.

She picked up one of the documents, read it, and tossed it aside. She picked up the next.

'Oh God,' she whispered. 'Everything he said was true. Mama did make him trustee.'

I picked up a sheaf of papers, clipped together, which were the deeds to Thornfield House.

'Your grandma left the house to you, Ellen,' I said.

'I don't want the house. I hate the house. What good is it to me?'

'You could sell it.'

'But that takes ages, doesn't it? Jago and I need the money now! How can I sell the house if I'm in America?' Her voice was panicky, verging on hysterical. 'What else is there?'

We looked through the other documents: several remortgages, loans taken out against the house, records of shares sold, deposit accounts emptied, overdraft agreements, credit bills.

I had a pain inside me. I felt sick. Ellen was white as a sheet.

'What is all this?' Ellen asked. 'What does it mean?'

I read a snippet of a document: *the charge taken out against Thornfield House to the value of £40,000 . . . as yet unpaid . . . further interest . . . fees incurred.*

'I don't know what it means,' I said, although I did know, it was obvious. 'You'll have to ask someone who understands these things.'

Ellen frowned. She bit her knuckles.

'None of these papers says anything about any money coming to me.'

'No.'

Ellen stared up at me. She looked very young, a child who has just understood something important about the world.

'There *is* no fortune, is there, Hannah?' she asked. 'There is no money. Even if I sold the house, there would be nothing. It's all debt. He's taken it all.'

I reached out my hand and touched her shoulder. She flinched away.

'Oh God!' she said. 'What are we going to do? What will Jago say? I've been telling him all this time that we were going to have thousands of pounds, and now . . . I don't want us to end up in some poky little apartment.'

'It's OK,' I said. 'Jago doesn't care about the money. He doesn't! Just keep calm, Ellen. Don't let your father see you're upset. As long as you keep your head, you can still go away. Nothing has really changed.'

'But—'

Mrs Todd called us from the front door.

'Just act normal,' I said. 'Don't do anything to rile him. Just get through this party and it will all be over. You'll be away. OK?'

Ellen nodded. She had been completely wrongfooted. She had thought she was directing the last scene in the last act of the story of her life there at Thornfield House, but suddenly the rules had been changed. She was looking to me for direction. Ellen Brecht had lost control entirely.

We went into the house and said goodbye to my mother, who had finished her cleaning. I ate some cold meat and salad Mrs Todd had prepared for lunch, although Ellen said her mouth was too dry to eat, and after that, for a while, I sat beside Ellen as she lay on her bed. She was exhausted but she would not sleep; she stared at the light from the sun reflected on the ceiling and her eyes were glassy and, for the first time ever, without passion.

'Just a few more hours,' I told her again. 'Just keep going for a few more hours, Ellen, and you'll be away from here. Don't give in now.'

As the afternoon wore on, Mrs Todd called us into the back garden to help decorate the marquee. Trestle tables had been laid along the back edge, and a smaller round table, which I thought must be for a cake, stood in the centre.

'Are we having a buffet?' I asked.

'Something's wrong,' Ellen said, and I thought, Everything is wrong. She bit her nails and looked around her. 'Something's terribly wrong!' she said again, and her voice was distressed. I took a step towards her and, at that moment, the canvas flap that was the door to the marquee flew back and Mr Brecht appeared with his arms full of white ribbons and yellow roses and lilies.

'The decorations have arrived,' he said. 'Aren't they beautiful!'

'But, Papa, we never have flowers.'

'It's your birthday! Every girl deserves flowers on her special day. Now don't turn your nose up at them, Ellen, they cost a fortune. I had to pay by credit card, but hey, what's a few more pounds in the red between family?'

He laid the flowers down on one of the tables.

'There are lanterns too,' said Mr Brecht. 'And candles. Make the garden beautiful, Ellen. Turn it into a backdrop that nobody who's here tonight will ever forget.'

Ellen's arms hung at her side.

'A backdrop for what, Papa?' she asked, without raising her eyes.

'Your birthday, of course!'

The roses were strongly scented, almost garish in colour against the pristine white of the tablecloth, and already the lilies were staining it with their brown pollen. I went into the house and returned with as many glass vases as I could carry in my arms. Inside I was panicking, but all I could think was that we had to carry on acting normally. It was the only way to make sure Ellen got away.

Ellen was quiet, biting at her lip.

'What now?' I asked. It seemed to me that things could hardly be any worse than they already were.

'Lilies are funeral flowers and yellow roses mean betrayal,' she said.

'They're only flowers.'

'He didn't choose them by accident, Hannah. Don't you see? Nothing he does is accidental. He's planning to kill someone!'

I tried to reassure her, but she wouldn't be reassured, and as the afternoon faded into evening her edginess began to infect me too. Neither of us knew what Mr Brecht was planning. We were afraid.

By late afternoon the garden and house were decorated, the caterers were busy in the food tent, the wine was chilling. Mr Brecht clapped his hands and told Ellen to go and change while Mrs Todd lit the candles and the lanterns.

Ellen's silver-grey evening dress, the one her father had given her the previous year, was hanging from the picture rail in her bedroom. The two of us went upstairs and I looked out of the window.

'Nobody's arrived yet.'

'I don't know what time he told them to come.'

'Maybe they're all going to come together in one great big convoy.'

'Or they might have hired a coach. Don't look.'

I turned my back while Ellen changed. When she was ready, I noticed how the dress clung to her. She had filled out, grown up. She did not look like a coltish young girl any longer. She looked like a woman. I helped her fasten her hair up and then she reached out and took hold of my hands.

'This is our last evening together,' she said. 'This is the end of you and me.'

'It's not the end,' I said. 'It's the beginning of a new phase.'

'I'll never have another friend like you, Hannah.'

'Me neither.'

We smiled at one another.

'I'm sorry,' we both said at exactly the same time, and I don't think either of us quite understood why we were apologizing, or why we were both so close to tears.

'You look beautiful,' I said, and it was true.

'I hate this dress.'

'You'll never have to wear it again.'

'I suppose we ought to go down,' she said, 'before any of the guests arrive.'

Outside, the light of day was fading and the candles were twinkling in their jars.

Mrs Todd, who had been given the evening off, kissed Ellen goodbye, and I told Ellen to stand in the rose bower so I could take her picture.

After that, we wandered around the garden. The smells

coming from the kitchen were mouthwatering. Music coiled from the marquee. Piano music. I recognized it, with a shudder, as the *Raindrop Prelude*, Mrs Brecht's death music.

Ellen looked around.

'Where is everyone?' she asked. She laughed nervously. 'Where are all my guests?'

'Perhaps they're hiding in the marquee?'

We crossed the lawn, the grass already dampening with dew. Ellen opened the canvas flap, and I followed her inside.

The air in the marquee was heady with the scent of the lilies and citronella candles. Flowers and ribbons and yellow and white balloons were strung from its canvas walls. A huge banner said: *Happy Birthday Ellen*. A pile of presents, all wrapped in gold paper and ribbon, was heaped on the trestle tables at the back and the music was being piped from somewhere. It filled the space; it was all around.

The small table in the centre of the marquee had been laid for two. There were two fancy red-and-gold antique chairs and a long-legged wine cooler, full of ice. An ornate chandelier hung above it. Apart from that, the marquee was empty.

'I don't understand,' said Ellen. She looked around her. 'Where is everyone else going to eat? Where *is* everyone?'

Her father had been waiting for us. Now he came through the entrance. He was wearing a morning suit, but it was not clean, and his hair was long and he hadn't shaved for a while. He looked creepy, like a character in a masque. He had a strange, wide smile on his face and the gun was in his hand. He propped it against the little round table, then stepped forward and took Ellen's hands in his.

'I know you weren't keen on having a party with lots of people and fuss,' he said. 'So I thought I'd give you what you wanted, *Schatzi*. A special dinner. Just the two of us.'

Ellen was trembling. She glanced over to me, panic in her eyes.

'What about Hannah? Where's Hannah going to sit?'

'Hannah hasn't been invited to this party,' said Mr Brecht. He led Ellen to one of the fancy chairs beside the table; dreamlike, she sat. 'It's exclusive. You and me, Ellen. Just you and me.'

'But—'

Mr Brecht looked at me. 'You're going home now, aren't you, Hannah?'

I nodded.

Mr Brecht smiled. He unfolded Ellen's napkin, shook it out and placed it on her lap. He sat in the other chair, beside her. He took the wine from the ice bucket and filled both Ellen's glass and his own.

'*Prost!*' he said. '*Zum Wohl!*'

'*Prost*,' Ellen repeated dully.

'Still here, Hannah?' Mr Brecht asked. He reached for the gun. I moved towards the door.

'Don't worry about us,' he said. 'We're perfectly safe. If anyone else should turn up – that half-naked burglar, for example – I'll be ready for him. And I won't mess about this time. Tonight,' he said, patting the gun, 'I'm in the mood for the kill.'

CHAPTER FIFTY-NINE

At the car park at the bottom of the hill that overlooked Magdeburg, we got into the car and John drove back along the winding road, pulling up at the entrance to Schloss Marien. The stone boar lay on their plinths and watched us with their stone eyes.

John leaned out and pressed the intercom button. There were a few moments' silence and then a friendly woman's voice came through the speaker.

'*Hallo?*'

'It's Karla,' I said. I leaned over John. 'Karla, hello! This is Hannah, Ellen's friend from Cornwall.'

There was a rustle and slight commotion at the other end of the intercom.

'Hannah? Little Hannah Brown?'

'Yes.'

'*Mein Gott!* Hannah, welcome, come in, come in!'

John smiled at me. I smiled back. The gates purred into life and slid back into their frames. John moved the car slowly into the drive.

I had been so bowled over by emotion when I saw Ellen, that now I felt almost empty, vertiginous. It had been too much, back there on the hilltop – too much emotion and too much confusion. I understood nothing. I didn't know how Ellen could be alive, I didn't know what had brought me here, to her, I didn't know how I should feel in this situation. It was too much for me and my cold, lonely heart. I was light and insubstantial, not made of flesh and blood, but pure spirit. Once more I thought: I've been given another chance. After all these years, I can make things right.

As the car wound along the narrow drive, in and out of the dappling sunlight, I thought not only of Ellen, but also of Jago and the loneliness in which he'd been mired for the past twenty years, and I wondered how I could ever explain all this to him. Could we be friends again, he and I? Was there the possibility of reconciliation? Was there any way back to how we used to be?

The drive seemed to go on for ever, through the lush park-land that surrounded the Schloss. At last it opened out into a wide, gravelled area in front of the grand facade of the house. Karla was standing at the top of a rank of wide stone steps. She was wearing a long-sleeved kaftan over a swim-suit, flip-flops and a large-brimmed sunhat.

She waved as I climbed out of the car, and then she came trotting down the steps and embraced me thoroughly. She must have been in her early sixties but she was still youthful in appearance and behaviour.

'My darling girl, how did you find us? How did you track us down?' she asked, holding onto my shoulders with both hands and looking me up and down.

'Ellen once sent a postcard from here.'

'And this?' Karla asked, beaming at John who was hover-ing just behind me. 'Who is this?'

'This is John.'

'What a handsome man. Your husband?'

'No, no.' I hid my embarrassment with a nervous laugh. 'Not my husband. We work together.'

'Her chauffeur,' John said.

'My friend.'

He and Karla shook hands. Then Karla kissed him on both cheeks anyway. 'It's the German way,' she explained. 'Come in, come through; the girls and I are sitting on the terrace. It's a sun-trap.'

We followed her into the cool gloom of the building. It was as I had expected it to be, high-ceilinged, with exposed beams and lots of stonework, but it had a friendly, welcoming feel to it. I would have liked to stop time, there and then, to hold onto the moment for ever, but I didn't. I kept walking, through a grand hallway and into an airy drawing room – the same room, I realized, where Anne Brecht had been photographed for the magazine – and out onto the terrace. There was the stone hart that Mr Brecht had been standing beside in the photograph. There was the fountain. And there, standing behind the fountain, smiling, waiting – was Ellen.

Except it wasn't Ellen.

It couldn't have been Ellen; Ellen was dead.

But she looked so like Ellen.

She was still a girl; her eyes were a little greener than Ellen's, and there was an auburn tinge to her hair. She was wearing make-up, red lipstick, but still I could see speckles of acne around her jawline. I didn't understand. I looked at Karla, who was beaming and clasping her hands to her chest with a mixture of pride and delight, at John who was watching me, and back to the young woman.

The girl stepped forward, holding out her hand towards me. She uncurled her fingers and there, crumpled in her palm, was the gold necklace with the treble clef charm.

'I'm so happy to meet you, Hannah,' she said. 'I'm Kirsten. I'm Ellen's daughter.'

CHAPTER SIXTY

I ran away from Thornfield House and the marquee and Mr Brecht and his gun. I ran all the way home, down the darkening lane. I threw back the gate to our cottage so hard that it slammed against the wall behind, and ran to the door.

Jago came round the side of the house, Trixie trotting after him, wagging her tail.

'What are you doing back here?' he asked. 'You're supposed to be at the party. Did you forget something?'

Then he looked at me more closely.

'Hannah? Are you all right?'

I shook my head and tried to catch my breath, leaning over to clutch a stitch in my side.

'You can't go,' I panted.

'What do you mean?'

'You can't go to Thornfield House tonight. You can't take Ellen away. You can't do anything now.'

'Hannah . . .'

'Her father knows about you and Ellen,' I gasped. 'He knows and he's ready for you. He's got his gun. He's going to kill you.'

'No, he's not.' Jago pulled a face. 'Don't be such a drama queen.'

That was what I used to call Ellen. I used to think she was making things up, that she was exaggerating. Shame and anger rattled through me.

I grabbed hold of Jago's arm. 'You mustn't go there, Jago. Not tonight. Do you hear me? You mustn't!'

I started to sob with frustration. Trixie sloped off with her ears flat against her head and her tail between her legs.

'Hannah, stop this,' Jago said. 'Stop being so weird. We have to leave tonight. The tickets are booked.'

'You're not listening to me!'

'Because you're not making any sense.'

'Ellen doesn't want you to go!' I cried.

Jago grabbed me by the shoulders. My arms were bare and his fingers hurt. 'What do you mean? What's wrong? What's he done to her?'

'Nothing, he hasn't done anything. But there's no party. It's just them – just the two of them. Just Ellen and her father, and she doesn't want you there.'

'Fuck him,' said Jago. 'Fuck the bastard. I'm going anyway. I'll walk in and take her out from under his nose if I have to. He can't stop us!'

'He'll shoot you and then he'll say it was self-defence! The police know you were there the other night. Oh Jago, please . . .'

Jago kicked open the front door to our house, sat down on the step and began to lace up his boots. I was crying properly now, great sobs. I was frantic; desperate.

'Jago, you can't go,' I said. 'Listen to me! Ellen doesn't want to see you.'

'You're lying.'

'I'm not.' I calmed myself a little. I wiped the snot from my nose on my arm. My body was still shaking. 'She told me to tell you she doesn't want to see you.'

'What are you talking about?' Jago frowned but he

dropped his laces. I saw a tiny window of hope. There was a chance I could stop him if I used the right words. 'You mean because she's scared of her father?'

'No. I mean she doesn't want to see you any more,' I said. 'It's over between you. It's finished.'

Jago laughed. 'Why would she tell you something important like that and not me, heh? She *loves* me, Hannah. She loves me! She tells me everything.'

I don't know what happened then. I can't explain it but my fear changed into a huge anger. All the jealousy I'd been containing for years, all the hurt, all the frustration came to the surface. In the beginning it had been Jago and me and then it had been Jago and Ellen and me, but for years now it had been Jago and Ellen with me on the outside looking in. I'd been their messenger, their helper, their confidante. I'd looked after them both, covered their tracks, lied for them and listened to them talking and agonizing for interminable hours. Ellen and Jago had hijacked my teenage years, they had consumed the best years of my life – and after all that sacrifice, my own brother thought I was so irrelevant that Ellen would never have told me anything without telling him first.

I'd never felt a fury like it. It blazed in me. It was cathartic. It was so powerful it was almost beautiful. And after that, it was easy. My fury made me calm and I knew what to say.

'She's changed her mind about going away with you,' I said. 'She got her inheritance this morning and that's changed everything. She doesn't want to live in some dump in New York with you when she can do whatever she wants without you. That's what she said.'

I enjoyed it. I enjoyed hurting him. Even as the words were coming out, I knew they were terrible, but they made me feel strong and clean, they purged that festering resentment. I reasoned, inasmuch as I could reason anything in the state

I was in, that I would recant the lies in the morning, when everything had calmed down and the immediate danger to Jago had passed.

Jago looked at me. He paused just long enough for me to see that my words were having an effect. He'd been abandoned before. He'd been rejected. His mother had died and his father had dumped him, and his uncle and aunt had treated him with cruelty. Deep down, I realized, Jago had always believed he was unlovable, not good enough. Despite what he said, he did not believe that Ellen loved him as he loved her. I took advantage of his vulnerability. I revelled in it.

'She could have anyone she wanted,' I said. 'Why would she want you?'

'No.' Jago shook his head. 'I don't believe you.'

'Jago, for fuck's sake!' I shouted. 'She doesn't love you! She's had an abortion!'

We both went still then. We stared at one another in mutual horror.

'No,' Jago said. '*No!*'

'She did! I was with her!'

He pushed me, hard. I stumbled backwards towards the garden gate, and fell.

'You're lying!'

'How can I be lying?' I asked, crawling towards him again. My voice was rising – ugly, mean. 'You told her not to tell anyone about the baby – not even me. But she did tell me, and she said she didn't want your bastard baby, and I was there when she had the abortion.'

'No.'

'She's changed her mind, Jago!' I shouted, grabbing hold of his knees and shaking them. 'She doesn't want you any more.' I pulled myself up until I was standing, and stood on tiptoe to put my face up close to his as I screamed: 'She doesn't care about you! She says you're boring and stupid! She says she can do better than you! That's why she's not going anywhere with you! That's why she doesn't want to see you again! That's why she killed your baby!'

CHAPTER SIXTY-ONE

Kirsten's fingers were slender and long, like Ellen's, her feet narrow. She had a tattoo around her left ankle, a Thai blessing rising up her leg, a pierced tongue and a bright pink streak under her hair – so, she explained, she could clip it to one side when she wasn't at work and transform herself into a wild child. She had straight white teeth and an easy smile and beautiful eyes. She had all Ellen's charm, and none of her angst. She seemed to have inherited or absorbed Karla's sunny disposition.

My mind was reeling, thoughts swirling around like fog. I couldn't hold onto anything, nothing made sense.

'I don't understand,' I said. 'How can you be Ellen's daughter? She couldn't have had a child. There wasn't time.'

A young woman came out of the Schloss with a tray of refreshments. John, who was perched on the side of the fountain, took it from her. There was iced coffee and more cake. The girl sat down with us. Her hair was very short and her ears and face glittered with body jewellery. She was dressed in punk clothes. She introduced herself as Dora and said she was Kirsten's friend. The girls had met at language school, where they were studying English.

'I don't understand,' I said again. I couldn't take my eyes off Kirsten. I felt as if I knew her, as if I had always known her, but at the same time she was a stranger to me. 'It's impossible.'

Kirsten took a deep breath. She glanced at her aunt.

'When did you last see Ellen?' Karla asked me gently.

'The last time . . .' I paused. It had been almost two decades ago and I had never once spoken to anyone about the encounter. I could not bear to go back to it, not even in my own mind. The last time I saw Ellen had been two days after her birthday. The morning before I left Trethene with Ricky to fly to South America.

I tried again. 'The last time I saw her . . .' but I couldn't do it. I couldn't speak. John came and sat next to me. He put his arm around me, his hand on my shoulder. The weight of it was a comfort to me. I could feel his thumb resting against the base of my neck. My pulse beat against it. He was all that was holding me together.

'It was just after her eighteenth birthday,' I managed.

'You didn't know she was pregnant?'

'She wasn't pregnant,' I said in a low voice. 'She had been, but she'd had an abortion.'

'No.' Kirsten shook her head. 'She didn't. She just made you believe that she had.'

Karla came closer to me. She sat in front of me and took hold of my hands. Hers were cool and dry. She reached up and stroked the side of my face.

'Convincing you and Mrs Todd that she'd had the abortion was the best way to protect Ellen's baby from her father. If there was any danger of the secret coming out, she knew the baby, and the baby's father, would be in danger. But if you all believed there was no baby, no problem.'

She smiled. 'She must have loved the baby's father very much to go so far to protect him.'

Kirsten hunched her shoulders. 'It's a shame he didn't feel

the same way about her.' She looked at me. 'He abandoned her, you know.'

'It wasn't his fault,' I whispered. The memory of what I had done, how I had driven Jago away, flooded back through me. Some of the words I had said, the cruel things I'd told him, crashed into me. I remembered Jago's face, his twenty-year-old face, his eyes, the conflict in them as he struggled not to believe me when I told him Ellen did not love him, did not want him, and had destroyed his child. I had stood and watched as his trust in her – in them, in their future – fractured and disintegrated, drained away. I had destroyed him. I had sent him away. It was my fault. It had been me, not him.

Oh dear God, I thought now. What have I done?

CHAPTER SIXTY-TWO

Jago went away that same night.

He drove off in the Escort and nobody knew where he had gone.

My mum and dad were beside themselves with worry. None of us slept that night, or the next. Trixie cowered beneath my bed. Mum and Dad did not know that he had chosen to leave, but I knew. The crib was gone from the shed and the baby clothes from his bedroom, but there was a pile of fresh, white-grey ash behind the hedge at the edge of the fields that backed onto Cross Hands Lane. In my mind's eye, I could see Jago lighting the fire, throwing the things he'd made so carefully, and chosen with so much love, into the flames. I could see him wiping the smuts from his eyes with the back of his arm as everything that reminded him of Ellen, or his hopes for the future, crackled and curled and charred. I could see the red glow of the fire reflected in the tears streaked across his face. Jago thought he was useless and he believed that's what Ellen thought too. He told himself he was shit, a waste of space: a loser.

Jago hadn't left a note. My parents were bewildered. They thought he must have had an accident, fallen from a cliff, or been swept out to sea. I said as little as possible. I made tea for my mother and covered my hands with my ears so I couldn't hear her frantic whispering to my father, or her prayers. Dad said little but I heard him too. The evening after Jago left, he went out with 10p in his pocket to call the coastguard from the phone box on the green. After that, he came back for his keys and drove off in the van without saying anything to us. Mum and I sat together in the living room, holding one another's hands, white-faced and silent while the clock ticked and the dawn gradually stained the night sky from black to grey. And then Dad came back and he sat in his chair, and for the first time in my whole life, I saw him cry, his big bear-body shaking with sobs he could not control.

A body had been washed up further along the coast, Dad told us; a young man's body. He shook his head and tried to stem the flow of his tears with a handkerchief.

Dad went into the mortuary.

The body wasn't Jago's.

I thought I couldn't leave my parents. I couldn't fly to Chile while all this was happening, but they wanted me to go. They didn't want Jago to ruin my future, they said. Dad almost pleaded with me and I realized that it would be easier for them, without me. They wouldn't have to take me into consideration, whatever happened. They could be less stoic. They could say what they really wanted to say to one another. They could voice their fears.

They were the innocent ones, my mum and dad. They knew nothing. They speculated and guessed. I knew.

I went to the beach, by myself, and sat and stared out to sea. In my mind I begged Jago to come home. I stood at the water's edge and I stretched out my arms and I screamed his name over and over into the wind, and I hoped the wind would carry my screams to Jago. It didn't.

And as the minutes turned into hours and the hours turned

into days, I tried not to think about Ellen, stuck up at Thornfield House with her father. I didn't want to have to worry about what she was thinking. She'd be all right, I thought. She'd be relieved that Jago had stayed away. She was probably occupied with sorting through those legal papers. And anyway, I was too busy to see her. I had so much to do, and my priority now was my own life. I packed my rucksack. I sorted out my bedroom. And soon enough, only a few hours were left before Ricky's father would pick me up to take the two of us to London to catch the plane to South America.

I didn't want to see Ellen, I didn't want to face her. I didn't want to have to tell her what I had done. She knew I was leaving. She knew which plane I was catching. She would understand if I didn't turn up.

I left my rucksack by the front door, went into the kitchen and put some bread into the toaster.

Mum looked up from her ironing. 'What are you doing?'

'I'm hungry.'

Mum glanced at the clock on the wall. 'Aren't you going to pop up to Thornfield House to say goodbye to Ellen?'

I turned my back to Mum and took a plate from the drainer.

'There's still time,' said Mum. 'I'll come with you if you like. I never gave her her birthday card and I—'

'No!' I cried. 'No, don't come. I'd like to have a bit of time on my own with Ellen.' I put the plate on the counter. 'I'll take the card. You can have the toast,' I said.

I heard the music before I reached the gates to Thornfield House. I followed the sound, dawdling across the drive to the front door. I was hoping something would happen to change the course of events, so that I would not have to go inside and face Ellen and confess what I had done. I closed my eyes and prayed for an earthquake, or a plane crash. But nothing happened. I opened my eyes and the day was still dreary grey, muggy with summer heat, the midges were still swarming and the music was still playing. Mrs Todd was at the door wearing her summer coat and her horseshoe headscarf, carrying her handbag and a wicker shopping basket with an umbrella tucked under her arm.

I smiled at her half-heartedly. She smiled back.

'I'm glad you're here, Hannah,' she said. 'Ellen's been very low. You can keep her company while I go to the supermarket.'

'Is Mr Brecht in?'

'He's upstairs,' said Mrs Todd, indicating with her eyes that Mr Brecht was above us, in the room where his wife died. 'Try not to disturb him.'

I went through the hall, and stood for a moment at the door to the front room, which was slightly ajar. I didn't like going into the room, knowing about the bloodstains that lay beneath the rug. My heart was beating fast, too fast. I touched the door with my fingertips and it swung open and I stepped inside. Ellen must have felt the draught, because she stopped playing at once and turned to me.

Her face was wan, her eyes dark, shadowed by circles of tiredness and stress, but she smiled when she saw me and slipped off the stool and came towards me, holding her arms out. She was wearing her shorts and a huge hooded sweatshirt that I recognized as one that had once belonged to Jago. I stepped back as she came towards me. I wouldn't let her touch me.

'Oh Hannah,' she said, dropping her arms by her side. 'Thank goodness you're here!'

I retracted a little, moved away, and she felt this and let me go. She smiled – her wide smile. She rubbed her nose with the back of her fingers, and scratched behind her knee with her toes.

'Here,' I said, holding out the birthday present I had never had a chance to give her. When Ellen reached out and took the small parcel, I noticed that her fingernails were bitten down to the quick and her cuticles were bloodied. She unwrapped the present. It was a photograph of the two of us on the beach in a small, heart-shaped frame that I'd made myself and decorated with drift-glass.

'It's so you don't forget me,' I said, 'when I'm in Chile.'

'I think it's more likely to be the other way round,' Ellen said. She was still smiling. She held the present to her heart. 'This is the best thing to come out of the shittest eighteenth birthday ever,' she said. I smiled a feeble smile.

Ellen put the photograph on top of the piano.

She was waiting for something. She was waiting for me to give her news.

'I . . . I'm leaving this afternoon,' I said. 'Ricky's father is driving us to the airport.'

Ellen bit her bottom lip. If she was envious of my freedom, my new start, my widening horizons, she did not show it.

'You're going to have an amazing time,' she said. 'I'm so proud of you. I knew you'd find a way to get out of here, somehow.'

'Ellen . . .'

She held a finger to her lips then pointed to the ceiling. 'I'll put some music on,' she said, 'then we can talk without *him* hearing us.'

She went over to the stereo, squatted, chose an album, slipped the disc from its sleeve and put it on the turntable. I watched as she set the record spinning, lifted the arm, blew dust from the needle, and dropped it onto the record. It was a Rolling Stones compilation. The first track was: 'Have You Seen Your Mother, Baby'. Ellen turned the sound up loud. At first she just nodded her head in time to the music, then she began to dance. She danced around the room in her bare feet, twirling like a dervish, her hair flying in all directons. I stood still, looking at my hands, still clutching Mum's card. Ellen grabbed hold of me and tried to make me dance with her, but I didn't; I couldn't.

'Come on,' she cried. 'Spoilsport! Who'm I going to dance with when you're in America?'

Then she dropped my hands. The record crackled for a moment and the next track began. 'Paint It Black'.

Ellen was panting. Her cheeks were flushed now and the hair closest to her scalp was damp with sweat. She smelled dirty, as if she had not bathed for days. This made me feel sad.

'How's Jago?' she asked. 'Is he OK? Was he devastated about us not leaving on my birthday? Does he have another plan? Because I don't think we should wait any longer. I think . . .' she reached behind her to turn up the music '. . . we should just go. We don't have to go to America. I don't care where we are. I don't care if we have to live in a barn! I'll climb out of the window one night. Or I'll sneak out when Papa's upstairs. I'll hide in the churchyard until the coast is clear. Will you tell Jago?'

'Ellen . . .' I said, as through the speakers the singer sang about how he wanted to escape his darkness. 'Ellen – Jago's gone.'

'Gone where?' she asked. She didn't get it. She had no inkling. She could no more conceive of Jago leaving without her than of the sun losing its fire and fading to nothing.

'He's gone away.'

She frowned. 'Gone away where? Why?'

I looked up at the ceiling, where the chandelier hung from a fancy plaster rose. The glass pieces had yellowed, and a broken spiderweb was collecting dust. I toed the edge of the rug that hid Adam Tremlett's bloodstains. Ellen came closer to me. She stood in front of me. Too close. She was taking the oxygen from me. Her breath was sour, it had a metallic tang.

'Hannah? Tell me! Where's Jago?'

'I don't know,' I said. 'He went away the night of your birthday and we haven't heard from him since. We don't know where he is.' I paused. I said, very quietly, 'I don't think he's coming back.'

Ellen looked at me intently. She tucked her hair behind her ears. Then she shook her head.

'No,' she said. 'No. Jago wouldn't have left without me. He just wouldn't.'

'He has,' I said. 'Ellen, I'm sorry but he has.'

She laughed, but now there was a nervous edge to her laughter. 'Why? Why would he do that?'

The record moved on to the next track.

Ellen's face looked so innocent, so blameless that I almost broke apart inside – but I reminded myself that it was her fault. If she had only told Jago the truth about the abortion, then I wouldn't have had to hurt him like I did. She'd been stringing him along for weeks, being Little Miss Perfect, acting all sweet and innocent and *pregnant*. If she'd been honest then I wouldn't have had to say those things to keep him away from Thornfield House. She couldn't blame me for what I'd done. What choice had I had?

'I told him about the abortion,' I said.

Horror crept into Ellen's eyes. It served her right, I told myself. She was the one who got rid of Jago's baby without so much as a word to him. She was the one who made me lie to him. It was her fault that Jago had gone.

Ellen stared at me as if she couldn't believe what I had said.

'But you promised you wouldn't tell him, Hannah! You swore you wouldn't.'

'And you promised me that you would!' I replied. 'You

should have told him, Ellen – you should have told him the truth. *You* might have been prepared to keep lying to Jago, but I wasn't. Did you know he'd been out buying baby clothes? Did you know he'd made a crib? He believed in a baby that didn't exist – he loved a ghost baby *because of you*!'

Ellen put her two hands over her mouth, the fingers splayed.

'Oh God,' she whispered.

'I'm sorry,' I said, more gently.

'Oh God,' Ellen repeated.

She was silent. Then she collapsed like a puppet. She fell down onto her heels and hid her head in her arms, grabbing fistfuls of hair. I watched her for a moment. I was wishing she'd stop being so dramatic, but then I realized that she wasn't putting it on. She wasn't acting. Ellen was disintegrating in front of me.

I didn't know what to do. I looked around helplessly as if I would find the answer in the fireplace, or the window – but before I could think of anything, Ellen uncurled herself and she started to scream.

I tried to stop her. I tried to hold her, to touch her, to console her, but she was beyond comfort. She was beyond anything I could do.

I had destroyed Ellen as comprehensively as I'd destroyed Jago.

It was something I would have to live with for the rest of my life.

CHAPTER SIXTY-THREE

I talked to Kirsten and Karla and Dora for a while and then I was exhausted, so Karla took me upstairs and showed me to a room where I could lie down. She drew the heavy curtains, and settled me on a bed that was big and soft as a cloud. Karla sat with me, saying nothing, but her presence was calming and for a while I slept.

When I woke I was alone, and the evening was beginning to draw in. I washed my face and went downstairs, out into the gardens, and followed a path down to the River Elbe. The meadow grass was long – it brushed my knees – and the air was full of soft sunlight and little moths and insects.

John was sitting on a huge old log stripping the bark from a twig, his legs stretched out in front of him. A few yards beyond, the river ran by, wide and calm, reflecting the sunlight. Insects danced on its surface and every now and then a fish leaped. I perched beside John, resting my bottom on the sun-warmed bark.

'Hi,' he said.

'Hi.'

'Did you manage to sleep?'

'A bit.'

A trout jumped out of the water and, for a brief moment,

light glistened on its pirouetting arc before it fell back into the river, ripples spreading wide.

I wrapped my arms about myself.

'This is a lovely spot,' John said. 'I saw a grey heron just now. A beautiful big bugger. That's supposed to be a portent of good luck.'

'I didn't have you down as the superstitious kind.'

'I'm not, as a rule.'

I looked out across the countryside. The leaves were beginning to turn in the trees, only a little, but the change was there. In the distance, the sounds of the city drifted across: cars and sirens and alarms.

'It's nice to think of Ellen being here,' I said. 'I bet she used to climb on this log when she was a child. '

'What was she like?' asked John.

'She was the most alive person I've ever known.'

We exchanged smiles.

'Karla told me they have some videos of her,' John said. 'Her grandparents took some cine-film when she was a child.'

'I don't think I could bear to watch the videos,' I said.

'No,' said John. 'That's perfectly understandable.'

For a while we sat on the fallen tree, looking out across the river. Two kingfishers chased one another across the surface of the water, flashing brilliant blue. I rubbed my eyes.

'Are you ready to let go of Ellen now?' John asked.

'Almost,' I said. 'There's one more thing I have to do.'

CHAPTER SIXTY-FOUR

This is what I knew.

After I left Ellen that day, the day I told her Jago was gone, I went back down the hill to number 8 Cross Hands Lane. I felt ill. Mum could see I was upset, but she put it down to the fact that I was worried about flying.

'Look at you,' she said, 'you're shaking like a leaf. Go and sit down and I'll make tea.'

I paced the front room, chewing my hair, telling myself over and over that it wasn't my fault, that if Ellen had only told the truth, none of this would have happened. She was to blame, not me. Mum came in with a tray and made me sit down. She told me about a conversation she'd had with someone from church who told her you were more likely to be kicked to death by a donkey than die in a plane crash.

'Are there many donkeys in Chile?' she asked. Normally I'd have felt irritated by her naivety, but that day I could hardly even bear to listen to her.

I thought that probably everything would be all right. Jago would come back and he and Ellen would just have to sort things out themselves, without me running around between them, keeping their secrets for them. It was up to them now. It was nothing to do with me any more.

But in my heart, I knew Jago wouldn't return.

I told my heart to shut up. I refused to hear it. I closed it down for good, packed it away and stitched it up tight so I wouldn't have to listen to it any more.

Each time we heard a car engine on the lane outside, which was not often, I leaped to my feet. I couldn't wait to be in Ricky's father's car powering out of Cornwall, I couldn't wait to be off. I wanted to be as far away from Trethene as I could be. While my mother fussed on about snakes and scorpions, I stared at the clock, oblivious to her. Every minute seemed to drag on. The big hand took an age to complete each circuit of the clockface, and the ticking was like torture to me.

While we waited in the cottage, Ellen picked up the fire poker, the same poker with which her father had tried to kill Adam Tremlett, and she smashed up the piano.

Nothing salvageable was left.

But I didn't know about that. I watched the clock and listened to my mother, and at last, at long last, the Land Rover arrived. Mum invited Ricky and Mr Wendon in for a cup of tea, but I think we were all relieved when he said we'd better be getting straight off. Dad came in from the garden, stiff and embarrassed in front of the senior officer. I kissed my parents goodbye quickly, and Ricky and his father shook their hands, then I sat in the back and watched as we drove out of Cross Hands Lane, waving to Mum and Dad through the rear window until they were out of sight. Then I slumped in the seat clutching the foil-wrapped sandwiches Mum had thrust into my lap at the last moment, and watched the Lizard peninsula go past. I was so relieved to be leaving, so glad that every second, the distance between Ellen and me was growing greater. Ricky and his father were talking, making conversation. I answered questions directed at me politely, but most of the time I was silent. When we finally crossed the Cornwall county boundary line, heading through

Devon towards the M5 motorway, I fell asleep, my head cushioned by my jumper.

Some time later, my parents received a postcard from New York. Jago reassured them that he was all right and promised he'd be in touch when he was settled somewhere. He did not ask after me.

They didn't hear from him again for ages, not until he found his feet in Newfoundland.

And I was in Chile. I had planned to go for a year, but when the time to return home approached, I could not bear the thought of it. I had become used to big skies and wide spaces, being part of an eclectic mixture of accents and personalities and cultures. I could not go back to Cornwall, the very idea was suffocating. So I agreed to stay on for another year. Ricky had to return to England to take up his university place. I didn't find it hard to say goodbye to him. I had stifled my capacity for feeling. We wrote to one another for a while, but it was half-hearted correspondence, and we soon lost touch.

But it was before then, months before, that I received the letter from my mother telling me that there had been an accident and that Ellen had drowned. There was no mention of a baby in the letter.

That was all I knew.

Karla and Kirsten told me the rest.

After I left Ellen, after she destroyed the piano, she did her best to carry on. She confronted her father about their financial situation, and he confirmed that Thornfield House had been remortgaged to the hilt and that they were as good as bankrupt. Ellen and her father sent Mrs Todd away to save money. The two of them lived together in that awful big house, hardly communicating, hardly existing. They were recluses, and once again, the people of the village turned a blind eye; they did not want to interfere.

Every day Ellen must have felt her body change. Every day the baby must have grown a little bigger, a little stronger. At night, she must have lain in bed and put her hands on her belly and felt the little kicks inside her. Ellen would have talked to the baby, she would have sung to her; she would have promised that her baby would be the most precious, beloved child ever.

It wasn't hard for her to hide the pregnancy. She hardly ever left the house, hardly saw anyone apart from her father, and winter was coming so if she went out, she wore big coats and her father's jackets. She probably blamed herself for the position she was in because she was no longer the attention-seeker, no longer the drama queen. Ellen was not herself any more. She was broken.

Destroying the piano, awful as it was, had brought about a kind of understanding between Ellen and her father. She no longer fought him; he stopped bullying her. He must have, there was no point in him hurting her because she was already at the nadir of hurt. He believed that everything had been taken from her. He accepted her act of vengeance because he understood it. In his mind, it helped lay the ghost of Anne Brecht to rest. His revenge had been exacted. He had, finally, taken complete control – or, at least, he thought he had. In disposing of his daughter's inheritance, he had taken away Ellen's independence and her future. He had scuppered Anne's plans for her daughter and he had put two fingers up at the ghost of Mrs Withiel.

Ellen kept her distance from him for the sake of her baby. She left the house rarely, isolating herself, arranging for pro-visions to be delivered. She cooked for her father, but ate alone, leaving his food in the kitchen for him to heat in the microwave when he was ready. In his mind, this small domestic act, those sad plates of toast and no-frills beans and cheap sausages that Ellen left out for him, were her way of showing contrition. He still slept during the day, and paced the house at night. She stayed out of his way. They no longer tormented one another; they left each other alone.

Ellen still believed in her lover. She believed he would come back for her: all she had to do was wait. She thought that sooner or later he would forgive her, and that once he returned, and realized the truth, then everything would be fine-and-dandy, hunky-dory, happy-ever-after. She didn't know – nobody knew – what I had said to him. She didn't know that I had dashed his belief in her. She hung on to her hope, her trust, her confidence in his love.

Only he didn't come.

In the end, growing desperate, Ellen wrote to Tante Karla. She didn't mention the pregnancy but said she needed help. Karla had some affairs to put in order, but she booked a flight to London at the earliest opportunity.

She was too late.

When the time came, Ellen must have known. On some deep level she must have known she was going to have the baby early.

One evening, while her father was sleeping, she put on her coat and her thick boots and as many sweaters as she could wear, and she walked out of Thornfield House. It was late autumn and she was a little over seven months pregnant. She could have walked into Trethene to ask for help, but she didn't. She had no friends, she didn't know anyone – perhaps she simply could not face explaining. Or perhaps, by then, Ellen was so worn down by life, so desperate that she was no longer thinking logically but relying on instinct, like an animal.

She went to the place where she had been happy, and where she felt safe.

She went to Bleached Scarp.

She made that arduous journey alone, through the bleak fields, across the marshy peatland and the coastal path, down to the cliffs. She negotiated the scree, found the cleft in the rock and climbed down the steps cut into the tunnel. It must have been cold as death that night, and the sky would have been wide and black, and apart from the sound of the sea and the wind, there would have been no company for Ellen. She put up the little two-man tent that I'd left for her, months before. She secured it to the sandy ground in the shelter of the cave, held it down with rocks to make sure it was stable. She made a nest inside of blankets, sleeping bags, coats and towels. Then she built a fire and she sat beneath the stars and listened to the rhythm of the waves rolling in from the sea.

She waited.

I couldn't imagine what it must have been like for Ellen on the beach, alone that night. She would not have been afraid of the sea or the sky or the animal noises, but she must have been afraid of what was happening to her. She might have cried out in labour, but maybe not. There was nobody to hear, nobody to notice. Somehow I imagine Ellen would have been quiet. She'd have wanted her baby to have a peaceful entry into the world.

The baby came. She was born beneath the moon and stars, to the sound of the sea and the smell of the breeze. I imagined Ellen wrapping her in the soft cotton blankets she'd brought with her. In the silver moonlight, the baby's tiny face was wrinkled and dazed, like the face of a fairy. She squinted her eyes against the cold and she turned her face towards Ellen's breast, and her lips searched and sucked against Ellen's skin.

Somehow Ellen knew what to do. She trusted her instinct – it was all she had to guide her. She must have been weak and exhausted but also, perhaps, exhilarated. She would have felt free. She would have felt happy. At last, she had achieved something wonderful all by herself, without reward, without duress. She was in a place she loved and she had a baby, a live, solid little creature, in her arms; someone of her own, someone who would love her unconditionally. She probably believed that now everything would be all right. She put the baby to the breast and the baby took the colostrum, the first milk. She must have done this, because otherwise she would not have survived. I don't know how Ellen knew how important this was, but she did.

The baby was fine, Ellen made sure of it. But she wasn't.

Sometime during that night, or the next morning, she bled to death on the beach.

Tante Karla arrived at Thornfield House in the afternoon of the following day. Mr Brecht had only just got out of bed, and was wandering around the house, smoking and dishevelled in his dressing-gown. Tante Karla assessed the situation at once. She assumed Ellen was lying in, so she made coffee and gave the filthy kitchen a cursory clean before she went upstairs to knock on Ellen's door.

Ellen had left a letter for Tante Karla on her pillow. It explained nothing, but gave directions to the beach, so Tante Karla knew where to go, where to look. It was late in the day. Almost sunset. Wind was gusting across the sea, picking up foam and blowing it. The hardy little plants that lined the cliff edge were pressed flat against the rock. Gulls wheeled and cawed, and high clouds hurried across the sky. Tante Karla went alone to the cliffs, following Ellen's instructions. At the edge, she looked down onto the lonely beach and saw Ellen's body, lying where she had collapsed at the point where the sea met the shore. Ellen was rising and falling to the rhythm of the small breaking waves, her extended arm seemingly beckoning to Karla as the sea pushed it in, and then drew it out again. Her hair was spread about her like seaweed.

She had been trying to clean herself up in the sea, trying to wash away the blood.

Tante Karla found her way down to the beach. She pulled Ellen's body from the water, laid it safely in the shadow of the cliff. She was a practical woman, who knew there was not much light left; there was no time for tears or grief. She knew she would have to walk half a mile along the coastal path until she reached the emergency phone box where she could call for help. She had to hurry. But first, she went to the tent, in search of a blanket or something with which to cover Ellen.

She unzipped the door. Inside, she found the baby, wrapped up warm and swaddled in amongst Ellen's bedding, like a little bird in a nest. She wasn't crying but watching the orange tent canvas move in and out with one eye open and the other closed, sucking her fist and making little clicking noises with her tongue.

CHAPTER SIXTY-FIVE

As night settled in over Magdeburg, I picked at the bread on my plate. The food was delicious, but I had little appetite. We were sitting on the terrace, the table lit by candles, and Dora, cross-legged on the bench, was hunched over her guitar, playing chords. Bats darted around us and the German moon was high in the sky. The night was dark and wide and beautiful. Dishes of salad, potatoes, cold meats, fruit, pickles and cheese were spread about the table, and bottles of wine and water. Karla was finishing the story of Kirsten.

'So I brought this beautiful baby – the most beautiful baby in the world – back to Germany with me,' she said. 'I told my friends, my colleagues, my family and the authorities that she was mine – that I had given birth to her unexpectedly in England, at seven months. I invented a love affair, a married lover who did not know about my pregnancy, and everyone believed me. My story worked perfectly. It was the only way to be sure Pieter could never get his hands on her.'

'Officially and legally, Karla is my mother,' said Kirsten. 'And I'm proud and pleased to be her daughter. But as soon as I was old enough to understand, she told me the truth. Any deception was only to protect me.'

She and Karla smiled at one another. They chinked their goblets together and then they drank wine, holding onto one another's eyes. Ellen had done the best for her daughter, I thought. She had arranged the best possible upbringing for her, away from Pieter, somewhere safe where she would be loved.

'But there must have been a coroner's enquiry. It must have come out that Ellen had – you know – given birth,' John said. He reached across me and helped himself to a slice of cheese from the board on the table.

Karla waved away a large moth, and nodded.

'It was assumed the child had drowned, been washed out to sea when Ellen collapsed. It was the obvious explanation. Nobody else knew about the existence of the beach, so how could the baby have been taken?'

A few months later, when she and the baby were settled, and the official paperwork had been sorted out, Karla tracked down Mrs Todd, brought her to Germany and made sure she had a peaceful retirement in a comfortable little house in the grounds of the Schloss.

'What about Mr Brecht?' I asked. 'What happened to him?'

'We brought him back here too,' said Karla. 'My brother was in a bad way, Hannah. He was committed to a psychiatric hospital for his own safety. He's still there.'

CHAPTER SIXTY-SIX

Karla insisted we stay at Schloss Marien, at least for the night, and I was grateful. A strange kind of peace had settled over me. I did not want to lose the feeling of being close to Ellen. I felt as if she were beside me, but gently now. I knew the truth about her death, and it was better than not knowing. I was not frightened of her any more. I just felt sad; terribly sad.

And there was Kirsten, who looked so like her mother had at the same age, who carried Ellen in her genes and her smile and her eyes, who played with her hair just as Ellen used to, who burned almost as brightly.

The kindness of the three German women soothed me. As the evening wore on, they told me stories of Kirsten's childhood. Karla said she had always been a show-off: she'd always wanted the starring role in school plays, always enjoyed attention. Kirsten laughed along with her almost-mother. She rested her head on Karla's shoulder and Karla leaned over and kissed her.

There was so much laughter.

John was adamant that he did not mind missing yet another opportunity to network with the curators of some of the best museums in Europe. He said he'd rather be with us instead. He was quiet, but I was glad he was there, beside me, and that he would know the story too.

I drank wine. John kept filling up my glass and I drank because it helped rub away at the sharp corners of my pain; it blunted my guilt. If I tried, I could almost imagine that Ellen was there with us, sitting just out of my eyeline, feeling proud of her daughter, happy to be with her family.

I had to ask, prove to myself that I wasn't crazy, so I turned to Kirsten and said, 'So it *was* you I saw in Bristol at the museum?'

She nodded. Told me: 'I came looking for you.'

'How did you know about me? How did you know where to look?'

Kirsten glanced at Karla, and Karla smiled and said, 'Show her.'

Kirsten slipped back inside the Schloss and returned moments later with something in her hand. She passed it to me. It was the photograph in the home-made, heart-shaped frame that I'd given to Ellen for her eighteenth birthday. Some of the drift-glass had come away, and the picture was faded, but I could still see us – Ellen and me – our faces pressed together, our arms around each other's shoulders, her dark hair mixed up with my fair. I turned the picture over. On the back were the words I'd written in black felt pen. They'd turned a pale orange colour now, but they were still legible. I'd drawn a crude heart with an arrow through it and on the top of the heart I'd written *Ellen Brecht*, on the bottom *Hannah Brown* and inside were the words: *friends always*.

Ellen had kept the photograph. She had kept it beside her bed, and Karla had picked it up and brought it back to Germany, together with Ellen's daughter.

'Karla remembered you, of course,' said Kirsten. 'I Googled your name. There were about seven thousand

Hannah Browns in England, but I kept modifying the search and eventually I found you on the museum's website. I showed Karla the picture. She said it was you.'

'Kirsten agonized for ages over whether she should come and find you,' Karla said.

'I was going to write first,' the girl said, 'but then I thought: What if she tells me she doesn't want to see me? Then I'll never know. So I decided to seek you out.'

'We rehearsed different scenarios,' Dora said with a laugh, 'me and Kirsten in her bedroom. I'd be you and she'd be herself, and sometimes you'd be shocked to find out that Ellen had had a daughter, but usually you were very happy and emotional and you kissed her and told her she was beautiful and took her out to dinner.'

'We never rehearsed what to do if you took one look at me and were so horrified you almost had a heart attack!' Kirsten joked.

'I'm so sorry,' I said.

'It's no problem,' said Kirsten, and she and Dora laughed together, and John laughed and finally I laughed too.

'And of course, that was you I saw in Berlin yesterday,' I said, and Kirsten nodded. 'And you were watching me from the clifftop when I was on the beach in Cornwall!'

Kirsten frowned. 'No. We flew straight home from Bristol. There didn't seem much point in staying.'

I made light of it. I said I must have been mistaken, but I wasn't. I knew who I had seen standing on the cliff at Bleached Scarp. *I knew*.

I watched the girls laughing, and I thought, Thank God. Thank God that Kirsten has Karla, and a friend like Dora who will always stand by her.

I thought, Kirsten is luckier than her mother ever was.

Ellen had deserved better than me.

Kirsten said, 'So, anyway, we came back here and I

thought that was the end of it – and then you found me.'

I was a little drunk, and very tired. 'Ellen brought me to you,' I said. 'I know she did.'

Karla patted my hand.

After that, I told Kirsten some of my story, but not all of it. I explained about Jago, how he had loved Ellen, how much he had wanted the baby, how he had believed it was gone. I explained that he had never recovered from losing Ellen and the child, how he was living a life in Newfoundland, but that it was not a whole life. I told her about our parents, how thrilled they would be to find out that they were, after all, grandparents – and how much they would love Kirsten.

There were some things I could not put into words, some things that would have to wait until they were told.

After that, the night became hazy. The black sky, the bats, more wine, the stars and the breeze, the smell of the river on the air, and John wandering off to speak to Charlotte on his phone. Dora sang, her voice low and tuneful. She sang songs of love and heartbreak, songs that I did not understand but which made me sad all the same.

The German women went to bed and John and I went for a walk by the river. The moon was full, its light so strong the trees, and even we ourselves, cast shadows across the grassy banks. Owls called from the trees. I felt Ellen was there too, walking beside us, knowing.

'You'll be OK now,' said John, and I said: 'I know.'

I crouched down to pick up a pebble and I threw it into the river, flicking my wrist as Jago had taught me. It bounced three times.

'I wish it had turned out differently for Ellen,' I said.

John replied, 'Hmm,' then he added, 'she left a wonderful legacy in Kirsten.'

'Yes, she did.'

John tried to skim a pebble. His attempt was feeble. I found a flatter, better one for him.

'How was Charlotte?' I asked.

'She was fine,' said John, 'on good form. She's been on the internet, booking a holiday.'

'For herself?'

'No.' John turned the pebble over in his hands. 'No, for all of us. She says she thinks we could do with some quality time together.'

'Oh.'

'A little resort in Turkey. I've always wanted to go to Turkey. They've got some great archaeological sites there.'

'I'm glad,' I said.

'Charlotte will probably be bored to tears if I drag her round them,' said John. 'She'll criticize and complain, and I'll have to sit on the beach bored out of my mind to compensate. We'll rub one another up the wrong way. But we'll laugh about it afterwards.'

I knew he was trying to explain his marriage to me. He was letting me know that things weren't perfect between him and Charlotte, that they were different people, but that they still worked as a couple. I wondered if he knew about her affairs, and realized that it didn't matter. He loved Charlotte as she was. That was the whole point of love: it did not judge or criticize, it was not jealous or defensive – it accepted.

John didn't want those of us on the periphery of his relationship with Charlotte to drag their secrets into the open where he would be forced to acknowledge them and to act upon them. He wanted to be married to Charlotte, whether she was faithful or not, because that was what made him happy.

It didn't seem too much to ask.

I also realized that there was no future for me and him, not in the way I had imagined. John would, I hoped, always be my friend and colleague, but he would never be more than that. It was doing me no good wishing he was mine, thinking about how happy I would make him, because that was never going to happen. The realization made me a little sad, but also it was a relief. I could let go. I didn't have to be on the outside of his marriage, looking in and thinking I knew best.

If I was going to love someone, I needed to find someone who was free to love me back.

'You're useless,' I said, as the second pebble belly-flopped into the river. 'Here.'

I took his wrist in my hand and, in the moonlight, on the bank of the Elbe, I taught him how to skim pebbles.

CHAPTER SIXTY-SEVEN

The next morning, I rose early. Karla had given me a lovely, east-facing room and the sun was low in the sky outside. I put on the dressing-gown she had lent me, picked up my phone, and crept from the room. Kirsten's bedroom was next to mine. The door was slightly ajar. I pushed it open, and she turned towards me in bed, smiling. She was awake; she'd been waiting for me.

I went downstairs, out through the doors, to sit on the terrace by the fountain. The sun was rising, lighting up the rooftops of the city of Magdeburg, casting a summery yellow light over the grounds of the Schloss. It was a beautiful morning. It was going to be a beautiful day.

I called Mum first. I didn't tell her anything about Kirsten; I just reassured her, once again, that I was fine and asked for the number I needed. She gave it to me.

'But it'll be the early hours there now,' said Mum. I thought, It doesn't matter. This can't wait another moment.

Kirsten came out in her pyjamas wearing flip-flops and carrying two mugs of coffee. She sat down beside me. Steam wisped from the surface of the coffee. Kirsten rubbed her nose.

The sun was sending long morning shadows across the

meadows below us. The whole area was tinted golden, dew glistened on the grass and the light picked out the intricate designs of the spiderwebs strung amongst the leaves of the shrubs. Beside us, the water in the fountain sparkled and twinkled; it was green-clear where it pooled in the stone basin. Kirsten trailed her fingers on its surface. She smiled at me, filling me with affection.

'Are you ready?' I asked.

She tucked her hair behind her ears so the dyed-pink flash showed, and she nodded. Her eyes were bright and wide.

'I'm ready,' she said.

I dialled the number. It took a while to connect, but eventually, at the other end of the line, a telephone rang. I crossed my fingers, and the call was picked up. I heard a man clear his throat and then a gruff, sleepy voice that was distant, but also dear and familiar to me, said: 'Hello?'

'Jago,' I said. 'It's me, Hannah.' I took a deep breath and I smiled at Kristen. 'There's somebody here who'd like to talk to you.'

ACKNOWLEDGEMENTS

A huge thank you to the talented and wonderful Sophie Wilson, who has made this book far better than it otherwise would have been, and to Cat Cobain for her constant wisdom and warmth. It's a complete joy working with you both.

To everyone at Transworld, especially Madeline Toy, Vivien Garrett and Elspeth Dougall. Thank you for everything – most of all for making me feel so much part of the team.

A million thanks, as always, to Marianne Gunn O'Connor, Vicki Satlow and Pat Lynch for your unfailing support.

Thank you to the wonderful Cathy Rentzenbrink for stories about Cornwall and more, and I'm sorry the trombone incident was lost in the final rewrite.

I have taken liberties with locations in this novel – some are genuine, some fictional. Bristol does have an excellent museum with an ancient Egypt gallery but many details have been changed.

Finally, thank you to my family and friends; you are the world to me – with a special mention for the lovely Georgia Adams.

Louise Douglas is a copywriter. She has three sons and lives in Bath with her partner. *In Her Shadow* is her fourth novel. Her first novel, *The Love of My Life*, was longlisted for both the Romantic Novel of the Year Award and the Waverton Good Read Award, and her second, *Missing You*, won the People's Choice Award at the Romantic Novelists' Association Pure Passion Awards 2010.